"*W*hat are you waiting for, MacLeod? Aren't you going to kiss the bride?"

Rory tensed. Cheeks flaming, Isabel stared at her toes, the tips of her silver slippers just peeking out from below the embroidered edge of her gown.

"Aye," he said, slipping a finger under her chin. "A kiss to seal our vows."

Slowly, he lowered his mouth, pausing for an instant to inhale her flowery scent before his lips touched hers. He almost moaned as the rush of desire flooded his body with heat. *Dear God,* she tasted sweet.

He lingered, the urge to deepen the kiss primal. He wanted to draw her into his arms and crush her full breasts against his hard chest. To feel the shape of her hips as she pressed against his heavy groin.

Yet somehow he held back.

For the first time in his life, Rory MacLeod—a man who'd faced scores of fearsome warriors on the battlefield and driven his enemies to their knees with terror—knew alarm.

"*Highlander Untamed* envelops the reader in a rich tapestry of passion and adventure. In this compelling, beautifully written debut novel, Monica McCarty brings Highland Scotland to life in all its glory with feuding clans, ancient secrets, and a pair of star-crossed lovers you'll root for even as you wonder how they can ever find their happy ending."

—TRACY GRANT, author of
Secrets of a Lady

Books published by The Random House Publishing Group
are available at quantity discounts on bulk purchases for
premium, educational, fund-raising, and special sales use.
For details, please call 1-800-733-3000.

HIGHLANDER
UNTAMED

A Novel

MONICA MCCARTY

BALLANTINE BOOKS • NEW YORK

Highlander Untamed is a work of fiction. Names, characters, places, and incidents are the products of the author's imagination or are used fictitiously. Any resemblance to actual events, locales, or persons, living or dead, is entirely coincidental.

A Ballantine Books Mass Market Original

Copyright © 2007 by Monica McCarty
Excerpt from *Highlander Unmasked* copyright © 2007 by Monica McCarty

Published in the United States by Ballantine Books, an imprint of The Random House Publishing Group, a division of Random House, Inc., New York.

BALLANTINE and colophon are registered trademarks of Random House, Inc.

This book contains an excerpt from the forthcoming mass market edition of *Highlander Unmasked* by Monica McCarty. This excerpt has been set for this edition only and may not reflect the final content of the forthcoming edition.

ISBN 978-0-345-49436-8

Cover illustration: Craig White

Printed in the United States of America

www.ballantinebooks.com

OPM   9   8   7   6   5   4   3   2   1

To Jami and Nyree, who have gone well beyond the call of CP duty. I promise, this is the *last* time you need to read it (I think a hundred times should suffice). Long live the SSRW!

And to my first two readers, my husband, Dave, and my sister, Nora: Your enthusiasm from the start made it all seem possible. And Dave, I'm sorry the Cover Model gig didn't work out, but I still love you anyway.

Acknowledgments

The road to publication is often a long and arduous journey, with many twists and turns along the way. Mine was no exception. There are, however, many people who have eased my travels.

First, I'd like to thank the entire team at Ballantine who made this dream a reality, especially my editor, Charlotte Herscher, whose comments are always dead-on. Thank you for your faith, enthusiasm, and hard work in making this project come to fruition.

The Fog City Divas, especially Barbara Freethy, Candice Hern, and Carol Culver, for taking me under your generous wings and sharing your wisdom about the *business* of writing—you guys are terrific.

A special thanks to Kathleen Givens; your kindness and encouragement to a newbie author (who also happened to be a huge fan) will never be forgotten.

Thanks to Annelise Robey and Maggie Kelly, who got it all started.

Finally, to my fabulous agents, Kelly Harms and Andrea Cirillo, who made it all possible—thank you.

Two households, both alike in dignity,
In fair Verona, where we lay our scene,
From ancient grudge break to new mutiny,
Where civil blood makes civil hands unclean.
From forth the fatal loins of these two foes
A pair of star-cross'd lovers take their life;
Whose misadventured piteous overthrows
Do with their death bury their parents' strife.
The fearful passage of their death-mark'd love,
And the continuance of their parents' rage,
Which, but their children's end, nought could remove,
Is now the two hours' traffic of our stage;
The which if you with patient ears attend,
What here shall miss, our toil shall strive to mend.

—William Shakespeare, *Romeo and Juliet,* Prologue

Prologue

❖

Dunscaith Castle, Isle of Skye, 1599

The ground shook with the heavy pounding of hooves as the score of warriors approached Dunscaith Castle. Their leader, Roderick MacLeod, Chief of MacLeod, urged his mount ahead, surging across the rocky crags at breakneck speed. He had to reach her before . . .

Just then a great roar rose above the thunder of the horses, and with it hope shattered. Rory cursed, knowing that the jubilant cries of the crowd could mean only one thing: The warning had come too late.

Refusing to accept what he already knew, Rory pushed the mighty destrier harder, climbing faster up the steep pathway. Finally, horse and rider crested the hill, at last giving vision to the cruel spectacle orchestrated by Rory's most despised enemy.

Not a furlong below them, Rory's sister sat atop a horse, slowly winding her way through a crowd of jeering villagers. She looked so tiny, so painfully alone among the madding crowd. Her hair, a thick, glorious halo of riotous curls, shone like white gold in the mid-summer sun. But neither the magnificence of her hair nor the remnants of her once fey beauty could distract the villagers from the conspicuous black patch that covered one eye.

Even from afar, Rory could see Margaret's pain. The rigid line of her spine, the nearly imperceptible shaking of her hands as she clenched the reins of her maimed horse, the slight flinch as the taunts pelted her pride like stones.

He could make out only snippets of their hateful words. "Face . . . hideous . . . one-eyed . . . mark of the devil . . ."

Rory pressed on, though the damage had already been done.

None but the MacDonald of Sleat could be capable of sending her away with such a monstrous procession. Sleat had gone to great lengths to shame his sister, mocking her misfortune with outrageous cruelty. For Margaret, who'd badly injured an eye in a horrible riding accident only a few months after arriving at Dunscaith, sat atop a one-eyed horse. A horse that was led by a one-eyed man and followed by a one-eyed dog.

It wasn't enough that Sleat had decided to repudiate the handfast and send Margaret back to her kinsmen. He did so in a manner designed for one purpose only—to strike right at the heart of the MacLeod pride in a way that could only demand retribution.

Damn Sleat, the devil's spawn, for dragging an innocent woman into a feud among men.

Rory's heart wrenched as a small tear slid down Margaret's pale cheek from behind the black patch. She wobbled, as if searching for strength. When she found none, her chin slumped forward to her chest.

Blood pounded in Rory's ears, rage finally quieting the cruel voices of the MacDonald clansmen. A piercing battle cry tore from his lungs as he raised his claymore to rally his clansmen. "Hold fast!" he roared the clan's motto. "To a MacLeod!"

Sleat would regret what he'd done. The MacLeods would be avenged.

Chapter 1

❖

That mighty stronghold of the west
In lonely grandeur reigns supreme;
A monument of feudal power,
And fitting haven for a king.

—M. C. MacLeod

Loch Dunvegan, Isle of Skye, July 1601

Isabel MacDonald had never thought of herself as lacking in courage, but over the past few days she'd begun to reconsider. The long hours of travel, with little to do but think, had tested her mettle. What had seemed in Edinburgh a well-conceived plan to help her clan, now, as they neared their final destination in the farthest outreaches of Scotland, felt more like a virgin being led to the sacrifice. An analogy, she feared, that was disturbingly close to the truth.

Huddled among her MacDonald clansmen on the small *birlinn,* Isabel felt strangely alone. Like her, the other occupants of the boat remained both watchful and silent as they approached their enemy's keep. Only the droning sound of the oars, plunging into the black depths beneath them, pierced the eerie quiet. Somewhere ahead of her in the loch beyond lay Castle Dunvegan, the impregnable stronghold of Clan MacLeod.

An icy wind swept over the loch, sending a chill deep into her bones. *Eilean a Cheo,* she recalled the Erse name for Skye. The "Isle of Mist"—what a prodigious

understatement. Cursing her inappropriate traveling attire, Isabel wrapped her fur-trimmed cloak—the only
warm garment she was wearing—tighter across her
body in a futile attempt to warm herself. But her garments provided such scant protection from the elements,
she might as well have been sitting here in a sark.

Given her perilous task, the foul weather seemed
somehow fitting.

Isabel had been promised in handfast to the powerful
MacLeod chief. Ostensibly, the handfast was a union
brokered by the king to end two long and bitter years of
feuding between the MacLeods and the MacDonalds. In
reality, it was a ruse to gain her access to their enemy's
keep and, if all went according to plan, his heart.

No wedding would follow this handfast. When Isabel
found what she came for, she would repudiate the handfast and return to her life at court as lady-in-waiting to
Queen Anne as if nothing had happened, secure in the
knowledge that she had helped her clan.

Assuming, of course, she wasn't discovered.

In retrospect, passing the days by thinking of the different ways a spy could be punished probably had not
been the most efficient use of her time.

Sensing Isabel's unease, her cherished nursemaid, Bessie,
reached down and gently squeezed her clenched fingers.

"Don't worry, poppet, it won't be that bad. You look
as if you are headed to the executioner instead of to a
handfast. It's not as if your bridegroom is England's old
King Henry."

He might as well be. If Isabel's perfidy was discovered,
the result could well be the same as the fate doled out to
many of Henry VIII's wives years ago. She would expect no
mercy from a fierce Highland chief. She could only trust

that King James, a man who'd welcomed her into his household like a daughter, would not see her tied to a vicious brute. "I'm fine," Isabel assured her, plastering a lighthearted smile on her face. As fine as she could be, she thought, given that she was about to be handfasted to a stranger.

It was thoughts of the man whom she must deceive that were partially responsible for her growing apprehension over the past few days. Her attempts to glean more insight into the MacLeod chief's character had proven largely unsuccessful. The king claimed he was an amiable enough man . . . for a barbarian. As the king considered all Highlanders barbarians, the description did not concern her overmuch.

Her father was equally circumspect, calling the MacLeod a "formidable enemy" with a "good sword arm." Hardly reassuring. Her brothers had been a little more forthcoming. They described the MacLeod as a cunning chief who was well respected among his clan and a fierce warrior who was unmatched on the battlefield. But she'd learned nothing of the man.

Too late, she realized Bessie was still watching her. "Are you sure nothing is wrong, Isabel?"

She shook her head. "It's only that I'm freezing and anxious to get off this boat."

Isabel watched with trepidation as Bessie's graying brows gathered over the elfin nose that made her aged face appear strangely youthful for her two and forty years. *God's breath, Bessie saw too much.* Those omniscient green eyes peered directly into her soul. Isabel knew that her nursemaid suspected something was afoot. From Isabel's hasty decision to handfast a man she'd never met to the inappropriate traveling attire her uncle had insisted she wear, Bessie had not been fooled by Isabel's vague explanations.

Isabel met Bessie's questioning gaze, imploring her silently not to ask what was really bothering her. The temptation to confide in the woman who'd cared for her like a mother was overpowering, but she dared not risk it. Only her father, brothers, and uncle were aware of her true purpose in agreeing to this handfast. It was safer that way.

For once, Bessie relented and pretended that she did not know that something beyond the nerves of a soon-to-be bride were at work. She squeezed Isabel's hand again. "I'll call for a bath as soon as we arrive, and you'll feel much better."

Isabel managed a smile. Dear Bessie thought every problem could be solved by a long soak in lavender-scented water. "That sounds divine," she murmured. But as soothing as a warm bath would feel to her aching, travel-weary bones, Isabel knew that her problems would not be so easily solved.

It had all seemed so straightforward a few weeks ago when her father, the MacDonald of Glengarry, had suddenly appeared at court. Her initial surprise and excitement at his unexpected visit, however, had quickly turned to wariness. Her father had never shown much interest in her before, so there had to be a catch. If he was in Edinburgh, it had to be for something important. And she had never been important.

Until now.

She'd been shocked but enormously pleased by his request. Her father had sought out *her* help! She'd been so thrilled by the prospect of his approaching her with such an important mission that she had jumped at the opportunity to help without much considering the particulars of her task.

It was not the first time Isabel's eagerness to impress her family had landed her into tricky situations—Bessie could attest to that. But even now, she could not regret her decision. Already her brothers were more relaxed around her, even going so far as to tease her about some silly nickname at court. Her father, too, seemed different. He actually looked at her for longer than a moment.

Unfortunately, he was not the only one.

The back of her neck prickled with awareness. Her uncle was watching her. Again. Since leaving Dunscaith Castle a few days ago, Isabel had often felt her uncle's heavy stare boring into her back. He unnerved her. Whenever she turned, he was there, watching her with those hard, unblinking eyes.

She'd tried to pretend that she didn't notice, but his oppressive presence made it impossible. She couldn't stand the constant staring any longer. Willing herself not to be intimidated, Isabel turned to face him.

"How much longer, Uncle?" she asked, hearing the slight tremble in her voice. Her uncle, the MacDonald of Sleat, hadn't missed it, either.

He frowned and crossed his thick arms forbiddingly across his chest. A ruddy freckled countenance and graying red hair that receded determinedly from a high broad forehead gave him an older appearance than was suggested by his six and thirty years. Isabel could not help focusing on the center of his face, where one too many drams had left his tremendous nose bright red and bulbous. Overall, he presented quite an imposing figure. Sleat was a great bear of a man, his large frame heavily

padded with thick muscle and blanketed with a generous layer of dark red hair. Her nose wrinkled with dis-
taste as his strong scent floated toward her. He even
reeked.

Her eyes flickered over his heavy features, searching
for a connection. It was so difficult to believe he was related to her mother. Isabel had been told that except for
their like coloring, her late mother, Janet, was the very
antithesis of her much younger brother. Whereas Janet
had been a willowy, delicate beauty, brutish Donald
Gorm Mor was far from a handsome man.

He was, however, a powerful one. And her clan desperately needed that power if it were to have any chance
of survival.

Uncomfortable under her uncle's heavy stare, Isabel
waited, trying not to fidget, for his response. She looked
to her father, but he seemed just as annoyed by her show
of nerves as her uncle. She would get no relief in that direction. Her father needed her uncle, and her uncle
needed Isabel.

His next words reminded her of that fact. "Do not
disappoint me, daughter."

Her chest twisted. That had always been the problem.

"I thought you were made of sterner stuff, little
niece," Sleat added. "Yet here we are not yet in sight of
the castle and you quiver like a scolded bairn. Make
yourself ready."

Isabel knew what he was trying to do—shame her
into being brave—but it wasn't working. She knew what
she was up against. Only a fool wouldn't be nervous,
even if only a wee bit.

"Look, my lady, there it is now," one of the clansmen

whispered softly, momentarily dropping an oar and pointing across the loch before them.

Isabel forced herself to follow the direction of his finger. Slowly, she lifted her gaze to the castle that was to be her new home—or, if she was caught, her dungeon.

It wasn't so bad, she tried to convince herself. There was nothing outwardly sinister about Dunvegan Castle, unless one considered imposing stone walls that seemed to reach clear to the menacing heavens. Perched high on the steep rocky cliffs of the seashore, long, angled curtain walls hugged the edge of the bluff, connecting a tall square keep on the left with a smaller turreted tower on the right. And if the structure weren't forbidding enough, the smaller tower appeared to be adorned with gargoyles.

It was a bleak fortification built solely for the purpose of defense that bid no welcome. The castle seemed invulnerable to an attack or, more important, to a rescue. Once she entered, there was no going back.

For a moment, Isabel imagined she heard the sound of fairies laughing through the wind as the *birlinn* glided toward the rocks at the foot of the sea-gate stairs. She'd heard tales of the mystical creatures who lived in the forests about the castle, and it was even rumored that the MacLeods had fairy blood. She usually dismissed such stories as the superstitious meanderings of old folk—believers in the old ways. But on a ghostly night like this, the idea did not seem quite so far-fetched.

Shaking off her fanciful imagination, she told herself it was probably just the haunting tones of the pipers bearing her greeting to Dunvegan.

But even so, she closed her eyes and said a quick prayer for strength.

It never hurt to be safe.

She drew her cloak protectively around her shoulders. The wispy hairs on her arms were sticking straight up. Every instinct clamored against this course of action, but she had no choice. The survival of her clan rested on her shoulders. Or, perhaps more accurately, on her face.

Isabel frowned. She might have been chosen by her uncle for her beauty, but she would succeed by her wits and raw determination. She'd always considered her face a nuisance. It had not helped her win the respect of her father and brothers in the past, but maybe now it would prove valuable in that regard. If she could use her charms to disarm, to entice, to seduce, to blind her husband from seeing her true purpose, then it would all be worth it.

Isabel sat up a little straighter on the hard wooden bench. This was her chance to prove herself. She had to take it. She forced her chin up and took a deep breath.

She was a MacDonald, and no one could stop her.

Certainly not her clan's most reviled enemy, Rory MacLeod. Her soon-to-be handfast husband. Her *temporary* handfast husband.

Determined, Isabel turned and met Sleat's fierce stare. "I'm ready, Uncle."

Alone in the mist-shrouded moonlight, Rory Mac-Leod strode vigorously back and forth across the deserted *barmkin,* his muscles taut with anticipation. His MacDonald bride approached somewhere in the darkness below. He paused long enough to peer over the battlements, searching for a glimpse of the *birlinn* in the murky black haze. But there was still no sign of the accursed MacDonalds and his unwanted handfast bride.

It still seemed impossible. For every day of the past two years, Rory had kept his vow of vengeance to destroy Sleat for the dishonor he'd done to Rory's sister Margaret and the MacLeods. But today the feuding would come to an end.

Temporarily, at least.

One year. That's all he owed the king. And when the year was done, Rory would resume his plan. He wouldn't rest until Sleat was destroyed and the MacLeods once again held the Trotternish peninsula, land seized by the MacDonalds that rightly belonged to the MacLeods.

Rory drove blunt, battle-scarred fingers harshly through his shoulder-length hair. He'd been damn close to bringing down his enemy—until Sleat had run to the king, and James had decided to interfere.

But if King James thought to end the feud with marriage, he was sorely mistaken. Not after what Sleat had done to Margaret. The hatred between the clans ran too deep.

Rory's eyes traveled up to the tower where Margaret slept. Could it be only three years ago that his beautiful, bright-eyed young sister had ridden away from Dunvegan, bound for Dunscaith Castle, the happy young handfast bride of the MacDonald of Sleat? It seemed impossible that so much could change in such a short time. Margaret had returned to Dunvegan a sad shell of the sweet, naïve, yet spirited little sister he remembered.

Not long after Margaret's return, the MacLeods had attacked the MacDonalds at Trotternish with fire and sword. And so it began, two long, bloody years of feuding. The MacDonalds called it *Cogadh na Cailliche Caime*, "the War of the One-Eyed Woman." Even the ridiculous epithet riled his anger.

Rory resumed his pacing. Although every fiber of his being rebelled against this alliance, he had no choice. The unrest in the Highlands made it look as if King James could not control his own kingdom. When the subject of marriage had first been broached by the king, Rory had refused to consider the proposition. The years of constant fighting had taken a toll on his clan, but he resisted being tied to a MacDonald—even to end the bloodshed. But James would not be gainsaid. So Rory had come up with a solution, one that would not see him tied forever to his enemies. He rejected marriage to the chit but negotiated a handfast. Unlike a wedding, the temporary bonds of a handfast were easily undone.

Rory rubbed his stubbled chin. That the MacDonalds had not demanded marriage was strange, especially after the devastation brought about by his sister's handfast. Perhaps Sleat was not as interested in ending the feud as he pretended. Did he, too, seek a way out of the alliance? If Sleat was up to something, it likely involved his new bride.

Rory would be wary of this Trojan horse.

A voice floated out of the darkness, interrupting his private rampage. "You have the look of a caged lion, Chief. I assume your bride has not yet arrived?"

Rory stopped pacing and turned to see his younger brother Alex striding toward him across the *barmkin* from the old keep. Rory cursed the MacDonalds again, this time for what they had done to Alex. Rory noticed the same roguish grin, but the thin veneer of lightheartedness could not hide the dark shadows under Alex's eyes and the hard lines around his mouth forged in a MacDonald dungeon.

"No," Rory said. "There is no sign of them yet, but I'm sure 'twill be soon enough."

Alex grunted. "MacDonalds at Dunvegan. It defies belief."

"Aye, but not for long," Rory promised.

Alex turned to meet his gaze. "Do you really think Sleat will dare show his face?"

Rory's mouth fell in a grim line. "Count on it. He'll not miss the opportunity to taunt us with his presence by taking refuge in the protection of Highland hospitality. He knows we are honor bound to do him no harm while he is at Dunvegan."

Alex sighed and shook his head. "Poor Margaret."

"Don't worry. I've seen to Margaret. She'll be kept far from Sleat."

"Damn King James for his interference," Alex swore.

Rory smiled dryly, having had the very same thought only moments ago. Even in the darkness, he could see the frustration etched on Alex's face. Like him, Alex detested the untenable position James had put them in. "'Tis only for a year," Rory offered, "and then we will resume our negotiations with Argyll for a more powerful alliance."

"Suggesting a handfast was a stroke of brilliance," Alex agreed. "But repudiating the lass will not sit well with the king. I hear she is a great favorite of both James and Anne."

Rory understood Alex's concern, but it could not be avoided. "'Tis a risk. But one that I'm willing to take. James demands an end to the feud, but the clan still thirsts for revenge against Sleat. And although I may be outlawed and our lands declared forfeit, the king has not sought to enforce his power against me. When the time comes, I will think of a way to mollify him."

"You always do," Alex said ruefully. "For some odd reason, the king seems to show you favor—despite your being put to the horn."

Rory shrugged. "The lass will not be harmed. At worst, I will have to go to Edinburgh to explain."

"And if you are imprisoned?"

"It won't come to prison." He caught Alex's skeptical look. "This time. James is only flexing his muscles, and I'm fulfilling my duty. I agreed only to a handfast."

Alex thought for a moment. "I wonder why the king agreed?"

Initially, Rory had wondered the same thing. "He seemed confident that a marriage would eventually take place. I did not dissuade him of his err."

"I don't envy you your position," Alex said. But his grave expression was broken by the grin that spread across his face. For a moment, Rory thought he was looking at the brother of his past. "Though perhaps I should," Alex continued. "I hear she is a great beauty, charming, and witty. When our cousin Douglas was at court, he said that he had never seen her like. The courtiers even had a name for her, the Virgin Siren— luring men to death with her innocence and beauty. Our Scot improvement over England's aging Virgin Queen. I for one am anxious to behold such a paragon of virtuous innocence and irresistible beauty. What will you do if you are attracted to her?"

Rory quirked a brow. His brother should know better. "A beautiful face will not turn me from my duty."

"It would turn me."

Rory laughed. Alex had a well-known weakness for a

pretty lass, but he knew his brother too well to believe that. Honor and duty were just as important to Alex as they were to him. "There is no requirement that I spend any time with her. I'm sure I'll barely notice her," he said dismissively. "Besides, no one could be as beautiful as the rumors suggest. Or as innocent. She's spent the last year at court, after all. But it makes no difference to me what she looks like or how witty and charming she may be. When I marry, it will be for the clan."

As if on cue, a guardsman shouted, "A *birlinn* is approaching, Chief."

Striding purposefully with long, muscular legs toward the sea-gate entrance, Rory glanced back over his shoulder at Alex and brought an end to their discussion. "We shall see for ourselves if the rumors are true. My *temporary* bride has arrived."

Chapter 2

❖

First thou wilt reach the Sirens, who bewitch
All human beings who approach their shore ...

—*The Odyssey*, 12:42

The soft orange glow of the torches formed a long bright snake illuminating the dark night as the parade of MacDonald clansmen wound up the steep stone stairs of the sea-gate. Already aching from the uncomfortable boat ride, Isabel was well past exhaustion as she stumbled up the path behind a young clansman.

"This way, my lady. Careful where you step. These rocks are sure to be slippery in this weather." Willie of Dunscaith smiled at her, his blue eyes wide with admiration.

Isabel shook her head with chagrin at Willie's besotted expression. She could only hope the MacLeod was as easy to impress.

She would never understand the ridiculous effect she seemed to have on men. *It was always like this,* she thought with considerable frustration. Silly gaping grins, shy fumblings, or sly, lecherous stares. Her brothers were the only young men she knew who didn't act witless around her. She was tired of being seen only on the outside. Just once she would like to meet someone willing to look beneath the pretty shell and see inside— virtues as well as faults.

Yet Isabel was keenly aware that the very thing that annoyed her was the only reason she'd been chosen to help her family. She'd fought for her family's attention for so long, it hurt to have them finally value her for the thing she valued least.

She snuffed the pang of disappointment and turned back to Willie, smiling. "Thank you, Willie, I'll be sure to tread carefully."

She continued her climb up the steep stairway leading from the loch to the sea-gate. From a purely defensive position, it made sense that the only entry to the castle was from the sea, where the MacLeod could easily observe friend or foe; but it certainly did not make for easy travel. The landward side of the keep was completely inaccessible, perched high above a steep gully. Thus, for the final portion of their journey from Dunscaith, they were forced to journey by boat.

The days of travel had definitely taken their toll. Isabel's body ached in places that she had never before noticed. Her feet were nearly frozen, the ridiculously thin slippers her uncle ordered her to wear providing neither protection from the dampness nor traction on the slick stairs. Sleat had attended to every detail of her appearance, every article chosen not to illustrate court fashion or for practicality, but to entice.

At last she reached the top of the sea-gate stairs. Looking up, she frowned. She would never be able to escape without being seen. There had to be another way out. And if she wanted to leave here in one piece, she'd better find it.

The feeling of foreboding only increased when she glimpsed the armed MacLeod clansmen lining the wall, still as the carved pieces of a chessboard, guarding patiently as her party approached. Isabel eyed them warily. Even from a distance she could see that their bodies were poised like lions ready to pounce—almost as if they were hoping for an attack.

Her nerves were already on edge, but Willie's next words shook her to her core. "Come, my lady, your betrothed waits to greet you."

A massive shadow moved to block the doorway ahead. The blood drained from her face.

Good God, he was huge.

She couldn't see his face, but his herculean shape and proud stance left no doubt that he was a powerful warrior to be feared.

Warily, Isabel followed her father and uncle through the arched entry and up yet more stairs to where the MacLeod waited. She wanted desperately to fall back in cowardly retreat but willed her feet to keep moving forward. With each footfall, he appeared taller and more broad shouldered. He even towered over her uncle, who was one of the largest men she had ever seen. Never before had she beheld such raw strength. No one at court could compare. His well-muscled physique was beyond intimidating. She was not surprised that her uncle had found it so difficult to vanquish the MacLeod chief.

Dread consumed her. How could she defend against this? Her skills would be practically useless against such a man.

But he was only a man, she reminded herself. Just like any other. With the same needs, the same desires, and the same weaknesses. Isabel swallowed hard, thinking about what she might have to do to ply those weaknesses.

Passing through the sea-gate, they followed the Mac-Leod through the dark courtyard and into the stone entry of the square keep. Relieved to be out of the icy, all-pervading mist, Isabel took a moment to warm herself, rubbing her hands together until her fingers tingled with sensation.

She stood half-hidden behind her uncle, father, brothers, Bessie, and the rest of her MacDonald clansmen. Her position afforded her a good vantage point from which to observe the MacLeod, although his face was still obscured in the shadows of the flickering candlelight. When he turned toward her uncle, she could just make out the strong angle of his cheekbone and squared jaw.

As if meeting in battle, the two clans had unconsciously formed two groups, facing each other from opposite sides. The MacLeod stood at the pinnacle of his men, with a pack of fierce-looking warriors at his flank. An aura of absolute authority emanated from him as he confronted her uncle chief to chief.

Isabel heard the grumbling from behind him as the MacLeods recognized her uncle. She could well understand their anger. Privately, she thought it warranted. After the abominable way her uncle had repudiated the handfast to Margaret MacLeod, she wondered that the MacLeod had not taken a dirk to him the moment he entered the castle. She glanced at the MacLeod chief again. No, he looked far too controlled for that. But some of his men didn't. A few of the MacLeod warriors looked as if they were itching to put a blade through her uncle's heart. She took note of the way they looked to him immediately for direction. In some silent form of communication, with one small movement of his hand, he quieted the men behind him.

Clearly his men obeyed him without question, but

whether it was from fear, as with those who followed her uncle, or from loyalty and respect, she did not know.

Ignoring her uncle, he dipped his head in a short nod as he addressed her father. "Welcome to Dunvegan, Glengarry. It has been some time since we last met." He paused, both men no doubt remembering their last meeting over a battlefield. "I trust you had an uneventful journey."

The MacLeod spoke in Erse, the language of the Highlanders and Islanders. It was a tongue now disfavored at court and the Lowlands in favor of Scots, a dialect of English. His proud, strong voice reverberated powerfully in the small stone entrance hall. He spoke with the assurance of a man who was accustomed to giving orders—and to being obeyed.

Her uncle did not demonstrate such control. Obviously annoyed at being ignored, he cut off her father before he could reply. "MacLeod. Thank you for your most gracious welcome. Our journey was indeed uneventful, if unseasonably cold."

The MacLeod leveled his gaze at her uncle. "Sleat. I don't recall sending you an invitation." It was not a welcome. "Though you were expected."

The MacLeod stood with his legs spread and his hands clasped behind his back, to all outward appearances completely relaxed. But on closer inspection, Isabel could see the slight bulging of his forearm muscles and a tension in his legs. He was prepared, ready to pounce on her uncle at the slightest provocation, but maintaining complete control.

Sleat frowned. Clearly, he'd hoped to take the MacLeod by surprise. Isabel knew enough of her uncle to understand that he did not like to be thought of as predictable. His mouth curled in an angry sneer, furious to have been deprived of his fun. "I simply could not miss the opportunity to share in this joyous occasion. Surely this joining means that our differences belong in the past. We will look to a brighter future. The king demanded my presence to seal our new alliance. Did he not mention so in his missive?"

Watching the silent battle of wills between these two chiefs from behind her kinsmen, Isabel couldn't fail to notice that the MacLeod hadn't bothered to look in her direction. She experienced a twinge of disappointment. Apparently he was not as anxious for this match as she had been led to believe.

A reluctant bridegroom would certainly make her job more difficult. The circumstances were less than ideal, but surely he should show a slight bit of interest in her. They were to be handfasted, after all—man and wife in everything but name. Isabel herself felt a perverse need to see his face, to look upon the man to whom she would be joined—to the man she must seduce.

At that moment, the MacLeod stepped into the light and his face slipped out of the shadows. Her heart slammed into her chest and seemed to stop beating. Her eyes widened in disbelief. If she dreamed for the rest of her life, she would never have been able to conjure the perfection of his face.

The Norse ancestry of his clan was obvious in the MacLeod's height and coloring. The Highlands were filled with braw men, but he towered over most, standing a good hand above six feet.

His straight chestnut hair was streaked with heavy chunks of golden blond that shimmered in the candle-

light. The thick golden mane was cut bluntly at his
shoulders and swept over a strong brow as it fell dramatically across his left eye from a high arched cowlick. Long
thick lashes framed eyes the color of dark sapphires.
Bronzed skin set off his chiseled features—high cheekbones and a classic aquiline nose above a wide mouth—
to perfection. A hint of dark stubble shadowed the
square jaw of his otherwise clean-shaven face. When he
opened his mouth to speak, white teeth flashed against
tanned skin. He was glorious. Incomprehensibly, Isabel
felt drawn to this man. And for once, she was the one
gaping.

"My, he's a handsome one, poppet," Bessie whispered
in her ear. "If I were a young lass . . ."

Isabel dared not respond with anything other than a
nod, as she doubted her ability to speak coherently, *but
oh, what a delicious understatement.*

Pulling her eyes from his face, she innocently feasted
on the rest of him. He was dressed in traditional clothing: the great plaid, the *breacan feile,* of soft blues and
greens over a midlength shirt of saffron linen, the *leine
croich.* The plaid was belted at the waist by a leather gir-
dle and fell in soft folds to his knees. It was secured at the
breast by the silver MacLeod chieftain pin. His powerful,
muscular legs were bare except for soft leather boots.

He was every inch the warrior. Every inch the chief. It
was impossible to imagine him dressed in anything else,
certainly not the elaborate costume of court that she was
used to with its lace ruff, puffed slops, loose canions,
and fancy embroidered doublet with peascod. The traditional dress of the Highlands suited him to perfection.
Realizing that her mouth was open, Isabel slammed her
lips closed.

Attraction was something she hadn't considered.

The MacLeod seemed oblivious to her interest, as his narrow gaze was still fixated on her uncle. He took an intimidating step closer.

"James did not mention that your presence would be required," he said in hard, clipped, emotionless tones. "But it makes no difference. You will enjoy our hospitality until the handfast ceremony is complete."

Her uncle well understood the custom and obligation of hospitality among the Highland and Island clans—or he wouldn't be here. By tradition, he would be safe while under the roof of the MacLeod. MacLeod's honor demanded it, and a clan chief lived by his honor.

Isabel could see her uncle's anger build at the Mac-Leod's quick dismissal. "Of course, we will leave at the conclusion of the celebration." Sleat gave the MacLeod a knowing, lecherous look. "You will no doubt want to have some time alone with your new handfast bride. Speaking of which, where is your sister Margaret? I'm surprised not to *see* her here to welcome us."

Isabel sucked in her breath as a deadly silence settled over the room. She stared at her uncle in disbelief. How could he be so cruel as to mention the MacLeod's sister? But if her uncle thought to provoke the MacLeod, he was to be disappointed. The MacLeod chief didn't move a muscle. The man at his side, however, was not so restrained.

"You bastard." He lunged forward but was prevented from moving farther by the steel restraint of the Mac-Leod's arm.

She hadn't noticed the man before, but he could have been the MacLeod's twin. She squinted into the soft light. Perhaps he was a wee bit fairer of coloring. He was also not quite as large of build, albeit still impressive. Though handsome, his face lacked the imposing authority of the MacLeod's. *Must be a brother,* Isabel thought.

Confirmation came quickly.

"I'll see to our guest, brother." Rory MacLeod smiled, though it did not reach his eyes. The cold intensity of his gaze was enough to freeze Loch Carron in midsummer.

By now, the undercurrent of hate flowing between the two men was palpable, the MacLeod's cold and controlled, Sleat's smug and cruel. Thankfully, Isabel's father intervened, preventing further offense from her uncle. Her brothers moved forward to be introduced. Isabel waited, both impatient and anxious. Her first impressions of the MacLeod had done little to ease her dread. Though his handsome face might make her task decidedly more palatable, her attraction to him was an unexpected complication. She could not delude herself: This was not a man to be ruled by lust. Still, she was anxious to gauge his reaction to her. Could she find a chink in his steely armor?

She took a deep breath. It was time to find out.

Rory clenched his fists at his side in a fury born of pure hatred. Sleat's predictability didn't make it any easier to welcome his enemy into his keep. If it weren't for the sacred obligation of Highland hospitality, Sleat would be a dead man. He would deal with the blackhearted whoreson later, when he could calm the fire raging in his blood.

"These are my sons, Angus, Alisdair, and Ian," Glengarry said.

The lads came forward in birth order, shaking Rory's

HIGHLANDER UNTAMED   23

hand one by one. Rory appraised Glengarry's sons with calculated interest. In a few years, these young men would be powerful Highland warriors—a force to be reckoned with. To a man they were tall, well built, and, he supposed, uncommonly fair of face.

In other circumstances, he might well be proud to have these men as brothers. But with what he planned to do to their sister, Rory knew he would be creating powerful enemies. Unfortunately, their anger could not be avoided. He had a responsibility as chief. His path was chosen, and it didn't involve marriage to a MacDonald.

The time had come. He could ignore her no longer. Glengarry grasped her hand and pulled her out from behind her brothers. "And my daughter, Isabel MacDonald. Your betrothed."

For one shocking moment, the steady hand of time stilled. He felt as if he'd been slammed across the chest with the heavy steel of a claymore. All he could do was stare at the most beautiful woman he'd ever beheld. The Greeks had gifted him not with a horse, but with Helen.

Tiny perfect features were arranged flawlessly on a canvas of soft white skin. Her nose was small and dainty, her eyes large and tilted seductively. He'd never seen eyes that color before; they were the most unusual blue. Wait—he squinted harder in the dim light. They weren't blue; they were violet. Like Skye heather. Dense black velvet lashes swept upward and grazed fine arched brows. Sensing his stare, she nervously flicked her tongue out to moisten full, sensuous red lips surrounding tiny perfect white teeth. Those lush lips could drive a man wild with prurient imaginings.

Her face was framed by shimmering dark copper gold tresses that looked unbelievably soft and lush. A vivid image of those locks fanned out across a pillow behind her head sprang to mind before he could prevent it.

An unexpected surge of lust hit him straight in the groin.

The swift strength of the reaction knocked him from his stupor. Rory tore his eyes from her face.

He reached out to take her hand and felt a shock run through his body as their skin touched. Her fingers were like ice, and he was more than tempted to warm them with his own.

"My lord, I am most pleased to meet you," she said with a sultry voice, drawing his eyes to her once again. It was a mistake. Isabel pushed back her cloak and curtsied, bowing slightly forward.

Rory thought he might choke. Alex coughed uncontrollably at his side. As she leaned forward, Rory was served the most delicious view of bosom that he had ever been fortunate enough to behold. Her firm, round breasts were near bursting from the tight, low-cut bodice of her gown. The creamy white skin, softly pink from the cold weather, begged to be touched . . . or kissed. The surge of lust he'd experienced before was nothing compared with the bolt that struck him now.

Her dress was on the edge of indecent, by no means as modest as the traditional loose-fitting Scottish *arisaidh,* yet he was glad she did not seem to favor the ridiculously elaborate stiff gowns with their wide skirts and large ruffs about the neck so favored by the court of Elizabeth and its northern neighbor in Edinburgh. This dress exhibited her gorgeous body to perfection, the thin satin fabric clinging to her curves, dangerously hinting at the glory to be discovered beneath.

God had certainly outdone Himself when He created

Isabel. *Although He's had a laugh at our expense,* Rory thought. It was such delicious irony. The face of an angel barely saved from holiness by a sensuous mouth paired with a figure that did not evoke any thoughts of religion. Rather, she was the embodiment of temptation.

His body responded to her beauty the way his mind would not. The traitorous heat of desire burned in his loins, but Rory realized he would get no relief in that area. Yet although the attraction angered him, it did not worry him. Lust was an annoyance he could control. His duty lay elsewhere.

Bedding Isabel MacDonald, tempting as it may be, was not an option. Though it was expected under the terms of the handfast, Rory would not take her to bed knowing that he intended to forsake her in the end. He would not risk getting her with his child. A child who would soon be left without a father was a complication he simply could not allow.

Noticing the wide-eyed stares of the men next to him, Rory felt a fierce urge to pull her into his arms and cover her up. To a one, he trusted his men with his life and knew none would dare offense. But he could hardly blame them for appreciating what was so freely offered.

The awkward silence continued. He realized that she was waiting for him to speak. Rory looked down and noticed that he was still holding her hand. It was as soft as rose petals and looked so small and white next to his large, tanned, battle-scarred fingers.

He dropped it as if scalded.

Annoyed by his reaction, Rory forced his voice back to its cold, emotionless timbre. "Mistress MacDonald. You must be tired from your journey and wish to retire to your room. Tomorrow there will be a feast after the contract has been signed and the ceremony completed."

"Thank you, my lord, I am tired, and rest would be most welcome."

"Is this your maidservant?" he asked brusquely, indicating the woman next to her.

"This is my nursemaid, Bessie MacDonald. She will be helping me get settled. I hope that is not a problem?"

"No. There is a pallet in your chamber. She may sleep there if she prefers."

Before she could reply, he turned away dismissively. But not before he noticed the way her hands twisted in her skirts with the curtness of his response.

Alex shot him a puzzled glance as he stepped forward with a conciliatory smile. "I'm Alex MacLeod, Rory's brother. Welcome, and if I can do anything to help get you settled . . ." His eyes twinkled mischievously.

"Thank you, Alex, *your* welcome is most appreciated," Isabel said pointedly, offering him her hand.

Aware of her none-too subtle set-down, Rory couldn't help admiring her fortitude. At court, his forbidding size and stern expression seemed to terrify the lasses, yet she didn't seem intimidated at all. The lass had some spirit.

"Of course, you'll be wanting some refreshment, and a bath can be arranged if you desire. Deidre," Alex motioned to their old nursemaid who'd just joined them, "can bring you anything else you need, you have but to ask." He finished with a courtly bow and a broad grin.

"That sounds divine," Isabel said warmly.

Rory's eyes narrowed, watching the easy interchange between the two of them. He didn't miss the grateful look she'd directed at Alex.

A look that should be directed toward him. Admittedly, it wasn't like Rory to be so abrupt, but the lass unnerved him. He was sure it was only temporary. Most men would be knocked senseless when faced with such beauty, he rationalized.

But still he frowned. He was not most men. He was immune to such nonsense, unlike his brother. Alex might be blown over by a pretty face, but Rory wasn't. Nonetheless, he felt what could only be described as a twinge of jealousy at the sight of her giving his affable brother a grateful smile. The ridiculous sentiment was both unwelcome and annoying.

With a look to show his displeasure, Rory took control of the situation. He would have to remind Alex that the lass was a MacDonald. And for better or worse, his handfast bride for a year. "Deidre will show you to your room *now*. Until the morning, Mistress *MacDonald*."

Turning to his men, he directed Colin and Douglas to show the rest of the party to their sleeping quarters— where they would be well watched. But then he found his attention returned to Isabel, his gaze following her as she was led away.

Isabel MacDonald had been a surprise. He refused to consider the unexpected surge of lust he'd felt at meeting his new "bride." He'd never thought to find himself in the position of being attracted to the woman. Still, it did not bother him overmuch. Rory had survived the vicious attacks of Sleat for the last two years, as well as the scheming of a hostile king. He could easily manage the wiles of one small lass.

But something else gnawed at him. He was uncomfortably surprised by his initial impression of his bride; she seemed so young and innocent—almost vulnerable. Hardly the type of woman to be doing Sleat's bidding. If she was innocent of Sleat's intrigue, Rory would do his best to see that she was not harmed and was treated fairly. Beautiful or not, he would keep his distance. And in a year, when the handfast period was over, he would return her to her kin with no harm done.

When his "guests" had cleared the entry, Rory headed back outside on his way to the Fairy Tower, followed closely by his brother.

"Well, I'll be damned, you're a lucky bastard, Rory. I hope those noble intentions of yours not to bed the chit are ready to be put to the test," Alex said, his voice rough with envy. "Those 'exaggerated rumors' did not do her justice."

Rory tried to ignore him, but Alex's obvious admiration pricked at him uncomfortably. Actually, it annoyed the hell out of him. He did not doubt his brother's loyalty, but it surprised him to realize how much he did not want to discuss the attributes of this particular woman with anyone . . . including his brother.

"I suppose she's attractive enough," he replied, knowing he sounded ridiculous.

Alex snorted his disbelief. "Well, at least we know why the king agreed to the handfast," he stated matter-of-factly.

Rory lifted a brow in question.

"No man in his right mind would repudiate such a beauty."

"A man of sound mind must act where his duty lies," Rory reminded him.

Alex shook his head with regret. A sentiment that Rory could well understand.

"How important is this alliance with the Campbell lass?" Alex asked.

Rory sighed. "Very." Only an alliance with Argyll would provide the sway they needed with the king. But Alex had a point. Keeping his distance was going to be a wee bit more difficult than he'd anticipated. But he could handle it. There was nothing Rory MacLeod couldn't handle.

Chapter 3

Here in Heaven's eye, and all Love's sacred powers . . .
I knit this holy hand fast, and with this hand
The Heart that owes this hand, ever binding . . .
Both heart and hand in love, faith and loyalty.

—FRANCIS BEAUMONT and JOHN FLETCHER,
Wit at Several Weapons, v:i

Isabel knew she was taking too long to get ready. But she was nervous. Needing some time to collect her thoughts, she'd sent Bessie on another frivolous errand as she finished preparing for the ceremony that would bind her to the MacLeod—for a year.

A year to slip under his defenses and discover his secrets. A task made all the more challenging after meeting him.

The MacLeod was a hard man forged of muscled steel. Clearly, he would not easily be duped. Nor did his authoritative and forbidding temperament bode well for leniency if she were caught. He possessed a daunting ability to mask his reactions. Although she'd sensed his attraction to her last night, he covered it up so quickly that she wondered whether she'd only imagined it. Otherwise, his expression was inscrutable.

Never had she met a man who seemed less inclined to "blindly" do anything—especially fall in love. Getting under his armor was going to be a challenge indeed.

She bit her lip. Though she sensed no animosity, his conversation had been a disappointment of brusque, cool politeness. Clearly, her uncle had misled her. Rory MacLeod was not eager for this match.

At least her fears of brutish barbarity did not seem warranted. She sensed an inherent civility in him. Although not as polished as a Lowlander, he would stand out at court not for his rough manners, but for his impressive size and the raw dignity of his bearing.

Although the MacLeod demonstrated many qualities that she admired, they were nonetheless obstacles to her goal. Earning his trust was going to be that much more difficult.

Gazing in the looking glass, she carefully pinned her hair at the crown and adjusted the diamond-encrusted wreath atop her head. She could not shake the unease, the feeling that she was doing something wrong. But what choice did she have? Without her help, her clan was doomed.

But Isabel knew it wasn't just the fate of her clan that had brought her here.

For as long as she could remember, she'd shadowed her older brothers, traipsing after them as they hunted, gamed, and practiced their sword skills. Jumping at the opportunity to participate whenever they tolerated her, hiding and spying on them whenever they excluded her.

More often than not, they had ignored her.

Desperate to be included, she'd tried anything to get them to notice her. But no matter how accomplished she became, neither her challenges nor her feats of bravery brought her any closer to her brothers or father. Instead, she was treated as an afterthought. An outsider. Irrelevant and unimportant. Her chest tightened as the familiar emptiness settled in her stomach.

That unhappy realization had come years ago, but it

still pained her. Her childhood tears had long since dried. She rarely allowed herself to wallow in such self-pity. But somehow she realized that these painful memories weren't really memories at all, they were the fractured remains of her childhood dreams. She *still* craved their love and respect. That craving had brought her to Dunvegan.

For the first time in her life, they needed her.

Without this handfast, her uncle refused to support her father in his feud with the Mackenzies over Castle Strome, her childhood home. Her clan needed the strength of her uncle to survive. And Sleat needed a beautiful woman. A beautiful woman to entice the MacLeod into sharing the clan secrets. Secrets that would enable her uncle to destroy the MacLeods for good and further his quest to reclaim the ancient fiefdom of the Lordship of the Isles.

Sleat had charged her with two tasks: to find a secret entrance into the impregnable castle and to steal their precious magical talisman—the Fairy Flag. If the legends were to be believed, it was the mystical source of their strength and had twice previously saved the MacLeods from destruction.

Even now her stomach churned uncomfortably when she thought of what had been left unsaid, but what had definitely been implied. She must use *all* her charms to get what they wanted, even seduction. How could she, who had never allowed any man close enough to steal a simple kiss, seduce a fierce and ruthless Highland chief?

Now, after having met the man, Isabel was even more certain that it would never work. Rory MacLeod was as rock hard as a stone parapet, seemingly impervious to a weakness like emotion.

Bessie bustled into the room. "They're waiting, poppet." She stopped abruptly, putting her hand to her heart with a dramatic exclamation. "Ah, Isabel, you are a vision. More beautiful than I've ever seen you." She dabbed at her eyes with a square of linen. "Oh, how your mother would have loved to see you on your wedding day."

A wave of emotion swept over Isabel. Hot tears gathered at the back of her throat. Bessie's joy only made Isabel feel worse for deceiving her—and the mention of her mother nearly undid her completely. She took a deep breath.

"Then we best not keep them waiting any longer." Alighting into the corridor, Isabel took her first step down a path that could only lead to betrayal.

Rory faced the day with a much clearer head, once again in control of his errant—and lustful—thoughts. Visions of his bride had haunted his dreams—erotic fantasies of a wedding night that was not to be. Vivid images of candlelight and silk. He pictured her standing before him, looking up at him with those seductive eyes full of invitation. He'd taken his time in undressing her, running his hands over the soft velvet of her skin, slipping the wispy *night rail* down her shoulders, revealing her tantalizing nakedness one lush inch at a time. The dream had been so vivid, so real, he'd awakened hard and throbbing, needing release. He attributed his unusual reaction to the MacDonald lass to the disquiet brought on by Sleat's presence in his keep and the girl's undeniably rare beauty.

Today, Rory was prepared to be awed by her beauty. He would admire her as one would admire a beautiful piece of art—an object to put on display. But that was all. Admiration need not breed intimacy. It was enough that she was a MacDonald and not a suitable alliance for his clan. He need know nothing else.

As was custom, the handfast ceremony would take place outside. Given the circumstances, Rory had decided on a small, private ceremony to be followed by a larger celebratory feast. Notwithstanding the enmity between the clans and the unwanted alliance, the clan would be disappointed with anything else. Feasting was an integral part of Highland life, and Highlanders welcomed any excuse to celebrate.

Thus, as the morning sun gathered intensity on the eastern horizon, Rory, Alex, Sleat, Glengarry, and Isabel's brothers gathered around the *barmkin* awaiting his bride.

His very late bride, the ten o'clock hour having come and gone some time ago. Perhaps she was having second thoughts? Oddly, the notion didn't relieve him as much as it should have.

Glengarry had glanced up at her chamber enough times for Rory to know that he was growing impatient and annoyed. Finally, Glengarry smiled with relief. "Ah, here she is now."

Rory turned, and all of his newfound clarity vanished.

He felt that same forceful blow to the chest, the same physical intensity of attraction. He was as overwhelmed as when he'd first beheld her last night, perhaps more so. In the clear light of day, Isabel MacDonald was breathtaking.

Her thick copper gold tresses blazed a fiery red in the bright sunlight. The long wavy strands were swept from the sides of her face and held in place with a silver-wired wreath heavily decorated with diamonds and tiny pearls. Her features were at once both delicate and vivid. The snowy whiteness of her skin contrasted with the dark brows and lashes that framed her lovely violet eyes and the bloodred pout of her sensual lips.

His gaze traveled down her face and halted at her breasts. He sucked in his breath and tried not to stare, feeling the hot blood flow to his loins as his cock thickened in appreciation.

Once again her dress bordered on indecent, something more suitable for one of King James's masques than a wedding. Most Scotswomen would choose to wear a brightly colored gown or *arisaidh* to their handfasting. But not Isabel. She had chosen an unadorned ivory damask gown that in its simplicity was anything but simple. The shimmering fabric draped provocatively across her shapely figure, tantalizing the senses with the glory of her lush body as the gown clung to her narrow hips and gently rounded bottom. The bodice was daringly low, cut in a deep square down the front of her chest. Her firm round breasts were barely covered, threatening to spill out at the slightest provocation. Rory thought, or just imagined, he could discern pale pink tips below the lacy edge of her bodice. Even as his body hardened with desire from all that bare skin, he had to acknowledge that there was something innocent and virginal about her dress. The unconventional bridal color suited her perfectly.

The realization hit him: Without a doubt, the next year was going to be the longest of his seven and twenty years.

Suddenly aware that her family was watching his reaction with unconcealed interest, he plastered a blank expression on his face. "Mistress MacDonald, I hope you have found your room to your liking."

"Yes, thank you. It was delightful. We were very comfortable."

Pleasantries dispensed with, he cast a glance around to make sure the others were ready. Out of the corner of his eye, he noticed Deidre standing next to Isabel's tiring woman.

Isabel caught his glance. "I hope you don't mind . . ." She hesitated. "But I invited her."

"So I see."

His tone must have alarmed her, because she began to fidget. "Well, when I sent for her this morning to thank her for arranging the bath at such a late hour, she mentioned that she'd served your family since your older brother was a bairn. I just thought she might want to be here."

Disconcerted by her kindness, Rory didn't speak. He looked into her eyes, seeing nothing but sincerity.

"Are you angry?" she asked in a small voice.

"No. Merely chastened not to have thought of it myself."

A wide smile lit her face, and Rory froze. Her eyes twinkled with a joyous effervescence that transformed her face from regally beautiful to playful and enchanting. A tiny dimple at the corner of her mouth lent a mischievous twist to her lips that made him think of naughtiness in other places. Like the bedchamber.

He shifted his gaze to Glengarry and spoke. "Let us begin."

Glengarry looked to his daughter. "Isabel?"

Rory's eyes narrowed. It seemed as if Glengarry were giving her an option. Seeming surprised but enormously pleased by the deferral, Isabel simply nodded.

With Glengarry officiating, Rory turned to face his bride, standing close enough to smell the sweet lavender of her hair and discern the previously unnoticed spattering of freckles across her nose. The freckles charmed him; the slight imperfection suggested a surprising lack of vanity in one so beautiful. This was a woman who enjoyed the outdoors, who valued the sun shining on her face more than the veneration of a flawless complexion. He scowled at the direction of his thoughts, realizing that he'd done just what he'd vowed not to do.

A beautiful object, he reminded himself.

Still, as they stood in the courtyard before the witnesses to their handfast, he was uncomfortably aware of how small and delicate she looked. And nervous. His hand moved about five inches before he pulled it back to his side.

What the hell was he doing?

He cleared his throat, telling himself to stop acting like a fool.

Clasping right hand to right and left to left, Glengarry took a piece of plaid and tied it around their hands, binding them together. Rory stared at her tiny hand in his, so soft and tender in his rough battle-scarred hands. Her fingers were like ice and he realized she was nervous— maybe even scared. He felt a strong swell of protectiveness, and couldn't remain unaffected by the symbolic allusion to the bond they were about to make. Though there would be no marriage, the handfast would be real enough.

He spoke the vows that would bind them together for a year. "I, Roderick MacLeod, Chief of MacLeod, do pledge my troth to Isabel MacDonald and with this handfast do hereby covenant to take her to wife for the period of no less than one year."

Isabel repeated the vows, and it was done. Except for one part.

"What are you waiting for, MacLeod?" Sleat taunted. "Aren't you going to kiss the bride?"

Rory tensed, knowing that it was necessary. He was reluctant. Not because he didn't want to kiss her, but because of how much he ached to do so. To taste her. To sample the forbidden fruit of her delectable mouth.

Cheeks flaming, Isabel stared at her toes, the tips of her silver slippers just peeking out from below the embroidered edge of her gown.

"Aye," he said, slipping a finger under her chin. "A kiss to seal our vows."

Slowly he lowered his mouth, pausing for an instant to inhale her flowery scent before his lips touched hers. He almost moaned as the rush of desire flooded his body with heat. *Dear God,* she tasted sweet.

And she was unbearably soft. Her skin was pure velvet under his fingertips.

He lingered, the urge to deepen the kiss primal. He wanted to draw her into his arms and crush her full breasts against his hard chest. To feel the shape of her hips as she pressed against his heavy groin. To plunge his tongue into the sweet cavern of her mouth and drink.

Yet somehow he held back.

Slowly, he lifted his mouth. Gazing at her face tilted to his, the rosy flush of passion spread across her cheeks, her lips still gently parted, Rory knew a dark moment of almost uncontrollable desire. Desire that gnawed at every inch of his body with a crushing, overpowering intensity.

For the first time in his life, Rory MacLeod—a man who'd faced scores of fearsome warriors on the battle-field and driven his enemies to their knees with terror—knew alarm.

He dropped his hand from her chin and took a step back. *That* wouldn't happen again.

Isabel had never been kissed before, and she was com-pletely unprepared for the all-consuming intensity of the experience. His rough fingers cradled her face with such tenderness, a sharp pang of longing tugged deep in her chest. And when his lips brushed hers, she knew a mo-ment of pure heaven. A moment of connection so pow-erful, it frightened her—making her body feel almost not her own. She'd never imagined how a kiss could possess.

With one gentle touch he branded her.

His lips were so much softer than she'd imagined, completely incongruous with the hard, implacable chief. He tasted . . . delicious. His warm, spicy breath engulfed her senses as he pressed his mouth more firmly against hers.

Her heart fluttered high in her chest and her body seemed to soften as sensation washed over her. She felt weak. Boneless. And wonderfully warm with the swell of burgeoning desire. For a moment she forgot the lie that had brought them together. She forgot the presence of her family and surrendered to the force of a more powerful calling.

She wanted more.

She sank against him, leaning her body closer to his. Close enough to feel the heat radiating from him and sense the strength barely harnessed under the powerful façade. He was big and hard, making her deeply aware of her own femininity.

For one precious instant it seemed as if he was going to wrap her in his muscular arms and deepen the kiss. His mouth moved over hers and the rough stubble of his jaw scraped over her skin, sending ripples of anticipation shuddering through her. His fingers tightened on her jaw as he pulled her closer. Unconsciously her lips parted, knowing there was something more.

Perhaps he noticed her reaction, for he stiffened and abruptly pulled his mouth from hers. Just before he released her, his dazzling sapphire eyes had briefly studied her upturned face. Her chin barely came to the middle of his chest. Isabel thought she glimpsed a smoldering fire in his gaze, but the aloof blank shutter dropped back into place, shielding any emotion.

He dropped his hand from her face, and the spell was broken.

He'd barely looked at her since. In fact, he seemed enthralled by the conversation of her father on his right and the lovely dark-haired woman seated next to Glengarry.

Unfortunately, Isabel was not nearly so indifferent.

Peering from under her thick eyelashes at the man seated next to her, she felt strangely aware of her new handfast husband. Indeed, she'd been aware of him since the moment she'd stepped out of the keep this morning, his tawny hair shimmering in the sunlight. He drew the eye like a fiery beacon on a moonless night, the magnificence of his presence not merely a result of his stature, but flowing from the aura of authority that surrounded him. He held himself like a king. A man born to rule.

Of all the men gathered in the *barmkin* for the ceremony, he was the only one who hadn't seemed bothered by her late arrival. Apparently, his confidence extended to her.

Hers, however, had been shattered. After that heart-stopping kiss, Isabel drifted through the rest of the day in a bewildered haze. Vaguely, she recalled sharing the ceremonial glass of wine and returning to the keep for the signing of the contract between her father and the MacLeod, making it official. She was his for a year.

But only a year. She'd do best to remember it, no matter how thrilling his kiss.

Although she knew that their handfast was but a temporary bond, sitting at the dais in the great hall observing the jubilant celebration feast around her, she felt oddly unsettled. She could almost believe it was a marriage in truth, blessed for eternity. Isabel forced herself to remember that it was all a sham, no matter how official it seemed. The contract, the ceremony, even the dress, were all part of her uncle's plan. The handfast was only a way out when her job was done.

This day was a farce. She had dreamed of the happiness of her wedding day since she was a little girl. Yet even with all the suitors she was presented with at court, she despaired of ever finding the right man. In many ways, Rory MacLeod epitomized the proud, handsome man she had imagined herself someday falling in love with and marrying. Just her luck. The first man to ever really intrigue her was the one she absolutely could not have. Of course, she reminded herself, he was not the man of her dreams.

In her dreams, her husband did not ignore her.

It was an unusual experience for her. Isabel was not used to complete indifference from men. He was unfailingly polite but distant. And annoyingly inscrutable. It was difficult to believe that this was the man who'd kissed her with such tenderness.

If only she could break through the icy shield he donned when around her and force him to take some notice of her. Not in the reckless way she drove herself to get attention from her family. No, for the first time in her life Isabel wanted a man to notice her as a woman.

That was going to be a challenge, if today was any indication.

In between the steady stream of well-wishers and the MacLeod's odd question—"More beef, Isabel?" or "Would you care for some wine, Isabel?"—she'd managed to count every window in the great hall. Twelve. Though it was a stretch to consider the narrow slits in the ten-foot-thick wall windows. It took a determined beam of sunlight to penetrate such a formidable impediment. Instead, the large room was lit by candles and the smoky glow of peat from the fireplace.

The walls were sparsely decorated with only the occasional threadbare tapestry of no great artistry, but hung prominently on the wall behind the dais was an ominous-looking three-foot-long *claidheamhmór*. The enormous two-handed cross-hilted sword looked far too unwieldy to be of use, but it still gave her pause.

Did it belong to him?

If anyone could lift that thing, he could. Isabel stole a glance at the man sitting beside her. She noticed the way his shoulders and arms strained against the fine linen of his shirt. The knowledge settled low in her belly. Rory

MacLeod was the most physically imposing man she'd ever met. Never had she been so aware of a man's size and strength. Though it would be impossible not to be. He dominated the space beside her.

His heavily muscled shoulders were so wide, they brushed against hers each time he reached to take a piece of beef or a bit of bread smeared with butter from their shared trencher, sending a thrill shooting through her. Even the air seemed filled with his distinctive masculine scent of sea and heather, an alluring mix that seemed to permeate her skin and sink deep into her consciousness. She found herself responding to his raw masculinity, not with fear, but with something akin to excited curiosity. She thought of touching him. To see whether he was as hard and strong as he looked. She shook off the strange yearning. What was the matter with her?

While they dined, she'd also had the opportunity to observe him with his clan. It was clear from the countless men who'd approached the dais to offer their congratulations with honest admiration and pride that he was both revered and loved. With his men, he had an easygoing banter that was friendly and relaxed.

The complete antithesis of how he was with her.

Stymied by his monosyllabic replies, she had finally given up and turned to Alex for relief from her boredom. At least Alex was welcoming. But for some reason, his handsome face did not stir her senses in the same way as his brother's. Nonetheless, Isabel relaxed a bit and found herself responding to his charming compliments with a smile.

After a few minutes, she turned to glance at Rory, expecting him to be ignoring her. Instead, she was surprised to find him watching her.

"Are you enjoying yourself, Isabel?"

She was taken aback by the chill in his voice. If she didn't know better, she could almost think he sounded jealous.

His blue eyes had turned black. The man could melt rock, Isabel thought as she squirmed under his intense glare. She would give her eyeteeth to know what he was thinking. Determined not to be intimidated by his forbidding demeanor, she ignored the sudden nervousness twisting in her stomach. *I have done nothing wrong,* she reminded herself.

Not yet, at least.

She lifted her chin, her gaze leveled unflinchingly to his. She spoke lightheartedly, as if she had noticed nothing amiss. "Yes, your brother is most kind. We have been discussing your talented pipers. They are wonderful."

He waited a long time to respond. When he did, she wondered if she'd only imagined his anger. "The Mac-Crimmons have played for the MacLeods for many years," he said. His expression was perfectly bland as he toyed with the heavily encrusted stem of his silver goblet, the pads of his fingers gently grazing over the smooth ridges of decorative relief. There was something deeply sensual about his movements, and she couldn't look away, imagining his fingers on her. Would he touch her with such care? A shiver of awareness slithered down her spine. The sound of his voice shook her from her musings. "They are the best pipers in Scotland," he finished.

Isabel heard the note of pride in his voice. The Isles were the last bastion of the Gaelic culture that had flourished under the Lords of the Isles. Pipers and bards were deeply important to the preservation of that tradition.

He started to turn back to the conversation with her father on his right. Not wanting the conversation to end so soon, Isabel asked, "Who is that charming child over there?"

Rory turned in the direction she indicated, and a broad smile spread across his face. Her heart stopped. If she had thought him handsome in his severity . . . the transformation was dazzling. The small lines around his eyes deepened. Entrancing dimples appeared at each side of his mouth. Bessie would say the fairies had kissed him. Perhaps the stories of his fairy blood were not that far off. His attractiveness certainly had a magical quality.

But it was the softness in his eyes when he looked at the little girl that struck her. He had a genuine fondness for the child. Isabel realized it was the first time she'd seen honest emotion behind that stoic reserve.

Unaware of his effect on her, he continued. "Ah, wee Mary MacLeod is already something of a legend around these parts. She has a talent that is quite rare for one so young. You will enjoy her stories."

"The child is a bard?" Isabel asked with genuine surprise.

"Mary is but five, but already she shows great promise. The clan is enchanted by her youth, and she often entertains us with her poems."

"I can see it is not only the clan who is enchanted," Isabel teased, and was rewarded with a boyish grin that caused her heart to beat erratically. "You like children?"

He seemed puzzled by her question. "Of course," he replied, as if there could be no other answer.

But Isabel knew there was. Not all men were comfortable around children, and few showed such obvious delight. She knew that only too well.

He never looked up when she entered.

"Father?"

"Not now, child. I'm busy."

"Then when?"

"Later."

But, of course, later never came. The memory dimmed and a very different thought struck her. She bit her lip, trying not to betray her sudden unease. "You will be wanting bairns, then?"

The softness around his eyes hardened, and the charming grin was gone. "Not for some time."

Furious to have angered him, Isabel turned back to their original conversation. "I thought the Irish O'Muireaghsain were the *seannachie* of the MacLeods."

Rory raised one eyebrow. "You have learned something of our family. Yes, the hereditary bards are the O'Muireaghsain. But they have been so long from Erin, I doubt they consider themselves anything but true Islanders."

"My knowledge of your family is quite limited. Nonetheless, you can't be a MacDonald and not learn something of the MacLeods." She met his gaze and added boldly, "Our clans share quite a history." *No need to hide from the obvious.*

He kicked his legs back under the table and took a long drink of *cuirm,* peering at her from over his glass. "I know you've had naught to do with the feud between our clans. I harbor no ill feelings toward you for what your uncle did to Margaret two years ago. But others may not be as accepting, Isabel."

Isabel nodded. Overcoming the prejudice of being a MacDonald would not be easy, but it was to be expected. "Well, at least everyone seems to be enjoying themselves right now," she said, indicating the mix of clansmen gathered for the feast. MacLeods, MacCrimmons, and MacAskills occupied one side of the hall, and her party of MacDonalds occupied the other. The former enemies kept to themselves, except for her three brothers. She shook her head with amusement as she watched them flirting shamelessly with the MacLeod serving girls. Those three never missed an opportunity to dally, even in the midst of a pack of wolves. She sighed.

He was watching her. "You must be exhausted."

She smiled and admitted, "Perhaps a bit."

"You may retire to your room at any time."

Isabel tried to control the fierce pounding of her heart. The night loomed before her. "Will my things be moved to another room this night, my lord?" she asked softly.

As soon as the words were out, she regretted them. His momentary good humor vanished. "I thought we might take some time to get to know each other. You will stay where you are for now." He spoke the last with cool finality.

Her eyes widened with shock, and her cheeks flushed with embarrassment. His reticence to consummate the handfast was unexpected, and unusual. She had been counting on the private time spent in their chamber to help him fall in love with her. She had even been preparing herself mentally for the possible bedding tonight.

She should be relieved. After that kiss, she'd been a mass of knots. If she reacted like that to a simple kiss, what would happen when he bedded her?

Isabel had hoped that he might give her some time to

get used to the idea. Now that he had, she didn't know what to think. Either he was very thoughtful or he was not attracted to her. She hoped it was the former—for the sake of the plan, of course. Still, she felt unaccountably disappointed.

A high-pitched tinkle of laughter mixed with Rory's husky voice drew her immediate attention. When she spied a beautiful dark-haired woman next to her father, another explanation crept forward. Her heart twisted in her chest. Isabel hoped he was not finding his pleasure elsewhere.

Rory hadn't missed the twinge of hurt in her eyes when he informed her they wouldn't be sharing a room. But he hadn't been prepared for the heat that surged through his body when she mentioned removing to his chamber. Extending his legs under the dais, he took another swig of *cuirm,* trying to repress the lust betraying his body. He could only imagine what it would be like to bed her when a chaste kiss set him on fire. Never had a kiss affected him so, setting off primal urges that had only worsened over the long meal. The sensual curve of her mouth taunted him. He wanted to taste her again. To feel her soft lips moving under his. She'd tasted so sweet and desire had hit him full force. His body hardened just looking at her. Damn. He shifted in his seat with renewed discomfort.

He was aware of the direction of her thoughts. He'd done his best to ignore her throughout the feast and had flirted shamelessly with the witless but beautiful Catriona MacCrimmon. He knew he was wrong to encourage Catriona, a past relationship that had outlived its initial excitement, but he had to find some way to distract himself.

He'd had to fight the urge to stare at his new bride all day. He told himself it was only because he had a duty to observe those around him—especially those whose very presence demanded a certain level of suspicion. Still, he wasn't nearly as indifferent as he pretended. He wished it was simply her beauty, but damned if he didn't find her intriguing for other reasons.

Rory found himself noticing little things, like the way she twisted her hair when she was nervous or bit her lip when she was thinking. But it wasn't just little things that intrigued him. He'd also witnessed her kindness and consideration in her dealings with strangers, like inviting Deidre to the handfast.

And after the ceremony, he'd noticed how she'd immediately sought approval from her father. There was such eagerness in her expression, it was almost hard to watch. But he had. So he hadn't missed her acute disappointment when none was forthcoming. Her relationship with her father and brothers seemed very awkward, almost stiff. As if she were a fragile piece of porcelain, and they didn't know quite what to do with her. Rory could commiserate.

Still, he felt sorry for her; he was close with all of his brothers and sisters. He stopped himself and frowned. Except the youngest. Flora had left with her mother as a child after the death of their father and rarely returned. It was a situation he intended to rectify to ensure that the girl didn't grow up without knowing her kin.

Isabel was endearingly vulnerable, but not timid. The strength with which she bore his uncharacteristic display of temper had proven that. Initially, he'd been relieved when she'd finally given up and turned to Alex.

Let her be a burr under his saddle for a while. Yet Alex seemed genuinely to enjoy her company, looking more relaxed than he had in some time. This should have made Rory happy, but instead he'd lashed out. Leaving him to wonder why.

He was loath to admit it, but the girl's bravery impressed him. The black look he threw her had felled many men much stronger and more experienced. Beneath that beautiful polished exterior there lurked an undeniable strength. Most lasses would have taken to the hills by now, but she somehow managed to make him feel to blame for intimidating her.

Such vulnerability mixed with spirit and courage was an unusual combination. He shook his head. Damned if she didn't remind him of his sister Margaret . . . before.

In truth, he didn't know what to make of her. She had far more substance than he'd expected and none of the haughty confidence of a beautiful woman. She surprised him, and Rory didn't like surprises. Isabel MacDonald was almost too good to be true, especially coming from Sleat. So far the lass had done nothing to deserve his mistrust, but it was early yet. She bore greater study; he would have to keep his eye on her. From a distance.

Sitting so close to her all afternoon and trying to ignore her had been a lesson in perseverance.

She looked enchantingly dainty next to him, and so damnably lovely. They were squeezed close together on the bench, and each time she moved she brushed against him, sending bolts of awareness shooting through him.

Isabel MacDonald was a woman who seduced by mere proximity. The subtle fragrance of lavender that wafted from her hair, the delicate way her fingers picked at the food on their trencher, the half-lidded expression of pleasure in her eyes as she savored a delicious morsel, the enticing way her tongue darted out to catch a stray grain of sugar on her lip. He couldn't watch her without imagining the same look on her face as he pleasured her or her tongue flicking out to taste other things with equal relish. The blatant sensuality of her movements was made all the more powerful by the simmering passion he'd detected in her kiss.

Everything about her screamed soft, sweet femininity and hot, passionate sex just waiting to be released. And Rory, or at least his body, was listening.

He couldn't look at her without getting hard. Her breasts were incredible, lush and round, displayed to mouth-watering perfection in her gown. He ached to feel them in his hands, in his mouth, and pressed against his naked chest. The temptation to take what was rightfully his proved more difficult than he'd imagined. He couldn't wait for the meal to end.

His lustful thoughts were turned by a loud crash from across the room, shattering the peace of the celebration. He heard a table turning over and the unmistakable thump of fists and the sounds of a skirmish. A quick glance told him all he needed to know—two men, MacDonald versus MacLeod.

Rory stood up, rigid with fury. *"Enough."* The boom of his voice snapped like a whip across the hall. The room fell to a deadly hush. The men stopped fighting as all eyes turned to him.

He heard Isabel gasp beside him. "Ian," she cried softly.

Rory recognized Isabel's youngest brother, still huffing from the exertion of the brawl, blood streaming down the side of his face from a cut at his temple. Opposite him stood Fergus MacLeod, one of his own men.

A fierce warrior, but also a quick-tempered one. Rory took in the situation, noting the horrified serving girl standing just to the side. Fergus's wife.

"Here." Rory pointed to the foot of the dais. "Both of you." When they stood before him, he ordered, "Explain."

Both men started at once.

"One at a time." When they'd finished, it was as Rory thought. Ian had flirted with the pretty serving girl a little too vehemently for the likes of her husband. Fergus had reacted by slamming his fist into Ian's face, breaking the peace.

Rory clenched his jaw and stared at his man, not bothering to hide his displeasure.

"I hope you intend to do something about this, MacLeod," Sleat said, obviously relishing the situation.

Rory ignored him. He did not need to be reminded of his duty.

The heat of the battle had worn off enough for Fergus to realize what he'd done.

"What have you to say for yourself?" Rory demanded. "You've broken the sacred obligation of Highland hospitality and disturbed the peace of this hall." He gestured to Ian. "This man is our guest."

Fergus bowed his head, knowing his actions had shamed the clan. "I acted without thought."

Before he could hand down the punishment, Isabel put a tiny hand on his arm. "Please—"

Rory stiffened. He knew what she was going to say. He was also aware of the eyes still upon them. "Don't interfere, Isabel."

"Please," she whispered in a soft voice. "It wasn't all his fault."

Gazing down at her hand on his arm, Rory felt something strange twist in his chest. He should be furious that she dared question his authority before his clan, but instead he admired her sense of justice. Even if it was misplaced. "Do I need to instruct you on the obligation of Highland hospitality?"

"No, it's only that—"

"Enough," he said, this time harsh enough for her to stop. He turned back to Fergus and made his ruling. "For your actions, you shall pay the fine of three spring calves. Two for the MacDonalds and one to me."

A collective gasp followed his ruling, but the angry glares were directed at the MacDonalds and not at Rory. He heard the serving girl begin to sob. It was a harsh punishment, but a fair one. He sat down to resume his meal, though in truth he'd lost his appetite.

Rory sat quietly for a long time, furious at having his decision questioned but struck by her compassion all the same. Especially since the man involved was her brother.

"My decision displeased you," he said. "You think it too harsh?"

She picked at the bits of food on their trencher before answering. "His family will suffer a substantial loss of income."

"Aye. It will cost them severely, but they will not starve. Fergus broke a sacred obligation, disparaged the honor of the clan, and must be punished accordingly. That is my duty." He cursed himself for explaining further. "What kind of chief would I be if I did not uphold our laws?"

"There is no shame in compassion."

"Compassion is for those not charged with responsibility," he said flatly. He didn't expect her to understand a chief's obligation to act decisively and forcefully. Women were softhearted creatures. He would have been within his rights to have Fergus flogged or put in irons. He looked her straight in the eyes. "The obligation of Highland hospitality is absolute. If you break the law, you suffer the consequences." The warning was unmistakable. "There is no mercy for wrongdoers."

Rory didn't fail to notice when she paled.

Chapter 4

❖

Late the next morning, Isabel stood alone on the battlements overlooking the sea loch, watching her family's departure with a heavy heart. Sheets of gray clouds blanketed the sky, dumping buckets of rain from the heavens, stirring the sea into a torrential frenzy. As the *birlinn* tossed atop the waves, it was difficult to tell where the rain ended and the loch began.

A long summer day on the Isle of Skye.

Wonderful.

Her hand darted from beneath the warm folds of her cloak, attempting to gather the errant strands of auburn that whipped across her face and tangled in her mouth. Her efforts were in vain. The wind blew mercilessly, tearing her hair from its bindings as soon as she'd finished.

Icy droplets pelted her raw cheeks, mingling with the tears that slid from the corners of her eyes. She sank deeper into her cloak, shielding herself as best she could from both the weather and the watchful eyes of the MacLeods. Isabel refused to let them witness her despair.

Her kinsmen's departure had come without warning. She had thought to have more time to get used to Dunvegan. And to Rory. But they were gone. And she was alone in a den of wolves.

On the dock below her, silent cheers of celebration trailed the *birlinn* of MacDonalds as it disappeared from view. The MacLeods were pleased to be rid of their enemies—storm or no storm. Their sentiments were hardly a surprise. Among the Scots, feuds were not easily forgotten or forgiven.

She wondered how many wished she were on that boat. Did Rory? Probably. Clearly, he was not eager for this handfast, and meeting her had not changed his opinion. For as impressed as she was by him, he seemed equally unimpressed by her. Precisely the opposite of what she'd hoped.

She knew her job wasn't going to be easy, and it wasn't. He suspected something, of that she was sure. His words of warning last night had been unequivocal. She didn't think she'd ever forget his face when he told her there was "no mercy for wrongdoers." She'd had the eerie sensation that he was peering right inside her.

She shivered, but not from the icy rain and wind. She would just have to find a way to slip under his considerable guard. The incident with her brother Ian and Fergus MacLeod had shaken her. If the MacLeod discovered her ruse, he would deal with her coolly and decisively. And fairly, she admitted. He was a man used to making hard decisions; he would not waver in his duty. Yesterday had shown her that. She would just have to make sure she wasn't discovered.

Not a simple proposition with a man who seemed to notice everything—like her earlier conversation with her uncle. Although he could not hear them from across the courtyard, Isabel had felt the heavy weight of the

MacLeod's gaze as her uncle cornered her, bidding her farewell with his usual aplomb. With one arm draped protectively about her shoulders, Sleat drew her aside in the courtyard for last minute instructions before his departure down the steep sea-gate stairs.

There was nothing subtle about Sleat's warning. Her uncle's words still rang in her ears: "Do what you must, but find the entrance and bring me the Fairy Flag within the year. The MacDonalds have been defeated by the flag once before; I want it in my hands. If you are successful, I will support your father against the Mackenzies." She tried not to stiffen under his heavy arm. In a thick voice dripping with menace, he leaned close to her, his putrid breath singeing her ear. "Do you get my meaning, Isabel? Do what you must. For when the time comes, I want no opposition to my claim for the Lordship. It is the hereditary right of the MacDonalds to rule these lands. With the MacLeods destroyed, there will be no one to interfere. Don't forget that you willingly agreed to help. It's too late for second-guessing. The lives of your clansmen are at stake, and it's up to you to do what it takes to save them. Fail me, and you fail your clan."

His words chilled her. "Don't worry, Uncle, I wasn't thinking of changing my mind. I know well what I must do. No one will suspect what I am about."

Realizing that Rory was still watching them, she patted the MacDonald's hand as a beloved niece might do to reassure a doting uncle. Her expression gave no hint of the consequence of her words.

Sleat appeared mollified. He relaxed his hold around her shoulders. "Be extremely cautious. And whatever you do, don't allow yourself to become seduced by the

MacLeod. You must be wary of him at all times—he knows well how to make a lass fall for his dubious charms." The MacDonald drew his fingers to his chin thoughtfully.

He continued as if thinking aloud to himself, "You are very beautiful, but young and innocent. Perhaps it would have been better . . . Well, no matter. It is too late now. I will send word to you soon, Isabel. As a precaution, I will use a waxed impression of this ring on my missives. Look on it well, memorize the design so that you will recognize it."

Isabel took his hand and scrutinized the large ring etched with the badge of Sleat. For Rory's benefit, she even leaned down to kiss his hand as if in homage to the chief of the family. If Rory were still watching, her study of the ring would not look too peculiar. The ring contained an armored fist holding a cross with the motto of Sleat scrolled across the top: *Per Mare per Terras*, "By Land or by Sea."

"I'll know it, Uncle. You'd best be on your way before I have to explain what we were talking about. I wouldn't want to arouse Rory's suspicions."

"Very well, then, good hunting to you, lass." The MacDonald snickered with a lewd yellow smirk.

With a heavy sigh of relief, Isabel watched him go. Something about the man made her skin crawl. Her uncle was undoubtedly a powerful chief. But he inspired fear, not devotion.

There was no denying Sleat's cruel edge. His brutal repudiation of Rory's sister proved that. It had been done for political purposes. The MacDonald had been carefully building support for his bid to reclaim the ancient fiefdom of the Lordship of the Isles lost by Clan Donald

over one hundred years ago. It was simple: The Mac-
Leods were out of the king's favor, and the Mackenzies
were not. Her uncle needed royal support if he was to
reclaim the political power that went with the title Lord
of the Isles. Thus, Margaret MacLeod became expend-
able. Isabel may have understood the motivation, but to
reject the woman by ridiculing her misfortune seemed
unduly harsh. Of course, that too must have been the
point. The MacLeod would be forced to retaliate, and
her uncle had hoped to destroy them with feuding. But
the MacLeod continued to be a thorn in the side of the
MacDonalds. A thorn that she was to remove.

Sleat did not want simply to increase the power of
the clan, he wanted to rule western Scotland and the
Isles without interference from the king—or MacLeod.
Knowing the king, Isabel thought the idea far-fetched.
Nevertheless, it wasn't her job to wonder about the le-
gitimacy of her uncle's plan; her job was to succeed. And
to succeed, she needed Rory. Or more precisely, she
needed Rory's love and trust.

Perhaps the MacDonald's quick departure was not
such a bad thing. Clearly, Rory loathed her uncle. Sleat's
presence undoubtedly reminded Rory of his sister's
tragedy. And that certainly wouldn't help her cause.

She drew up her shoulders and shook off her despon-
dency. It would do no good to brood. She had a job to
do. She would make her family proud of her, and then
she could leave this dismal place. A year would not
come soon enough. At least she hadn't been completely
abandoned. Bessie had agreed to stay for a few months
to help her get settled.

"You shouldn't be standing out here in the rain."

Startled, Isabel jumped, her feet skidding on the stone

walk of the battlements. She felt the heat of his body and the hard shield of his chest behind her as he steadied and then promptly released her.

She knew who it was before she turned.

Her heart had leapt for a moment, thinking from his words that he might be concerned. But when she met his blank gaze, she knew it was not so. The man had a face about as yielding as stone.

"I wanted to make sure my kinsmen departed safely. I hoped that they might reconsider and remain at Dunvegan until the storm passed."

She winced, knowing that she sounded defensive.

"Well, you can see that they have gone. Return to the keep and dry yourself before you catch a chill."

His brusque tone, coupled with the acute loneliness she was feeling at the moment, stung. She nodded, unable to keep the wounded expression from her face.

He must have noticed, for he let out an exasperated sigh and offered her some semblance of reassurance. " 'Tis for the best, lass. Your uncle will never be welcome at Dunvegan. And after the trouble yesterday, tensions between the clans were running high. The MacLeods and MacDonalds will never be friends."

Isabel thought she detected another warning in his voice. "Friends perhaps not. But no longer enemies. Our handfast has put an end to the feud."

His mouth tightened. "For a year, at least," he qualified. Isabel experienced a moment of panic, thinking that perhaps he'd overheard something. But then he continued, "It will take longer than a year to repair the damage of a lifetime of feuding."

"But it is a good beginning," she said. Something else was bothering her. "About what happened yesterday . . .

it was wrong of me to try to interfere. Nor did I intend to question your decision." It had been wrong of her. She was chastened to realize that despite the harsh punishment, there were no grumblings among the MacLeods. His decisions were respected.

Rory nodded, accepting her apology. "Why did you?"

"I didn't want anything to mar the celebration. And when I saw my brother, I guessed what had happened. I know my brothers. They mean no harm, but I realized that your men do not know them as I do. Ian was very sorry for the trouble he caused."

"He told me so himself." Rory must have seen her look of surprise. "He apologized for disrupting the celebration and admitted he did not know the lass was wed. He is young yet, but I admire his integrity."

Isabel smiled, pleased that the MacLeod acknowledged how difficult it must have been for Ian to apologize after the matter had already been decided in his favor.

"You are fond of your brothers?" he asked.

Isabel nodded. "Very much so."

He stared at her intently. "And they of you?"

She hesitated. "Of course."

Rory must have heard the uncertainty in her voice. "I am sure it was difficult for them to leave you as well. But it is for the best. With your family gone, your adjustment at Dunvegan will be easier. Unless you are having second thoughts?"

"No, of course not," she said too quickly.

He lifted a brow that suggested he did not believe her. "I noticed your intense conversation with your uncle. I thought perhaps you might be reconsidering."

Isabel felt her pulse quicken.

He stared at her hard, waiting for her to explain, which of course she could not. "If you were watching, then you must know I was simply bidding my uncle farewell."

"It seemed rather more than a simple farewell. He appeared to be giving you some sort of instructions."

Isabel sucked in her breath, her pulse now racing frantically. How could he have possibly guessed? Rory MacLeod was much too observant.

Think, Isabel.

Well, she thought, *men loved obedient women, didn't they?*

She smiled demurely, fluttering her long lashes at him. "Very well, you are right, Rory."

His brows lifted in surprise.

She forced what she hoped was a becoming blush. "My uncle was giving me instructions." She paused. "Instructions on how to be a proper and obedient wife. Instructions on how to please you."

He seemed to tense, as if her words had knocked the breath from him. His eyes met hers. This time, there was no mistaking the flash of heat. "I would like to hear those instructions." His gaze slipped to her mouth and down the length of her body, lingering on her breasts. "On how exactly you intend to please me."

Isabel felt her insides quiver, not missing the sexual innuendo in his words. Her cheeks flamed. "That's not what I meant."

"Then what did you mean, Isabel?" The huskiness in his voice sent a shiver of awareness down her spine.

Dear God, he was standing close to her. So close that she could feel the heat from his body and smell the alluring scent of sea and spice that was strangely his. She wanted to sink against him, dissolve into that heat, and feel the strength of his arms around her. She wanted it with an intensity that was nearly overwhelming.

His wet hair fell in thick chunks across his ruggedly handsome face. She had a brazen urge to reach out and tuck it behind his ear. Anything to touch him.

Isabel couldn't answer. The air between them crackled. Unconsciously, she leaned closer, caught in a warm magnetic pull that seemed to draw her in.

He continued to stare at her, looking deep into her eyes. His mouth was achingly close. She could see the stubble along his jaw and remembered how it felt scraping over her skin when he'd kissed her. She remembered the softness of his lips. The spicy taste of him. Her lips parted, waiting.

Did he see how much she wanted him to kiss her? How all she could think about was the taste of his mouth on hers? For a long moment, they stood like that, staring at each other in the rain. Isabel searched for something, anything, to suggest that he felt it, too. She was to be disappointed. He deliberately broke the connection, turning his gaze from hers.

"Now we are both soaked," he said sternly. "Return to the keep. I have work to do. And in the future, stay inside during dangerous storms. I don't want to have to fetch you again."

He turned on his heel and left her feeling even more alone than before.

The MacDonald of Sleat watched Dunvegan sink into the gray mists of the storm clouds, but not before he caught sight of the two people standing on the battlements. A sight that brought a satisfied smirk to his mouth. There was no mistaking the identity of the woman or the man. His plan was progressing smoothly. The MacLeod would fight his attraction, but in the end, Sleat had no doubt that Rory MacLeod would succumb.

Sleat still could not believe the good fortune that had brought his niece to his attention. Isabel MacDonald was a rare beauty indeed. A redheaded Helen of Troy. Men would see her and want her. Wars could be fought over her. She embodied the perfect combination of innocence and sexuality. Aye, his niece would serve their needs well. Very well, he congratulated himself.

Rory MacLeod had been a thorn in his side for too long. It would amuse him to see his enemy, the great "Rory Mor," brought down by a mere lass. The MacLeod had put up quite a show pretending not to notice her, but Sleat knew better. His indifference had been his unmasking. The MacLeod wanted her. Badly. Who wouldn't? What man could refuse such riches? Sleat chuckled, well pleased with himself.

Aye, using a woman to get inside the MacLeod's stronghold had been a stroke of genius.

The MacDonald scratched his scraggly beard, absently flicking the crumbs from this morning's bread into the churning sea. He frowned. There was one weakness in his plan. His little niece. The ultimate success of his plan depended on her. He abhorred relying on a woman for anything, useless creatures that they were, but in this it was necessary. There was no other way.

Was the chit strong enough to do her part? She was very young and inexperienced. It was part of her charm. But it also made her a liability. He hadn't missed her fascination with the MacLeod chief. Sleat would keep a close eye on her progress and make sure she understood the consequences for her clan if she failed.

For this Helen would not start a war, but end one. And in the process deliver him a kingdom.

Chapter 5

❖

Since the afternoon of the MacDonalds' departure three weeks ago, Rory had done his best to keep his distance from his new bride. The more time he spent with her, the more he learned about her. And the more he learned about her, the more he wanted to know. It was a vicious circle that would lead him nowhere but to perdition.

Even on that day of her family's leaving, he hadn't intended to go to her. But did the woman have no sense, standing on the slippery battlements in a torrential storm? He would have left her to the mercy of the elements, but that damn vulnerability had eaten away at his reserve. He'd spied her sad leavetaking from her family and tried not to be moved. Yet there was a poignancy to the moment that could not be ignored. Her father gave her an awkward pat on the head, and Isabel looked as though she wanted to throw her arms around him. Each of her brothers did give her a quick hug, but Isabel held on just a tad too long. She wanted to stretch out every minute, while the MacDonalds looked as if they couldn't leave fast enough. She fought tears watching them make their way down the sea-gate stairs, as they left with nary a backward glance.

Damn fools. Couldn't they see how difficult this was

for her? She'd seemed so alone and desolate as the boats departed that he couldn't stand back and watch her catch ill. He knew she must be feeling abandoned and a bit scared at being left on her own with a group of strangers. Strangers who only days ago were her enemies. When she'd turned to face him, her luminous violet eyes blurry and red rimmed from crying, Rory could not remain unaffected. He'd felt sorry for the lass.

But sorrow quickly turned to something else when she'd talked of pleasuring him. His mind had momentarily gone blank with erotic images. Of her beneath him, on top of him, wrapped around him. Images that were only too easy to imagine with her lush mouth a tantalizing few inches below his. The force of his lust for this woman annoyed the hell out of him.

Only later did he wonder if her suggestive comment was meant to distract him from further inquiry into the strange conversation he'd witnessed with her uncle. Something about this handfast and Isabel didn't sit right.

He didn't trust her. And with her living in the old keep, and him in the newer Fairy Tower, it wasn't as easy to keep an eye on her. From Deidre, he learned that she'd been spending an inordinate amount of time in the kitchens. The information had piqued his curiosity, as did her current crouched position peering under the shelves in the storeroom.

Rory waited until he was standing right behind her. "What are you looking for?"

Startled, Isabel jumped. Her eyes widened, and her mouth opened into a wide O.

He crossed his arms and stared at her. Hard. "Well?"

"I . . . I . . . d-d-dropped something."

She was lying. "What?"

Collecting herself, she pursed her lips, put her hands on her hips, and lifted a decidedly obstinate chin to his. "Why are you questioning me?"

"I find you on your hands and knees in the storeroom looking under shelves and you have to ask?"

She seemed to find humor in his description and grinned. "Oh, very well." She paused, making a great show of brushing the dust off her skirts. "You found me out. Colum has promised to teach me how he makes his delicious marzipan cakes, and I've been sent to the stores to requisition the almonds and sugar."

Rory had learned from Deidre that Isabel had made a quick admirer of his taciturn and cantankerous old cook. "A good excuse for finding you in the storeroom, perhaps, but that does not explain what you were looking for under those shelves."

"I was getting to that," she said haughtily. "While I was collecting the ingredients, I heard something drop and roll under the shelves. I feared it must be a pearl from my earring."

"Hmm," Rory murmured. "Shall we see?" Slowly he reached out, slipping his hand through her hair to pull it away from her ear. The soft, silken waves slid across his skin and sent a shock rippling through him. Gently, he gripped the velvety skin of her neck with his fingers, breathing in the sweet bouquet of lavender as he bent to examine her earrings. The temptation to loosen the ribbon that bound her hair and bury his hands in the silken warmth was almost overpowering.

His voice sounded unnaturally deep. "You don't appear to be missing anything."

"I know I heard something drop." She sounded flustered, but whether it was from his touch or her lie he could not tell. "Perhaps it was from my brooch," she offered quickly.

His eyes slid down to the piece of jewelry fastened between her breasts. Eyes wide, she followed the movement of his hand as it trailed from her ear to her bodice. When he brushed the heavy curve of her breast with the back of his finger, he heard her sharp intake of breath. The erotic sound filled him with heat—as did the immediate tightening of her nipple. Her gaze flew to his and awareness stretched taut between them. He could hear the unevenness of her breath coming between her softly parted lips as he inspected the brooch with his fingers. It would be so easy to slip his hand under the bodice of her gown, to feel the velvet of her skin, to massage his thumb across the hard tip. To feel the shudder of passion sweep through her.

He leaned closer, inhaling the sweet perfume of her skin, feeling the heat of desire swirl over him. His cock thickened, and his loins grew heavy with need. Just one little stroke . . .

But he knew it would not be enough. He'd want more. Much more.

God's wounds, no woman had ever affected him so effortlessly.

Taking a step back, he removed his hand and allowed his pulse to return to normal, waiting for the vise hold of lust to dissipate before he spoke. "Again, there appears to be nothing missing."

"I know I heard something," she insisted, a pink flush still staining her cheeks. But rather than offer another paltry excuse, she asked instead, "Why are you here?"

His gaze sharpened. *A good tactic,* he thought, but

one that did not fool him. He studied her, wishing he could see inside that beautiful head. Why was she spending so much time in the underground kitchens, and what was she really looking for? He didn't think it was a missing pearl. Allowing her to stay in the old keep by herself was an unnecessary risk. There was an easy solution, one that shouldn't be difficult to make. Rory knew what he had to do, unreasonable lust or not.

"I was looking for you," he said.

"You were?"

He nodded. "It's time." It had been for a while. The servants, he knew, had begun to gossip. He might not intend to wed the lass, but he would not shame her. In all but one way, she would be his wife.

"Time for what?" she asked cautiously.

"It has been long enough. You shall move your things into my chamber in the Fairy Tower." Where it would be easier to keep an eye on her. Keeping everything else off her was going to be the difficulty.

That was a close call. Isabel exhaled slowly, noting the rigid set of his broad shoulders as he disappeared up the kitchen stairs. It shook her to realize just how close she'd come to discovery. As she'd done every day since her family's departure, Isabel had been exploring the old keep from top to bottom, paying particular attention to the catacomb of tunnels located near the kitchens and dungeon for a secret entry. Rory, materializing out of nowhere, had startled and thoroughly discomposed her. Isabel's heart had about dropped to her toes when he started questioning her . . . and then for other reasons.

She hadn't set out to entice him with her explanation, only distract him. Instead it was she who had been distracted. The attraction that sizzled between them still warmed her. He radiated heat. Heat that drew her in. When he'd put his hand on her neck and brushed his finger over her breast, she'd felt a strange pull from deep inside her. Her skin prickled with awareness. Every movement, every touch, every hesitation, seemed emblazoned on her skin.

He left her wanting more. She'd wanted him to pull her into his arms and kiss her. To touch her. To ease the tension coiling inside her.

But she'd seen the flash of desire in his gaze and knew that he was not unaffected. And now he wanted her in his room. It could only mean one thing. He intended to make her his bride in truth.

For the rest of the day, Isabel was a bundle of nerves. All she could think about was what would happen that night. She might be innocent, but she was not without knowledge of what occurred between men and women. Traipsing after her profligate brothers had unintentionally taught her much.

Her virginity was a natural casualty of their plan. But she'd always imagined it would be a sacrifice. That she would have to grit her teeth and bear it. Never did she imagine the knot of anticipation swirling in her belly. Anticipation that had nothing to do with the plan and everything to do with the man who with only a touch made her tremble with newly awakened passion. She could not deny that he affected her. She would just have to make sure that she didn't allow herself to get caught up in the unfamiliar sensations but stayed focused on her goal.

With Bessie's and Deidre's help, Isabel moved her belongings to his room. After instructing Deidre where to have her trunks placed, Isabel busied herself about the room placing her hairbrush and mirror on the large table beside the fireplace and the book of sonnets that she was currently reading on the table next to the bed. She was scattering her belongings among his just as if she were a young bride happily sharing a bower with her new husband.

Her new living space impressed her. Rory's chamber, on the third floor of the modern Fairy Tower, was a beautiful, albeit definitely masculine, room sparsely furnished with heavy wooden furniture. Large windows provided a panoramic view of the loch. A small fireplace supplied heat. The wooden walls were painted a soft yellow but otherwise unadorned. Colorful jewel-toned carpets similar to those in the downstairs hall covered the floor.

But the enormous four-posted bed dominated the room. It was similar to the bed in her old chamber with its luxurious thick feather mattress and pillows, except that it did not have the colorful silk hangings surrounding it. There was a simple wool coverlet and cozy fur pelt for cold nights. A tall stack of books and haphazardly strewn parchments littered the top of the table that must serve as his desk. Another small table near the window held a basin for washing, and a large chest sufficed for storing his clothes.

Though stark, the room was warm and comfortable and a welcome departure from the rustic old keep. But all day long, her eyes kept drifting back to the bed. And her mouth went dry, as she wondered what the night would bring.

The little flutter in her chest started as soon as she took her seat next to him at the dais for the evening meal. He acknowledged her arrival with a curt nod of his head and immediately returned his attention to Alex. Isabel tried to hide her disappointment. Part of her had hoped today would be a turning point. That the virtually silent meals she'd endured for the past three weeks would be at an end.

Other than an occasional banality about her meal or other meaningless pleasantry, Rory paid her no attention and spoke mostly with his men at mealtimes. Occasionally, she would spy Alex sitting with the other warriors, watching her. As if understanding her loneliness, he would give her an encouraging lopsided grin. But even Alex assiduously avoided long conversations. Today was no different.

Rory's courteous indifference frustrated her. Especially tonight, when every nerve ending in her body seemed set on edge. Still, sitting so close to him, her body tingling with awareness, Isabel kept thinking of the night to come. She peeked up at him from under her lashes. What would it be like? Would he have care for her innocence? Her thoughts stole to his impressive physique. His size intimidated her; she hoped he would not crush her with all that muscle. Yet as her questions multiplied, Rory seemed entirely unaffected. There was no indication that he anticipated tonight more than any other.

He must have felt the weight of her eyes on him, as finally he turned and addressed her. "Are you finding everything to your liking?" He paused significantly. Isabel blushed to have been caught so obviously staring. "In the new tower?" He finished with a smile, clearly amused by her discomfort.

"Yes, the bed is—" She stopped, mortified. Her cheeks burned. "I mean, the room is delightful."

Something flickered in his gaze. "I'm glad you are pleased," he said. Before she could respond, he turned back to Alex.

Somehow, she made it through the evening meal. For once, she was grateful that he ignored her. Her mind was racing in every direction, and she feared a repeat of her earlier blunder.

With Bessie's help, Isabel donned a beautiful *night rail* of ivory silk, chosen by her uncle for this very occasion. Not surprisingly, there wasn't much to it. The thin swath of cloth clung to all her womanly parts in a manner that left little to the imagination. Isabel felt a bit like a trussed-up goose, but she set aside her qualms and allowed Bessie to fuss over her.

After some uncomfortable last-minute explanations from Bessie that made her want to laugh and cry at the same time, Isabel was alone. She slid under the covers and waited.

And waited.

For hours, Isabel lay in bed clutching the coverlet to her chin, her nerves as sharp as the edge of a blade. Her heart pounded frantically. Her ears strained to hear the sound of booted footsteps from the corridor. But it was a sound that never came.

Eventually, it became painfully obvious that he did not intend to join her.

More disappointed than she wanted to acknowledge, Isabel blew out the single taper next to the big bed and slept. Restlessly.

Seven long nights later, Rory stared at the woman sleeping not five feet away and told himself he was being ridiculous. One wee lass should not keep him from his bed.

He hadn't slept more than a few hours since he'd ordered her to his room. Isabel had invaded his room, his bed, and his thoughts. The room even smelled of her, enticing him with the sweet, seductive scent of lavender. Night after night, he found himself sitting by the fire, drinking whisky by the bottle to dull the edge of desire, gazing at the comfortable bed, and devising reasons why he should not sleep there.

Last night had nearly proved too much. She'd kicked off the covers in her sleep and lay on her side with her arm stretched above her head, her full breasts high and beckoning. Rory could see every curve of her lush figure, clad only in a wispy *night rail*. He ached to test the soft roundness of her breast in his palm, to run his hands along the curve of her hips and bottom, and to wrap those long slim legs around his waist as he plunged inside her. The images haunted him all night—it had proved to be a very long night.

But not tonight. Tonight he was sleeping in his own bed.

Rory removed his shirt and plaid, placed them over the chair, and, careful not to disturb her, slid under the coverlet. He held perfectly still. When nothing happened, he relaxed. Grinning, he called himself a fool. What had he thought? That lying beside her would be a temptation too impossible to resist? Ridiculous. He closed his eyes and slept.

The soft rays of morning teased his eyelids. But Rory didn't want to wake up; he was too damn comfortable. He snuggled closer to the smooth silk coverlet. He buried his nose deeper into the soft spray of lavender that filled his pillow and inhaled deeply.

His eyes popped open. He didn't have lavender in his pillows. Nor did he have a silk coverlet. The soft bundle in his arms was not a coverlet, but a scantily clad Isabel. And the lavender wafted from her hair and not from his pillow. It took him a moment to realize that his arm was tucked under her plump breasts, that she had her bottom pressed firmly against his groin, and that he had an erection the size of Mt. Olympus.

The weight of her breasts on his arm was too much. One hand slid up to cup her. He muffled a groan as all that soft, deliciously heavy flesh filled his hand. It felt too damn good. Her nipple hardened in his palm, and Rory ached to rub it between his fingers, to stroke her until she arched against him. She was so warm and soft, so sweetly feminine. And he'd been waiting too long. His hips moved closer, increasing the pressure of her tight bottom pressed against his now throbbing erection.

His little bundle sighed and wiggled mercilessly against him. His body clenched with agony as he thought how easy it would be to grab her hips and ease himself in from behind. He squeezed her a little harder, lifting her breasts together in his palms. The urge for relief roared through him.

Hell.

He quickly unfolded himself from her silken web before he did something he would regret.

Chapter 6

❖

Lips pursed with frustration, Isabel stormed around the spacious bedchamber.

Moving to his chamber in the Fairy Tower was supposed to have solved her problems. But what was the use of sharing his room if he was hardly ever there? He spent just as little time with her as he had before. She'd begun to suspect that he'd moved her only to keep an eye on her.

Over a week in his bed and a month at Dunvegan, and she was no closer to her goal than when she'd first arrived. The MacLeod's secrets were well hidden. Since her move, she'd conducted a few basic searches of the chamber for the Fairy Flag but didn't dare attempt more. The MacLeod was suspicious of her enough already.

But the failure to advance her plan was not the only cause of her frustration. Her nervous excitement at the prospect of what *might* happen once her things were moved to his chamber had been completely unwarranted. It seemed he had no intention of bedding her.

For the first few nights she'd tried to wait up, but sleep appeared before he did. When he did come in, it was in the dead of the night, and by time she woke, he was gone. Until last night, she hadn't even been certain he slept there. But this morning, she'd woken with a start. Chilled. And with a strange sense of emptiness, as if she missed the comforting shield of his presence. Somehow she'd known he slept beside her. The large indentation in the feather bed next to her confirmed it.

Isabel didn't know whether to be angry or disappointed by his lack of attention. Probably a little of both. The worst part was that she had nothing to truly be angry for. He treated her with perfect civility. Given the history of their clans and her relationship to Sleat, it could have been much worse. Then why was she so disappointed? Because he'd not taken one look at her and fallen to his knees in besotted supplication as her uncle hoped? After meeting him, she had to laugh at the image, it was so ridiculous. Though the failure to advance her plan *should* be the reason, it was not.

What truly frustrated her was her own lack of indifference. The more she had learned of him and observed him, the more she had come to realize that Rory MacLeod was unlike anyone she'd ever met. She was attracted to him, she admired him, and it pained her to realize she'd made no impression on him at all.

Not only did he avoid her at night, he avoided her the rest of the time as well. If she did happen to see him during the day, after a few polite inquiries, he removed himself.

Being left on her own most of the day wasn't aiding her in her quest at all. What had become painfully clear was that she could not succeed on her own. She needed him to confide in her. Earning his trust, to allay that suspicion, was what she must concentrate on. But how could she when he seemed determined to keep distance between them?

Indeed, Isabel felt less like a wife and more like a temporary guest. If she was to have any hope of success, she would need to change that. She must take the reins of the household by securing the keys that he'd neglected to give her after their handfast. She sat on the edge of the bed to think, twirling a long strand of silky hair through her fingers. She had to insert herself in his life whether he liked it or not.

She looked around at the stark masculine chamber. What better place to start than with his room?

She would ask Rory for leave to add some womanly touches to his room, and then perhaps she would bring up the matter of the chatelaine's keys.

Isabel stood up with a new sense of resolve and headed to the door. She had every right to make her request. She *was* the new mistress, after all, even if no one was treating her as such.

She hadn't taken two steps down the corridor when she heard a voice behind her.

"Good day, mistress. May I be of some help?"

Since she'd moved to the Fairy Tower, someone always seemed to be watching her the moment she stepped outside the door. Isabel turned to find Deidre right on her heels. Deidre was short and round, with hair so white, it seemed that it must have always been that way. Since that first morning, Deidre was one of the few friendly faces around this dismal place. The others being Colum the cook, Alex, and Bessie.

At first she'd befriended the crusty old cook because she thought it might help explain why she was spending so much time in the kitchens. But that was not why she kept returning. Bessie, Colum, and Deidre were comfortable to be around since she was used to spending her days with servants. Before her time at court, it was all she'd known.

"No, no, I'm just looking for Rory. I need to speak with him about a matter of some import. Do you know where I can find him?"

"By this time he is already outside training with the men."

"Thank you, Deidre, I will look for him in the court-yard."

"Very well, if there is nothing else, then."

Deidre turned and continued about her business—assuming that her business included shadowing Isabel until she left the building.

As Isabel headed down the stairs, she considered her treatment this past month by the MacLeods. By and large, the clan had taken its lead from Rory. They were polite but distant. Considering the history of feuding between the MacDonalds and the MacLeods, it was more than she'd expected. The feud might have nominally ended with their handfast, but only time would heal the damage wrought by years of bloodshed, and Isabel did not have that particular luxury.

Initially, being left to her own devices was fine, as it had provided her an easy opportunity to explore the old keep and search for the flag. But it was also lonely, reminding her distinctly of home. Left with nothing to do, she grew bored, and the days moved slowly.

By now, she'd hoped to be well on the way to having Rory fall in love with her. Men were simple creatures, the ladies at court had assured her. Isabel would compliment him on his prowess as a warrior, admire his superior intellect, and remark upon his handsome countenance. For good measure, she would act her most charming, agreeable, complacent self—giving him nothing to object to. Simple. But all the planning in the world was useless if they never spent any time together.

That was about to change.

Isabel stepped into the courtyard from the darkness of the great hall, squinting from the sharp contrast of bright sunlight. The unusually dreary weather that had descended over Dunvegan since her arrival was readily forgotten with the promise of a beautiful summer day. The full bloom of August was evidenced all around by the lush green of the grasses and the vivid saturated color of the wildflowers that peppered the coastal hilltops. A sprinkling of woolly clouds enhanced the crystal perfection of the crisp blue sky.

She sighed, letting the fresh air flow over her body. The salt from the sea spray tickled her nose as she inhaled deeply.

Already her heart felt lighter.

Surprisingly, there were few people about. Two women were hauling water to the keep from the main well near the sea-gate, but otherwise the courtyard appeared deserted.

She looked around for Rory. A great cloud of dust rising near the south side of the courtyard looked promising. As she drew closer, she could hear the sounds of raucous laughter interspersed with the clatter of steel crashing against steel.

As was true of all Highland clans, the MacLeods were clearly divided into two groups: those who fought and those who tilled the land or tended the livestock. Feuding and foraying were a way of life for the warriors of the clan. When idle, they practiced their fighting skills or devised organized trials of strength and skill. As a girl, Isabel had loved to watch the MacDonald warriors go through their exercises. There was nothing quite like watching Highlanders demonstrate their impressive strength and prowess with a claymore.

Isabel turned the corner and stuttered in midstep. The warm salty air heavy with the toil and pungent scent of well-worked bodies enveloped her senses, but it was her eyes that were fixed on the display before her. A group of half-naked men stood in a circle, cheering on a pair of fierce combatants. It wasn't the lack of clothing that startled her. The MacDonalds also practiced without their saffron shirts on warm days. Rather, it was one broad, tanned, tightly muscled chest in particular.

At the center—figuratively and literally—was Rory MacLeod.

She couldn't take her eyes off him, mesmerized by the raw masculinity of his bare chest. He could have been cut from stone; there wasn't an ounce of extra flesh on him. The sun highlighted the hard, chiseled edges of his muscles. A thin sheen of perspiration made his body glisten like a bronze statue. His shoulders and arms were as thick and hard as granite, tapering to a flat stomach banded in tight layers. Very little hair marred the clean bronzed lines of his broad torso. The tops of his shoulders were burnished red from the sun, and the veins in his thick forearms bulged from the exertion of the sword practice.

But it was not merely his powerful form that captured her admiration. His strength and prowess were utterly magnificent to behold as he took command of the warriors around him. One by one, his men entered the circle to take a turn at their champion. Rory thrust and parried, lifting the enormous sword as if it were no heavier than a feather. She recognized the claymore he wielded at once as the one she'd noticed hanging on the wall in the great hall, proving that it wasn't merely decoration or fodder for boasting of the great strength of some illustrious ancestor. His arms flexed as he fought off the blows, though he made it seem effortless.

He was a pillar of strength, immovable and unbending. Isabel didn't think she'd ever get used to his size. Yet there was a sensuality to Rory's movements, a grace that belied his muscular form.

Whether inexperienced or experienced, the MacLeod treated each challenger with respect, relaying instructions as he deftly moved his opponent on the defensive. Not once did he grow impatient. Nor did he merely toy with his opponent as an opportunity to display his skills. He adjusted his approach with each man, finding a particular weakness and training the man first to identify it and second to conquer it. As the game continued, the relative skill of his opponent increased. But rather than tire, the MacLeod only seemed to grow stronger. Finally it was Alex's turn.

The two men circled each other, as if gladiators in an arena of ancient Rome. Engaged in their deadly dance, they moved with the pride of lions. Alex attacked first, the crash of steel on steel ringing in Isabel's ears. At first she thought they were evenly matched, but as the game drew on, it looked as if Alex held the edge. Alex had Rory on the defensive, backing him to the wall of the battlements.

She didn't understand it when Rory smiled. "Very impressive, little brother," he said, breathing hard. "You'll force me to use my right."

Isabel gasped when he switched hands. She hadn't noticed, but Rory had been using his left hand the whole time—and he was right-handed.

Rory must have heard her because he turned to look at her, suffering a knock of Alex's claymore on his shoulder for his distraction.

"Damn," he swore, rubbing his shoulder. He didn't look pleased to see her. "What are you doing here?"

"I—I wish to discuss something with you, my lord," she stammered shyly. "In private, if you please."

As she spoke, Isabel took a tentative step closer. She broke her stare and looked over his shoulder at the men who had gathered around to follow the exchange. Though perhaps only forty men were present today, she knew that his warriors numbered about four hundred— a considerable force, larger than her father's and not much smaller than Sleat's. He hadn't introduced her to any of his men, but she had discovered some of their names. Rory was most often with Alex and two of his *luchd-taighe* guardsmen, Colin and Douglas.

They made an imposing foursome. With his white blond hair and the pointed marquisotte beard, Colin had the look of a Viking. And with the perpetual frown he wore, a very angry Viking. She remembered Douglas from his short visit to court. He'd caused quite a stir with his untamed dark good looks and brusque Highland manners. He was quiet, but not shy. A man of few words. The ladies at court were intrigued by both his savage good looks and the exciting air of wildness that seemed to surround him. She recalled hearing that he was a cousin to Rory and Alex.

"As you can see, I'm busy right now," he said abruptly.

"Please, it's important."

"It will have to wait—"

He seemed poised to deny her request when Alex interrupted.

"Surely you can attend your bride for a few minutes, Rory. We were just about finished here, weren't we?"

Rory glared at his grinning brother. With obvious unwillingness, he lifted a dark eyebrow to Isabel and reluctantly accepted her invitation. "It seems I may have a few minutes to spare," he said sarcastically, tossing his claymore to Alex.

Rory pointed in the direction of the battlements. "Would you care to stroll around the courtyard while you talk?"

Before the words had even left his mouth, he started to move away. Taken aback by his lack of gallantry, she followed, practically running as she tried to keep up with his much longer strides. He led her toward the battlements along the coastline. Well, she thought, catching her breath, at least the view from behind was every bit as impressive as the naked chest she had admired earlier. His back was equally tanned and well muscled, narrowing at the waist above a tight backside. He strode forward with the assurance of one who was born to lead—the unqualified authority of his ancestors trailing behind him. Even if she did not know he was chief, the pride of his carriage left no doubt.

Rory finally stopped at a point overlooking the sea loch and allowed her to catch up. He gazed pensively out past the curtain walls to the loch beyond. Small, feathery lines around his eyes shone stark white against his tanned skin as he squinted into the sun. He looked so content that Isabel almost hesitated to intrude. Her shoulder grazed his shirtless side as she moved next to him, wondering what had captured his interest.

Ignoring the flutter in her stomach from the touch of his skin and the hypnotic scent of sun, sweat, and a hint of heather that filled her nose, she turned her eyes to follow his gaze, sucking in her breath in awe at the splendor unfolded beneath them. The jagged, rocky coast shimmered like polished stone against the teal blue waves capped with delicate white froth that marched in flawless symmetry toward the shore. The juxtaposition of the deep teal blue of the sea against the clear azure sky was breathtaking. It seemed unreal, as if she were looking at a painting where the colors were too vivid, too sharp, too perfect. It was simply beautiful.

Notwithstanding the stunning display of natural beauty before them, the pronounced silence was awkward. He was obviously waiting for her to speak.

"I'm sorry to interrupt your training. I hope I have not ruined your practice." Isabel paused, waiting for a polite response.

He looked at her blankly.

When no assurance was forthcoming, she shuffled her slipper-clad feet nervously beneath his hard, penetrating gaze.

Try compliments, she reminded herself. "Your sword skills are quite remarkable. I enjoyed watching you practice with your men."

He shrugged.

"I couldn't believe it when you switched hands. I've never seen anything like it. It must have taken you years of practice to master using both hands."

"Yes."

So much for compliments. This was like talking to a

stone wall. "I have some experience with a blade myself," she offered casually, "though I'm better with a bow." Trying to get the attention of three brothers did have some benefits.

He stared at her, his shock patent. "You are serious?"

She met his gaze with a proud tilt of her chin. "Perfectly."

He gave her a quick glance up and down. "You look like you could barely lift a sword."

"I'm stronger than I look," she said, standing a little straighter.

Now he looked amused. "And what use could a wee lass have for swordplay?"

"You'd be surprised."

He shook his head, looking as though he wanted to laugh. Isabel fought to control her temper, but she was used to such masculine condescension from her brothers. It had only made her work harder.

"And your father approved of this unusual pastime?"

"You're making a nuisance of yourself, lass. You're brothers need to practice."

Isabel hated that word, *nuisance*. She heard it enough. *"But I just want—"*

"Your mother was a real lady. You must be as well."

But Isabel was ten years old and she didn't want to be a lady. She wanted to play with her brothers.

"Not at first," she admitted. Never. "But I believe he saw the wisdom in a woman learning how to defend herself." She hoped.

"Well, you've no need of that while you are here," he said. "I will protect you. And my warriors do not have the time to waste on child's play."

Isabel bit back her pert reply, but his attitude set her

teeth on edge. "Actually, I've been meaning to ask whether I could arrange some short hunting excursions—"

He crossed his arms. She tried not to stare, but the display of muscles made her feel slightly warm and fuzzy all over. "No."

His terse denial surprised her. Her eyes shot to his face. "Why not? I believe hunting is a suitable activity for a 'wee lass.' " And it would do much to relieve her boredom.

"It's much too dangerous."

"I would have an escort—"

"I said no."

He was being unreasonable. But now was not the time to argue, so she fumed silently.

"Was there a reason you wanted to speak with me?" he asked impatiently, looking as if he'd rather be anywhere than standing here with her.

Isabel thought quickly. "Yes, I would like to make a few minor changes to our chamber to make the room more comfortable, and I thought it best that I seek your permission before I did so. Even though," she couldn't resist adding, "you spend so little time there." An unmistakable trace of reproach colored her voice as she glanced at his stern face from under her long eyelashes—implicitly offering him a chance to explain their sleeping arrangements. But he didn't take the bait. "I assume that you want me to take over the duties of chatelaine. If you could direct me to the appropriate person, as I do not know who is currently administering the castle—"

"You need not worry about that." He cut her off. "My sister Margaret has handled those duties for the last two years." He looked at her grimly. "Since her return to Dunvegan."

Isabel blanched, instantly realizing her error. She should have guessed that his sister would be acting as mistress, and now her innocent reminder of her family connection to his sister's disgrace had ignited his anger. But it was easy to forget Margaret's presence at the castle, as she had not even been introduced to her. It was an omission that she would have to remedy.

"Of course your sister should remain chatelaine. I'm sorry, as I have yet to meet Margaret, I didn't realize. Should I address my requests to make some changes to the chamber to her?" Even though she asked politely, Isabel knew that by all rights she should be insulted—his refusal to bestow the position that was her due as his bride was a serious affront. She was the new mistress, and as such she should have the duties of chatelaine. Her smooth features betrayed nothing of her feelings, but suppressing her natural propensity for argument was more difficult than she had anticipated.

He was obviously displeased by her request. "Tonight, Eoin Og O'Muireaghsain will entertain us with his verse of the history of the clan. I will ask that Margaret sit with us for the evening meal."

"Wonderful." She couldn't hide the eagerness from her voice.

"Was there anything else?"

She twisted her hands. He certainly wasn't making this easy on her. "I'd hoped that we would be able to spend some time together to get to know each other," she ventured.

"Why?"

Was he serious? She bit back a sarcastic retort, tamping down the flicker of anger. She *was* trying to make him fall in love with her, after all. She must do her best to be charming and complacent, even if it killed her. "It just seemed natural that we would get to know each other since we are recently handfasted."

"I'm very busy, Isabel. You must know that as chief I have responsibilities and duties that require my attention. We take meals together, what more can you require? I assumed, as the daughter of a chief, you would understand the limited time I have to engage in mere frivolity."

Mere frivolity! The arrogance of this man was beyond compare. So much for compliments and platitudes. This conversation was not progressing at all as she had hoped. Her mind raced, searching for what had gone wrong. Perhaps he misunderstood her intent.

She reached out and touched his arm imploringly, her fingers momentarily shocked by the heat of his bare skin. He was just as hard and strong as she'd anticipated. She could feel the power radiating under her fingertips. She noticed that the hairs on his arms stood up at her touch, almost as if she chilled him.

"I'm sorry, I did not mean to imply that I am not familiar with the demands upon your time. Indeed, my father is a very busy man and did not spend much time with me—I mean us," she corrected hastily, "as busy as he was with his duties at Strome Castle. It's just that I have not had much company other than Bessie this last month, and I was hoping you might spare a few minutes to show me around."

Rory lifted a dark arched brow. "I am not a nursemaid and did not realize that you would require one."

Isabel felt her cheeks grow hot with indignation. "Well, perhaps if you could spare a moment to glance in my direction now and again, you would see that I am well past the age for a nursemaid." She resisted the feminine urge to stick out her chest and force him to notice just how far from a child she truly was.

Ah, Rory thought, *there was the spark.* He was beginning to think that he had imagined the spirit he'd glimpsed before. She'd been acting remarkably sweet in the face of his increasing rudeness. She seemed to be trying awfully hard to please him. Her blandishments might have amused him if he weren't so aggravated. He hadn't set out to provoke her, but finding himself face-to-face with the recent source of his woes did nothing to improve his already bad temper.

The memory of her soft backside pressed snugly against his groin was not easily dismissed. Nor was the constant reminder throbbing beneath his plaid.

Being so close to her at night and not being able to do anything about it was wearing on him. Rory damned himself for his unusual impulsivity. Moving Isabel to his room had been a hasty decision brought about by her interest in his kitchens and his swift reaction to touching her in the storeroom. His error in judgment, his unreasonable fascination with her every movement, and his unsated lust had all combined to put him in a foul mood.

A foul mood that he'd sought to erase on the lists, only to find his beautiful bride invading his peace again.

When he'd first caught sight of her, he froze, captivated by her lustrous hair blazing in the sun with intertwined hues of copper, fiery red gold, and deep bronze—suffering the blow of a sword for his stupidity in allowing himself to be distracted. But she looked as fresh as the first dew of spring in her simple green woolen gown. Her eyes seemed lighter in the daylight, more lavender than violet.

An uncomfortable tightness pulled in his chest. He wished it were simply her beauty that called to him. But the more he watched her, the more she entranced him. Even the gentle lilt of her voice enticed him.

Out of the corner of his eye, he could see her simmering next to him. He could tell by the way her hands clenched that she was furious. Furious and adorable with her pursed lips and stubborn chin. A sweet Isabel was intriguing, but with fire she was irresistible. Oh, he'd noticed that she was well past the age for a nursemaid all right, but he still had to keep his distance.

"Well?" she asked.

"I did not realize your statement required a reply. But if you must know, I have noticed that at least *physically* you appear of age to not require a nursemaid."

Her frustration at his inept responses had clearly turned to anger. "I was only asking that we spend some time together because I just thought—"

"What did you think, Isabel?" he snapped, refusing to look at her beautiful upturned face. Rory was not nearly as indifferent as he pretended. He forced a coolness to his words that belied the heated awareness her touch brought to his body. He knew she was lonely, but he could not allow himself to feel sympathy.

She needed to know how it would be.

He knew that if he looked, he would see the hurt in those haunting lavender eyes. *Duty,* he reminded himself silently. The sooner she realized this was not an ordinary union the better.

Still, he was finding it increasingly difficult to act the cold stranger in the face of her innocent friendliness.

And why did he feel like he was pulling the tail of a defenseless puppy?

He felt a strange urge to protect her. To wrap her in his arms and discover what made the shadow cross her face when she thought no one else was looking. Even more, he wanted to make sure nothing ever troubled her again.

He sighed, the frustration of the situation getting to him. "This is a political arrangement. King James ordered our handfast to settle the feud between our clans. Do not try to make it into something more. If you are expecting love and romance, you will only be disappointed."

Isabel stiffened from the blunt shock of his words. "What do you mean?"

He finally turned from the sea to look at her. "This is a political match. Love is not part of the bargain." He deliberately pulled his arm away from her touch and tried to ignore her quick intake of breath at the insult of his words and brusque movements.

"But it need not be so," she argued. "My father was deeply in love with my mother."

Her words took him aback. It was difficult to imagine the sober, battle-hardened MacDonald of Glengarry as a besotted husband. "When did she die?" he found himself asking.

"My birth was a difficult one," she answered softly. "She never recovered. I barely knew her, though my father says I am much like her."

Rory steeled himself against the sadness he heard in her voice. He didn't know that she'd lost her mother so young. And with what he'd witnessed of her relationship with her father and brothers, he could imagine how difficult—and lonely—that must have been for her. It was also obvious that she blamed herself for her mother's death. Did Glengarry as well? Was that what explained his reserve around his daughter? Rory didn't think so. There was something in the older man's gaze when he looked at his daughter, as if it pained him. Perhaps Isabel was right and Glengarry had loved his wife. If Isabel resembled her, it explained much. *Damn,* he thought with frustration. This was precisely the sort of information he didn't want to know. This was what happened from spending time with her.

"What of your parents?" She persisted. "Were they not in love?"

"My parents got along well enough," he answered. "But in love, no. They respected each other, but led relatively separate lives. Over time, I'm sure they developed a certain fondness."

"But don't you want someone to love? To have someone love you? To have someone to trust with your innermost secrets, someone to confide in, someone completely and utterly loyal?"

"I am chief. I have the love, trust, and loyalty of my clan and family. MacLeods are unfailingly loyal. I neither need nor desire anything more. And a chief doesn't confide his secrets to anyone. A chief keeps his own counsel. What use does a warrior have for love? Does love win battles? Settle grievances? No, love is a fanciful ideal invented by the troubadours to tell pretty stories. Love has no place in marriage—even the troubadours would tell you that. Nobility marry for land and wealth, or as we have done, to settle a feud. We do our duty to the clan by handfasting, Isabel, nothing more, nothing less."

All this talk of love made him uncomfortable. Rory was a warrior, not a courtier. He had a duty to his clan that took precedent over anything else, personal desires included. No, love had no place in his life. He wanted Isabel only as he would desire any beautiful woman. The reason he seemed to be unable to focus on anything else was that this beautiful woman was not for him. A simple case of wanting what he couldn't have, he reasoned.

She appeared visibly distressed by his words, as if she had hoped for something more. He considered for the first time that he might have been wrong to suspect her. Of late, she'd done nothing to give him cause for concern. He'd watched her, noting her kindness and sweet attempts to befriend his clan. It had not escaped his notice that Fergus's wife left the castle daily with extra food in her pack. Maybe Isabel was exactly what she seemed: an innocent, sweet young lass being forced into a situation not of her making.

It suddenly occurred to him that his indifferent behavior and blunt honesty could be hurting her when all he'd sought to do was protect her from harm. He wouldn't bed her, not because he didn't want to, but because he didn't want to hurt her when he sent her home, as he must.

"But surely we should try—"

He stopped her. "This was not an alliance of my making." He lowered his voice and said more kindly, "I only agreed to a handfast, Isabel. You understand the terms of a handfast. It is for one year."

"Of course." But then it dawned on her, and the color slid from her face. "So you intend to repudiate me," she whispered, incredulous.

He didn't need to answer. She understood.

"But what about . . . ," she stammered, color flooding her cheeks.

He knew what she was thinking. "In all *other* respects, we will live together as man and wife."

She looked down at her toes, clearly discomfited. "But what about passion—what about your needs?" she asked in an embarrassed whisper.

If only she knew how badly he wanted her. Even now, just standing so near her, smelling her, he felt the heat of desire stir his blood. The memory of waking with her bundled in his arms, her soft bottom pressed hard against him, was still too fresh. One glance at her lush breasts was enough to recall the feel of all that tender flesh filling his hand. His time on the lists had not freed him from his torment. What he needed was to carry her up to his room, toss her on his bed, and take her in a storm of red-hot passion.

Instead he said, "You need not concern yourself with that. I assure you, my needs are being met. Very well met," he lied. He hadn't had a woman since a week before she'd arrived. Each time he thought about sating his lust between a willing pair of thighs, something stopped him. He took the edge off in his hand, since he knew there was only one person who could ease his pain. The realization surprised him. Never before had he focused so intently on one woman.

Venturing a quick glance, Rory just glimpsed her openmouthed stare of hurt disbelief. He felt a stab in his chest. *Damn,* he thought, *I knew I should not look at her.*

"But I thought . . ." She hesitated. "I thought you might—" Her voice broke, and she didn't finish.

Their eyes met. Tension as mysterious and powerful

as lightning crackled in the quiet morning air. Rory warred with every instinct in his body. He'd hurt her. And the realization of how much he hated doing so disconcerted him. He yearned to pull her into his arms and wipe away the sting of his lie even as he felt her slanted eyes locking on his, drawing him into the depths of her soul.

The urge to wipe away the hurt was too powerful. As if in slow motion, he reached out to cup her face, stroking the curve of her cheek with his thumb. Her skin was unreal. Baby soft and so smooth to the touch. She leaned toward him, and the press of her breasts against his bare arm sent a shock of wanting so acute, it hurt physically not to take her in his arms. Every instinct clamored to hold her. He hesitated for an instant before he lowered his hand to his side.

His duty was clear. He knew what he had to do. Isabel MacDonald would go back to her family at the end of the year, and Rory would form a more advantageous alliance with the Campbells and continue his plans to destroy Sleat. As much as he wanted her, she was not for him.

He didn't want to risk an emotional entanglement, so he'd best make sure there was no confusion about his intentions. "You are an exceptionally beautiful woman, Isabel. But that does not change anything. When the year is over, my duty is done."

Chapter 7

❖

If, as her uncle believed, beauty was the way to a man's heart, then she would use everything at her disposal to entice Rory MacLeod.

Even if the hypocrisy of it killed her.

Isabel dressed with the utmost care for her appearance as she prepared for the evening meal. Since he declined to spend any other time with her, meals were her chance to change his mind about their relationship. He thought her beautiful, but not enough to tempt him from the bed of his leman. She hoped this dress would change his mind.

Isabel still couldn't believe what he'd told her. Or how much it hurt. She couldn't get the image out of her mind or shake the sense of emptiness that had gripped her when he'd confessed to finding his pleasure elsewhere. She knew he must be referring to the dark-haired beauty she had seen him with earlier. To have her suspicions confirmed felt as though someone had clamped an icy claw around her heart and squeezed.

Moreover, she'd practically offered herself to him, and he'd rejected her. He didn't want her. The realization stung far more than she wanted to acknowledge.

Isabel drew up her shoulders protectively and shook off the hurt. It was ironic. The only man she had ever set out deliberately to entice was impervious to her charms. Hadn't she wished to meet a man who did not want her simply for the pretty package? *Be careful what you wish for, Isabel,* she thought dryly.

She should be more concerned with what else he'd revealed.

He intended to send her back in a year, untouched. She'd laugh if it wasn't so painful. Her own handfast husband didn't want her. What bitter irony: They'd both entered the handfast with every intention of repudiating it in the end. Rory simply thought to do his duty to his king, while she intended treachery and betrayal. His honesty shamed her, though with what she'd learned of his character this past month, it could not surprise her.

There was only one thing she could do: She had to convince him to change his mind. At least now she knew what she was up against. He'd admitted he thought her beautiful, so she would start with that. She would find a way to make him fall in love with her despite his avowed sentiments on the subject.

Isabel had gathered the tatters of her resolve all afternoon, after he left her standing there by herself, holding her cheek and trying not to burst into tears. Her skin felt scorched where the same strong, callused fingers that wielded a claymore with such deadly skill had gently swept the side of her cheek. She'd just barely glimpsed the tinge of regret that crossed his features even as that austere, emotionless façade dropped back into place.

But she'd seen it, and it gave her reason to hope.

As Bessie finished lacing her gown, Isabel reached for her silver hand mirror. She held her arm out straight and took a step backward to get a broader view.

" 'Tis not at all proper, poppet."

Isabel gazed into the mirror. "Nonsense, Bessie. There's nothing wrong with this dress, it's beautiful." But the flush heating her cheeks belied her words.

Bessie tsked and shook her head. "It's indecent, is what it is. I can't imagine what compelled your uncle to provide such a gown for an innocent young lass."

Isabel could. And if her reflection was any indication, he'd succeeded. The woman who looked back at her definitely did not look innocent. Her auburn hair was coiled high on her head, framed by the pearl-encrusted headpiece that she'd worn to the handfast. The soft gold silk gown emphasized the creamy ivory of her skin and the redness of her full lips. The subtle tilt of her violet eyes gave her the look of a seductress.

But it was the style of the dress that made the greatest impact. She looked like a debauched wanton. The gown provided by her uncle was not the least bit fashionable. In many respects, it was like the gown she'd worn when she arrived at Dunvegan. She wore no bolster, no stomacher, and no ruff. Only a thin sark separated her skin from the smooth silk of the dress. The soft gold fabric clung to her body, emphasizing every curve, leaving very little to the imagination.

But that was not what caused her to blush. Rather, it was the way that the tight bodice emphasized and exposed her breasts. There was so little fabric covering her bodice that if she took a deep breath, she would likely fall out of the dress completely.

Isabel rarely wore jewelry, but tonight she made an exception. She donned an exquisite set of emeralds in a delicate gold setting left to her by her mother: teardrop earrings, a bracelet, and a pendant. The jewels were all she had of her mother, and she treasured them not for their value, but for their connection with a past she would never know.

A bit shocked by her reflection, Isabel tried to control the tremor in her voice. She knew that she needed to jolt Rory from his indifference and attract his attention, but she realized just what sort of attention this dress might bring. That thought made her tingle with apprehension and something else. Anticipation.

"Well, I think this dress is beautiful, Bessie."

"I did not say that the dress was not beautiful, poppet. I said 'twas indecent. The two are not the same." Bessie gave her a long look. "I do not think your handfast husband will approve of that dress."

"I doubt he will even notice."

"Oh, he'll notice. Have no fear of *that,*" Bessie warned.

Isabel took one last long look and replaced the mirror in her trunk. She supposed this was the best she could do, but displaying her body in a manner calculated to seduce made her uncomfortable. She knew that she had to use what she had at her disposal, but that didn't make it any easier.

Isabel was in an untenable position. To achieve her purpose, she must get closer to him, but the more she learned of Rory, the more difficult it was becoming to think of betraying him in the end. She couldn't ignore what she'd observed of him. Rory MacLeod was the type of leader who inspired devotion, a steadying force in times of trouble. A rock. And the sort of man she had only dreamed of. But if she was going to have any hope of success, it would serve her well to take a lesson from him in indifference. She must harden her heart and not allow herself to be distracted from her goal.

Isabel had a mission, and it definitely didn't include *her* falling in love. This was a one-sided proposition. She must ignore her silly girlish qualms about drawing this sort of attention to herself and use what God had given her for the greater good of her family. The MacLeod wanted to send her back, and she must change his mind. Being charming hadn't gotten her anywhere—it was time for something more drastic . . . like this dress.

She knew something of lust, of seduction. A touch here, a suggestive word there, a sly, knowing smile. Isabel had been at court long enough to learn a few tricks, to learn how some women used their bodies to get what they wanted, to learn to play the game of seduction. It was not in her nature to be so aggressive, but the battleground was clear. He didn't want her, but he lusted for her. So be it.

At least now she knew where she stood. Wasn't that what her uncle had warned she might have to do all along?

Bessie was still speaking. "Your new husband will not be able to tear his eyes away from you." She lifted her fingers to her chin, considering. "Perhaps this dress is not such a bad idea after all."

Isabel stiffened. She knew what was coming next.

Bessie continued fussing with her hair and turned to repeat yet again the same statement Isabel had heard at least a dozen times over the past month. "It is not right that he has not made you his bride in truth. You must realize how the servants are whispering."

Isabel's flush deepened. "Bessie dearest, I have explained this to you before. Rory told me he wishes to give me time to adjust to my new home. That is all. I'm sure he is just being considerate of my innocence. He moved me into his room, didn't he?"

Bessie raised her thin eyebrows with skepticism. A look that said she could not believe Isabel would be so naïve as to believe Rory's explanation. "It's not natural, the man not wanting you in his bed. You are his wife. Well, his handfast wife, at least. Something is not right." When Bessie got hold of something, she was like a dog with a meaty bone. "I'm worried. What if he does not intend to keep up his end of the bargain?"

"What do you mean?" Isabel pretended ignorance. She should have known that Bessie would figure it out.

"I've heard rumors."

"What rumors?" Isabel asked, intrigued.

"Of another alliance."

Isabel's heart dropped. She waited for Bessie to explain.

"The MacLeod was rumored to have been negotiating an alliance with the Campbells."

Her heart was pounding fast, but she forced herself to sound nonchalant as she dismissed Bessie's concerns. "Oh, I'm sure that is all in the past."

But what if it wasn't?

A sick feeling settled in her stomach. Had she upset his plans for another alliance?

It was all she could think of as she approached the hall. Did that explain his reticence? Was he enamored of someone else? The thought disturbed her more than she wanted to acknowledge.

Isabel paused as yet unnoticed at the entrance. A sea of swarming faces assaulted her resolve, causing her a long moment of trepidation. Suddenly, she felt naked and exposed. Wearing this dress no longer seemed like such a good idea. Her confidence faltered.

Gathering the slippery reins of her courage, she took in the achingly familiar scene. The great hall overflowed with boisterous men and women enjoying the easy camaraderie of friends and family. Everywhere she looked, people were laughing, drinking, feasting, and swapping stories. The scene that unfurled before her presented a poignant picture of ordinary Highland life.

A sharp stab of pain in her chest recalled her lifetime longing to be a part of such ordinariness. But it was the same at Dunvegan as it was at Strome. She was alone, an outsider. She would never be a part of this particular happy scene of domestic tranquillity, and she'd do better to remember that. But perhaps if she succeeded, she could find such happiness at Strome.

With renewed determination, she lifted her chin and started toward the dais.

For the first time in over a month, Rory was enjoying himself. Now that Isabel understood what he intended to do, he could relax. He would treat her with the respect that was due his wife, but there need be no pretense of anything more between them. In fact, he was fairly sure she'd do her best to steer clear of him. Of course, he would keep her close until he could assuage his suspicions, but perhaps now he could even sleep in his bed again.

Well satisfied, he took a long drink of *cuirm*, sat back in his chair and smiled, relieved to have taken control of the situation and put the matter decisively behind him.

His contentment, however, did not last long. Rory noticed the disturbance in the hall immediately. He glanced up just as Isabel began her regal procession toward him. It was impossible not to admire the pride and strength in her carriage. She moved with such grace, she practically floated across the floor.

All of a sudden he felt his body go rigid. His eyes locked on a superfluity of pale ivory skin. *What in the bloody hell was she wearing?*

Unlike her previous gowns, this gown no longer teetered on the edge of indecent, it *was* indecent, and left very little to the imagination. The bodice dipped low, exceedingly low, and the thin silken fabric clung to every delectable inch of her womanly charms. His reaction was visceral. Every muscle in his body clenched with awareness and restraint, as he fought to control both the anger and the desire that her appearance wrought within him.

A multitude of conflicting emotions raged through him: He wanted to leap up and cover her, he wanted to pull her into his arms, he wanted to order her to never wear that dress in public again, and he wanted to worship her like the goddess she evoked. Mired in a tempest of bodily conflict, Rory was certain of one thing: If she ever donned that gown again, he would rip it from her body. To hell with the consequences.

He wanted her. He could not deny it. Nor apparently was he alone in his desire. Rory tore his eyes from Isabel and glanced about the room at the gawking stares of his clansmen. Even Alex could not look away. A violent surge of possession took hold of him. He felt a strange primal craving to exert complete dominion, a feeling so alien that it shook him. She did not, and could not, belong to him.

God's wounds, was it her intent to drive him mad with longing?

His eyes narrowed. *Yes.* After what he'd told her today, she was trying either to not so subtly change his mind or to rub his nose in his losses. Neither sat well with him.

What was her game?

Rory's fingers clenched the stem of his goblet. He held his face impassive as she moved to stand before him; he felt the pulse tick in his neck as he fought to douse the fiery blast of anger. He thought a bit of her bravado slipped as his eyes scanned the length of her body, lingering on her breasts. Good, she should be nervous. If he were any other man, he'd take what she offered.

But he would not fall prey to such tactics.

"Good evening," she said, bowing slightly, her breasts nearly spilling forth from their delicate confinement.

His breath seized, emitting a harsh sound reminiscent of a hiss. He could see the damn pink edges of her nipples, perched invitingly only inches from his mouth. His cock rose in appreciation as he imagined running his tongue along the delicate ridge before slipping the hardened tip in his mouth and sucking until she writhed in fervent entreaty. Isabel had a body built for sexual fantasies. And the knowledge that he was not the only one engaging in those fantasies right now enraged him beyond all endurance. By all that was holy, this woman had pushed him too far.

Her cheeks turned pink as she tried circumspectly to adjust her gown.

When the bolt of lust dissipated, Rory saw red. He'd had enough. No wife of his would flaunt herself in such a manner. The ripe fullness of her breasts, the narrow circle of her waist, the slim curve of her hips, and the soft pink of her nipples were not for public display. She belonged to him—for now, at least. And he would not share.

"I'm sorry I'm late," she offered. "It took me some time to get dressed."

Without a word, he stood up, took her arm, and unceremoniously led her from the room. Only when they were out of earshot of the clan did he respond. "I don't think you've finished."

"What do you mean?"

He did not bother to hide his fury. His voice was every bit as dark and dangerous as the strange emotions she evoked in him. "Do not test my patience, Isabel."

From her silence, he knew she'd heeded his warning. He sensed her nervousness as he steered her outside toward the Fairy Tower, through the entry, and up the stairs. He pulled open the door to his solar, pushed her inside, and slammed the door behind them with a resounding thud.

She stood in the middle of the room, her hands fumbling in her skirt. Venturing a cautious peek from under her lashes, she asked, "What do you mean to do?"

"Not what I should do," he snapped. His gaze burned down the length of her body. She shivered in its wake. "That gown is indecent. What could you be thinking wearing something so inappropriate?"

"It's a bit revealing, perhaps—"

"A bit revealing?" he exploded. "I can see the damn edge of your nipples!"

Her cheeks blazed. "Don't yell at me."

Rory forced himself to calm. "I'm not yelling," he said in a lower voice. *I'm so aroused, I can barely think.*

"I didn't think you'd notice what I wear," she said defiantly.

"Oh, I noticed all right. As did every man in the hall with a pulse. My wife, the lady of this keep, will not flaunt herself like a wanton before my men."

He saw a spark of defiance flare in her eyes. "Temporary wife," she corrected.

"Is that what this is about?" His gaze sharpened. "You'll learn that I cannot be manipulated, Isabel. Not by you and certainly not by a scrap of fabric. No matter how revealing."

"You're wrong." She stuck up that adorable chin. "I like this dress, that is all."

He grabbed her by the arm and looked right in her eyes so there would be no mistaking his meaning. "You'll never wear that dress again, or you'll suffer the consequences."

"What consequences?" she asked with a rebellious toss of her flaming hair.

The lass didn't know how precariously close she was to finding out. Every nerve ending in his body was set on edge, primed for release. He wanted to rip the dress from her body and cover every inch of that velvety skin with his. He wanted her hot and aching, throbbing with need, just like him. Instead, he ignored her reckless challenge and moved to the adjoining chamber where their clothes were stored, threw open the door, and yanked out a gown. A sufficiently modest gown of green velvet.

"Change," he ordered. "Now."

"But Bessie—"

A slow smile curved his lips as he met her anxious gaze. "You won't be needing a serving woman."

* * *

Isabel withered under the heat of his predatory stare. She realized belatedly that she'd pushed him too far. The look of raw possession in his eyes sent a chill down her spine. The primal intensity she read there made her think he'd like to do nothing more than toss her on the bed and ravish her like a hell-bent marauding Viking. For the first time since she'd come to Dunvegan, Isabel sensed danger. This man she could not control.

She bit her lip and took a step back. Perhaps she'd miscalculated slightly. The wisdom of wearing this dress suddenly escaped her.

"Take it off," he ordered.

"I c-c-can't."

She heard him curse as he grabbed her by the waist, turned her around, and began unlacing her gown with undeniable skill. Rory MacLeod had had plenty of practice unlacing ladies' gowns. She felt a pang suspiciously like jealousy.

Still, there was something incredibly intimate about his fingers working the laces of her dress. He stood so close, she could smell the distinctive scent of his soap. She felt every touch, every gentle press of his fingers, as he slowly made a path down the length of her spine. His hands came to rest around her waist and she was deeply aware of how close his fingers were to her breasts. How easy it would be for him to stroke her. He moved closer and her breath caught. He, too, was not unaffected. His breath, suddenly uneven, warmed the bare skin of her neck and shoulders, making her skin prickle.

His touch was driving her mad with longing. She felt so strange, boneless, as if she had melted into a deep, warm puddle. Her body flooded with sensations that she didn't understand.

His lips hovered achingly close to her neck as his fingers slid along her back. She sank against him, closing her eyes, silently begging for more. He slid the sleeves past her shoulders, his fingers singeing a path along her sensitive skin. She moaned when his lips finally touched her neck in a soft caress. The scrape of his chin sent a rush of heat through her veins. Her nipples hardened. And God, he knew. With one swipe of his thumb across the throbbing peak, she dissolved against him, taking refuge in the solid strength of his chest and arms.

She sensed his urgency as he kissed her harder, his hot mouth climbing the length of her neck, savaging the tender skin with the force of his desire. His hunger for her had broken free, unleashing a fierce passion that she never would have imagined. Perversely, this dangerous, unpredictable side of him excited her. Her body drenched with heat, savoring the press of his muscled body behind her. The thick column of his arousal against her bottom gave hard proof to his desire.

She felt his tongue, his lips, and every scratch of his stubbled jaw with a startling intensity. Her skin seemed so incredibly sensitive—so alive. He drew her earlobe between his teeth, tugging gently as his tongue circled her ear, his ragged breath making her tremble and shiver.

But it wasn't enough.

She wanted his mouth on hers, his arms around her, his hands covering her body. She wanted relief for the clawing need rising inside her. His mouth slid to her jaw, close to her mouth, while he eased the gown past her hips. Her heart raced and nervous excitement bundled low in her stomach. Every nerve ending was set on edge

in anticipation as she stretched against him in silent surrender. Before she could think to tell him that the gown
must be removed by lifting it over her head, she heard
the unmistakable sound of fabric tearing.

The ruined dress fell to her feet, and Rory promptly
released her. For a moment, he seemed almost as
shocked as she. He stared at her until her breathing returned to normal and glanced meaningfully at the ball of
fabric on the floor. He'd nearly ripped it in two.

"A dress like that is an invitation," he said flatly.
"Have care what you offer, Isabel. You just might get
it."

Isabel swallowed hard and nodded.

Without another word, he tossed her the dress he'd
chosen for her, thankfully one that laced in the front,
and watched—from a distance—her struggle to clothe
herself. The heat in his penetrating gaze was contained,
but no less volatile.

When she'd finished he led her from the room as if
nothing had happened, which, given her confused state
of mind, was just as well. Had he just intended to teach
her a lesson, or had she finally managed a chink in his
impenetrable armor?

Chapter 8

❖

The crowd gathered in the great hall was conspicuously quiet as Rory led Isabel back to the dais, though
no one stared too openly. Everyone in the room was
keenly aware of what had happened, but none would
dare shame his lady by making it known. Returning to
the table, Rory offered Isabel a seat beside him, sat
down, and resumed his meal as if he hadn't just ripped
her gown from her body and ravished her honey-sweet
skin with his mouth. And as if she hadn't just combusted
like wildfire in his hands.

He'd made his point. She'd overstepped the bounds
with that dress and pushed him too hard. Isabel had
learned her lesson, but, he realized, so had he.

Not wanting to think any further about what had
happened, Rory turned back to his conversation with
Alex, engaging him in a heated debate about the fastest
roads to Edinburgh. A good argument was exactly what
he needed to release some of his pent-up tension.

Isabel must have been listening, because when he'd
finished she asked, "Have you visited court recently, my
lord?"

Rory relaxed. It seemed she, too, was anxious to put
what had just happened behind them. It was a warning,
nothing more. "No," he said. "Though I must return

soon." He masked his annoyance at having to present himself to the king.

Her face lit up. "Oh, how I envy you."

Rory ignored the strange pull in his chest at the burst of pleasure on her face. But he'd also heard the longing in her voice. "You were fond of court?"

She nodded enthusiastically. "Very much so."

"You were a lady-in-waiting to Queen Anne, I believe?"

"Yes, for almost a year." She sighed. "It was a difficult adjustment at first, but I grew to love my time there."

Rory realized it had probably been hard for her to leave her family. "You did not find it tiresome, all that pomp and formality?"

"It wasn't like that at all," she said. "The queen and king are very different when they are with their family."

Her choice of words was telling. Rory was beginning to understand what she'd found at Holyrood. "And you were part of the family?" he asked gently.

He noticed the flash of loneliness cross her eyes, before she covered it with a wobbly smile. "Of course not," she chided as if he'd only been jesting. "Though I was made to feel as if I were."

And Rory realized how much she'd savored the experience. At court, she'd found what she'd been missing with her own family. She'd found happiness, but he also sensed a sadness—a certain vulnerability—in her, as if she were used to being on the outside and wanted desperately to be included but didn't know whether she deserved to be. He guessed that although she approached things openly and enthusiastically, she pushed herself recklessly at times in response to those feelings of insignificance.

"And I learned so much," she continued. "The king considers himself quite a devotee of literature and learning. He openly encourages the queen to pursue her scholarly endeavors. I was fortunate enough to join along."

Rory lifted his brow. "You read?" When she nodded, he asked, "What are your favorites?"

"The great romances and the old chansons de geste, especially *Le Morte d'Arthur* and *La Chanson de Roland*." The tempo of her speech increased with her passion on the subject. "I also fell in love with a new playwright from England. Have you heard of William Shakespeare?" He answered yes. "My favorite is *Romeo and Juliet*."

"I'm familiar with the work," Rory said carefully. He did not miss the irony of her choice. Like King James, Queen Elizabeth detested feuding. It was to please his royal patron that Shakespeare had written the cautionary tale of star-crossed lovers fated to die as a result of their families' incessant feuding.

Rory was impressed. Not many women of his acquaintance were proficient readers, and none, with the exception of Margaret, were as voracious. He shared her appetite for literature and added to his extensive library whenever he traveled. He found himself offering, "There is a library in the Fairy Tower. You may borrow whatever you like."

When she smiled, his chest constricted until the air left him. Her delight was so poignant, he had to turn away or he'd find himself devising ways of keeping her happy.

Isabel was disappointed when Rory returned to his conversation with Alex. She thought he'd been enjoying talking to her. But her heart fell when she saw the beautiful dark-haired woman, Catriona—Isabel had learned her name—approach the dais. This was the first time they'd crossed paths since the handfast ceremony. Though they spoke for only a few moments, the reminder of his liaison shattered whatever joy she'd experienced from his kind offer to allow her access to his library.

He might have kissed Isabel's shoulder and ripped off her dress, but he was taking his pleasure with someone else.

There was no denying that Rory seemed extremely comfortable—no, intimate—with the woman. Isabel's already shaky confidence crumbled. The unexpected burst of passion she'd felt in his arms tonight had confused her. She'd hoped she'd found a crack in his reserve, but now it seemed he'd only been trying to teach her a lesson. She'd embarrassed him before his clan, and that was all.

Trying to hide her disappointment, she turned away, only to watch as someone slipped from the shadows into the seat next to her. She smothered the gasp that rose involuntarily to her throat as she noticed the large black patch that covered half her face. It could only be Margaret.

She was grateful that Bessie had forewarned her of the lass's disturbing appearance. Even so, Isabel was taken aback, but she managed to hide her consternation with a serene smile. The patch was as loud as a blaring trumpet heralding her disfigurement. She wondered whether the damage to the eye was worse to look upon than the menacing mask that was meant to hide it.

Isabel had been very nervous to meet her new sister,

fearing that Margaret would attribute the sins of her uncle to her. But Isabel's nervousness vanished at the sight of the timid creature next to her. Once she noticed Margaret's discomfort, her heart immediately went out to her.

"You must be Margaret," she said. "I've so looked forward to meeting you."

Margaret peered shyly at her from beneath her lashes.

Without thinking, Isabel reached out and covered Margaret's shaking fingers with her own. "I have never had a sister, but I know I should like one."

Margaret stared at her hand in shock, but after a minute she seemed to relax. Her voice quivered when she spoke. "It is a pleasure to meet you as well, Isabel. I apologize for missing the celebration of your handfast, but my sister Christina had sent for me during her confinement." She met Isabel's friendly gaze with a feeble smile.

Isabel knew that Margaret's journey to the neighboring Isle of Lewis, home to the Lewis branch of the MacLeods, had probably been conveniently arranged, but she could not blame the poor lass for wanting to avoid such proximity to Sleat. Isabel took a closer look at her new sister. Except for the patch, Rory's sister was quite lovely. Long golden blond curls cascaded in soft ringlets down her slender back. Dainty fair features were somewhat hidden but still evident. Her one visible eye was the same transfixing deep sapphire hue of Alex's and Rory's eyes. Although Isabel was small of frame, Margaret was much smaller. Why, Isabel thought, grinning at the obvious similarity, she was as sprite as a wee fairy—compliments of her supposed ancestors, perhaps?

Once again, Isabel questioned her uncle's actions.

How could he have treated Margaret so harshly? She couldn't reconcile her uncle's handling of Margaret with the deeds of a worthy chief. It was unsettling, especially when compared with the strength and honor of the man beside her.

"I hope the birthing went well?" Isabel inquired politely.

"Yes, thank you, but I'm sorry to have missed your arrival."

Isabel made a dismissive gesture with her free hand. "A babe is much more important. What did she have?"

Margaret smiled. "A girl."

"I hope to meet her one day," she remarked. "And Christina as well. How many sisters and brothers do you have?"

"Only one other. My youngest sister Flora. But she resides with her mother." Margaret gave her a hesitant look. "Are you finding Dunvegan to your liking? I know you have just come from court," she continued with a far-off look in her eye. "I doubt I'll ever have the chance to travel to Edinburgh."

"Whyever not? I would be happy to escort you to court and make the proper introductions. Queen Anne would be most happy to meet you, I'm sure. She is wonderful; I know you would like her. And of course I shall tell you all about my time at court whenever you wish. But I know you are busy with your duties, so you must tell me when it's convenient."

Margaret squirmed a bit in her seat, as if the fact that she was still chatelaine made her uncomfortable. "I've been very busy of late, but I'll certainly find the time to hear about your stay at court. It sounds so exciting. But

I could never show myself there . . . with the way I look and all."

Isabel heard the deep sorrow and shame in Margaret's softly lilting voice. She took hold of Margaret's tiny other hand and said with complete sincerity, "You are lovely, Margaret. If you want to go to court, you should. Don't let the unkindness of others dissuade you from living your life with purpose. There are many cruel people at court, but I think you'll find there are many more who are good and compassionate."

"You are kind, Isabel, but I have not the strength to bear the inevitable gossip."

There was such sadness in her that Isabel could not resist trying to find some way to help. Her uncle was to blame for the shame that must have turned Margaret into this wounded fey creature. She sensed a kindred spirit in the young woman and thought perhaps she could right a wrong while she was here. It was the least she could do, since she would be making an enemy of Margaret's brother.

Her mind was made up. She wanted to help Margaret find the strength that Isabel could sense was buried within her. Isabel did not wish to examine her own motives. If she did, she would probably recognize the guilt she assumed for the actions of her uncle. And for her relationship with him.

"The women who are inclined to gossip will always find something to gossip about. I don't know if they even realize how hurtful it can be, especially to someone unfamiliar with life at court. When I first arrived at court, they laughed at my rough Highland manners. I seemed to always say the wrong thing, as I was used to speaking my mind when at home with only a father and three brothers. Not the most appropriate behavior for a woman, I assure you. Then the next new person arrived and they forgot about me."

Margaret looked at her with a mixture of admiration and awe.

Isabel chuckled. "I don't mean to suggest that I was immune to the gossip. I admit I was hurt initially, but that's because I didn't anticipate that I would be so different from the other ladies at court. I felt rejected, but I soon realized they weren't rejecting me personally but merely finding something interesting to talk about. But you'll know what to expect and will not be as unprepared as I was."

"I don't know. You make it sound so simple, yet I am not at all brave, Isabel."

Neither am I, Isabel thought. Instead she said, "Don't worry. If you want to go to court, we will find a way. I'm sure that with the two of us working together, we will be able to devise a plan of attack."

Isabel's confidence must have been contagious because Margaret smiled.

From his seat on her right, Rory observed the conversation between Isabel and Margaret. He was concerned about Margaret's reaction to Isabel. His first instinct was to protect his sister from the pain of her memories that seeing a MacDonald was sure to evoke, but he knew they would have to meet eventually so he forced himself not to interfere.

Isabel's kindness was immediately apparent. He noticed the way she looked Margaret directly in the eye and unconsciously touched her hand, not shying away as most did from Margaret's injury. Not many had offered their friendship since Margaret's return; his sister's disfigurement made people nervous and uncomfortable. It infuriated him, but he could not force people to treat her as before. Fear and superstition were powerful forces. He felt the tightness in his shoulders dissipate, not realizing how tense he'd been while observing the two women.

Rory couldn't hear their discussion, but he was amazed after only a few minutes to see a carefree smile transform Margaret's face. He was flabbergasted. Margaret hadn't smiled like that in two years. By all appearances, they seemed to be fast friends. It warmed him to see his sister relaxed and enjoying herself; it had been far too long.

"Did you speak with Margaret about your ideas for our chamber, Isabel?" he asked, more curious than he wanted to admit about what they were discussing.

"Not yet. Margaret and I were discussing court."

"The latest fashion?" he asked, a sardonic reference to her dress.

Isabel blushed, realized he was teasing her, then shook her head and laughed. "No, only that I think Margaret would enjoy it."

Rory stiffened. The thought of his shattered sister set free among the vicious ladies of court made his protective instincts flare. What could Isabel be thinking to encourage Margaret's hopes like that? His sister was incredibly fragile as it was; court would destroy her. Not wanting to hurt his sister's feelings, however, he quickly turned the subject. "Aye, but my sister is needed at Dunvegan. I could not spare her." He smiled encouragingly to Margaret. "Wasn't there something you wanted to ask Margaret about my solar?"

Isabel gave him a small questioning frown, then turned to Margaret. "I just wanted to make a few wee changes to *our* room," she corrected, "but I wanted to ask your permission before I do so. We can discuss it another time if you wish."

Margaret looked to Rory for approval, and he nodded. "What did you have in mind?" she asked.

"Just a few things to make the room more comfortable, perhaps a few soft pillows, some bed hangings"—Isabel shrugged—"Things like that."

Margaret was immediately ensnared. Rory was amazed how the topic of decoration could inspire such fervor in the female mind. "Rory's room is entirely too austere," she agreed. "I've been trying to change things for years. But he'll hear nothing of it."

Rory crossed his arms over his chest. "That's the way I like it. Plain and simple."

Both women made faces. Margaret met his gaze. "Yes, well, you are handfasted now. You will have to adjust."

Rory couldn't believe it. His timid little sister had just stood up to him. It was . . . wonderful.

Margaret continued, "What colors were you thinking?"

"Hmm. Maybe soft roses and lavenders with floral fabric, laces, and needlepoint, what do you think?"

God's wounds, it sounded like Margaret's frilly boudoir.

Both women took one look at his expression and burst into laughter.

Rory started to frown until he caught the mischievous twinkle in Isabel's eye. Surprisingly, he didn't mind their teasing at all. Some of Margaret's spirit that had been eviscerated from two years ago was returning after only minutes in Isabel's company.

Her spirited playfulness was infectious, and he found himself smiling.

Rory thought of the sweet but timid Campbell lass who would be his bride and couldn't help comparing her with another. Would she embrace his sister and bring a smile to her face?

Watching Rory with Margaret offered Isabel a side of him that she had never seen. That Rory cared deeply for his sister was obvious. It impressed her that this hard, formidable warrior could also be gentle and considerate.

A sharp pang of longing hit her square in the chest. Isabel yearned for her own brothers to look at her the same way. Given the lengths she had gone to to evoke such feelings from them, that Rory showed his love for Margaret so readily was yet another attribute in his favor. This man had so many layers, and the more she peeled away, the more there was to admire.

A buzz of anticipation rippled through the hall, abruptly ending their conversation. The night's entertainment was set to begin. A bearish white-haired man rose from the trestle table below the dais and moved purposefully across the room to stand before the fire. He was dressed in a simple long plaid, but it was his knee-length beard that drew Isabel's attention. It was thick and fluffy, as pure white as freshly fallen snow. He raised his grizzled, pawlike hands and loudly cleared his throat to quiet the room. Eoin Og O'Muireaghsain, *seannachie* of the MacLeods, began to speak in a strong, melodious voice that reverberated throughout the crowded hall, in sharp contrast with his aged appearance.

"This night, our chief has requested the story of how the great *Bratach Shi,* the Fairy Flag of the MacLeod, was brought to the clan."

Isabel blanched. Her heart quickened as she realized the subject matter of this night's entertainment. Rory couldn't know. *It's only a coincidence,* she told herself, trying to calm the rising panic. But her palms grew damp from being clenched so tight. She forced herself not to look around and see if anyone was watching her reaction, but she could feel the weight of Rory's eyes on her.

"A long, long time ago, not long after the time of Leod, a handsome young chief fell in love with a beautiful fairy princess—one of the *bean sidhe.* The couple wished to marry and sought permission from the princess's father, the king of the fairies. Much to their surprise, the king was against the match. For he knew that in the end, to marry a mortal man would cause his beloved daughter infinite unhappiness, for unlike the princess, the young chief would eventually grow old and die.

"Darkness and unhappiness shadowed Skye, for theirs was the truest unrequited love. The weeping of the princess filled the loch, threatening to flood the land, until the king at last capitulated. The princess could handfast with the MacLeod. But there was one condition. She had to promise to return to her people in one year and a day. The couple was so happy to be together, they readily agreed to the king's condition."

Isabel had not heard the enchanting tale before, but she was finding it extremely difficult to relax. She glanced furtively around the room, grateful that no one seemed to notice her turmoil. The clan appeared enthralled by the story even though they had surely heard the tale countless times. Afraid that he would somehow notice her anxiety, Isabel dared not look at Rory.

"The people rejoiced with the happiness of the couple, and before the year was out a cherished son was born. But the joy of the birth of the child was tempered with the knowledge that soon the princess must return to her people and leave her beloved husband and precious son forever.

"As they knew it would, the day for her departure to the land of the fairies arrived. The fairy princess and the chief were brokenhearted but knew that they must honor their promise. For once given, the word of the MacLeod was absolute and could not be broken. At her leavetaking, the princess sought a promise from her husband. He must vow to never let their son be alone, for the fairy princess could not bear to hear the crying of her precious child. At last, with a desperate, bittersweet kiss intended to last a lifetime, the princess left her beloved husband and son behind, fading into the mist over the bridge that we now call the Fairy Bridge in memory of their parting, returning sorrowfully to the fairy folk."

The *seannachie* paused dramatically. Silence filled the hall. He motioned for a goblet and ever so slowly took a seemingly endless gulp of ale. The hall was heavy with the dull drumming sound of silence. He looked like a druid from another time, with swirls of smoke from the peat fires spinning mystically over his head. He wiped his mouth with the back of his furry hand and looked carefully about the room to ensure that his audience was listening.

They were.

"The pain of the chief was immeasurable. His beloved

wife was lost to him forever. But he consoled himself with the fact that at least he had his son. He kept his promise to his wife, and the child was never left alone. Never, that is, until the night of the celebration of the chief's day of birth. That night, a great feast was held to cheer the despondent chief. The pipers filled the air with the magic of their music, and the chief at last allowed himself to dance and sing. But, alas, the joyful sounds drew the attention of the nursemaid whose duty it was to watch over the child. She left the wee bairn unattended, and he began to cry. Far, far away in the land of the fairy folk, the princess heard the pitiful wailings of her child and her heart was struck with an intolerable pain. She rushed to her child and comforted him with whispered words of magic. The princess wrapped him securely in her shawl and gently kissed his tears, singing him sweet fairy songs to calm his crying. The words she sang, her fairy charm, are still sung to the MacLeod's heirs to this day.

"Later, when the nursemaid finally returned, she found the child sleeping peacefully wrapped in a fine ethereal crimson-and-yellow swath of fabric.

"Many years later, the boy told his father what had happened that night—the night his mother returned to Dunvegan and left her shawl, the *Bratach Shi*, for her son. The princess bestowed the Fairy Flag upon her child to protect the clan. If the MacLeods were ever in great jeopardy, the flag must be unfurled and waved three times, and the knights of the fairies would appear to their defense. But as we know is always true with the fairies, there were conditions. If anyone other than a MacLeod should touch the flag, that person would immediately perish. And most important of all, the magic of the flag would work only three times. So it should be used only in the direst of circumstances."

His voice had dropped to barely a whisper, but his words were heard by all. The *seannachie* had spun a web of magic of his own throughout the hall. Isabel scooted forward in her seat, anxiously awaiting the rest.

"The flag is kept in a secret place known only to the chief, safely tucked away in a locked box but ready to be unfurled if the clan should ever again need its fairy magic. There is but one unfurling left in the flag, for its powers were needed twice in the time of Alasdair Crotach— once to save the clan from sure defeat at the hands of Clan Donald and again to save the clan from starvation. But I will save those tales for another night."

Disappointed groans echoed throughout the great hall, and not just from the wee lads and lassies. But in the tradition of all great bards, Eoin Og O'Muireagh-sain left his audience wanting. Regal as a king, he slowly returned to his seat, basking proudly in the thunderous applause.

Isabel was moved, held spellbound by the charming tale of lost love and maternal protection by the fairy princess for her child. The story touched a chord in the heart of the girl who had lost her own mother at birth and the woman who yearned for the romantic love of troubadours. Looking around the room at the happy, cheering faces of the MacLeod clansmen, Isabel could see that she was not the only one affected by the tale. The MacLeods treasured the famous Fairy Flag, and she could see from their proud faces that they believed in its magic.

She knew that in the end it did not matter whether the flag really possessed fairy magic. The MacLeods *believed* in its magic, and faith could be every bit as powerful as truth. Her uncle wanted that power—whether to wield for the MacDonalds or simply to destroy the MacLeods. It did not matter. The MacLeods would not have a talisman to rally around, and that would be enough for their ultimate ruin and destruction. Of course, it wouldn't hurt if she also managed to locate a secret entrance to their stronghold.

Guiltily, she lowered her gaze from the cheering clansmen. She felt almost as if she were violating a private moment—intruding on a sacred ritual. Now that she better understood the origins of the flag, Isabel was filled with a sense of dread. She would be the instrument of their destruction. And she realized there was yet another complication, as if locating the flag and fleeing the castle without being caught weren't enough. She also had to avoid death.

Chancing a sideways glance at the powerful man seated next to her, Isabel knew that if the flag didn't kill her, Rory well could.

Chapter 9

❖

Perhaps the dress had served its purpose after all, Isabel thought as she caught sight of the discarded gown still lying in a heap on the floor of their bedchamber. Though it had not exactly elicited the reaction she'd hoped for, it had elicited a reaction. And as the night had drawn on, she had detected a subtle thawing in Rory. For the first time, their conversation had been relaxed and at times even playful. He was no less imposing than before, but not quite so remote. She'd been enjoying herself with both Rory and his sister.

The story of the Fairy Flag, however, had jarred her back to reality. If the tale spun by the *seannachie* was to be believed, she knew where the flag was kept: a locked box in a secret location safeguarded by Rory. Now all she had to do was get Rory to tell her where he kept the box, retrieve it, find the secret entrance, and leave. Simple.

She scoffed. The man intended to send her home in eleven months, but would he confide the clan's most precious secrets? Not likely. But she had to try. The only other choice was to return home to face defeat and the destruction of her clan at the hands of the Mackenzies. In other words, she had no choice.

She dared not think of what Rory would do if he discovered her subterfuge. How would he deal with a traitor? Would she be killed? Maimed? Imprisoned? She didn't think so. Even in the beginning, when he had been so remote and cold, she had not sensed ruthlessness in his character, and less so now. He did not seem the type to enjoy violence toward women. In fact, he showed his love for his sister quite openly, something most men in his position would be reluctant to do for fear of being thought weak. Perhaps he would be able to forgive her? She laughed scornfully. Highlanders did not forgive—it was not in their vocabulary. No, he was a proud man, and what she intended would be a blow to his pride. He would never forgive her.

The forlorn hollowness in her heart at the thought of betraying Rory tore bitterly at her sense of duty, her sense of responsibility. Like a coward, she wanted to run from here, return to court as if nothing had happened. Unfortunately, either way the result would be the same. She would never see him again.

Isabel doubted she would be able to look at herself in the mirror when this was all over, but the thought of the destruction her failure would bring to her own clan was equally unpleasant. She had to proceed with her plan.

She had to get closer to him, to change his mind. To make him forget she was a MacDonald. Tonight she intended to wait up for him, even if it took all night. He might be bedding another woman, but she wouldn't let that stop her. He was not completely indifferent to her.

Nor was she to him. Tonight had established that well enough. Her response to his touch earlier had given her more than a twinge of apprehension. Even simply sitting beside him, she flushed with awareness. When he smiled, she remembered the feel of his mouth on hers, and when his eyes lingered on her breasts, she remembered the brush of his finger and the intimate longing from within. No, she was hardly indifferent. She just couldn't let her attraction get in the way of what she had to do.

She must analyze her plan of action methodically. If she was going to truly search for the Fairy Flag, it seemed logical to begin with Rory. A talisman must be accessible to be of use in an emergency. She would have to search the areas that Rory frequented but that were private enough not to be subject to accidental discovery. Somewhere in his rooms seemed the most likely hiding place. It was named the Fairy Tower after all.

Isabel lay in bed gazing at the ceiling, watching the flickering shadows of candlelight, waiting. She rolled from side to side, trying to get comfortable. When that proved futile, she tossed off the coverlet, alighted from bed, and moved to stand before the window. But not even the soft glow of moonlight or the tranquillity of a bright starry night could calm her strange restlessness.

What was keeping him? As if she couldn't guess. Catriona. A sick, queasy feeling knit low in her belly. Admittedly, she intended much worse, but why did it feel like a betrayal?

Frustrated and angry, Isabel hurriedly donned her slippers and robe. If she sat here all night with nothing to do, she'd go mad just thinking about it. She had to relax. What she needed was a good book. Something to free her mind from Dunvegan, from Rory, and from her wretched plight while she waited. He'd offered her the use of his library; she wished she'd thought to ask him where it was, but it shouldn't be too difficult to find.

Isabel frowned as she looked down at her wrap. It

was another of her uncle's purchases. The sheer ivory silk did little to hide her near undressed state. Despite the modest *night rail* that she wore to sleep, the robe clung to her at all her most intimate parts as if she wore nothing underneath. She pulled the sides of the gown tighter across her chest, attempting to further cover herself, but she only exacerbated the problem.

Isabel tiptoed softly across the room and hesitated for a moment, Rory's warning not to flaunt herself echoing in her ears. If she were caught in her present ensemble, it would be embarrassing. But she couldn't wait up with nothing to do, and she dearly missed her nightly read that had become an enjoyable ritual in Edinburgh. Besides, she reasoned, the noise had quieted considerably in the last hour. Certainly everyone except for Rory would be in bed by now.

But what if he caught her?

He wouldn't be happy to see her traipsing around in her nightclothes. A spark of recklessness kindled inside her. She'd pushed him tonight with the dress, but perhaps not hard enough. What would happen if she pushed harder? It was what she wanted, wasn't it? For her plan. Memories of hot kisses along her neck and his finger sweeping her nipple assailed her, calling that theory into question. A shiver of fear and anticipation shot through her. It appeared Isabel had a heretofore unknown penchant for courting danger.

She moved purposefully toward the door, then paused to rest her hands on the wooden slats, listening with her ear to the door to make sure no one was about. Hearing nothing, she cautiously opened the door.

She slid from her room and began the quest to find the library. As she had yet to explore the Fairy Tower, she didn't know where to begin. Rory's room occupied the third floor, and she knew that both Alex and Margaret had chambers on the second floor, so she decided to start with the bottom and work her way up. Keeping to the shadows, she carefully began her long journey down the steep curved stairs to the lower level.

Despite her fear of being caught, Isabel felt a surge of excitement. Her skin tingled. Her body felt wonderfully alive, wonderfully sensitive. She grinned mischievously. It had been quite some time since she had embarked on a nighttime adventure.

Wandering around in the middle of the night through dark corridors reminded her of sneaking after her brothers when she was a girl. Unbeknownst to both her father and uncle when they had sought her cooperation, she made an excellent spy. She'd had more than enough practice. Even Bessie was not aware of how many times she had escaped her chamber at Strome Castle to follow her brothers on their midnight raids or their illicit trysts with the conquest of the week. Early on, she'd been caught following them once or twice, earning her a sore backside for a few days, but she soon grew far more adept at her game.

As she grew older and realized the danger, she carried along her bow for protection. On her last raid before leaving for Edinburgh, she'd followed her brothers, who had been "borrowing" some cattle from the Mackenzie of Kintail but had been surprised in the act by a handful of Mackenzie clansmen. Her youngest brother, Ian, had been forced from the protective core of fighting Mac-Donald clansmen, and Isabel watched in horror as a Mackenzie warrior lifted his arrow and aimed it straight at Ian's heart. Without thinking, she released her own arrow from her hiding place in the trees. As always, her aim was true, and the arrow struck the Mackenzie warrior right between the eyes. She'd been sick on the spot. The sound of the arrow sinking into flesh and bone was one she would never forget.

Ian had been so shocked that he had not turned around right away to see who had rescued him from death. Only later, when he realized that none of his brothers or clansmen had noticed his troubles, had he figured out someone else had been there.

He might have suspected who it was, but he never said a word. After that night, however, Isabel detected a subtle change in Ian's attitude toward her. From that day forward, he offered her a small token of respect.

Isabel was severely shaken by the incident. When she followed her brothers on their adventures, she'd wanted only to be included; she'd never contemplated having to kill anyone. She matured much in that moment, realizing by experience that her childish games had very adult consequences. She vowed to leave her brothers be, but at the same time she couldn't resist a wee bit of pride that her arrow had saved Ian, even if he didn't know it.

Exiting the stairwell, she wandered through the half-lit corridors of the lower level, cautiously opening doors, finding nothing, making her way to the familiar entry hall of the tower.

It was a charming space, as beautiful as any of the private chambers of the queen. Torches in iron sconces lined the walls, having not yet been extinguished for the night. Intricately designed tapestries, likely Flemish in origin from their great beauty, hung on thick plastered walls painted a rich gold. She recognized many of the scenes as depictions of famous chansons. Scenes of great battles. Scenes of great love. Fresh rushes woven into mats on the floor were topped with fine colorful carpets, no doubt brought back from the Holy Land hundreds of years ago by a crusading ancestor. Delicately carved wooden chairs, upholstered with cushions of rich emerald velvet, formed a small seating area before the fire. Isabel moved to the fire, thinking to warm herself before resuming her search on the upper levels.

It took her a moment to realize that she was no longer alone.

"What are you doing here?"

Rory's voice snapped like a whip across the silent night. Despite the fire, the hair on the backs of her arms stood up. From his tone, Isabel knew something was wrong. Very wrong. She turned, cautious, her gaze flickering over his rigid stance and fierce, unyielding jaw. The flames from the torches cast shadows across his ruggedly handsome face. Her chest clenched. He looked like a stranger. Like the ruthless warrior she'd once feared. Internal warning bells clanged.

She looked to him for reassurance. Her tentative smile, an attempted greeting, wobbled and then fell. His eyes were as hard as sapphires, and her blood ran cold. The aura of safety and security she'd unknowingly grown accustomed to fled. The solid, steady veneer was gone, replaced by a penetrating fury that cut her to the bone. Fury that, unlike earlier, had nothing to do with lust. He wasn't even looking at her ensemble—or lack thereof.

Her heart dropped to her feet. *Dear God, had he discovered her subterfuge?*

*   *   *

Suspicion coiled in him like a poisonous snake, ready to strike at the faintest spark.

Too many things didn't add up. And finding her sneaking around the tower in the middle of the night had sent him over the edge.

Rory had returned to his chamber, deeply troubled by the inconsistencies he perceived in his observations of Isabel. On the one hand, she seemed a kind, innocent, and vulnerable young woman eager to find a place in her new clan. But at other times, her actions were decidedly suspicious, made more so by her connection to Sleat. Despite what he'd told her about returning her to her kin at the end of the handfast period, she'd set out to entice him with her revealing dress. Could her attempt to tempt him with the dress have something to do with her uncle and her reasons for being here? Sleat had another purpose with this handfast, of that Rory was sure; what he didn't know was whether Isabel was part of it.

He'd also noticed her face pale when the tale of the Fairy Flag began—indeed, her discomfort throughout the rest of the evening was obvious. But it wasn't until he'd entered his solar and found her gone that his already simmering doubts flared. He had not forgotten her strange behavior in the kitchens. And when he went searching for her, only to find her wandering the corridors of the keep, opening doors as if she were looking for something, his suspicions intensified. Now he was furious—not just with her, but also with himself for how much he didn't want to believe she was anything other than what she seemed.

She stood unsteadily before him, the fire behind her forming a halo around her flaming hair. She gazed at him warily, like a fawn sensing danger. He took a step closer.

"What are you doing here?" he repeated. She flinched at the sound of his voice. But fear would not distract him. She'd do well to witness his wrath. To know the consequences of betrayal. This time, Rory would not be put off by suggestive comments; he would have answers. This was not the first time she'd acted strangely or been looking in places she shouldn't.

"I couldn't sleep," she explained nervously. "I was looking for the library you mentioned; I thought I might find a book to read."

"You should have asked Deidre to bring you one. Or waited for me to return."

"It was late, I didn't want to wake her." She met his gaze with a defiant thrust of her chin. "And I wasn't sure that you would return."

A plausible excuse, but could he believe her? His penetrating gaze raked her face for signs of deceit. But when his eyes lowered, his body leapt to attention. His muscles tensed, and a small pulse beat at his throat. Rory had been so focused on his finding her sneaking around his corridors that he hadn't noticed how she was dressed. Or rather undressed. *Dear God, he could see everything*.

With the backlight of the fire lighting his way, he could see the curves and contours of her form so clearly, she could have been standing before him naked. He saw the high firmness of her breasts. The creamy perfection of her velvety soft skin. The small, tight nipples the size of tiny pearls that stood out from the cold. Her waist was small and her hips gently curved.

His eyes stopped their hungry descent. He dared not lower his gaze any farther or he wouldn't be able to resist taking her right there. He couldn't look at that delicate apex where her legs joined. He stepped back, his body so tense with lust that he thought he might explode. Fine beads of sweat formed on his forehead. His physical reaction to her was so strong, for a moment he forgot his anger.

But it soon came back to him full force. *By God, I warned her.* "Why are you out of your room dressed like that?" He made a harsh gesture with his hand. "Did you hear nothing of what I said earlier?" *Didn't she realize what she did to him?*

Perhaps she did.

Instinctively, she pulled her robe closer. He nearly groaned. The fabric stretched taut over her full, succulent breasts. The sweet buds of her nipples teased him. The force of his desire rose hard beneath his plaid.

"I heard, but I d-d-didn't expect to see anyone," she stuttered. "If you would show me the library, I will return to my room."

"Didn't expect to see anyone? Don't you understand"—his voice shook—"*I* could have been anyone." Any one of his men could have seen her nakedness just as clearly as he could. The thought made him halfcrazed.

Had she set out to entice him again? To drive him mad with longing? Rory struggled with the conflicting emotions battling inside him. Frustration and lingering doubt gave his voice the sharp edge of a blade. "Why do I find you searching the dark corridors of my keep? What are you looking for?"

Her eyes widened with alarm. She tried to explain.

"You misunderstand me, Rory. I was only looking for a book. I didn't know where to find the library. It's late, and the noise had died down. I thought all were abed."

He whipped around to grasp her arms. His hold tightened with the roughness of his voice. "What game are you playing, Isabel? Was the damn dress not enough?"

"You have the wrong of it. I certainly didn't seek you out." Her voice lowered to almost a whisper. "You have made it very clear that you do not want me."

It was the wrong thing to say. He was only a man, and she'd prodded him one too many times. Teasing him with her beauty, her provocative clothing, her naughty innuendo, her seductive smiles. The press of her soft buttocks against his rock-hard cock. Her soulful eyes, eyes that tore through his indifference. She was his handfast bride. Who would blame him if he took her? No one. It was expected. She belonged to him—for a year.

Restraint exploded inside him. He did want her. He wanted her more than he had ever wanted a woman before. He felt none of the careful reserve that he usually felt with the lasses. None of the distance. None of the control. Right now, his body raged with a fire that could not be contained.

He pulled her into his embrace, holding her firmly against his chest and groin, skimming his hands down her hips. Savoring the soft sensation of her body molded against his, he gripped the tight curves of her buttocks in his hands as he lifted her against him. He pulsed with need. "You are wrong, Isabel. I do want you." His voice grew thick. "Can't you feel how much I want you?"

Her eyes widened.

"Is this what you wanted, Isabel? Did you want me to touch you?" He moved one hand around to cup her breast, rubbing his thumb across the hard tip, smiling when she gasped with shocked pleasure. He lowered his head to the curve of her neck, burying his nose in the warm lavender essence of her silky curls. His mouth brushed along her neck and throat, trailing kisses until he reached her ear. Pulling the tender lobe between his teeth, he felt her shiver. "I don't just want to touch you, I want to taste every inch of you." The soft burr of his speech became more pronounced with the sensual promise of his words, rolling off his tongue in a caressing whisper.

He felt the wild flutter of her heart against his chest. Finally, unable to resist any longer, he lowered his head, covering her trembling lips with his. This time, he kissed her with all the passion he'd held inside since he'd first seen her. For every time she'd tempted him to kiss her, to touch her, to make her his. His mouth moved against hers, demanding. Tasting. Devouring.

The innocence of her response nearly brought him to his knees.

His heart raced, and blood pounded in his ears. Rory couldn't get enough. He kissed her with an urgency that could not be denied. Deftly easing her lips apart, he slid in his tongue. The honey taste of her only made him want more. *God, she was sweet.* The kiss went deeper, hotter, more desperate. He delved in the sweet caverns of her mouth and stroked her tongue until it entwined with his.

Rory groaned, surprised by the intensity of her sensual response. He pulled her even closer. Her breasts

pushed hard up against his chest, the heat between their
bodies nearly dissolving the thin layers of cloth that
stood between them. He was burning up. He ached to
feel the rake of her tight nipples on his bare skin as he
slid against her.

Soon, kissing wasn't enough. He needed to see her, to
touch her, to drive her mad with desire as she'd done to
him. He slid his hands over the soft silk of her wrap and
pulled it aside. After working the silk ties at her neck, he
opened her chemise.

He sucked in his breath. His imagination had not
done her justice. Her breasts were perfect—high, round,
and sinfully generous. Reverently he cupped her, testing
their weight in his callused palms. Her skin was the
finest alabaster, tipped with delicate pink. Their eyes
met. He held her stunned gaze as his fingers caressed the
velvety skin, watching as her eyes filled with passion
when he rolled the hard peak between his fingers and
squeezed ever so gently, the nipple puckering and turning a deep, mouthwatering red. And God, he was going
to taste her.

Her back arched, and she pressed her breast more
firmly against his hand.

Her response turned his mind to black. The swift kick
of pure lust hit him hard, and desire gripped him like an
iron claw as he descended into the realm of no return.

Isabel felt as though her body were not her own. He
held complete dominion over her. She was powerless.
Consumed. Wave after wave of unfamiliar sensations
crashed over her. From the first taste of his mouth to the
demanding sweep of his tongue, her body awakened
under his masterful touch.

Her initial shock at the scalding heat of his hand cupping her breast had turned to wonder. She fought to catch her breath as his fingers lightly rubbed her new hardness and his hand kneaded the fullness of her breast.

But when his mouth slid over her sensitive tip, she was lost. A sharp, wondrous pang surged straight to her heart. She was afraid to move, not wanting to shatter the beauty of this spectacular moment of awakening. An awakening that burned a trail of fire from her chest to the juncture at her legs, making her aware that the area between her legs was alive—its innocent slumber shattered by a frantic, quivering pulse. Alive and tingling with anticipation for she knew not what. He sucked, circling the hardened peak with his tongue, nipping her with his teeth until a dam exploded inside her. Heat spread across her skin and rushed between her legs. Never had she imagined how something could feel so perfect. So right.

Her legs shook. She clutched his broad shoulders to brace herself. He sucked her harder, and she arched her back, her hips shifting closer to his heat. His demands grew more frenzied.

The initial shock she'd first felt when he'd held her so intimately and pressed the proof of his desire against her had turned to unconscious need. She wanted him firm and hard between her thighs, wanted to feel the power of his arousal. To know that he wanted her as much as she wanted him. Her hips swayed against him. When he groaned, pleasure spread inside her like molten lava.

He was supporting her now. Her hands splayed across the granite muscle of his arms and shoulders. She wanted to feel him, to take strength from his powerful body. His muscles flexed beneath her fingertips, and with a masculine growl he tightened his hold. God, he was amazing. She didn't know what was happening to her. This strange feeling of powerlessness. All she could think of was him. Hot and hard, surrounding her.

She felt his hand on her leg, under her chemise, sliding up her thigh. Isabel froze. Growing hotter, wetter, as desire flooded between her legs. Her mind raced in a thousand directions. A twinge of uncertainty tugged in the recesses of her consciousness.

He wouldn't.

He would.

With one last tug on her breast, he lifted his head to watch her face as his finger swept over her. A small sound escaped from deep in her throat. Her eyes flew open, stunned by the intimate contact. She felt confused as the desire of her body quickly outpaced the knowledge of her mind. It was too much, too quick. Despite her mission, she was, after all, an innocent. A woman who not so long ago had never been kissed. For a moment, innocence intervened. She grabbed his wrist. Her body squirmed in confused anguish. *Please,* she thought. Please stop, or please more? She didn't know. This was what she'd wanted, tempting fate by wearing her nightclothes, but why did she feel so unsure?

She must have spoken her thoughts aloud, shattering their all too brief moment of connection, for as suddenly as it had begun, it ended. Rory raised his head, his brilliant blue eyes heavy with passion, and roughly released her.

Please more, she realized. But it was too late.

She stumbled backward. Her legs were as weak as a newborn foal's. She brought her hand to her mouth, sure that it must be dark red and bruised from the pressure of his lips. She felt a vicious yearning for something that she didn't understand and wanted nothing more than to be swept up once again in the sweetness of his powerful embrace.

"That should never have happened." His breathing was ragged and his voice rough.

He was not unaffected. She took a cautious step toward him, placing her hands on his chest, offering herself to him once again. "But it did."

"An unfortunate occurrence that will not be repeated." This time, she heard the iron determination in his voice as he deliberately removed her hands.

He doesn't want me. Rejection throbbed like an open wound. "Did I do something wrong? Do I not please you?"

He took a long look at her disheveled nightclothes. Self-conscious, she quickly tied the strings of her sark. And when his steely eyes turned to her again, she felt something else. Shame. Shame for her response and the shocking intimacies she'd allowed him, for how quickly and thoroughly she'd succumbed to his touch, for the eager sounds of pleasure that had escaped her lips. What must he think of her? She'd moaned and clutched at him like a harlot. Even knowing that he intended to send her back.

Her eyes fell to the floor. She was humiliated by the betrayal of her body. She didn't think she could ever look at his face again and not be thinking of what he'd done to her. The way his mouth had pleasured her breast, how his finger had swept her very core.

He studied her face. "You please me well enough. As you would any man. You're a beautiful woman with a body made for pleasure." The whiplash of pain knocked her back. His words flayed her, reopening wounds that had never healed. He saw only her face. She thought what they'd just shared was special. "Every man has his breaking point. If you want to be a maid when you leave here, you'll stop your dangerous game."

Isabel swallowed, tentatively lifting her eyes in question.

He pinned her with a look that seemed to see right through her. Her heart skipped a beat. "I'm not a man to toy with, Isabel. You'd do best to remember it." He paused, flicking one last glance over her nightclothes. "For your sake, I hope you were only looking for a book."

He spun on his heel and left her alone with the crackle of the fire. She shivered, with need or fear she did not know.

Chapter 10

❖

Rory did not return to their room that night, and for once his absence did not bother her. Isabel didn't know if she could face him. Her emotions were still too raw.

She'd wept silently in the darkness for hours, as she had too often as a child, until exhaustion finally overwhelmed the hurt. She must have slept, but for how long she knew not. When she woke, the sting of his rejection had not lessened. She lay in bed, reluctant to get up. For if she did, she must face the mess of her own making.

Isabel had confused lust with something more. A deeper connection. In the shelter of his embrace, she'd felt a sense of security and belonging she'd never experienced before. Like a fool, she'd allowed herself to believe, if only for a heated moment, that someone like Rory MacLeod might care for her. She'd spent a lifetime trying recklessly to prove herself to her family. If the people closest to her did not care about her, why would he?

The MacLeod desired her, nothing more.

She'd felt his desire. Felt it wedged hard against her body. He'd wanted her.

But clearly, he didn't trust her. And not without reason, she admitted. Guilt needled her conscience. Though she had not necessarily set out to seduce him last night, seduction was part of her plan. She'd wanted to press him and had known he might come upon her wandering around scantily dressed. She'd flirted with danger and had been burned. He had every right to question her and to hurl his accusations. She deserved all that he thought of her, and worse.

The true horror of the situation had only begun to dawn on her. She'd known what she would have to do, but never had she imagined how cold and calculating it would feel to use her body to prey upon his attraction. To use their passion to manipulate. A wave of self-revulsion washed over her.

His words came back to her. He'd only taken what was offered. She cringed. Had her desire been so obvious? If she had responded to him inappropriately, it was only because she'd acted instinctively. Innocently. Fresh shame burned her cheeks. She wanted to bury her head under her pillow and hide from the vivid memories.

But he was wrong in his suspicion. Last night had not been an act. Her response had been freely given. Never had she thought herself capable of such feelings. And their intensity terrified her, for it indicated just how susceptible she was to him. And just how easy it would be for her to lose her head.

Isabel felt a pang of regret. If circumstances were different . . . She shook her head. But they weren't. She had a job to do, though she now realized it would not be done without a price. When the year was over, she would not walk away unscathed.

Something else gnawed at her. Isabel knew it was not only suspicion, or her unconscious plea, that had made him push her away. It was his honor. He would not take her virginity knowing he intended to send her back.

Isabel threw back the covers and pulled herself together. It would do no good to hide from her problems. She needed to clear the air between them. And suddenly it had become important that he not think the worst of her. She wanted him to know that she'd set out to find the library last night and nothing more. It was time for a little honesty on her part. She still had a job to do, but she was no longer certain she could use her body to accomplish it.

There had to be another way.

By the time Rory returned to their chamber to wash the remnants of a sleepless night from his face, Isabel had already left to break her fast. He hadn't trusted himself to return to their solar last night, not when his body still raged with lust. Instead, he'd spent an uncomfortable night before the fire in the library with a bottle for company. But not even strong drink could dull the honey taste of her that seemed branded on his lips.

He'd allowed his anger at finding her sneaking around the tower to cloud his judgment, and then seeing her in that flimsy *night rail* had pushed him too far. But he should never have kissed her. Isabel had him so twisted up in knots, he didn't know what in Hades had come over him. Her response had made him half-crazed. The sweet dart of her tongue. The tentative movement of her hips. The arch of her back as he'd kissed her lush breasts. The dampness between her legs that nearly drove him over the edge.

He had a duty to his clan to repudiate the handfast and forge an alliance that would help in his quest to destroy Sleat. His vow of revenge against Sleat did not include despoiling an innocent lass. Or getting her with child. Although he knew there were other pleasures they could share, last night had proved that one taste of her was not enough. He could not trust himself to show restraint. What would he have done had she not uttered her innocent plea, knocking him back to his senses? He couldn't be sure.

Standing at the window in his chambers, watching the morning sun climb over the distant horizon, Rory hardly recognized himself. Never had he felt unsure of his ability to control his baser instincts. Of his ability to do his duty for the clan. Never had he questioned his role as chief.

But when he'd enfolded her in his arms, crushed his lips to hers, run his fingers through the silky thick veil of her unbound hair, and found himself overcome with the heady sweet scent of her, he'd done just that.

At that moment, lost in the fever of their embrace, he had wanted her more than he wanted revenge. And he might have thrown it all away, tossed away his heritage as fast as he could unbelt his plaid, for the moment of sweet pleasure waiting between her slender thighs. The proud heritage that had passed from his father, Tormod, to his elder brother, William. A heritage that had never been meant for Rory, but one he had fully embraced upon the untimely tragic deaths of his brother and his young nephew John.

The welfare of the clan depended on the strength of its chief. In return for their absolute loyalty, the clan expected the chief to protect and to provide. The chief was the leader in war, the holder of land, the judge and jury—with absolute authority over the clan. A chief without honor, a man who was not true to his word, failed his clan.

Rory's heritage as Chief of the MacLeod was of duty to the clan above all else. Duty above personal desire.

The MacLeods had been shamed by the MacDonalds, and he must restore the honor of the clan. He shook his head with disgust. He had nearly forgotten this, until her unconscious plea had broken the spell and brought his responsibilities back to him in full force.

But she played with fire. He'd warned her not to tempt him again. He'd been furious with her, and with himself, for falling into her trap so damn easily, causing him to strike out in a blind rage. And if the look on her face was any indication, his words had found their mark.

His rejection had hurt her. She'd stared at him as if he were a hunter who had just released an arrow straight to her heart. Her anguish had been real.

He pressed his hands against the cold, unbending rock of the stone windowsill. Usually the sea gave him a modicum of peace, but today it deserted him.

As a child, full of the fanciful tales of the bards, he'd imagined that he glimpsed the shimmering scales of mermaid's tails, the *Maighdean na Tuinne,* beckoning him from the sun-splayed iridescent sea. Of course, now he realized he had seen only gray seals—not mermaids. How long ago that seemed; he barely remembered the carefree child he'd been before he'd been consumed by responsibility.

A heron dipped in a perfect arch down and up again, clutching a fish in its mouth. Rory savored the sights of nature displayed before him, as he knew that soon the days would shorten and the majestic colors before him would be hidden behind a curtain of gray mist and heavy rain. Summer's reluctant parting beckoned, its chilling wind breathing down the neck of a still sunny day.

Yet even as he beheld the tranquil roll of the waves climbing and cresting in a perfect, almost musical tempo, he could not rid himself of those luminous violet eyes so filled with pain.

Had she really only been looking for a book? It surprised him to realize how much he wanted to believe her. Perhaps Isabel deserved the benefit of the doubt.

He rubbed his unshaven chin thoughtfully. He'd never considered a learned wife but found that he liked the idea. It bespoke a certain fortitude. He was the first of his clan to have had the benefit of a university education. Reading was a passion and his one escape—other than the passion of a good woman. Rory was quite proud of the depth of his library and made new acquisitions whenever and wherever he traveled. There was more depth to Isabel than he'd expected.

He moved away from the window and strode purposefully toward the basin on the other side of the room. The cold water splashed unmercifully against his skin, shocking the weariness from his face. He dressed quickly and unthinkingly, the complicated wrap of the plaid now routine after years of practice.

Perhaps he'd bring her a book, then. On his last trip to London a few years back, he had purchased the recently published epic poem by Edmund Spenser, *The Faerie Queene*. A romance of King Arthur and his glorious faerie queen, an open allusion to Queen Elizabeth, told in the tradition of Virgil. It was one of his favorites, and somehow he knew instinctively that Isabel would love it. It reminded him of her:

Her angel face,
As the great eye of heaven, shyned bright,
And made a sunshine in the shady place;
Did never mortall eye behold such heavenly grace.

Having completed his morning dress with a quick tie-back of his hair, Rory headed to the library. The sooner he took care of this the better. Last night was best put to rest.

Ironically, in her search for Rory, Isabel discovered the very library that she'd set out for last night, on the second floor of the Fairy Tower. The room was small but charming. Shelves of leather-bound books lined the tapestry-covered walls, large windows provided abundant natural light, and comfortable chairs surrounded a large, highly polished wooden table.

Margaret, looking no bigger than a child, was seated at the large table and obviously engrossed in a matter of some import, for she did not notice Isabel standing at the door. Isabel watched with amusement as Margaret repeatedly tapped the feather of the quill against her temple, immersed in thought. Her nose wrinkled and her lips quirked perplexingly as she studied the rolls.

"I hope I'm not disturbing you," Isabel said.

Margaret lifted her shiny blond head, the flowing curls neatly tied back in a long braid. The black patch hid most of her features, but not the shaky smile of greeting. "Good morning, Isabel. What a wonderful surprise. And in truth I'd welcome anything to get me away from these accounts." She pushed back from the table with obvious delight. "My head hurts from the strain of trying to keep all these numbers straight. I must admit, I find this the most tiresome and difficult part of my duties since Geoffrey, the old seneschal, passed on. We have not been able to find a replacement as yet, and I have been forced to keep the accounts. And with Michaelmas approaching, the accounts for this year must be finished before I can begin the accounts for next year."

Isabel moved around the table to look at the ledgers. She turned to Margaret with an embarrassed but understanding smile. "I hope you do not consider this too forward, but I could help you with the accounts." Somewhat abashed, she elucidated, "At court, I discovered that I have a rather peculiar skill for such work. I see sums clearly in my head without much thought. Queen Anne often had me look over her own household accounts. Truth be told, you'd be doing me a favor. It would bring me pleasure to have something to occupy my time."

Margaret looked at her as though she had suddenly grown wings and a halo. She grinned, and deep dimples like Rory's appeared in her face. "You are not serious. You wish to do this drudgery? You would be the first in this keep for as long as I can remember. We have always struggled to find someone to manage the accounts. James, the bailiff, can help you with the rents from the lands and livestock, and Deidre can help you with the expenditures for food, supplies, and visitors this year. Are you sure you would not mind?"

"Consider it done." Isabel smiled broadly.

Margaret was so excited, she jumped out and gave Isabel a quick hug before seeming to realize what she had done. "Forgive me." She blushed. "I don't know what came over me."

Isabel dismissed her embarrassment with a smile. "Nonsense. I told you I've always wanted a sister." She took Margaret's hands in hers. "And now I have one."

Margaret beamed.

Alex stuck his head in the door. "What are you two

conspiring about?" he asked, his voice laden with exaggerated concern.

Both women jumped apart guiltily, Isabel recovering first. "Good morning, Alex. Margaret and I have just decided on a most opportune arrangement. A way in which I might help her with her duties."

His face immediately lost its jocularity. "Are you feeling well, sister?" he asked, concerned. "Have you been working too hard?"

"Stop fussing over me, Alex. I'm fine. It's only that I've never had a head for numbers." Instinctively, Margaret looked to Isabel for help. Isabel understood her frustration. Big braw men like Alex and Rory's first instinct was to protect. But their oversolicitousness in treating Margaret as if she were a fragile piece of porcelain that could break at the wrong word was surely not only tiresome, but, Isabel suspected, also prevented her from healing.

"We've decided that I'll keep the accounts," Isabel said. At Alex's look of surprise, she explained. "I know, it must seem odd, but surely as Margaret was already performing these duties, it must not be impermissible to have a woman act as seneschal."

"It's not that, Isabel." Alex turned to Margaret with a meaningful stare. "Have you cleared this with our brother, Margaret?"

Margaret's face fell. "I had not thought of that, Alex. Of course, you are right. I need to speak with Rory. Isabel, I'm afraid that I've accepted your generous offer without aforethought. I must obtain Rory's permission first." She paused and continued in a contrite, weak voice, "I'm not sure he'll approve of our arrangement."

Isabel knew why. Not only would Rory be wary of

her poking into his financial concerns, he also wouldn't want her involved in the household management when he intended to send her back.

Responding to his sister's obvious distress, Alex said, "Well, maybe we could keep it a secret amongst ourselves for a little while. Rory has been very busy, and perhaps we might wait a wee while to bring it up. Until then, there is no reason why Isabel could not help you with the ledgers."

Both women smiled at him, but it was Isabel who moved quickly across the room to place a soft, grateful kiss on his cheek. Isabel was moved by Alex's desire to bolster his sister's newfound confidence. But she didn't anticipate the movement of his head, and her lips landed near the edge of his mouth.

Rory heard none of their conversation as he entered the library.

His attention was held by the sight of Isabel's full, sensual lips landing precipitously close to his brother's mouth. He froze. Something akin to a gunshot exploded in his chest.

It took him a minute to clear through the haze of rage. He'd seen enough to know that the kiss was nothing more than a spontaneous show of gratitude for something, but the effect was no less devastating. The strength and intensity of his reaction told him far more than he wanted to know.

He clenched his jaw and cleared his throat.

Isabel jumped back with such a show of guilt on her face that Rory wondered how he could ever have suspected her of snooping last night. She gave away her emotions on her face—even when, like now, they weren't warranted. Though he'd have to insist that she not bestow kisses, harmless or not, on anyone.

"I hope I'm not interrupting anything?" he asked lazily, masking his reaction.

"No, of course not," Isabel said too quickly.

"No," Margaret assured him at the same time. They looked at each other, and Rory watched them exchange some silent form of communication.

They were up to something. But when he looked to Alex, his damn brother just grinned.

He'd deal with Margaret and Alex later, but right now he needed to speak with Isabel. He hadn't come directly to the library. Colin had intercepted him with a missive that he could not ignore.

"If you two aren't too busy, I need to speak with Isabel." Rory thought he detected a bit of reluctance, but they did his bidding. When they'd left, he turned to notice Isabel eyeing him warily.

"It was nothing," she explained.

"I know. But you shouldn't be kissing anyone other than your husband."

She lifted a brow at that and seemed about to offer a reply, but she refrained. Instead she said, "I was looking for you."

"Why?"

She put her hand on his arm. "I wanted you to know that I truly was searching for the library last night. And nothing else."

They stared at each other for a long while, and something passed between them. He believed her. One side of his mouth lifted in a half-smile. "Well, it looks like you've found it."

Isabel returned his smile, and Rory felt a strange skip

in his chest. A skip that turned into a full-fledged leap when she reached out to tuck a strand of his hair behind his ear. He wasn't sure whom she'd shocked more. The strange intimacy of the act took away his breath.

Heat filled her cheeks. "It had come loose."

His throat thickened. Nonplussed, he turned his gaze. "I came to tell you that I must be away."

The blush slid from her face. "What?"

"I'd planned to take the cattle to the fair at Port Righ next week, but it appears I cannot delay." Though only twenty years old, the fair at Port Righ grew each year in popularity, attracting more and more people from beyond the Isle. The Islanders brought their goods, usually sheep, cows, linen, and cheese, twice a year to sell or trade.

"You will be back soon?"

Rory shook his head. "I must leave for Edinburgh directly after the fair." He masked his anger. James's missive had reminded him of the onerous duty of all the Island chiefs to present themselves in Edinburgh once a year before the Privy Council to show their "good behavior." Ever since James had assumed power in his own right nearly fifteen years ago, he'd been tightening his grip on the Highlands and the Isles with a series of new laws—the General Band—aimed straight at the heart of the clan chief's authority.

Rory and the other Highland chiefs chafed uncomfortably under James's unwelcome bridle. For hundreds of years, the Highlands and Isles had existed almost as their own fiefdom: a Gaelic kingdom under the dominion of Clan Donald, the Lords of the Isles. But since the forfeiture of the Lordship over a hundred years ago, the largely ineffective Scottish central government had, by necessity, led to the rise in power of the clan chief. Now the king sought to change that shift in power by weakening the authority of the clan chief. Presenting themselves at court was just another way James sought to remind them all of that shift.

Instead of giving voice to his frustration, he said simply, "The king has requested my immediate presence."

Her eyes lit up, and she clapped her hands together. "You're going to court!"

"Unfortunately, yes."

"But this is grand. I was just telling Margaret—"

Rory told her brusquely, "I'm afraid I must travel alone," and he could read her disappointment.

"I see," she said. But she didn't.

"Alex will be in charge while I am gone."

She didn't say anything. He turned to leave, but something held him back. The memory of last night was still too fresh in his mind, as were the sensations that rocked his body. He'd leave the book for her, but she needed to know something else. He tipped her chin and forced her gaze to his. "Never believe that I didn't want you."

Her gaze softened. Before he could stop himself, he pulled her into his arms and gave her a hard, fast kiss. A real kiss, not like the one she'd given his brother. This kiss was of possession. A reminder to leave her with.

When at last he released her, he left without a backward glance. Not wanting her to see how difficult it was for him to do so.

Chapter 11

❖

"Margaret, I must venture beyond the walls of this castle before the winter storms come or I shall surely turn half-crazed."

Margaret, who was sitting at the large library table across from Isabel, lifted her face from the ledgers and grinned broadly. Little was left of the shy, tentative creature to whom Isabel had first been introduced. Except for the patch. Margaret's nose wrinkled.

"Isabel dearest, you know what Alex said. It is not safe to travel about the forests right now with the Mackenzie's recent attacks." Her eyes twinkled mischievously. "Of course, if *you* ask, mayhap Alex will agree to a short outing. He seems unable to refuse you anything."

Isabel laughed uncomfortably at Margaret's gibe. Although Alex did not show it openly, she sensed something beyond brotherly affection reflected in his dark blue eyes when he looked at her. Isabel suspected that he thought himself infatuated with her. She would have to speak with him soon, but she wanted to give him time to work it out on his own. Shaking off the discomfiting feelings, Isabel stood up from the table and crossed her arms with resolve.

"Very well, I'll ask Alex this time. Anything to breach

these walls. It's been so long since I've sat upon a horse, I may well have forgotten how. Perhaps we might convince Alex to let us have a wee hunt."

Margaret clapped her hands like the excited bairn that her willowy delicate beauty so resembled. She seemed young, even though she was older than Isabel by some five years. "I should love to hunt, but . . ." Her expression fell, her elfin face suddenly devoid of its endearing childish glee. "I don't know how I ever shall learn with—"

Isabel threw her a withering stare that stopped her cold. She pursed her lips tightly and lifted an eyebrow in mock surprise. Margaret got the message and laughed, the happiness returning in an instant.

"Very well, Isabel, I know. You are no better than Bessie, that old taskmaster. Of course I should love to learn to hunt. It will surely not hurt to try."

Isabel gave her a fond hug. She was pleasantly surprised by the pronounced changes in Margaret. Nearly every vestige of shame over her injury had disappeared. The transformation was so dramatic that even the household servants had commented to Isabel on the difference. Perhaps they gave her some credit for the improvement, as their friendliness had increased noticeably over the last few weeks. Isabel had a plan where Margaret was concerned, but it would take some time yet. "Never underestimate yourself, Margaret. You'll be surprised what you can accomplish once you set your mind to a task. And by the by, Bessie thinks herself a lambkin—as do I!"

Both girls looked at each other and burst into hearty peals of laughter.

Margaret recovered first. "I don't know why I'm

laughing, Bessie has been fussing over me just as much as you lately. We'll have to think of something to distract her. I've seen the way Robert watches her of late. Maybe we shall dissuade her hovering with romance."

Shocked, Isabel's eyes grew round. "The porter Robert and Bessie! I hadn't noticed any particular regard from him toward her." Her fingers stroked her chin. "But now that you mention it, he is very solicitous and helpful. And he has seemed to be hanging about more often of late. I did not realize . . . I doubt even Bessie has realized." She dropped her hands to her hips. "You are a sly one, Margaret MacLeod, seeing what others do not."

Margaret grinned. "Maybe the loss of the sight in my right eye has forced my left eye to work stronger. I do seem to observe more now than I did before. In fact, most of my senses seem sharper since the accident."

Margaret looked as though she wanted to say something more. "What is it?" Isabel asked.

"Nothing, I was just thinking how refreshing it is that you do not censor your language by avoiding all reference to sight. You would never believe how awkward it can be. Before you arrived, I never spoke of the accident." She took Isabel's hands. "I don't know what I would have done without you."

Isabel smiled. "You would have found your way soon enough. You have too much spirit to have lain dormant for long." She closed the book she had been working on. "And speaking of dormant, I'm about to burst. I must get out of here."

Margaret's brow wrinkled with mild concern. "You know, Isabel, even if Alex agrees, Rory will be furious to discover we have left the castle even for a hunt. He expressly warned Alex not to let us out of the keep for fear that one of us might be kidnapped by the Mackenzies and held for ransom. Or worse."

Isabel tossed her hair and moved to the window, gazing at the sea. "The Mackenzies wouldn't dare an attack this late in the season, not when their escape could be cut off by storms. We will be well guarded and stay close to the castle. And since Rory is not here, he can hardly expect us to seek his permission, can he?"

Isabel couldn't hide her irritation. It was almost November, and Rory had been gone for nearly two months. Leaving her with only the memory of that confusing, heart-stopping kiss. A memory she'd tried to hold on to, but that with each passing day grew more faint. She'd wanted to believe that after the disaster of the night before, he'd been trying to reach out to her. And that belief had been bolstered when she'd returned to their room and found *The Faerie Queene* propped up in the middle of the bed. Her mercurial heart had leapt, thinking it was surely a truce offering or maybe even his way of apologizing. She'd hoped for something more. But although Rory had sent brief missives to Alex and Margaret, Isabel had heard not a word.

Now, she didn't know what to think.

And more frustrating was that Isabel realized she missed him.

She'd spent much of the two months devouring first *The Faerie Queene* and later other books she'd discovered in Rory's vast library, working on the accounts as she and Margaret did now, and getting to know Margaret and Alex better.

She and Margaret had spent countless hours as they were now, working, chatting, and laughing. Once Isabel had exhausted the stories of her time at court, which the enthralled Margaret couldn't get enough of whether scandalous or mundane, they took turns regaling each other with anecdotes from their childhood.

Isabel had especially enjoyed stories of the youthful Rory, the carefree lad who had roamed the Isle before the role of serious chief was thrust upon him so unexpectedly following the death of his brother. She also realized that even though she had not explicitly told her, Margaret had probably deduced among the silly stories of her childish escapades what her own situation had been like.

With Margaret she'd found the first real friend she'd ever had. And a sister.

Margaret was studying her intently. "What is it?" Isabel covered her cheeks with her hands. "Do I have ink on my face?"

"He doesn't know what to say, Isabel," she said quietly.

Isabel's eyes jumped to her friend's face. Had her thoughts been so transparent? Margaret did see too much. Her back straightened. "I don't know what you mean."

"You hide your disappointment well, but I see how much it hurts you when each day passes and you do not hear from my brother."

"You see all that, do you," Isabel said wryly.

"Rory cares for you more than he wants to admit. There's a softness in his gaze when he looks at you that I've never seen before."

Isabel tried to cover her hope, but Margaret gathered her hands and forced her to meet her gaze. "I don't want to see you get hurt, Isabel."

"He intends to send me back," she said hollowly.

"I know. The feud will only be over when your uncle is destroyed and the MacLeods hold Trotternish. The only way for that to happen is with the Earl of Argyll's sway with the king. An alliance with Argyll's cousin Elizabeth Campbell will provide that sway."

Isabel turned her eyes away. It hurt too much to see Margaret's sympathy. "Does he care for her very much?" Her voice sounded very small.

"He barely knows her. It will be a horrible match. The lass has not the fortitude you do to stand toe-to-toe with my imposing brother. Elizabeth Campbell is a sweet but timid little thing. Rory will terrify her." Margaret sighed. "But it matters not. Rory will always do his duty, even at the expense of his own happiness."

Isabel knew Margaret was right. She'd thought quite a bit about Rory in his absence. More than she wanted to. The night before he left, she'd caught a glimpse of the passionate man behind the revered chief. But his position as chief would always dominate. His clan called him "Rory Mor"—Rory the Great. The title fit. Even if she succeeded in making him fall in love with her, he would send her back if his duty demanded it.

"You're not angry with me, are you?" Margaret asked.

"How could I be angry with you for speaking the truth?" Isabel managed a wry smile. She tried to pretend that her friend's words did not bother her, but Margaret was not fooled.

Isabel moved back to the table and began closing the ledgers that she had been working on, carefully returning the parchments to their place on the bookshelf. She was grateful for the distraction of the accounts. Even with Michaelmas behind her, there was much to be done. Managing the rents from Rory's lands, the livestock, and the household accounts took a large portion of her days. She fought back an unwelcome twinge of guilt. She'd been so busy, she'd not found much time to search for the flag or a secret passage out of the castle.

With Rory gone, it should have proved an opportune time. But she was no closer to achieving her goal, and nearly three months had gone by since she'd arrived. Time enough for her to form strong friendships and attachments that made the thought of betraying the MacLeods unbearable. It wasn't just the lives of her clan that were at stake, but the lives of the MacLeods. If she failed, her clan would be left landless and at the mercy of the heartless Mackenzies. But if she succeeded, it would be at the expense of the MacLeods. If only she could think of a way to help her clan that did not involve harming the MacLeods. Perhaps it was time to write to her father.

She looked back to Margaret. "Well, are you going to break out of this keep with me or must I go alone?"

Margaret's moment of seriousness fled, and she turned to Isabel with a wide grin. "If you are game, I am willing to brave the tempest."

Isabel watched the impish yet confident expression traverse the fey features of her new sister. What only weeks ago would have terrified Margaret now seemed an exciting adventure. At least she'd done one good thing in coming here.

With a last brave hoorah, she turned to wave to Margaret, who was still sitting at the table, smiling. "It's settled, then, I'm off to find Alex. Wish me luck!"

They both knew she would not need any.

Chapter 12

❖

"Isabel, slow your pace this instant or we'll return immediately."

The wind ripped through her hair as she leaned even farther forward on the beautiful Arabian palfrey's long elegant neck, urging her faster while pretending not to hear Alex's angry shout. It had taken her only one week of cajoling to persuade Alex to a hunt.

It was too tempting: a beautiful day, a fast horse, and finally freedom from the oppressive gray walls of that grim dungeon. She felt alive, reborn, and it was wonderful. Laughing, she turned her head to look at Alex, Margaret, and the dour Viking Colin trailing in the dust behind her.

The black scowl on Alex's face gave her pause. She was struck by how alike the two brothers were in temperament—much more than they realized. Both were strong, confident leaders with a healthy dose of fierce Highland pride and, Isabel realized as she gazed at Alex's expression, a tendency toward pigheadedness. But there were differences. Alex was always there to offer kindness and on the surface seemed more lighthearted than his formidable brother, but Isabel caught glimpses of the dark, restless turmoil that Rory lacked lurking under the roguish façade.

Isabel had learned the source of that turmoil a few weeks ago. She'd been teasing Alex about how capably he'd slid into his role as temporary chief, when a strange look came over his face. He'd mentioned that it had not been the first time he'd acted as chief. Not long before she'd arrived at Dunvegan, Rory had been taken prisoner by Argyll at the king's directive for Rory's failure to comply with the terms of the General Band. During his brother's confinement, Alex had led the MacLeods in a battle against the MacDonalds at Binquihillin. The MacLeods were defeated, and two of his cousins were killed. Alex blamed himself and had taken the losses hard. She knew how important it was that nothing go wrong this time. She pushed aside the twinge of guilt. Nothing would happen.

She pulled lightly on the reins to slow her mare, allowing Alex to catch up to her. She didn't want to press her luck this day. But she was an accomplished horsewoman used to racing her brothers, and it irked her to play the proper lady after such a long sojourn. If Alex would only stop acting like an overprotective nursemaid, he would recognize that she was in no danger.

"Very well, Alex. But you are acting as tiresome as that tyrant brother of yours with your disapproving glower. I'm an excellent rider. I could even take a turn on that spectacular Andalusian destrier you are seated upon." At his look of disbelief, she continued, "Please, let's relish this beautiful day."

Alex shook his head. "I don't know why I let you talk me into this, Isabel. Rory will be furious. If you think I look grim, wait until my brother gets wind of our 'wee hunt.' "

"Well, I'll not worry about an eventuality that may

never occur. He's been gone so long, maybe he's decided not to return," she responded primly, feigning indifference.

"Oh, he'll return," Alex warned. "I expect him back at any time. But after this outing today, you and I might wish it differently."

Isabel halted her palfrey and reached for Alex's hand as he stopped his black destrier alongside the mare. He'd been a good friend to her. Giving his hand an appreciative squeeze, Isabel apologized. "I'm sorry, Alex. I know you've some qualms about our outing. You must think me a thankless ninny. But surely Rory did not realize how long he would be gone or he would not have ordered us chained to the castle. He could not expect us to remain inside for so long. And we did take precautions," she said, referring to the group of warriors who followed them. She waved her hand around at the beautiful ash and wych elm trees surrounding them, the amber light of late autumn lending mellow warmth to the chilly day. Her cheeks bloomed pink from exertion and joy. "With these beautiful forests in our very backyard. It would be sheer torture not to enjoy a hunt while we can."

Alex shook his head in mock defeat. "All right, Isabel, you win. If I thought it would do any good, I should ask for quarter. We shall enjoy our hunt and worry about the repercussions later. But at least let us rest for a bit. We'll water the horses, and Margaret can practice her skill with the bow that we borrowed from young squire Tom."

Isabel was about to argue but belatedly noticed Margaret's pleading look and realized that her wild ride had not terrified only Alex. Reluctantly, she yielded with a nod of her head.

"I did it!" The arrow arched beautifully, if not accurately, against the clear azure sky before landing harmlessly in the moss and fallen leaves encircling the tree.

Isabel watched as surprised delight spread over Margaret's face. With her hands on her hips, she intonated with a perfect impression of Bessie's voice, "I told you, poppet, if you put your mind to it, you can do anything."

Margaret rolled her eyes and giggled at Isabel's mimicry. She turned to her brother. "Alex, did you see, did you see? I shot the arrow!"

Alex laughed, his deep blue eyes twinkling with delight. "I must say that I am impressed, sister. I see that next I shall have to hide my squire's sword. You seem to have found quite an accomplished instructor in warfare."

Isabel grinned at the sudden image of Margaret with a claymore. She doubted Margaret would be able to lift it off the floor, let alone threaten anyone with it. But one never knew. Margaret had shown remarkable strength for her size; even the child's bow they had borrowed required considerable strength to maneuver. "Margaret deserves all the credit. I did no more than show her how to hold the bow, the rest was up to her. Well done, Margaret." She briskly stood up from the bright green moss-covered tree trunk she had been sitting on as she watched Margaret's practice, shaking the dirt off the skirt of her luxurious amethyst velvet habit. "I think that is enough practice for now. Perhaps we are ready to hunt for a deer or two to augment the winter reserves?"

Apparently having anticipated her eagerness, Alex was already leading her palfrey forward. She lifted a gently arched eyebrow in surprise, then chuckled at her obvious transparency. She shrugged but offered no defense; she *was* anxious to be off before the day was done. Looking up through the trees at the sun directly above her, she knew there were only a few hours remaining before Alex would insist that they return to the castle. The days were already unbearably short.

Two hours passed in an instant. Isabel couldn't remember the last time she'd enjoyed herself as much. Except for . . . a memory of devouring lips and caressing fingers flashed in her mind before she could brush it away. Rory was gone, remembering wouldn't bring him back any faster.

She felt the full measure of Alex's gaze upon her. "Have you had enough?" he asked. "The hour grows late, and I fear the weather has taken a turn." He looked up to indicate the gathering clouds.

It still amazed her how fast bright sun could change to dark rain on Skye.

Isabel grinned. "No, I haven't. But I know we must return."

With an authoritative gesture of his hand that distinctly reminded her of his brother, Alex ordered the men to start back toward the waiting *birlinn*.

They rode in companionable silence for a while before Isabel spoke. "Thank you, Alex. I cannot tell you what this day has meant to me."

Alex gazed meaningfully at his sister Margaret, who rode ahead with Colin. "It is I who should thank you.

For what you've done for Margaret. My brother's wrath is a small price to pay for the happiness on my sister's face. It's almost as if the last few years have faded into a bad dream. The change in her is remarkable." He nodded his head to indicate Colin. "Even the Viking has seemed to take notice."

They shared a smile. "I thought much the same myself," Isabel said. "Though he seeks to hide his interest, it is as plain as the scowl on his face."

Alex chuckled, and they continued on. As daylight faded, Alex ordered some of the men-at-arms who accompanied them to push ahead and ready the boats. They were safe this close to Dunvegan, but Alex said he didn't want to have the women out on the loch any longer than was necessary in the event of a storm. Isabel didn't realize how far they'd fallen behind until they entered the forest and she could see only Margaret and Colin ahead of her and Alex.

Colin led the small group along the narrow path deeper into the forest. The light wind gently rustled the leaves on the forest floor. The bluebells and primroses of spring were long forgotten, replaced by foxglove, thistles, wood sage, and now russet-colored clumps of heather. The floor of the forest was peppered with large black mushrooms. Relaxed by the lush beauty surrounding her and the gentle sway of her palfrey as the horse expertly picked along the uneven path, lost in daydreams, Isabel startled at the sudden standstill. She glanced up to see Colin raise his hand in warning for silence.

Something was wrong.

An unnatural quiet seemed to have smothered the small chirping sounds of the forest, eerily reminding Isabel of the strange stillness in the air that often preceded a fearsome storm—when the creatures of nature flee, having sensed danger before man. Instinctively, she held her breath, straining to hear something. Now fully alert, she searched the trees but found nothing out of the ordinary. Assuming that perhaps Colin had just spotted a deer in the foliage ahead, she exhaled and slowly relaxed back in the saddle.

Right before the gates of hell flew open.

Alex's arm unexpectedly whipped out to push her face forward against her horse only moments before the quiet hiss of an arrow whizzed above her. Precisely in the space previously occupied by her head.

"Damn." She heard Alex swear, her head still planted firmly on the mane of the mare. The gentle teasing voice was gone, replaced by the hard, decisive voice of authority. "Colin, take Margaret and Isabel and make for the landing. Bring help. I'll stay behind and try to hold them back." He swatted Isabel's mare on the rump. "Go. Quick. Ride as fast as you can."

At the harsh physical command, her mare leapt forward frantically. Fighting to stay seated, Isabel grabbed the reins of the terrified horse while trying desperately to settle it down. She eased back the reins, gradually able to slow the frenzied pace. Just ahead of her, Colin yanked Margaret's horse forward and disappeared into the dense forest. *Wait,* she scolded herself as a flash of clearheadedness broke through the chaos. This was her fault. She couldn't leave Alex alone. Heedless of the danger, she turned the horse around and started back toward Alex.

They had surrounded him, but Alex was holding his own, fighting the men back with the broad swing of his sword. He'd almost broken free when he caught sight of her, and his eyes narrowed ominously. "What the hell do you think you are doing—" His voice broke off as the blow of a claymore on his back stunned him, but it was the following blow to the head that knocked him from his saddle. He fell unconscious to the ground.

"*Nooooo!* Alex. Oh God, please." Her hands flew to her face in horror as she opened her mouth to scream, and for a moment the shock was so great that no sound came forth. She was nearly overcome with fear for Alex, but after a brief feeling of paralysis, something akin to calmness took over her movements. Strangely disembodied from the horror and fear surrounding her, Isabel found herself filled with a fierce determination, like a warrior in the midst of battle—she knew what she had to do. She had to compose herself and help him.

She jumped from the saddle, hastening to where Alex lay twisted and dreadfully still in a pile of dirt and leaves. She was so focused on reaching Alex, she didn't notice that she was surrounded by a handful of terrifying-looking clansmen until it was too late. She was just about to reach out for Alex when she was jerked harshly into the hold of a dirty, crude-looking warrior. When she met his gaze, she flinched. He had the eyes of a dead herring.

"What have we here? Looks like a wee bit of bonny entertainment for the afternoon." His ugly, lecherous gaze traveled down her face. "Seems we have found ourselves a fine beauty. I'll wager whoever you belong to will be anxious to get you back and willing to pay for it. Although I hope it's not that one, lass," he said, motioning to where Alex lay. "He's not likely to claim you anytime soon . . . if ever." His sour breath hissed in her ear.

Isabel recoiled visibly from the menace curdling his voice.

Inwardly, she cursed her foolishness in leaving her bow and arrows on the palfrey. Her instincts had failed her, but the attack had happened so quickly. "Unhand me. Can't you see this man is hurt? He needs me. Let me go." She tried to wrench her body away from his hold, but he was too strong and was gripping her too tightly.

The warrior laughed unpleasantly. "Don't you worry about him. He won't need you where he is going." Cruelly, he kicked Alex's unmoving body.

Isabel was relieved to hear the pained groan. Alex had been lying so still, she'd been afraid he was already dead. The blow had probably just knocked him out, but they would not let him live. She had to do something. If she hadn't begged Alex to leave Dunvegan, none of this would have happened. Anguished guilt mingled with helplessness. "Who are you? What do you want with me?"

"I've already told you what we want from you, a wee bit of sport." He smiled, revealing the stumps of his crooked brown teeth. "As for the other, who do *you* think we are? Who would be bold enough to raid MacLeod lands in the middle of the day?" The arrogance spewing from the swarthy clansman was great.

"Mackenzies," Isabel hissed.

"Ah, so our reputation precedes us. And who might you be, my beauty?" He considered her appearance, noting the quality of her garments. "Obviously a lady." He reached out to stroke her breast with his rough, dirty fingers. "A lady with the body of a whore."

Instinctively, Isabel swatted his hand away. He retaliated swiftly, cuffing her brutally on the chin. Her head whipped backward with the power of the blow, knocking her hair loose from its ribbons. If possible, the lewd stares of the men became even more filled with lust.

Although dazed from the blow, she swore, "If you touch me again, I'll kill you."

A deadly silence followed her pronouncement, as the rest of the men waited for the reaction of their leader. His bawdy laughter rang out at her threat. "Ah, we have found ourselves a wee firebrand. You'll be a pleasure to tame, my sweet, but heed this warning. Do not anger me, or I may begin your lessons right here. I ask you again, what is your name and who will claim you? The truth, gel, or you will know my wrath."

Isabel debated her answer, quickly weighing whether the truth would help or hinder her in this situation. Apparently, she was taking more time than he had allotted, because she found herself yanked back by her hair, pulled against his sweaty body as his hand ripped open the bodice of her riding habit. His grimy fingers reached under her sark and clawed roughly at her breast, jagged nails scratching the delicate skin. Isabel felt sickened by his touch; nausea spread up her throat, and she knew she was near to retching.

"Enough. Your name, or do you require more persuasion?"

"Isabel."

"Well, Isabel, who will claim you?"

"Rory MacLeod. I am wife to the MacLeod." She lifted her chin as if to challenge him. Her voice sounded small but held a touch of defiance.

Astonished by her claim, the man abruptly released her. He was obviously displeased and appeared uncertain as to whether she should be believed. Isabel could see the thoughts running through his mind. Rory MacLeod was a powerful adversary. Relieving him of a few head of cattle was one thing, relieving him of his wife . . . Well, he would be a hunted man. Taking his wife would make him an enemy for a lifetime—likely a short lifetime.

The Mackenzie clansman crossed his arms and stared at her for a moment before coming to his decision. "You lie. The wife of the MacLeod would never be left to roam the forests with such a paltry escort. He would be a foolish man to leave such a tempting treat behind while he dallies with Argyll. More likely is that you are his leman." He reached out and twisted a clump of her unbound hair painfully in his fist. His eyes filled with lust and excitement as he said with a chilling leer, "I did warn you to speak the truth."

Isabel tried to talk, tried to explain that she was speaking true, but his fetid mouth pressed against hers, crushing her lips violently as she was thrown roughly to the ground. His huge body landed in a harsh thud on top of hers. The weight of his limbs crushed her, pushing her deep into the unforgiving ground. His beard tore at her face as he kissed her.

For a moment she wanted to die, before the fight for life took over.

She fought like a tiger, scratching and clawing at his face, but he clasped her hands above her head and tossed up her skirt, tearing quickly through the layers of undergarments to reach bare skin. Panic rose in her throat and threatened to spill. She felt his fingers grabbing at the soft skin of her bottom, lifting her hips toward his. Through a tunnel of disbelief, she heard his lusty groans mixed with the laughter of his men as he raised his plaid and pushed his hard member against her closed legs, trying to force them open. She felt his coarse hair against her legs as one hand reached down to try to separate her clamped legs.

Lewd voices urged him on.

When she realized what he was about to do, horror unlike any she'd ever experienced chilled her soul. For a paralyzing moment, she couldn't move. She was suffocating, spiraling downward in a helpless free fall toward hell.

She heard Alex curse and then moan as her screams roused him. But his efforts to help her were thwarted by the fists of the Mackenzies.

Her body gave one last surge—a reflexive fight for survival. She kicked and wiggled against the unyielding weight of his body. But her movements seemed only to excite him. She bit the snakelike tongue that crawled down her throat, tasting blood.

He yelped in pain. "Damn bitch!"

Her head flipped to the side with the first blow. His fist slammed into her face again. And again. The pain was unbearable.

She was powerless.

Oh God, no, she prayed. *Please, no.*

"No!" She heard her muffled scream from the distance of her descent into hell. A hell that smelled like a sweaty swine.

Time stood still as she waited for the release of death.

But nothing happened.

Suddenly, amid the terror, she recognized the distant whiz of an arrow in flight, and the ruffian collapsed hard on her chest, nearly smothering her with the dead weight of his body. His herring eyes fixed in eternity with a startled stare. Confused and in terrible pain from the blows to her face, she barely registered the sound of steel clashing against steel. She looked away from the eyes of the dead man. A lightning flash of steel formed before her eyes like a silver cross. Was she in heaven, then? No, the crosses were swords. A battle, she realized slowly. Perhaps it was hell. The sound of the slash of a blade as it slid through a man mingled with the gurgling cries of death.

Moments later, the Mackenzie's body was pulled from her. Her first thought was that she could breathe. She was alive. Cool air accosted her bare legs.

Still stunned by what had nearly happened and that it was apparently over, Isabel was unable to focus on her rescuer. For a moment she was confused, until strong arms pulled her into a fierce embrace.

Rory.

His mouth was against her head, buried in her hair. She could feel the furious hammering of his heart against her cheek. She could smell the distinctive scent of heather and sun. Her eyes locked with his, holding his gaze. He looked at her as if he wanted to memorize her features. And she recognized an emotion she had never thought to see on his face. He looked scared. For her.

Rory knew a long moment of gut-checking fear. Fear that he'd arrived too late. The race of his heart had not yet begun to slow. He stroked the side of her ravaged face with his thumb. "Thank God. When I realized who it was beneath that devil's spawn . . ." He tipped her chin and looked deep into her eyes. "Isabel, are you all right?"

His eyes practically gorged on the face that had

haunted his dreams over the last two months, taking in the cuts and bruises and trying to convince himself that she would not die. Blood streaked her face. Dark shadows surrounded her sunken eyes. An unhealthy gray pallor marred the creamy ivory perfection of her soft skin. There was an angry bruise along her jaw, flecked with spots of black and red, and the area had already swelled. Her glorious hair was tangled and matted, and her riding habit was in shreds. Rory thought she had never looked more beautiful. She was safe.

Tumultuous violet eyes flickered across his face. Disbelief clouded her vision. She reached up to touch the side of his unshaven cheek as if willing him to be real.

"Rory, is it really you? But how?" She clutched at him as if terrified that he might disappear.

"Later. I'll explain everything later. First we must get you back to the castle."

She seemed to calm as he carried her to his horse, but in the next instant, the horror returned. "Oh God, Rory. Alex. We must help Alex." She let go of her death grip on his arms and looked about, searching frantically for Alex.

Rory buried her face in his shoulder, trying to prevent her from seeing the bloody carnage that surrounded them. The proof of his rage. Dead Mackenzies littered the forest floor, their bodies twisted in unnatural positions, riddled with arrows and sword gashes. Blood had turned the orange brown autumn leaves scattering the forest floor a deep burnished red.

"It's all right, Isabel, Alex will be fine." He'd suffered a severe knock on the head and some other cuts and bruises from the beating, but he would recover. "Douglas is already carrying him back to the landing." The very landing where Rory had been surprised to come across a group of his warriors waiting for the return of a small hunting party.

Blood surged through his body at the memory of Colin and Margaret bursting through the trees, telling him of the attack. Praying he would arrive in time, the fury and helplessness he'd felt when he'd seen his brother lying lifeless on the forest floor and Isabel wedged under the vile Mackenzie. Rory's mind had gone black. The primal thirst for blood penetrated every fiber of his being. Half-crazed, he'd attacked like the Berserker warriors from whom he was descended.

"Rory, I'm sorry. It's all my fault, please . . . I never meant . . ." She wept softly on his shoulder, small tremors wracking her body.

"Shhhh, shush. We'll not speak of it now. Later, Isabel," Rory crooned, stroking her silky hair. His first instinct was to put his mouth on hers and kiss away her memories. Selfishly, he wanted to stamp the proof of his possession all over her, wiping away the taint of another. But after what she'd just been through, he knew it was too soon. She was too fragile.

But once again, Isabel surprised him.

Her hands clasped his shoulders. She lifted her mouth to his. "Please." She shivered. "That man." Rory could see the horror in her eyes. "Please, Rory, kiss me?"

His heart lurched. 'Twas an offer he was only too willing to accept. "Aye, lass, with pleasure."

He knew what she needed. Gently, he covered her lips with his.

Isabel couldn't believe her boldness. But she needed to know that she was alive and safe. To erase the horror with pleasure.

The first brush of his lips was like a feather. The second was achingly tender. Never had she imagined this fierce warrior could be capable of such heart-stopping gentleness. His lips were so soft and yet so strong. And healing. The taste of him was every bit as warm as she remembered. He cradled her in his arms and kissed her with a raw emotion that took her breath away.

And when it was done, Isabel did not trust herself to speak. For fear that the emotion squeezing her chest would break free.

He lifted her onto his horse. Scant seconds later, Isabel felt his strong arms encircling her waist and his hard body behind her. He wrapped his plaid around her torn bodice as lovingly as if she were a newborn bairn. Isabel was too overcome with emotion to feel any modesty for her disheveled appearance. *Dear God, she had nearly been raped.* If Rory had not arrived when he had . . .

His destrier pounded through the forest, heedless of the added weight of its extra rider. The wind ripped through her hair as it had only hours before—a lifetime ago. Isabel felt herself relax against his habergeon-clad chest, felt her body slipping deeper into the lulling sway of the horse and the warm, protective enclosure of her handfast husband's strength.

Almost asleep and somewhat disoriented, she inexplicably remembered what she wanted to tell him when she saw him next. "Thank you for the book, it was wonderful." Her voice sounded soft and drowsy.

She felt the warmth of his breath by her ear. "You're welcome."

Safe at last, she collapsed into an exhausted sleep.

Chapter 13

❖

Five days later, he found her at Alex's bedside. The same spot she'd been stationed at day and night since he'd rescued her from rape at the hands of Murdock Mackenzie. Despite the pandemonium surrounding the attack, Rory had recognized the Mackenzie's youngest son immediately—and had not hesitated to put an end to his foul life. The man was the worst sort, the type who took immense pleasure in the pain of another; but even so, Rory knew there would be a reckoning with the Mackenzie chief over the life of his son. But it did not matter. Standing in the doorway watching Isabel as she bent over the unmoving figure of his brother, wiping his brow repeatedly with a damp, cool cloth, Rory knew he would happily kill the fiend again and again for what he had nearly done.

The knock on Alex's head had been more severe than they'd initially realized. He had a knot on his head the size of an egg and had remained unconscious for almost two days. Even now, when he woke, it was not for long and was usually accompanied by dizziness and strong bouts of nausea.

Isabel turned, somehow sensing his presence, although he'd made no sound as he entered. A weak smile of greeting lit her weary face.

"The swelling has gone down considerably." Relief was evident within the exhaustion clouding her voice. Her finely defined brows drew tight over her nose. "But he still does not wake for long."

Rory approached the bed and gazed fondly at his peacefully sleeping brother. "He looks much better. 'Tis best to let him sleep. When he wakes he'll have one roaring headache. Besides," he said with a grin, "Alex has much too hard a head to let a knock on the pate get him down for long."

Her smile grew stronger. "Aye, he's not the only hardheaded, stubborn man in this keep." At his exaggerated look of affront, she laughed, her eyes sparkling, looking more like herself for a moment.

Rory moved closer to her, his hand reaching down to rest tentatively on her shoulder. Ever since that day in the forest, he could not resist any excuse to touch her. He could feel the tension from her tireless vigil under his fingertips. Despite her obvious weariness, desire hit him hard. He longed to knead the tightness from her body, to run his fingers in a gentle caress over her soft skin, to erase the fatigue of the last few days with his hands—and then his mouth.

But first they needed to talk.

Anticipating his thoughts, she clutched Alex's hand protectively like a mother protecting her child, a defiant gleam in her haggard eyes, her stance evidence of her obstinate refusal to relinquish her position as head nurse.

Rory knew she blamed herself and had taken Alex's injury extremely hard. But he refused to allow her to wallow in her guilt any longer. "Isabel, we must talk. Margaret will take over nursing Alex for a bit. His body needs rest to recover. You can do nothing for him right now. Come."

"But I can't leave him yet. I must be sure that I'm here if he wakes and needs anything. Please, just a wee bit longer."

"Isabel, you can't avoid this. We will talk. Tonight, no later. I've already sent for Margaret. She is most anxious to help nurse Alex. She's taken much of the blame for what happened upon herself and longs to atone for her part. We'll talk, but first you will bathe, rest, and have something to eat or you'll make yourself ill. Go to our chamber. Now." His clipped voice left little room for argument.

Her beautiful copper gold hair fell limp around her face, covering her features from his view as she made a great show of pondering his request. A request that they both knew was a command. She fumbled distractedly with Alex's blankets, but it did not take long for a sigh of resignation to escape the contrary set of her lips.

She flipped her hair behind her shoulders, lifted her chin resolutely, and replied, "As you wish, *Chief*. We will speak this evening. I will return to our chambers now to do as you have *ordered*." Emphasizing the last word, she rose from her post beside Alex, placed the cool cloth on his brow once more, turned her back to him, and glided regally out of the room.

Rory's mouth quirked. Her reprimand amused him. But he was chief, and used to giving orders. Truth be told, he did not have much experience with gentle requests to ladies. And he had waited too long to find out what had occurred in the forests about Dunvegan.

The shock of the attack had faded, to be replaced by thinly constrained anger. But he would hear her out.

One thing was obvious: His orders not to leave the castle had been blatantly ignored.

He sat in the small wooden chair positioned next to the bed, its soft velvet cushion still warm, and gazed thoughtfully at his sleeping brother. At the haggard face that was so familiar. A small frown betrayed his thoughts. He had been more shaken by Alex's injuries than he had let on. In addition to the knock on the head, he'd suffered a severe beating at the hands of the Mackenzies. That Isabel blamed herself for Alex's injury was evident. He ran his fingers abstractedly through his hair, pushing it back from his face and shaking his head as if he were trying to sort out the mixed thoughts in his mind. Rory did not know whom to blame.

The corners of his lips lifted with a bemused smile. Apparently, many were fighting for that particular honor. In addition to Isabel and Margaret, Colin had also sought to take the blame for Alex's injury and Isabel's near rape. And knowing his brother, when he woke long enough for coherent thought, Alex would surely take full responsibility for the happenings on that day as well. That horrible day. He couldn't think about it without his stomach turning at the involuntary picture that came to mind of Isabel fighting wildly beneath Mackenzie with her skirts around her neck, her face beaten, and her violet eyes murky with terror. Yet he knew it could have been worse, much worse. If he and his men had not arrived when they had, if Margaret and Colin had not escaped to warn them . . .

They were lucky.

Rory wet a cloth with cool water from the basin, squeezed it out, and pressed it lightly to Alex's forehead as he had observed Isabel do before she involuntarily relinquished her post.

Colin had provided him with a brief account of what they were doing in the forest but failed to explain adequately how the group had come to be outside the walls of the castle in direct contravention of Rory's express orders—not to mention how the group had become separated from their escort. Alex had much to account for when he woke. But for now, Rory wanted to hear an explanation from Isabel's own lips of how she could possibly justify being so foolish.

Despite his anger, he could not forget the sense of connection he'd felt for her that day amid the carnage. She'd reached for him without thought. It was almost as if there were a fine silken thread holding them together— so fine that it could be easily snapped if pulled too taut or woven with more threads into something much stronger. He shook his head at his romantic musings.

The attack had forced Rory to confront his growing feelings for Isabel—feelings he'd hoped to escape on his journey. He hadn't meant to be gone for so many weeks, but his business in Edinburgh had taken longer than expected. In addition to presenting himself to the king to account for his good behavior in compliance with the General Band, he had resumed negotiations with the Earl of Argyll. After assuring himself that Rory intended to go ahead with the alliance with his cousin Elizabeth Campbell, Argyll had promised to urge the king to decide on the disposition of Trotternish. James's continued refusal to take sides on the matter—even after what Sleat did to Margaret—infuriated Rory to no end.

But as the direction of Rory's duty became more clear, he realized just how much he'd come to care for the lass he still could not trust. The primal intensity of his reaction to her near rape only clarified the depth of those feelings.

He bowed his head in his hands, but he couldn't escape the truth. Nothing had changed. He still had his duty to his clan to marry the Campbell lass. Isabel was not for him. But for the first time, he wondered whether there might be another way—to both destroy Sleat and reclaim Trotternish—that didn't involve Elizabeth Campbell.

Rory continued to wonder throughout the long evening, an evening made even longer by the punishing pleasure of Isabel's presence at his side.

Even now, a sultry smell of lavender filled his nose. He knew that if he leaned down close to her loose damp hair and inhaled, the smell would be even stronger. And stronger still if he leaned down farther and burrowed his face in the graceful, elegant curves of her long, ivory neck. And if he kept lowering his face down her body, smelling all the areas of warmth . . . He groaned and shifted in his seat, adjusting the sudden discomfort he found hardening in his lap. A perpetual discomfort, it seemed, since the arrival of his bride.

"Is something wrong, Rory? You sound as if you are in pain." Isabel placed her fingers on his arm and looked up at him, her eyes wide with sudden concern.

"No," he said a shade too roughly. He took her warm fingers, the touch that was only increasing his pain, and gently unfurled them from his arm. "I knocked my knee on the table, that is all."

He groaned again. *Bloody hell, wrong thing to say.* Immediately her attention flew to his supposedly injured leg. He grabbed her wrist as her hand landed perilously close to the real "injury," preventing her fingers from further investigation. "It's fine. Only a small bump, do not concern yourself."

"Are you sure? If you let me lift your plaid a bit, I can see whether there is any swelling. You might need some ointment, and I could rub it in for you."

He nearly choked. *Curse the woman!* Her innocent innuendo was driving him mad with lust. His hand tightened on her wrist, and he moved her hand back into her own lap. His voice sounded forced and ragged even to his own ears. "It's nothing." He needed to change the subject. She was getting that determined set to her face that he was beginning to recognize too well. Her stubborn expression made him want to laugh. Her tenacity reminded him of the mothers of his acquaintance with marriageable daughters. "How about you, are you feeling better after a respite from my brother's side?"

His eyes trailed slowly down her face. The bath and rest he had forced on her appeared to have provided some measure of rejuvenation. Overall, she looked much better. Her hair shone fiery copper, her mouth was soft and relaxed, the tiny worry lines etched around her eyes had disappeared, and the dark shadows lurking beneath her skin were nearly invisible—unless one looked closely, as he did. He was not surprised to see subtle signs of torment hidden beneath the otherwise composed façade. She had been through a lot these past few days; certainly strain and anxiety were to be expected. He even felt a bit of pride when he looked at her calm demeanor. Most women would still be bedridden after what she had been through. He admired her fortitude.

Nonetheless, any sign of distress, no matter how minor, gnawed at him.

The distraction provided by his question worked. Her embarrassing concern for his leg turned to anger at the reminder of his brusquely imposed exile from Alex's side. Her gaze sharpened for a moment. She turned an angry frown toward him before apparently reconsidering, and her mouth curled into an adorably shy grin. She tilted her head so that she looked up at him from under her long lashes. "All right, I do feel better. That tub of warm water felt delightful. I fell asleep before I even realized I was lying down. I must have been more exhausted than I realized," she admitted grudgingly, "and hungry. If the cleaned-off tray of food was any indication."

He laughed, and before he realized what he was doing, he covered her hand with his. The stubborn lass did not like to admit she was wrong. "It may have seemed I acted harshly, but it was for your own good. You looked exhausted; I feared you could faint from weariness at any moment. I'd watched you working tirelessly at Alex's side for five days and nights. You needed rest."

"I think you just like giving orders."

Rory chuckled. "I'll not deny it. But it comes with the position."

Isabel's mouth quirked. "I think it came with birth."

Isabel could watch Rory forever. The twinkle in his eyes and the deep dimples in his cheeks created by his easy grin were alluring. If he was impossibly handsome when stern, when relaxed and smiling he was absolutely irresistible. She looked at his large, battle-scarred hand covering hers, and her heart rose in her throat. She felt the full force of his reputed charm directed at her. And the feeling of helplessness that the attraction induced in her was terrifying.

"If you're finished, we'll retire to my solar, where we can converse in private."

Isabel swallowed and allowed herself to be escorted from the dais. She knew the time had come. She would bear her punishment for disobeying his instructions. His gentle behavior in the forest and the peaceful lull that had existed the past few days were at an end. It was time to pay the piper for her impulsiveness.

Isabel accepted the blame, but her frustration at being confined to the castle for so long was not without justification. He had left her alone, without communication, for months.

She accepted Rory's hand, and he led her out of the hall. She wasn't unaware of the speculative glances thrown their way; the clan had noticed the blossoming intimacy between their chief and his bride.

They made their way outside, along the passageway connecting the two towers. She shivered in the cold night air. Instinctively, he pulled her closer to his side. It seemed so natural, as though their bodies slipped into perfect alignment. But even with his warmth to shield her, it was freezing.

"I've often thought to connect the two towers with an indoor corridor. I hope to hire a mason to look at the project within the next few years."

Isabel's teeth rattled. "Sounds like a wonderful idea. Perhaps you might consider finding someone sooner?"

Rory chuckled. "I'll consider it."

They entered the inviting warmth of the Fairy Tower, and she was glad when he led her up the spiral staircase to the library and not their chamber. Neutral ground. Whenever she stepped into the tower, Isabel experienced a sharp twinge of guilt. While Rory was gone to the fair at Port Righ and on to Edinburgh, she'd hoped to have the opportunity to search this tower as she had the old keep, but an appropriate time never seemed to present itself.

Or perhaps, she admitted, she had not wanted to find the time.

Isabel moved across the room and headed directly for the large, inviting window looking out over the loch.

"It's lovely." She realized she'd spoken her thoughts aloud.

"It is." But Isabel realized he was not looking at the view. A shiver of awareness slid down her spine, as it always did when he stood so near. He cleared his throat. "On a clear day, you can see north to the Isles of Harris and North Uist. To the west is a beautiful view of the Tables."

"The Tables?"

"MacLeod's Tables. Two flat-topped hills so named after a trick played by my grandfather, who promised an arrogant English nobleman that there was not a more beautiful table or spectacular candelabrum than the one on Skye. When the nobleman arrived to prove him wrong, my grandfather held a lavish feast on those hills, and the sky was illuminated with hundreds of sparkling stars, forcing the Englishman to agree with him."

Isabel clapped her hands and laughed. "Your grandfather sounds like a wily old fox."

Rory chuckled. "He was at that." He motioned toward the window and redirected her attention to the blackness below them. "But the view of the sea is my favorite."

Isabel gazed straight down the side of the bluff below them to the swirling blackness of the sea, the sliver of the moon providing little light to pierce the darkness of the misty night. She nodded in agreement. "I think that I must always live by the water. Although the gardens at court were beautiful, I missed Loch Carron. It was strange not looking out my window and finding water." She sighed dreamily. "There is nothing as magically soothing as the rhythmic crashing of waves against the rocks."

Rory looked surprised by her heartfelt words. "I feel much the same. Living on an isle, I feel a part of the sea—it flows through my blood. Whenever I am away from Skye, it calls to me."

Isabel realized that Rory had just shown her a little corner of his heart. He felt things more deeply than he wanted others to see. It warmed her, even as she wanted to laugh at the uncomfortable surprised expression on his face.

Clearly disconcerted, he pulled out a chair from under the table and changed the subject. "Please sit. I'd like to ask you a few questions about what went on in the forest the day Alex was injured and you were nearly—"

The blood slid from her face.

"When you were set upon by the Mackenzies," he amended quickly.

She accepted the proffered chair and folded her hands demurely in her lap to stop their shaking. He sounded calm, but she was nervous all the same. She took a deep breath. "What is it that you would like to know? I'm sure Colin and Margaret have told you that I asked Alex to take us hunting."

"Yes, Colin explained what you were doing in the forest, but not why you put yourself and the others in such danger by leaving the castle in the first place."

She briefly recounted the events of that day. When she had finished and he did not say anything but simply stared at her, she continued nervously, "Alex took proper precautions. I only thought to provide a brief respite from the monotony of weeks spent inside the castle walls. You see, we'd been working so hard getting the accounts in order for Michaelmas." She knew her explanation sounded ridiculous—which it was. She was ashamed of her part in instigating their adventure.

"Were you unaware, then, of my orders that you and Margaret remain at Dunvegan while I was gone? Did Alex not explain this to you? Did he not warn you about the danger presented by the Mackenzies?"

"Of course Alex explained your wishes. It's just that, well, I assumed you did not realize you would be gone so long . . . and, uh, that you would not mind under the circumstances. It was such a beautiful day, we were having such fun—and we did not stray too far from the castle. I never dreamed the Mackenzies would be so bold and venture so close. It seemed harmless enough." She was a bairn again, standing before her father, twisting her hands in frustration while trying to explain yet another questionable decision that she could not rationalize even to herself.

"What I don't understand is why Alex agreed to this. Why would he disobey my express orders?"

She bit her lip. Rory was watching her changing expressions closely and mistook the guilt on her face for an answer.

His eyes narrowed. "What did you do?"

"No, you misunderstand. It's difficult to explain. It's just that, well, I feel guilty. You see . . ." The twisting of her hands intensified. "Alex may have some tender feelings toward me, and, well, I did beg him, and I know it wasn't right." Her cheeks flamed with embarrassment and shame.

Rory threaded his fingers through his hair and glared at her. "No, it reeks of manipulation. If what you say about Alex's sentiments are correct, you should not have encouraged him."

"I didn't encourage him. I did not set out to purposefully use his feelings in that way. You make it sound so calculated. It's just that when you mentioned it now, I felt guilty—that in retrospect I probably should not have gone to Alex, knowing how he feels."

"No, you shouldn't have. You will discover that not all men will do your bidding, Isabel. Not all men will be led about by a pretty smile or a well-placed touch. Indeed, I am surprised my brother fell for such an obvious ploy. But I will not." His voice was as rigid as steel. "You will find that I am not as easy to persuade."

"What do you mean?"

"Do not try to deceive me. Ever."

A chill slid down her spine. "Are you finished?"

"No." The anger Isabel dreaded came full force. His eyes blazed. "Don't you realize what would have happened had I not arrived when I did? They would have killed Alex, and you would have wished for it. To go hunting? You could have waited for my return."

"Your return?" Her hurt at his abandonment finally

burst forth. "You stayed so long, I questioned whether you intended to return at all." Her throat tightened. "You never thought to write me. Not one word."

Her eyes were glued to her feet. She dared not meet his gaze for fear that he would see how perilously close to tears she was.

"What do you want from me?" he asked roughly. "I've told you it cannot be."

Suddenly, she found herself in his arms, where he clearly intended to vent his frustration on her person. Her head tipped back as she searched his face for some sign of understanding. But there was no evidence of compassion in the harsh, tightly drawn lines of his face: his eyes narrow slits, his mouth clenched firmly in a straight line, his arms rigid and unforgiving.

He looked as though he couldn't decide whether he wanted to shake her or kiss her. They stood staring at each other for some time, balancing on the precarious precipice of indecision. Isabel held her breath, aware that he was fighting a fierce internal battle. Not content to wait, she made the decision for him.

Circling her arms around his neck, she lifted up on her toes and leaned her mouth closer to his. Her curves molded perfectly to his thick, hard muscle.

"I want this," she said, and kissed him.

He swore softly and drew her closer to him, not simply returning her kiss, but taking control. His kiss was full of hunger bordering on starvation.

Bold and frenzied.

His mouth moved over hers possessively, searching for relief. There was an urgency to his movements, as if the sands of time were an enemy that could only thwart his intentions. The furious quickening of her heart—

beating now with excitement and not fear—matched his.

Anticipation was a potent aphrodisiac. The touch of his lips on hers instantly rekindled the passion invoked by their last heated kiss. Isabel felt a powerful bolt of desire shoot through her body. She knew that she wanted him, and her wanting had nothing to do with her uncle's plan. Her need was primitive. She wanted him as a woman wants a man.

Rory overwhelmed her senses, rendering her limp with desire, unable to form a coherent thought other than hunger for the man holding her. The weighty feel of his demanding mouth, the soft tickle of his golden chestnut hair slipping forward against her cheek, the friction of his day-old beard against her tender skin, the intoxicating scent of salt and sea that seemed to permeate his skin, and the taste of wine lingering on his lips dissolved all thoughts of her plan.

Slowly, he relaxed his hold. His rough fingers traced a surprisingly feathery, light path up her arm, across her shoulder, and up the side of her neck to finally cup her chin. Her skin tingled where he left his touch as he gently tilted her chin upward, forcing her to deepen the embrace.

She knew he would not be content with innocent kisses. His passion had broken free of its tight rein and the repressed desire she felt exploding within him would not be quenched by a gentle wooing. She felt the power of his desire as his fingers and mouth worked in tandem to open her lips to the thrusting invasion of his tongue, plundering and pillaging with each swirling stroke. Unable to contain her own passion, she responded instinctively, her tongue joining his, meeting and matching his desire with her innocent but knowing rejoinder.

Her back was pressed hard against the wall next to the window as the full length of his body crushed against hers. The force of his powerful build, so muscular and strong, touched a primitive longing for protection that she would have scoffed at only months before. Before she had learned of her own vulnerability at the hands of Murdock Mackenzie. With Rory, she felt completely feminine. Vulnerable, but safe. And most of all, wanted. He ravished as if he could not have enough of her.

His hands were everywhere, exploring the sleek contours of her body. Like a conqueror—with each touch, he branded her as his. His movements were rougher, harder, and more frenzied than before. As if he feared the intervention of rational thought. He slipped his fingers beneath the bodice of her gown to caress her breast, and her nipple hardened, awaiting the touch of his tongue. He took her in his mouth and sucked, rolling the throbbing peak between his teeth and tongue until she writhed in frustration.

Cool air chilled her heated skin as he lifted her skirts and exposed one leg. She felt his hand caress her naked bottom and purposefully tilted her hips toward his length. She shivered with the tingling rush of excited anticipation growing where their bodies now touched. The heated pulse between her legs felt so sensitive, tingling with heightened awareness.

His lips found her mouth again as his hand boldly climbed the inside of her thigh. She tensed, heart pounding. Wanting. Waiting. Aching for his touch. Oh God, how he teased her. His torturous stroking, sweeping, brushing, slowly increased the divine pressure until she shook with need. Until she was damp and hot, weeping for more. His tongue flicked in and out of her mouth, and suddenly she knew—knew what he would do. She pressed her hips against his hand in silent entreaty.

She moaned, reveling in the sharp surge of relief when his finger plunged swiftly into the dampness between her legs.

"God, you're tight." His voice sounded strained, as if he were in pain.

The feelings of near ecstasy he was arousing easily outweighed all other thought. Or any qualms. Nothing that felt this wonderful could be wrong. Her breathing quickened in short gasps as he continued his intimate stroking, stirring her body into a wicked frenzy of need. The pressure built and built, until she thought she would burst. She felt strange, impatient for something she didn't understand.

"Relax," he whispered encouragingly. "Don't fight it, allow your mind to let go. Just concentrate on the feelings of pleasure where I touch you. I'm going to make you come."

Isabel gave over to the soothing caress of his voice. It didn't take long for her to understand what he meant, as the pressure built inside her. His finger plunged inside her, and when his thumb massaged her most sensitive spot, she clenched and, finally, shattered.

Rory watched the celestial wave of Isabel's release crash over her, sweeping her up in its powerful wake.

The wonder and ecstasy that flushed across her face was the most beautiful thing he'd ever seen. As the sensations began to ebb, the rise and fall of her chest slowed and her color returned to normal.

"I never imagined . . . ," she said, her voice soft with awe. "Is it always like that?"

He wanted to lie but instead spoke the truth that had lodged firmly in his chest. "Not always." *Never.* He'd never felt like that as he brought a woman to release.

She seemed to take his words to heart. Her smile encompassed her entire face.

Rory hadn't wanted this to happen.

He'd wanted only to shake some sense into her, but when she'd pressed her sweet lips to his, he was lost. He knew he could not—and would not—fight the powerful attraction that seemed to pull them together. He could still give her pleasure and not take her innocence.

Or so he thought. But her next words changed everything.

"I want to touch you, too. Show me how to give you pleasure."

His honorable intentions flew right out the window. He held his breath as her hand moved innocently to his thigh. He should be shocked by her boldness, but he was too damned aroused. He wanted her hand on him. Taking her wrist, he moved her hand over his plaid, stopping at his bulging erection. Her fingers curled instinctively around his length.

He tensed, waiting for her next move—thankful for the length of cloth separating her hand from his cock. He was so hard, so filled with lust, that even the simple touch of her hand on his hot, sensitive skin might make him lose control. Innocently, she caressed him, tentatively explored his length, and with his help began to stroke him. His buttocks clenched as he fought the urge to explode in her hand. Or lift her skirts and slide into her tight heat. The thought of all that softness surrounding him brought a bead of anticipation to his tip.

Rory knew he was going too fast, but he felt his experience incinerated by the blazing inferno between them. No woman had ever made him feel like this—made him lose all control. The fever of her response was driving him mad. He had been down this road many times before, but never had he traveled like this—with a woman who met his every stroke with a parry of her own. He was in danger of taking her right here, pressed against the window. Either that or risk shaming himself like an untried lad by the sweet circle of her hand.

He forced himself to slow the pace. Easing her away from the window, he lowered her to a nearby cushioned bench. Bending over her, he kissed her gently as he began working the laces of her gown. His lips moved across her face, toward the sensitive nape of her neck. She sighed as his tongue tasted the honey-sweet silk of her skin.

Rory hadn't intended to take it this far, but his body would not be denied. Desire warred with honor.

His head jerked up, and he felt as if he'd been dunked in a tub of cold reality. He knew what he had to do, though it was undoubtedly the hardest thing he'd ever done. He was so close to releasing the nearly unbearable pressure.

But honor, it seemed, had won.

He couldn't do this. Not when she was still vulnerable from her attack. Not when there were so many questions between them.

She deserved more than he could give her.

He stood up, his gaze held captive by what he'd forsaken for duty. She was temptation personified—her eyes half-closed with passion, her sensuous lips bruised by his kisses, her breathing ragged and shallow. He raked his gaze down to the soft ivory skin of her partially exposed breasts, the nipples dark and tight from his kisses.

He must be insane.

Isabel opened her eyes wide with surprise at his abrupt curtailment of the pleasure he was giving only moments before. "Why are you looking at me like that? Did I do something wrong?" She sat up, fumbling self-consciously with the laces on her bodice.

Wrong? She was so damn innocent.

Rory turned, gazing out the window into the darkness, allowing his breathing to slow. Finally, he looked back to her. "I've told you how it must be."

She stood up, sliding her hands around his neck. "It doesn't need to be."

It was almost too much. Perhaps he should just take what she offered, to hell with the consequences. But Rory would not act rashly when it came to the clan, not even with a woman he wanted above all others.

Carefully he unfolded her arms from around his neck. He couldn't think with her so near. "Why did you kiss me?"

Her mouth dropped open. "What are you implying?"

"Nothing."

"You don't trust me," she said flatly.

"Should I? You are a MacDonald."

Their eyes met, and he could see that his frank words had hurt her, but her answer was important to him. More important than he wanted to acknowledge.

She lifted her chin, but the tremble of her bottom lip betrayed her distress. "Have I given you reason not to?"

Rory stroked his jaw but didn't answer. He wasn't sure. "You've pushed me before," he said, referring to the dress and flimsy *night rail*. "And you haven't answered my question."

Isabel flushed, but whether from anger or guilt he did not know. "I kissed you because I wanted to. That is the only reason. If you will remember, we were discussing the attack at your request. Your suggestion." She lifted her chin and looked down her nose at him. "And *if* I choose to seduce you, you will know." The sensuous, womanly confidence in her eyes took him aback.

Rory almost smiled at her bravado, even as her threat sent a shiver of trepidation winding through him. He suspected that she was right. This woman was lethal.

She let her threat hang for a moment before continuing. "Maybe I should question your motives. Why did you bring me here tonight?"

"I asked you here to discuss the attack. Perhaps we should return to that and talk about the ramifications of your actions." He paused, deliberating what those consequences might be.

Isabel stood before him proudly, her hair disheveled and her cheeks flushed, but otherwise little evidence remained of her near undressed state of a few minutes ago.

"I admit responsibility. Do what you will."

Rory shook his head. "I do not like your part in this, but it was Alex who was responsible. He was left in charge while I was away, and he will answer for his actions when he wakes. You have already suffered punishment enough at the hands of the Mackenzies. However, if you ever choose to disobey me again, mark me, Isabel, there will be severe consequences. I trust you will not do anything so reckless again."

It was not a question.

"You may return to your chamber," he said more gently. It wasn't only Alex and Isabel to blame. Rory felt some responsibility for what had almost happened to her. He had not spread the news of their handfast, and this had contributed to Murdock Mackenzie's suspicions that Isabel was not who she'd claimed to be. He'd also left her alone too long. The memory of her bitter accusation had not faded—his long silence had hurt her.

Isabel ventured one last glance, pleading for understanding. He held her gaze but kept his expression inscrutable. The memory of what they'd shared stretched uncomfortably between them. Chastened, she turned and started to leave.

He watched her go, his body still smoldering with unspent desire. The memory of her face as she'd shattered in his arms would haunt him for every day that remained of this damned handfast.

He stopped her before she reached the door. "Why are you *really* here, Isabel? Why did you agree to the handfast?"

She seemed surprised by his question. " 'Twas my father's wish."

"But what about *you*, what do you want?"

"My clan to prosper, the love of my family."

"Is that all? Do you not want a man to love? Bairns to care for?"

"Of course, but you've made it very clear that is not your intention." Their eyes met and held. "Why did *you* agree to this handfast?"

"I had no choice, the king demanded it," he answered

automatically. He saw the flicker of something in her eyes. Pain?

"By handfasting with me, you did your duty to your king, but there is nothing to say that you may not enjoy it." Her voice was very quiet. "I did."

He was silent for a moment, remembering the intensity of what they'd shared. "It doesn't change anything." He didn't realize he'd spoken his words aloud until he noticed her expression. She looked as though he'd struck her.

After a moment, she smiled sadly. "You're wrong. It changes everything."

Chapter 14

❖

Isabel awoke as she'd done every day for the past month—cradled in Rory's arms. She feigned sleep for a few minutes longer, relishing the sensation of those strong steel bands encircling her, the heat of his hard chest against her back, the spicy masculine scent of him, and the deep soothing sound of his even breathing. Safe. Warm. Content. She could stay like this forever.

And today, like every day, she experienced the same sharp pang of disappointment and loss when he slid out of bed the instant he hardened against her, dressed quickly, and left. Some days it seemed he hesitated, but his honor was strong, and inevitably, she heard the door close with a definitive click behind him.

Isabel never let him know that she was awake. As if by acknowledging the unspoken lure of their bodies, she might shatter the growing intimacy between them. The connection forged in the wee hours of the night, when she unconsciously reached for him, seeking the warmth of his body and the heat of his skin, and nothing else mattered but the press of his body against hers. And in those long, slow days spent awaiting the Christmas celebration, Isabel had come to realize how much she treasured his strength beside her.

She'd been correct. That night in the library had changed everything.

His gift to her had opened up an entirely new world. One that she didn't know how she could possibly leave behind. She couldn't stop thinking about what he'd done. How it felt to be in his arms, the closeness, the ecstasy, and the magic. Though rightfully placed, his distrust afterward was the only thing to mar the beauty of her release. She wanted nothing more than to prove to him that he could trust her. But how could she, when he could not?

The unspoken truce had created a pleasant lull, but one she knew could not go on forever.

She dressed quickly, broke her fast with a small tray of food brought up by Deidre, and headed to the library to begin her tasks for the day.

In the month since Rory's return, Isabel's daily activities had settled into a comfortable pattern. Alex's recovery had progressed remarkably fast given the severity of the injury. She and Margaret had taken turns nursing him until one day, fed up with their "incessant hovering," he threw them out of his room, declaring that he had been subjected to enough humiliation and was more than capable of bathing and feeding himself. His exact phrase actually contained the terms *clean* and *arse,* but suffice it to say, he was feeling much better.

When they weren't busy with their duties attending to the management of the castle, she and Margaret enjoyed reading or playing chess near the hearth of the crackling fire in the library. The disaster of their hunting adventure now behind them, the two had resumed a rigorous practice schedule with the bow—albeit within the safe confines of the castle walls. Margaret's skills had improved dramatically. She was proving to be quite the apt pupil, and Isabel suspected that Margaret's ability would soon surpass that of her instructor.

Bessie had become fast friends with Deidre and was largely accepted by the MacLeod household servants. During Alex's illness she had taken to clucking and fussing over him, and although he pretended to be annoyed at being treated as if he were little older than a "wet-behind-the-ear squire," Isabel knew that he was growing to love Bessie as much as she and Margaret did. Robert, the porter, still seemed to manage to find tasks that would require his presence in the tower—not coincidentally in close proximity to where Bessie happened to be working.

Rory spent most of his days in the yard, training his warriors for the inevitable retaliation by the Mackenzies for the death of the chief's son Murdock. It was not a matter of *if*, but *when* retribution would come, and Rory would be prepared. He refused any requests that would take her beyond the gates of the castle, and Isabel was still so upset with what had happened last time she'd ventured out, she did not press him.

She dropped her quill carelessly on the table and slumped back in her chair, pondering the situation. She knew she had to do something soon. Her uncle would be expecting a report of her progress. She was amazed Sleat had left her alone this long, with Christmas only one week away. Time was slipping away from her, and the pressure of her precarious predicament was building. She'd expected danger, yes, but she had not anticipated the painful emotional costs that would be involved with her treachery. How could she betray Margaret and Alex, who had welcomed her and treated her as more of a sister than her own family? How could she betray Rory, a man who she admired above all others? A man who'd rescued her from rape and then wiped away the horrible memories by awakening her passion.

She couldn't. And the realization was like a physical blow.

How would she fulfill her duty to her clan? She'd hoped Rory would make it easy on her by wresting the decision from her hands, but he had a will of steel. He wanted her, but his honor prevented him from acting on his desires. She considered claiming that she was unable to locate the flag or the secret entrance, but there was too much at stake. She could not yet concede to such absolute failure in her family's eyes or to the inevitable destruction her failure would bring.

Isabel still held out hope that circumstances might have changed or that her father would have devised another way to repulse the Mackenzies' attacks on Strome. She frowned. Her father's failure to respond to her letters, another one written after her attack, concerned her, although the delay of his response helped her justify her reluctance to search the castle further and her failure to seduce Rory as she'd planned.

Isabel glanced down at the piles of parchments before her and returned to her work. She'd spent most of the morning conferring with James, the bailiff, about the rents for the month. She was in the process of making the appropriate notations in the ledgers reflecting the new information when Margaret bounded into the library, laughing excitedly. She had obviously come from outside; her golden curls were hopelessly mussed from the wind, a slight glow of perspiration shone on her brow, and her cheeks bloomed bright pink from exertion. Looking down, Isabel could see the telltale mud splattered on the edge of her gown and slippers. As doggedly determined as the most ambitious mercenary, Isabel knew Margaret had been at it again.

"What are you laughing about on this cold and dreary day?" Peering out the window, Isabel could barely see the loch, as the mist cloaked the castle in a thick, dense fog. Despite the warm fire in the room, she wore an extra plaid about her shoulders.

"You will never guess." Margaret giggled, pulling up a chair next to Isabel at the table.

Isabel looked at her pointedly, pretending to consider her answer. "Let's see . . . you have decided to put that devilish pirate-looking suitor of yours out of his misery and marry him."

Margaret blushed. "No. Isabel, your teasing is just as bad as Alex's. You know Colin is only being considerate. He could not be interested in me the way you suggest. Guess again."

Isabel lifted an eyebrow skeptically. Margaret was quite deluded where Colin's interests lay. "Hmmm. Let me think. I know, Catriona has decided to defy the kirk and become a nun." Isabel could joke about Catriona now, since Margaret had assured her that Rory's involvement with the woman had ended long ago.

Margaret gave a loud guffaw that was decidedly incongruous with her size. "Isabel, you are a wicked one! Imagine that shameless woman forsaking the more earthly pleasures in which she so continuously delights. I know many a wife who would be overjoyed to have that husband-tempting harlot out of the way. All right, I suppose I shall have to tell you, since I can hardly wait for you to guess. I challenged Alex to a contest with the bow and won!"

Isabel threw up her hands and gave her a tight hug. "How wonderful! I told you your skills have improved." Her lips lifted mischievously. "I'm sure Alex had something to say about your victory. He has been relentless in his horrible teasing about your diligent practice schedule. Serves him right." She could clearly visualize his bewildered shock. "I remember my brothers' reactions when I bested them. Their pride always bristled at being set down by a *mere lass*." She emphasized the last words with mock haughty condescension. "And you being such a spry wee thing—hardly a likely challenger to a fierce, proud MacLeod warrior."

Margaret's face flushed crimson with delight, and her uncovered sapphire blue eye sparkled. "Oh, Isabel, you should have seen Alex. The look on his face was worth a king's ransom. When I hit the target dead center, I thought his eyes might pop from his head. And you should have heard the men who were standing around watching. I'm sure he will not hear the end of this for days."

"Well done, Margaret. You have earned your victory. Mayhap this will teach Alex to curb his teasing tongue." They looked at each other, paused for a moment, and broke out in fresh laughter. Alex was a born instigator, a born tease; it was part of his charm, and they relished the lighthearted moments that seemed to come so infrequently. Isabel also suspected that although he might feign indignation, Alex was extremely proud of his sister's burgeoning accomplishment with a bow. She had progressed at an amazing pace. The change in her was so striking, the new pride and self-confidence she exhibited was incredible to behold. Alex would not begrudge her a win, even at the expense of some relentless ribbing by the clansmen for his foreseeable future.

Rory stood at the doorway watching the two women bursting in great peals of laughter. His chest tightened to see the joy on his sister's face, joy he had never thought to see again. And he knew Isabel was responsible for the happy return of his lost sister. How could it have happened in such a short time? It seemed that almost overnight, Margaret had discarded the cloak of shame and timorousness that she had worn for the last two years, to revel like a pagan at Beltane in her newfound confidence. Even in the midst of the bleak, frozen darkness of winter, Dunvegan seemed to burst with the warm spring light of their laughter and smiles. He had not realized how much he'd missed the laughter of happy women until it returned so unexpectedly.

His gaze fell on Isabel. She'd also changed, perhaps not as dramatically as Margaret, but just as importantly. The loneliness and vulnerability that hovered around her on her arrival seemed to have faded as she'd carved out a growing place in his family. Knowing that her time at Dunvegan was only brief, it troubled him. In truth, the plan to repudiate the handfast weighed on him heavily.

He would never tire of looking at her. She was exquisite—the way she moved, the way she laughed. Each time he looked at her, her beauty seemed to change. It's not that she became less beautiful with acquaintance the way some women did. No, he thought, rather the opposite occurred—she grew even more beautiful. With each meeting she became more real, as if aspects of her unique character broke through the mask of perfect features.

He was not the only one to notice her. Rory had caught most of his men casting her admiring glances when they thought he was not watching. It riled him, but he did not attribute it to a lack of loyalty. They were not bloody eunuchs. He could hardly blame them for something that he found impossible to avoid doing himself. Even sitting behind a table stacked with parchment, she was stunning, her shining copper gold hair floating around her shoulders, her ivory skin smudged with black ink, her full lips twitching mischievously, the defiant lift of her chin. Her beauty was magnetic—a rare gift meant to be admired.

His thoughts strayed to this morning, when he'd woken to find her nestled in his arms. His body warmed at the memory. The last month had been exquisite torture. He'd hoped that it would grow easier, that he would get used to sharing a bed, but each day he wanted her more than the day before. Their bodies had found each other and wouldn't let go. Abstinence was doing crazy things to him; Rory didn't know how much more he could take.

She was still a maid, but if she pushed him again, he would not be held accountable.

His distrust had eased over the last month, though he still couldn't forget that she was a MacDonald and the niece of his enemy. He'd watched her closely these past few weeks and was relieved not to find her searching through any more dark corridors. Nor had she made a further attempt to press him. Though sleeping beside her every night was temptation enough.

Rory observed the two young women who seemed as

comfortable as two cagey old dowagers who had been friends from the nursery. They still had yet to notice him.

He wasn't surprised to find the accomplices here in his library. From the stack of ledgers piled next to Isabel and the black smears on her fingertips, he deduced that she had been working on the accounts again. First his room, then his sister, now his accounts. Isabel had woven her way into the fabric of his castle—into his life. Pretty soon she'd be sitting in his chair. The image made him smile.

"What are you two hoydens laughing about?"

Isabel turned in surprise as Rory entered the library. His visits to the library were more infrequent now that she and Margaret had largely taken over the room. Even more unusual was that it was still the middle of the day, a time usually devoted to waging war with his warriors in the courtyard. Apparently, he'd just come from the lists, as he'd yet to wash the toil of his practice from his well-worked body.

Her heart skipped a beat as it always did when she recalled his prowess on the lists. And something warm and tingly curled inside her stomach when she thought of this fierce warrior cradling her gently in his arms.

Isabel's strong physical reaction to him did not lessen with familiarity. She still had to pull her eyes away from staring at his ruggedly handsome face—still deeply tanned despite the lack of sun these past few months. Nor would she ever get used to the way his very presence filled a room—not just the result of his broad shoulders and powerfully muscled body, but also from the raw heat that seemed to radiate from him.

Since Margaret appeared conveniently mute, reluctant to admit they'd been laughing at Alex, Isabel decided to let him in on the joke. "It seems Margaret has defeated Alex in an impromptu archery contest."

He turned and looked pointedly at Margaret. Uncertain of his reaction—he was a man, after all—they waited patiently for some sign. Slowly, his lips curved into a devilish grin, his dimples piercing deep craters in his cheeks.

"So Margaret has managed to trap that taunting scoundrel with his own words. I've heard his incessant boasting that no matter how diligent the practice schedule, he would never be beaten by a mere lass. Perhaps he'll learn a valuable lesson: to expect the unexpected. It's an arrogant mistake to underestimate your opponent—one that can lead to death." He gazed over Margaret's head and fixed his gorgeous eyes on Isabel. "I never underestimate my opponent."

She flushed guiltily. Now why had he said that?

He appeared not to notice her reaction. "Well done, Margaret, you have made me proud. Our braggart brother could stand to be knocked down a peg or two." Laughing, Rory lifted his sister into a warm, brotherly embrace.

Margaret's smile seemed to fill her face. "Maybe I'll be ready to challenge you, Rory, by the time we host the gathering this spring," she teased.

He released Margaret from his embrace, and the smile that transcended his face matched hers in its infinite joy. "I would be honored to accept your challenge, Margaret. Alex is a very good bowman, little one, so I know you must have become quite accomplished in a very short time. But I have not been beaten in a contest with the bow since I was a lad, so you would be wise to increase your practice schedule." He turned his smile to Isabel.

She felt as if she were melting under its warmth.

"I hope your instructor can find the time in her schedule?" he queried.

Isabel grinned and nodded.

He turned back to Margaret and said, sounding almost apologetic, "But it may not be at the gathering. You know very well that a lass may not participate in the Highland gathering—by long tradition, it is a contest reserved for warriors to test their skills, strength, and agility." Isabel knew the gatherings were begun over five hundred years ago by Malcolm Canmore to identify the best warriors among his men. Rory's eyes twinkled under the black wings of his raised brow. "Besides, what if you were to win? The fierce pride of the Scots would be irreparably damaged by a mere slip of a lass. It would be a blow that we men would likely never recover from."

Isabel was mesmerized by the playful teasing of the siblings. It was a side of Rory that was so rarely exposed; she knew she would never tire of listening to their loving banter. He could be so devilishly charming—acting like this, he was irresistible. Her chest squeezed with longing.

Margaret nearly jumped up and down with exuberance. She began her preparations for extra practice immediately—talking to herself excitedly. They both listened, amused, as she ran from the room. "I will have to find someone to oversee the kitchens in the morning and take over the meal planning . . ."

Still grinning, Rory said, "Margaret seems to have

found her calling." The full force of his attractiveness hit her with his next words. "I thank you, Isabel. You have accomplished what I thought was impossible. You have given me back my sister." The warmth and sincerity in his voice were like an enchanted spell binding her to him.

Isabel warmed under his praise. Rory constantly surprised her. She could not recall ever being honestly thanked for anything by a man in his position. Most men would never consider being beholden to a woman for anything. But such graciousness only increased his estimation in her eyes; the power to recognize another's worth in no way diminished his own, it only made him appear stronger.

She stood up and stepped toward him, struggling to find her voice. "I've done nothing but be a friend, and that was simple enough with Margaret. I feel like I've known her my whole life. It's difficult to believe it's only been a few months."

Isabel paused, debating whether to say something further. She might never have a better opportunity, and she wanted him to understand about Margaret. "I think the end to the feud has helped her enormously," she added hesitantly.

Rory tensed as he did at any mention of the feud. "What do you mean?"

Isabel took a deep breath, deciding it was worth the risk to state her opinion, even if it ruined his good mood. She looked down at her feet, not wanting his reaction to stop what she had to say. "I think the feud and the quest for revenge has made it impossible for Margaret to put the past behind her. I know she feels responsible for the death and destruction done in her name."

Isabel's clenched hands betrayed her anxiety at mentioning the forbidden subject of her uncle.

After a moment of unbearable silence, she dared to peek at his face. But instead of the anger she'd expected, Rory appeared thoughtful.

"And the feud was a constant reminder of Sleat's cruelty," he finished. "But it was not only Margaret who was shamed, the honor of the clan demanded retribution."

Isabel nodded. "You were attending to your duty as chief, Margaret knows that"—her voice lowered—"and so does Alex."

"What does Alex have to do with this?" When she appeared reluctant to say anything further, he added, "Speak freely, Isabel, I would like to hear what you have to say."

There was no easy way to say this, so she just blurted it out. "Alex needs to feel that he is important to you and the clan."

"Of course he's important. He is my *tanaiste*." She felt the full measure of his attention on her. "Go on," he urged.

"I know you think that he is important, but I don't think Alex does. What duties have you delegated to him?"

Rory was silent for a moment. "Not many," he admitted. Isabel waited for him to finish the thought. "And by my not doing so, he believes that I do not think he is capable."

Isabel nodded. "If you do not give him more responsibility, he will never be able to resolve his defeat at the hands of the MacDonalds."

Rory leaned back, assessing her with an appreciative

gaze. "If Alex has discussed his loss at Binquihillin and the death of our cousins, you truly must have earned his confidence. I know he blames himself, but I do not. I would have done the same in his stead."

"But if you do not allow him the responsibilities worthy of your *tanaiste*, are you not telling him by your actions that you do not trust him? That you do blame him?" she asked quietly.

Rory drew himself up to his full height and crossed his arms over his chest. "I am chief, I do not delegate my duties and responsibilities."

Isabel tried not to be distracted by the impressive display of muscle straining against saffron linen. "I know that you would not be so arrogant as to believe that you must personally attend to all the matters of the clan and that you are the only one qualified to make decisions."

He quirked his mouth, seemingly amused by her sarcastic set-down. But he appeared to at least consider what she said. "I will think on it." Apparently, turnabout was fair play. "And what of you, Isabel? What of your family?"

It was Isabel's turn to bristle defensively. "What of it?"

"Tell me why the mere mention of your family causes pain to flicker in your eyes," he urged, this time gently.

She looked away, embarrassed that her loneliness was so obvious. "There's not much to tell," she said carefully. "You know that my mother died when I was young, my father had his duty to the clan, and my brothers . . . well, they had their own pursuits. Pursuits that were not appropriate for a young girl." She saw something resembling sympathy in his eyes, and she quickly tried to explain, lest he get the wrong impression. "My father was not cruel. Just busy. And I always had Bessie looking after me."

His soft voice drew her eyes back to his. "Your father is not unusual, Isabel. Most men do not concern themselves with the raising of their girl children. 'Tis the way of the world. As chief of a clan facing constant attacks, no doubt your father did not have much time for you *or* your brothers. He had his duty to the clan."

"You are not that way," she pointed out. "I see how you care for your family, including your sisters."

Rory smiled. "I didn't say I agreed with it, I said 'twas the way of the world. My father was much as yours."

"But you had your brothers and sisters."

"Didn't you?"

She thought for a second. "For a while, but as I got older they changed. My mother was a lady. My father thought that I should be one, which meant that I was no longer able to spend as much time with three older brothers."

His fingers reached out to cup her chin, tilting it upward until their eyes met. "Perhaps they did not realize how lonely you were, perhaps they did not know any other way. I watched your family with you. To me it looked more awkwardness than lack of regard."

His words startled her. Was he right? Was it simply that the men in her family didn't know how to deal with a young girl? Could she have misinterpreted her family's feelings so greatly? Memories, snippets of conversations, shuffled through her mind. Reframed with Rory's perspective, it felt right. Isabel allowed a glimmer of hope to build in her chest.

He looked at her as though he wanted to say more, but instead he chose to let the subject drop. They merely stared at each other, each afraid to move and break the spell of connection that had sprouted between them.

"Was there something you wanted?" she asked breathlessly, more moved by the moment than she thought possible.

"Yes. I would ask a boon of you. As Margaret has been so busy with her duties and her new practice schedule, I was wondering whether you might find the time to help me organize the Highland gathering that will be held at Dunvegan in the spring."

He was including her. She thought her heart would burst with happiness. "Of course, I would love to help. What can I do?"

Rory returned her smile. "First, we will need to prepare a list of the clans that will be asked to participate and send a messenger with an invitation."

Isabel was already making a mental list of the surrounding clans: MacCrimmons, Mackinnons, MacLeans, Argyll and the Campbells, Ramsays, MacDonalds. MacDonalds. Her brows shot together with the sudden realization. Her heart sank with dread. If her family were here, she would be forced to provide a report of her progress—or lack thereof.

"Does that mean my family will be invited?"

"Of course, Glengarry and even Sleat must be invited. Our recent handfast has made allies of former enemies. Is that not what the king has ordered?" He looked at her with a challenge in his eye.

Given his good mood, Isabel decided not to point out that Rory had once questioned that very premise.

Another thought occurred to her, this one even more

treacherous and unwelcome than the last. "What about the Mackenzies?"

"*All* the local clans, Isabel." He placed his hand over hers in a gesture of reassurance. "All feuds will be set aside for the duration of the gathering."

"But what if they try to retaliate?"

"They would not dare break the sacred obligation of Highland hospitality. They'll come and seek to best the MacLeods on the field of games. We can expect an attack from the Mackenzie, but not at the gathering."

His confidence calmed her anxiety. "What types of games should we organize?"

"The usual challenges: the tossing of the caber, throwing the hammer, archery, stone throwing, wrestling, swimming, leaping, and hill running. Most of the games will be held in the village or in the forest. Of course, the swimming will be in the loch. We'll also need to provide for accommodations both here and in the village, as well as coordinate the food and drink for the feast. Are you sure you'll have time to help?"

"Very sure. I'll get started immediately preparing a list of guests for your approval. Then I can begin drafting the invitations. Whom shall I send to deliver them?"

Before he could answer, a knock came upon the door. He bade them entry, and Isabel was surprised to see Colin.

Displeased, Rory frowned at the interruption.

Colin explained, "A missive has arrived for the lady."

Finally a letter from my father, she thought. But her relief was short-lived.

"From your uncle, my lady," Colin said, handing her the folded parchment with the waxed seal. A seal that she recognized immediately: *Per Mare per Terras,* the badge of Sleat.

She turned to Rory in time to notice the almost imperceptible sharpening of his gaze. "How convenient. If you prepare the invitation for your uncle, you can give it to his messenger personally."

The false sense of tranquillity she had been experiencing for the last few weeks was instantly shattered by one innocuous folded piece of parchment. Isabel knew what she held in her hands.

Her reminder had come.

Chapter 15

❖

Isabel knew it was bound to happen sometime. But why did it have to be just when she and Rory had found a new intimacy and she was starting to feel that she had established a place for herself at Dunvegan? A place that mattered.

The forced reminder of her true purpose in handfasting with Rory MacLeod was a bitter draught to swallow. She had almost succeeded in convincing herself that it might never come. That perhaps they would forget about her. *Fool.* This was not some silly game; her clan's fortunes would rise or fall based on her success. Her uncle had not forgotten her or devised another way to claim the Lordship of the Isles for himself.

Thankfully, Rory had left her alone in the library to read the letter. She could tell by the speculative turn of his brow that he was curious—but he did not inquire into the contents of the missive. And she did not volunteer the information.

She settled back in her chair before the fire, cracked the seal carefully, and began to read.

Her uncle sent a thinly veiled reprimand for her failure to report her progress at Dunvegan. Claiming that he was "dismayed" not to have heard from his "dear niece" since the handfast, he hoped that she might find the time to assure her "concerned family" that she was adjusting to her new married life at Dunvegan and that she had "found all that she was looking for" with her new husband. He also mentioned that he had heard "rumors" that the Mackenzies were readying to mobilize an attack on the MacDonald clan and Strome Castle.

So much for subtlety.

The letter fell to her lap as she stared in a daze at the glowing embers of the once blazing fire. Suddenly shivering, she tightened the plaid about her shoulders.

The moment had come. She had to make an impossible choice—one surely fit for the wisdom of King Solomon. Either way, it meant betrayal. Betrayal for the MacLeods or betrayal for the MacDonalds. She must choose between the family she'd grown up with or the family she'd always wanted.

At Dunvegan, she'd found friendship, happiness, and something else that she dared not contemplate. Of Margaret's friendship, she was sure. And so too of Alex's. Rory's feelings were more complicated. But somehow, in her heart, she knew that he too had softened toward her. Otherwise, he would not have asked her to help organize the games. A task that would bring them into close contact during the day—something he had previously sought to avoid.

But perhaps it was what he had not done that was the most persuasive evidence of his changing affections. He had not moved her from his room, forbade her from taking over the accounts, discouraged her from instructing Margaret with a bow, or prohibited her from nursing Alex. Indeed, in the days following the attack in the forest, he'd treated her gently and with the utmost consideration. She could only conclude that he was beginning to accept her place in his family.

But he still intended to send her away.

And though he wanted her, and the passion between them could not be denied, he'd yet to make her his bride in truth.

Her brow furled with frustration. Each time she felt their connection growing strong, something always seemed to interfere. Like this letter, reminding him of her connection to his enemy. She grabbed a lock of hair, twisting it around her finger as she grappled with her uncomfortable thoughts.

How could she align herself with a man like her uncle against a man like Rory? If it were only a matter of her uncle's quest for the Lordship of the Isles, her choice would be clear in favor of Rory. But there was her clan to consider. The MacDonalds of Glengarry desperately needed Sleat's men to withstand a prolonged attack by the Mackenzies. Without her uncle's help, her clan was doomed to lose its lands. And a clan without land was a broken clan. Their people would be forced to scavenge for food, land, and protection from another clan. The thought was too horrible to contemplate.

Isabel had a duty to her family, but deep down she wanted to be selfish. She wanted to be happy. She wanted Rory for herself. But though she no longer felt an overwhelming drive to be the savior of her clan, she didn't want to let down her family. She could not live happily knowing that her failure had led to the destruction of her people. She desperately needed to find an alternative solution to help her family defend against the Mackenzies. As at Dunvegan, the Mackenzie attack on Strome Castle could come at any time.

Something clicked, and a kernel of an idea began to take hold. The Mackenzies. They were the key. Her father and the MacLeod shared the same enemy. *The enemy of my enemy is my friend.* The ancient Arab proverb brought back from the Crusades could be her salvation. She tried to contain the burgeoning hope brimming inside her.

Maybe she didn't have to choose.

Rory's fighting force was nearly as large as her uncle's. If her father had the MacLeod's support, he would not need Sleat. And Isabel would not need to betray the MacLeods by stealing the Fairy Flag or disclosing the location of a secret entrance—if one existed.

Her mind raced as she began to consider the possibilities. Could this work? It might be the perfect solution. But how could she get Rory to agree? She couldn't just go to him with her request. Not while he still intended to send her back. Not while his alliance with her family was temporary.

So how, then, to prevent him from sending her back?

He had to fall in love with her. If he fell in love with her, he would not *want* to send her back. She frowned, realizing it was not simply a matter of earning his love. She knew Rory was counting on the alliance with Argyll to help sway the king to decide in his favor on the disposition of the disputed Trotternish peninsula. She would have to find a way to make the union with her equally as profitable.

However, there was also the fact that she was a Mac-Donald. Rory hated Sleat. But perhaps if Rory fell in love with her, he would be willing to forgive the connection.

One thing was certain: She knew Rory would never

forgive betrayal. She shuddered, remembering his face when he'd discovered her searching the Fairy Tower. She dared not contemplate his fury if he ever found out she'd handfasted with him intending to deceive him. But if she was successful, maybe he need never find out about her treacherous purpose. She considered confessing, but she dared not. Not while she was uncertain of his feelings. And she couldn't take the chance that her plan wouldn't work.

It wasn't perfect, but she had to try.

And if she succeeded, she would have her heart's desire: a place at Dunvegan and the respect of her family. And most important, Rory's love. For deep down, Isabel realized that earning his love had become vital. As necessary as the food she ate or the air she breathed. He'd become a part of her.

Letting her hair fall from her fingers, she stood up, suddenly anxious to begin. She looked down and watched as the wretched letter floated to the ground. Uttering a small oath, she picked it up, crumpled it in her fist, and tossed it into the fire. She smiled grimly as the flame caught the parchment, curling the edges with blackness until it vanished into a small billow of gray smoke—the hateful words of betrayal obliterated into nothingness.

Her decision freed her from the inertia of the past few months. It gave her the excuse she needed to go after what she really wanted. Simply waking up in Rory's arms wasn't enough. She wanted the intimacy and closeness that could come only from making love.

Isabel knew what she had to do; he would not come to her. Seduction it must be. She tried not to think about his warning not to manipulate him. Her motives were pure. She would fight for Rory's love and seduce him—not to betray him, but because she wanted to hold on to him.

She squared her shoulders and headed up the stairs to change for the evening repast. Tonight. After the meal, she would retire to their room and wait.

She bit her lip. What was she going to do when he got there? She had learned much about kissing over the last few months and had a vague idea of the rest courtesy of their previous interludes. But there was a vast difference between knowing in the abstract and instigating in the reality. How would she let him know that she was ready to take the final step?

Isabel took her time winding through the dimly lit corridors. Though it was only late afternoon, the days were exceedingly short in the wintertime and dusk had already fallen.

She opened the door.

A taper flickered. Warm, steamy air entwined with a delicious masculine scent of spice enveloped her.

She knew he was there even before she looked. When she did, her heart dropped to her toes.

Rory had just stepped out of his bath. He wore a drying cloth slung low on his hips and—she swallowed—nothing else.

Her eyes gorged on the rugged masculinity of his powerful physique. He was magnificent. His broad naked chest, glistening with tiny droplets of water, tapered to a narrow waist above powerfully muscled legs. There was not one inch of him that was not cut and hard as rock. His body was a finely honed weapon of warfare, the numerous scars that crossed his chest evidence of his hard-earned prowess. The damp linen hugged his hips, dipping low above his groin, and outlined every ridge of his . . . Her eyes dropped farther, and her mouth went dry. Of his enormous arousal. The thick column strained against the thin cloth, leaving her no doubt of his desire.

Isabel flooded with heat. Awareness crackled in the sultry room like dry kindling in a hot fire. Her heart was pounding so loudly, she was sure he must hear. She lifted her eyes to his and nearly withered under the force of his penetrating stare. Never had she been the focus of such all-encompassing desire. She felt the hunger, the need. The whiplash of raw heat. His gaze possessed her. Like an animal caught in a trap, she was paralyzed by all that sexual potency fastened on her, claiming her. He looked as though he wanted to tear off her clothes and ravish her. It was a side of him—a wild, primitive, uncontrolled side—that she'd never seen. And for a moment, the intensity frightened her, even as it humbled her with its strength.

They stood perfectly still, staring at each other. His eyes glowed like sapphire coals. As he'd removed the leather thong that usually bound it back, his damp golden chestnut hair slumped forward across his face to his chin. The shadows that partially hid his face hardened his features into sharp angles—making him appear even more menacing than his large physique would suggest.

Isabel shivered with anticipation. Never had she been more certain of anything in her life. The intensity of his desire only emboldened her. She wanted to tame this man, to claim this warrior for her own.

All thoughts of a well-planned seduction fled. The

time was now. Gathering the reins of her courage, she lifted her chin and took a small step toward him.

His body went rigid, every muscle taut with restraint. A tic in his jaw pulsed as she drew near. Slowly, she removed the plaid she wore for warmth and draped it over the chair.

"What are you doing?" he asked through clenched teeth, his voice strained.

"I came to dress for dinner. I didn't realize you had called for a bath."

"It's too cold to swim in the loch."

"Of course."

"You should leave."

She shook her head and took another step toward him. She was standing so close, she could hear the harsh unevenness of his breath. He was holding himself by a thread, and she knew it. Relished it. Savored it. And yearned to make it snap.

He stepped toward her, and she could see that his eyes were dark and heavy with desire. He reached down to cup her chin as he looked deep into her eyes. "Are you sure?" His voice was husky and full of promise, the soft brogue more pronounced. "My duty lies elsewhere. This will not change anything, Isabel. Even if I wish it differently."

Isabel's heart tugged. Did he wish differently? The glimmer of hope gave her all the encouragement she needed.

The polite small talk had drained every ounce of Rory's reserves. He was running out of patience. Surely she could see how his pulse raced, how he struggled to breathe the sultry air between them, how he fought the urge to take her into his arms the very moment she entered the room.

The beauty that filled his eyes when she opened the door had nearly felled him—as if someone had unexpectedly punched him in the stomach. And then he picked up her scent. The beguiling perfume of lavender ensnared him, but it was the sensual promise in those damn violet eyes as she admired his body that made him realize he'd never stood a chance. There was an inevitability to this moment, probably from the first. Fate.

Rory waited, every muscle in his body clenched, for her response. He fought to contain the hunger pounding through his body. She must come to him knowingly and without pretense; nothing else would assuage his guilt. He would not take her virginity from her unless she understood. There was still the issue of a child, but Rory could prevent that. The questions kindled by her uncle's letter would be left for another day.

His weeks of holding her in his arms like a bloody eunuch had come to an end. He would not fight this overpowering, mind-numbing attraction any longer.

Her hand touched his arm, and he flinched, shocked. The simple press of her fingers on his skin ignited an inferno that spread like wildfire through his body.

"I understand," she said simply. "No promises."

That was enough.

He swept her in his arms, crushing her in a fierce embrace. So thick was the tension that had built between them, she sighed audibly with relief. He knew she wanted him as he wanted her.

His fingers wove through her glorious hair, the thick tresses sliding like satin ribbons through his hands. Clenching a fistful of the smooth, glossy locks, he eased her head back, tilting her parted lips to his. Lowering his mouth, he drank. His thirst unquenchable. The honey-sweet taste of her lips was like the nectar of gods. With the first touch of her tongue, a deep groan of triumph at her surrender shuddered through his body.

He couldn't contain his need. Never had he felt lust this powerful, this uncontrollable. This primal. All the passion, all the desire he'd restrained for so long, burst free in a savage storm. He wanted to possess her body and soul.

He felt like a caged wild beast, frantic for escape. Hunger drove his mouth over hers, rough and hard. Deeper and deeper, devouring her, consuming her, and claiming her for his own. Boldly she met the thrust of his tongue with her own. Her immediate response only increased the agony building in his loins, only incited the meager restraint he was just barely containing in deference to her innocence.

He knew he was out of control, rough and moving too fast, but she responded on every level. He wanted nothing more than to tear off her clothes, toss her on the bed, and bury himself deep inside her. He wanted to take her hard and fast, pounding and thrusting until she clenched around him, until he buried himself full hilt and came in a torrential explosion of relief. What had this woman done to him? Knowledge of how close to the edge he teetered gave him the strength to find control.

He would make sure her first time was perfect even if it killed him.

He released her mouth, his head sinking lower as he devoured her neck, tasting the unbelievable sweetness of her feverish skin. Impatient to taste more of her, he did not linger long but slid down past the base of her throat.

Her head fell back in complete abandon. He felt her shiver under the press of his mouth. He nuzzled the deep cleft between her breasts, breathing deeply of her lavender scent. He teased her mercilessly, sliding his tongue along the edge of her bodice, delving achingly close to the wrinkled edge of her nipple.

She moaned her frustration.

He slid his thumb under the lace, lifting the tight pink pearl to his tongue. He sucked in his breath at the knowledge that she was just as aroused as he was. Teasingly he blew, flicking his tongue across the taut peak, then nibbling her softly between his teeth. She arched her back, begging for more. And he complied. Sinking his lips around her and sucking, sucking until he heard her sharp intake of breath and knew she was close. Not yet.

"I want to see you naked," he said.

Cheeks flushed with passion and embarrassment, she shyly nodded her acquiescence.

With the finesse of years of experience, he quickly removed her gown, stomacher, and bolster, unlaced her stays, slid down her hose, and in one smooth motion lifted her sark over her head.

His eyes widened with awe at the bountiful treasure before him. Blood surged to his already engorged staff. He was so hard, it hurt. Completely naked, she was even more beautiful than he'd imagined, slim and gently curved, her flawless ivory skin smooth and creamy. Her breasts were generously rounded, high, and firm, her stomach flat, her hips small, and her legs lean and gently muscled. She looked like a marble statue of Aphrodite. But this goddess was very much alive. Smiling devilishly, he watched as the pink blush spread over her body wherever his eyes lingered. There would be plenty of time later to memorize every part of her. To stroke that velvety skin with his hands and mouth.

Taking pity on her obvious embarrassment, he scooped her in his arms and lowered her gently on the bed. Mindful of her innocence, he bent over her, kissing her softly, touching her, quickly rousing her passion again.

Seeing her naked had sapped what was left of his patience. "I want you so badly"—his voice was ragged and uneven—"I don't think I can wait."

"Then don't," she gasped. It was all the invitation he needed.

His drying cloth disappeared. Her eyes fell, then widened.

Understanding her sudden hesitation, Rory lowered his body next to her and whispered, "Don't worry, it will be all right."

"But, how . . ."

Tightly, he thought in answer to her unspoken words. Rory was barely able to resist a lust-filled shudder as he imagined her soft heat closed around him. "It will be all right, Isabel. The first time there's pain, but it will lessen. Trust me."

In answer, she lifted her face to his in guileless invitation. The erstwhile seductress had vanished, replaced by the innocent woman yearning for a fulfillment that only he could give her.

No enticement was necessary. He kissed her again, his mouth moving over hers possessively. He pulled her closer, and the shock of her bare skin pressed against his produced a sensation unlike any he'd ever felt. Hot and sensitive, their bodies merged like molten lava, skin to skin. His hands roamed her body, stoking the fire. Her breasts, her hips, her stomach, the long length of her legs, the delicate curve of the arch of her tiny foot . . . he wanted to touch every inch of her.

She writhed in sweet agony, leaning her hips toward his. He knew what she wanted. He gave it to her. With a soft chuckle of pure masculine pride, his mouth closed over one breast as his hand began its tormentingly slow crawl down her flat stomach. Too aroused for any more teasing, he slid his hand between her legs, finding her already damp with desire.

He increased the pressure on her breast with his mouth as his finger slid inside her, and he began the merciless stroking. He heard her startled gasp when he slid in another finger, stretching her gently. She clenched her thighs around his hand, and her hips began to move in a sensual rhythm.

He watched her head fall back against the pillow, eyes closed, lips parted, the soft, husky panting of her breath urging him on. He found the center of her pulse, and his knowing fingers brought her to the edge of a storming frenzy.

Sweat beaded on his brow. For each minute delayed, the pain of his desire was nearly unbearable. He wanted nothing more than to slide into her silken heat, but something held him back. It was important that she enjoy this as much as he was about to.

He began to trail kisses down her velvet stomach. Bracing her hips with his hands, before she guessed, he moved his mouth between her thighs and nuzzled her softly. Shocked, she bucked and murmured an embarrassed protest, but he held firm. She was deliciously wet, and he couldn't wait to taste her passion.

* * *

Instantly mortified, Isabel could not believe his intimate kiss. But her resistance was futile—like the sun refusing the moon its entry into the evening sky. She couldn't push him away, her body wouldn't let her. The pressure built inside her with each wicked stroke of his tongue. She felt possessed by pleasure, mindless with need. She yearned to move her hips, to clench her thighs around his head and release the exquisite torture. He teased her until she quivered, until she unconsciously pressed against his mouth, wanting more.

"Tell me what you want, Isabel."

She writhed as his tongue flicked out to tease her again.

"Tell me," he ordered, his voice sinfully dark and wicked.

"I want—" Her voice broke. "Like last time."

"You want me to make you come?"

His voice spread an erotic veil around her, freeing her inhibitions. Never could she imagine such intimacy. All modesty vanished in the face of the desperate cravings of her body. "Please," she begged.

He chuckled and buried his face against her. He kissed her harder, as if he couldn't get enough of her. "I love the way you taste, like warm honey." His words drove her wild, but his tongue made her touch heaven. Sensation gripped her, and she felt the desperate climb as the tingling turned into a frantic pulse. Just when she thought she could not take any more, his mouth pressed against her most sensitive spot and sucked. She exploded, pulsing her release against his wicked mouth.

Isabel felt boneless, utterly spent. As contented as a well-fed cat. He read her expression and laughed. "I'm not done with you yet, my sweet. That was just the beginning."

He braced himself above her, lifting his chest and extending his arms, one hand placed on each side of her shoulders.

She opened her eyes, struggling to pierce the haze of passion that had engulfed her. With his body braced above hers, she had a perfect view of his powerful chest. Her hands moved slowly up his arms, caressing the hard muscle under her fingertips. Just touching him roused her passion. She took the time to examine the various scars peppering his torso, tracing them gently with her fingers. He embodied power and virility. Under the shield of his broad, powerful chest, paradoxically both warm and as hard as cold steel, she felt incredibly vulnerable, but completely safe. Power *was* intoxicating, she realized, but not in the way her uncle desired. The raw strength she felt as she explored his body was much more enticing, much more overwhelming. His was a power of protection. She sensed that when he held her in his arms, nothing would ever harm her.

She knew her touch was making him crazy. But she wanted more. Aching to feel him, she reached between them and traced a light trail down the cords of muscle lining his stomach. His body clenched. He seemed unable to move or breathe as her hand slid down his belly. Isabel smiled, enjoying the moment of control.

Slowly, she found him.

This time, no plaid separated the feel of her hand encircling him. She felt his body stiffen as her hand wrapped around the velvety skin of his arousal. Isabel was shocked at the feel of rigid steel surrounded by the softest skin she could imagine. She explored his length with her fingers. Glancing shyly at him from under her long lashes, she was surprised to see his face contorted in pain. His eyes were hooded, his teeth clenched, the hollows beneath his high cheekbones even more pronounced.

"Show me."

She didn't know if he heard her. Then he slowly opened his eyes. "I don't think I can," he whispered tightly.

"Please."

The small entreaty seemed to break him. He taught her to find his rhythm. Fascinated, she watched his face as she brought him to the edge of surrender—astonished by her ability to arouse him. She felt the power in him waiting to explode. A warm feeling of tenderness enveloped her heart as she watched the pleasure of her touch transform his features with unbridled passion. She was the master of this powerful warrior. She held him in her hand. He was hers.

"Enough." He unfurled her fingers from his length. "I cannot wait any longer."

His hand moved between her legs. He eased a finger between her folds and groaned. "Do you see how your body wants me?" He leaned down to kiss her. "You're already wet for me again."

He grabbed her hips and lifted her to him, slowly moving his staff between her legs. He teased her with the thick round head, sliding along her damp opening until heat flooded between her legs. She opened wider, and he eased himself in inch by inch. Her body tensed, instinctively fighting the invasion. He was too big. Too thick. Too much. Sensing her fear, jaw clenched with restraint, he lowered his mouth to her ear and whispered, "Isabel, trust me. It will hurt only for a moment."

And before she could think, he plunged deep inside her, tearing through the web of her innocence.

He covered her cry with his mouth. Isabel stiffened with the pain. She felt as though she'd been ripped in two. She pressed against his chest, trying to push him off her. But he wouldn't budge.

"God, you feel good," he groaned. "Trust me, Isabel. Relax. Feel me in you. Concentrate on my mouth." He kissed her again, wooing her. Teasing her, making her forget, and, finally, easing the pain.

Slowly, she felt her body come alive again. The sensation of him inside her was unlike anything she'd ever imagined. He filled her, claimed part of her that she never knew existed.

He began to move, easing himself in and out. She felt the fever return as the movements quickened. She reached up to grab his shoulders, steadying herself against his hard thrusts. Instinctively, she lifted her hips to meet his masterful strokes.

Isabel was acutely aware of the slow building within her, a building even more intense than before. He pounded harder, faster, deeper. Frantically, she raked her fingers down his back, clutching his rock hard buttocks as she felt it coming closer. And closer. Her pulse contracted. Heart beating rapidly, she clasped her legs around him and let herself go, exploding with a violent release. Shattering into thousands of pieces like shards of broken glass tossed over a cliff.

As she quivered with the contractions of her exploding passion, he clutched her bottom and lifted her hips, driving into her one last time, filling her completely.

Throwing his head back with a roar, he stiffened with his release, spilling his seed deep in her. They clutched each other, rolling on the tide of their shared climax. Where there had been two, there was now one. Joined together in perfect surrender, floating on the crashing waves of heaven's most magnificent ocean.

Rory collapsed on top of her. Neither wanted to break the connection that joined them in the sultry cocoon of the silk-curtained bed. The warm air was thick and damp, burgeoning with the musky scent of spent passion. Still tingling, Isabel felt the waves of passion slowly ebb around him. The fevered pace of her heart began to slow. Her breathing steadied. Finally, with seeming reluctance, Rory rolled off her, gently pulling her naked body close to his. Isabel savored the way their damp bodies slid together—molding perfectly in a delightful tangle of limbs.

A warm, prickly happiness unlike anything she had ever experienced crept through her weary bones. Sighing with contentment, she snuggled closer to the warm strength next to her and closed her eyes. Never had she suspected that such beauty or closeness could exist. She wanted to hold on to this man forever.

But could it last? Refusing to allow any nefarious implications to cloud the blissful moment, she concentrated instead on the steady beat of his heart—lulling her into a wonderfully exhausted and well-sated sleep.

Chapter 16

❖

Isabel woke to the gentle warmth of the morning sun streaming through her window and to Rory awakening her in an altogether different manner. She felt his arousal pressed firmly against her bottom, but this time he did not jump from bed. This time she felt his fingers caress her until her body dampened with desire. Holding her hips, he slid in from behind. Filling her. Wedged between her thighs, he felt even bigger and thicker than before, but rather than cause pain, the sensation took her breath away.

His hands stroked her breasts, lightly circling her nipples, cupping and squeezing her harder as he slowly slid in and out, drawing himself to his full length before quickly sinking back inside.

She felt the tickle of his breath at her ear. "Have I shocked you?" he asked softly, holding her hips tight against him for a moment. He was planted so deeply, he seemed to touch the very heart of her.

"No. Yes. Maybe a little bit," she admitted shyly. "But I like it." She trusted him completely. There was so much that she did not know, Isabel didn't bother being embarrassed or shy. Rory had opened an entirely new sensual world for her, and she wanted to explore every inch of it with him. She made a small sound of pleasure as, still holding her tight, he circled and rocked his hips, stirring her to an erotic frenzy.

"Do you know how long I've ached to do this?" He thrust hard to emphasize his words. "Do you know what torture it was for me not to slide into you when you snuggled your bottom against me this last month?"

"I didn't know," she gasped between slow, deep thrusts.

"There are many things you do not know, my sweet. But I intend to teach you all of them." The sensual promise of his words sent a thrill shooting through her. He nuzzled her neck and kissed the curve of her shoulder. No longer content with lazy strokes, he increased his rhythm, and when he knew she was approaching release, his hand reached around in front of her. With one deft caress of his thumb, Isabel felt herself tremble, shudder, and break apart. He stiffened from behind her, but instead of spilling himself inside her as he'd done last night, he withdrew at the last minute and pulsed his release onto the bedding.

Fighting the haze of delirium, Isabel needed a moment to realize what he'd done. Despite the euphoria of her release, she felt strangely empty. As if he'd deprived her of part of himself. When the rise and fall of his chest slowed and his breathing returned to normal, she turned to him with the question in her eyes.

He took a long look at her and sighed. Clearly, he would rather not have this conversation. "I've taken your innocence, Isabel, but I will not risk getting you with child."

A sharp pain twisted in her chest. To hear his intentions spoken with such brutal honesty after the intimacies they'd just shared knocked the air right out of her.

Emotion burned behind her eyes, and she rolled on her back to hide her disappointment. What had she thought? That he would change his mind just by making love to her? That he would fall in love with her as easily as she had him?

The errant thought stopped her cold.

She loved him. The truth hit her square in the heart with a certainty that could not be denied. After last night, she could no longer pretend, even to herself. She'd fallen hopelessly, deeply in love with her handfast husband. Each time she looked at him, her heart flipped. Each time he smiled, she felt as if the sun were shining just for her. His merest touch set her aflame.

She loved his strength, his honor, his prowess, but most of all the solid, steadying force of his presence. She loved the way this fierce warrior could touch her with such gentleness. She loved the way he made her feel warm and protected, as if nothing could ever harm her.

At Dunvegan, she'd found what she'd spent a lifetime longing for. Rory had given her a family and provided a place for her to feel needed and protected. And he'd given her a new perspective on her own family, making her realize that her perception of her own father's and brothers' feelings might be more complicated than a simple matter of not loving her.

But he would not give her his child.

She should admire his honor and nobility but was instead stung by his ability to think rationally while she was in the throes of newly discovered love. At the most amazing moment of her life, when she'd given him her heart, he'd hit her with the hard truth. Unless she changed his mind, the man she loved would marry another in a little over six months.

"Second thoughts?" he asked softly.

She shook her head, emotion gathering at the back of her throat threatening to spill. She could not allow him to see how much his forthrightness had affected her. Most important, she didn't want to give him any reason to think she would not be content with their arrangement. She knew Rory. He would stop if he realized how much he was hurting her. She pasted a happy smile on her face. "Of course not. I merely did not understand how these things worked."

Rory looked relieved and let the matter drop.

As he took her in his arms again, Isabel fought the rise of panic in her chest. Time was running out. What if her plan did not work? What if he did not fall in love with her? He kissed her with such tenderness that Isabel understood the only thing she could do. She must squeeze every bit of happiness she could out of the next few months, because it might need to last her a lifetime.

Hours later, Rory dragged himself from bed. He could linger no longer, no matter how tempted. His gaze fell on the naked siren on his bed. He dressed quickly and quietly so as not to wake her. The lass deserved her rest.

They'd made love more times than he could count, but still it was not enough. His hunger for her seemed insatiable. Her openness and her uninhibited passion astounded him. This morning when he woke with her soft bottom nestled against his arousal, he'd wickedly done what he'd wanted to do for the past month. He'd thought he would shock her, but she'd welcomed him, returning his eagerness with her own.

How could he defend himself against such a gift?

But something bothered him. He hadn't missed the

flash of pain in her eyes when he'd reminded her of his duty. He didn't want to hurt her, but he also did not want to encourage false hope. If he could find a way to persuade the king to return Trotternish to the MacLeods without Argyll's help, then maybe it would be possible. He'd been racking his brain for another way, and so far nothing had come to him. But he had some time to think, as King James had yet to agree to hear the matter—even with Argyll's support.

Still, Rory wondered whether he'd done the right thing in making love to her. For either of them. The intimacy, the connection between them, was already strong. What would it be like in six months' time? It was only sex, he told himself. But he knew that for the lie it was. What he'd shared with Isabel was unlike anything he'd ever experienced before. Raw, shattering, soul-encompassing sex. Sex that made him lose control and spill his seed inside her. A mistake he'd never made before. Ever.

He slipped out of the room and headed down the winding stairs, making his way outside and down the path to the old keep. His men would be waiting for him. He'd just entered the hall when his brother caught his eye.

"Sleep well?" Alex asked innocently.

Rory frowned. "It's none of your damn business. Where are Douglas and Colin?"

"Waiting for you in the private dining room."

He followed Rory into the small room behind the great hall. With Alex recovered, they'd gathered to discuss the threat of attack by the Mackenzies.

His guardsmen rose as he entered. Another of the king's damn restrictions, Rory thought. Limiting the number of his household men. Colin stepped forward with a letter in his hand. "It arrived only this morning," he explained. "I did not think you wished to be disturbed."

Apparently, the entire castle was aware of what had transpired last night. If Colin had an opinion on the matter, he kept it well hidden. Like Rory's other men, he would never question his chief.

Rory nodded, flipped over the parchment, and recognized Argyll's seal. *Damn.* He opened the missive and read. It was the news he'd been waiting for. News that should make him happy. Instead, he felt the noose of duty closing around him. Argyll wrote that the next time the MacLeod presented himself at court, the king would agree to hear the matter of Trotternish. Isabel was slipping through his fingers. He related the contents to his men, and they all fell silent.

Finally, Alex asked the question they all were thinking. "You will still repudiate the handfast?"

Rory smothered the almost visceral response to deny. Instead he said, "Aye. It is necessary. Argyll has proved his sway with the king by getting him to agree to hear the matter at all—something James has previously refused to do. With the Mackenzie supporting Sleat's claim, we need Argyll's influence."

"If only there was another way to make James see Sleat for the overreaching tyrant that he is," Alex said.

Rory smiled at his brother who was so infuriated on his behalf. "Be assured, if there is another way, I will find it."

He put aside the disturbing emotions evoked by the contents of Argyll's letter, and returned to the discussion for which they'd gathered—defending against an attack by the Mackenzies. Rory didn't want any more surprises. The Mackenzies' boldness in attacking so close to the castle concerned him. Alex relayed the events of the attack as he'd done earlier, including the conversation between Isabel and Murdock Mackenzie. Something Alex said stopped Rory cold.

"You're sure?" Rory asked.

Alex nodded. "I was in and out of consciousness, but Murdock knew that you had delayed your stay in Edinburgh with Argyll."

Rory felt a flicker of unease. How the Mackenzies knew of his plans bothered him. He'd purposefully kept his stay with Argyll quiet.

Rory thought for a moment, his eye catching Argyll's letter on the table. Suddenly, he recalled another letter, one received by his bride only yesterday. He'd realized just how much he'd grown to trust her when Sleat's letter yesterday caused barely a flicker of unease.

Rory held his face impassive. "Did my bride send any letters while I was gone?"

The men looked distinctly uncomfortable. Douglas answered. "Only one. To her father, Glengarry."

"I'm sure it was a coincidence," Alex said, jumping to Isabel's defense.

Rory didn't believe in coincidences, but for her sake, he hoped it was.

"The lass is a MacDonald. Can we trust her?" Douglas asked the question Rory did not want to voice himself.

Rory thought for a moment. The memories of last night assailed him. He thought of the woman who'd given herself to him freely and without conditions. He thought of the contentment he'd known while holding her in his arms, the strange sense of peace that had settled over him. He thought of her kindness to Margaret, her radiant charm, her loneliness, and the happiness she'd found at Dunvegan. If not in his mind, Rory knew the answer in his heart.

"Aye, I trust her."

But if he ever found out she'd deceived him, her loss of innocence would be the least of her problems.

Chapter 17

❖

As the yule celebration gave way to Hogmanay, and winter faded into spring, Isabel kept her vow to squeeze every bit of happiness she could out of her time at Dunvegan with Rory. They made love every day except . . . Isabel sighed wistfully, recalling the day a couple of weeks after Christmas when she'd gotten her flux. Though she did not want a child without a husband, she felt strangely disappointed. And hurt by Rory's visible relief—relief she understood, but which pained her nonetheless.

At times, Isabel felt her new plan was working and that Rory had begun to love her. Alone at night, cradled in his arms, she believed nothing could ever come between them. At meals, or over the long hours spent planning the festivities for the Highland games, he would laugh and tease her as if she were part of the family. And occasionally, she would catch him looking at her with something akin to tenderness in his eyes.

But other times, she was not so sure. He had not discussed a change of intent or broached the subject of their handfast at all. She wanted to believe he'd reconsidered, but any casual reference that she made to a future beyond July was ignored or met with an uncomfortable smile and a swift change of subject. And then there was that odd conversation about the letter she'd written to her father. He'd seemed to think she might have told her father something of import, but what? He'd started to question her, but her answers had seemed to satisfy him and he'd dropped the subject.

There were so many times Isabel wanted to declare her love. But the knowledge that her words would only cause him discomfort, and perhaps even guilt, held her back. She wanted honesty between them more than she wanted anything else, but until she secured an alternative to the alliance with Argyll, she dared not risk it. Nor could she risk upsetting the delicate balance they'd fought so hard to achieve.

Time slipped away too quickly. Especially the nights. Her cheeks reddened. And sometimes the days, she thought, recalling the fragrant, downy meadow of heather. A few weeks into March, Rory had finally relented and allowed her to spend a day outside the castle walls. Little did she know that behind his acquiescence lay an ulterior motive. Making love outside had been an entirely new experience for her. She smiled. Rory had kept his word to teach her much, and Isabel had proved an apt, and attentive, pupil. So much had changed since that wild, passion-filled night before Christmas. Gone was the nervous virgin, replaced by a confident, sensual woman. A confident, sexually adventuresome woman.

When she wasn't occupied tumbling through meadows of heather, Isabel kept herself busy with the accounts and organizing the festivities for the Highland gathering and, much to her delight, a wedding. Since Margaret had pointed it out to her those many months ago, Isabel had noticed Robert's blatant interest in Bessie. Nevertheless, she was surprised when Bessie

came to her with the news of her proposal. She was
overjoyed for her dear nurse, but Isabel would miss her
terribly if Rory repudiated the handfast.

She was painfully aware that only three months remained in their handfast period. With the Highland gathering fast approaching, Isabel would be forced to see her
family and report her progress. She hoped to broach the
subject to her father about shifting alliances.

But today, Isabel's mind was turned to other matters.
After much anxious preparation, the day of Bessie's
wedding had finally arrived. Following the small ceremony, long tables and benches had been set up in the
courtyard for the celebration to take advantage of the
favorable weather. Isabel knew she wasn't the only one
tired of being cooped up in the castle.

Standing in the crowded courtyard, she leisurely
swept her eyes over the scenic vistas surrounding her.
She inhaled the fresh breath of spring that was in evidence all around. The lemon yellow sun hung all alone
in its azure frame, its extreme brightness seeming to defy
heavenly competition. The sea rolled and glistened, its
turquoise waters unusually clear and vivid. Behind her,
the landscape seemed to turn more colorful by the moment, the forests flourishing green, the horsetail standing proud on the heathered hillsides, the purple thrift
and yellow iris blanketing the coastal cliffs. A lazy
breeze tickled the rustling leaves and gently cleared
away the vestiges of winter dankness.

Spring had certainly arrived.

Lost in thought, Isabel didn't notice when Margaret
moved to stand beside her. " 'Tis a beautiful day for a
wedding," she said.

She grinned at Margaret. "It's absolutely perfect."

Isabel couldn't have asked for a more fitting stage for this special occasion. She and Margaret had worked tirelessly in preparation, with very little time. She shook her head with bemused chagrin, only two weeks to plan a wedding as important as this. Bessie had complained that she was far too old to wait any longer; she didn't want to give Robert time to change his mind.

Isabel's gaze fell on her beloved nurse. Her heart swelled with pride as she watched the beaming bride and groom greet their guests. "I'll miss her." Isabel didn't realize she'd spoken her thoughts aloud.

She felt Margaret's sympathy as surely as if she'd put her arms around her. Margaret knew Isabel had not told Bessie of Rory's plan to repudiate the handfast. Only those closest to Rory knew of his intentions: Alex, Margaret, and Rory's guardsmen. Fortunately, Bessie's curiosity had waned after Rory had made Isabel a bride in truth.

"Bessie will always belong to you. She loves you as if you were her own child."

"For so many years, she was all I had."

"I know."

Margaret didn't need to say more. Isabel knew she understood. Margaret was the best friend Isabel had ever had; she knew her almost as well as Isabel knew herself.

Almost. There was one thing they never spoke of directly: Rory's plan to send her back and repudiate the handfast. It was a subject too painful for them both.

"Enough of these maudlin thoughts. This is a day for celebration. By the way, where is your Viking?" She expected that Margaret would also have some happy news soon. The Viking's interest in her was as plain as the per-

petual scowl on his face. And Isabel's secret plan for
Margaret was about to be divulged.

It was Margaret's turn to blush. "He's not *my*
Viking," she said primly.

Isabel raised an eyebrow. "He's not?"

"Well, at least not in so many words."

"I suspect that will change soon."

Margaret was saved from replying by the arrival of
her brother.

Rory made a sweeping motion with his hand. "Is
everything as you wished, Isabel? I see even the weather
has followed your directives."

"Oh, Rory, it's perfect. Thank you so much for making this such a special day for Bessie. It has meant so
much to her, and to me."

Rory grinned broadly. "I'm glad you are well pleased.
Between planning a wedding and planning for the gathering, you have not had much time to rest."

He was so irresistibly handsome and charming, the
thought flashed through her mind for perhaps only the
hundredth time. His hair glimmered more golden than
brown in the bright sunlight. So tall and muscular, he
looked like a bronzed god. That this man belonged to
her was overwhelming. She loved him beyond measure.

Still, she frowned. "That reminds me, I'd almost forgotten something I meant to do today for the gathering.
The clans will start to arrive in a few days, and I have
not yet checked to make sure we have enough space to
stable all the horses in the village."

Rory interrupted her. "Not today, Isabel. Today you
will enjoy this wedding that you and Margaret have
worked so hard on. It's almost time for the dancing to
begin, and I'll not let you go." To demonstrate, he

twirled her around in the air as if she weighed no more than a bairn.

"Put me down right now, Rory MacLeod!" She laughed, banging on his arms for release. "I have work to do. I will make you regret this high-handedness."

Watching him now, so playful, Isabel was struck by just how much he'd changed in the past few months. He was lighter, happier. She wanted desperately to believe that she was the cause of the change.

"Promise?" He smiled wickedly.

"I promise," she whispered breathlessly. Locked in the blue twinkling of his eyes, she felt her heart flutter at the sensuous promise lacing his words.

"Leave be, you two." Margaret giggled. "Please try to refrain from discussing your private bedroom exploits before my innocent, burning ears."

Rory dropped his head and pressed a light kiss on Isabel's parted lips before releasing her. "Oh, very well, Margaret. I never knew you were such a tight-laced prude. I'll have to warn Colin to temper any illicit advances he has planned."

"I'm sure I don't know to what you are referring, brother," Margaret said primly, hands on her hips.

"Don't you? Hmm. We'll see."

Isabel still loved to stand witness to their lighthearted sibling teasing.

"Do you know something, Rory? What are you not telling me?" Margaret narrowed her eye threateningly at her much larger brother, looking as though she might attack.

"Patience, Margaret. You always were a demanding little brat."

"How dare you, Rory MacLeod! Brat, was I? You'll

regret those words." She pounced on him, beating his arms with her tiny fists where Isabel had left off.

"Margaret, you should not punch the chief. It's not seemly," Colin interrupted.

Speak of the devil, Isabel thought. Another booming, proud voice of authority—how many could this castle possibly hold? She smiled at the handsome Viking. Even when he was teasing, Colin frowned forebodingly. Well, Margaret cared for him, and that was all that mattered.

"I was not punching the chief, Colin. I was merely reminding my brother that I am no longer a bairn."

"Ouch. I'll try to remember that in the future, Margaret," Rory said, holding his arm. "You've a heavy fist for such a wee lass."

Isabel turned to Rory, clasping her hands together with excitement. "Before the dancing begins, Margaret and I have one more surprise for this day of celebration. Are you ready, Margaret?"

Margaret glanced at Colin as if she were going to be ill, then drew up her shoulders with forced confidence. "I think so, yes."

Isabel motioned to Rory, Colin, and Alex, who had just walked up. "You stay right here. We'll be right back."

"What are those two up to this time?" Alex asked, confused.

Rory looked at the two men next to him and shook his head. "I can't even hazard a guess. But we better do as we were told. Margaret looked quite serious. For a moment, I thought she seemed almost frightened." His gaze fell back to the Fairy Tower, where Isabel and Margaret had just disappeared inside.

Moments later, he was the only one facing them when they alighted from the tower. He blinked in disbelief, then reached up to shield his eyes from the sun. It was not an apparition. His heart stalled. All he could think to say was, "Dear God in heaven. How did she do it?"

"Do what?" Colin and Alex asked in unison before they turned to follow Rory's gaze.

Three men stood stunned as the women came toward them. Others around them began to realize that something important was happening, and as quick as summer fire, an unnatural silence spread through the crowd.

Silence, before the dam burst and a resounding cheer pierced the air.

With his long stride, Rory reached Margaret first. Tentatively, as if she could not be real, he placed his hand on her cheek. His fingers brushed the now empty place where the monstrous patch had once covered his sister's injured eye. A thin, star-shaped white scar trailed from the inner corner of her eyelid up to the brow. Although he knew she had lost the vision in her eye, it was impossible to tell from looking at her. Two round sapphire blue eyes sparkled directly into his. His throat tightened as he let the shock filter through his body. Margaret was just as bonny as he remembered. The scar in no way detracted from her beauty. It was barely noticeable.

He turned to Isabel and asked in a voice rough with emotion, "How did you do it?"

"All Margaret needed was a wee bit of encouragement"—she laughed—"and a looking glass. I just convinced her that what was under the patch was not nearly as terrible as what hid it. The rest was up to Margaret."

Colin descended upon them and ignobly pushed his chief to the side. He reached for Margaret's hand and raised it to his lips reverently. His gaze locked with hers. "What fairy spell is this? I had never thought . . . Margaret, you are even more beautiful than I remember you before the accident." His hushed voice was full of admiration.

He said it with such sincerity that Isabel knew Margaret could not doubt his words. She smiled shyly but proudly. "Thank you, Colin. I assure you there is no fairy magic, but only my stubborn sister to blame. Isabel has badgered me for months to remove the patch and show her the scar. That first step proved the most difficult. I haven't looked in a mirror for years, so even I was surprised to see how much the scars had faded. 'Tis not nearly as bad as I remember. I must admit, I was very nervous just now to see your reaction. I've been wearing that horrible patch for so long."

Isabel watched with amusement as the corners of Colin's lips lifted up in what could only be described as a smile. *Inconceivable,* she thought, now *there* is a true bit of fairy magic.

Alex interrupted to lift Margaret in a great hug, her feet dangling in the air. "I hate to think what this will mean for your archery skills. I fear I have lost my only advantage," he teased. "As you will not be needing it any longer, perhaps I can borrow your patch and try my luck?"

Margaret leaned her head back and laughed. "Alex MacLeod, you are incorrigible. It is yours, I have need of it no longer."

Rory was overwhelmed.

He thought Isabel could not surprise him, but she

had. He had learned so much these past few months. Not just the feel of her skin melting against his or the erotic sensation of himself rock hard deep inside her; no, he had learned much more. It was not just lust that propelled him to her over and over. He'd been a fool to think once would be enough. With Isabel, a thousand times would not be enough—he should know. He'd come to care for her more than he had ever thought possible, more than he had ever cared for another person.

Over the last few months, Rory had taken pleasure in discovering all the little things that made Isabel unique. He knew that she crinkled one side of her nose when she was displeased, that she twirled her hair when she was anxious, that if she said "as you wish," he was in trouble. He'd learned that she was truly interested in the business side of the castle, enthusiastically suggesting improvements in efficiency. He'd come to respect her mind, finding pleasure simply in her company.

What was so special about her? Undoubtedly, he was attracted to her beautiful face, but there was so much more. She was kind, charmingly stubborn, quick-witted, and spirited. The vulnerability and loneliness he'd noticed on her arrival had faded.

She made love with such openness and sharing, it humbled him.

Moreover, Isabel had helped him realize that by his unrelenting focus on duty, he'd lost sight of what else was important. His family. Rory's quest for revenge had the unintentional consequence of prolonging his sister's shame. And his reluctance to cede control of his duties had prevented Alex from forgiving himself for his losses on the battlefield. He'd begun to delegate more to Alex, and already Rory noticed that Alex seemed to thrive on the responsibility. For the first time since he'd become chief, Rory was beginning to relax.

Isabel had brought laughter back to Dunvegan.

She'd given him so much, but still he could not give her what he knew she wanted. He'd purposely kept a tight rein on his growing affection over the past few months, not wanting to give her false hope. He knew how much his reluctance to talk about the future pained her. He wanted to reassure her, but how could he when he couldn't reassure himself?

Thus far, his attempts to find alternative means to sway the king had proved fruitless. He was no closer today than he was that first night to finding a way to avoid the alliance with Argyll. But how could he send her away? With each day that passed, their attachment deepened.

If there was a way to hold on to her, he would find it.

He reached for Isabel and pulled her against him without care for such a public display. His fingers found her chin and tilted up her face so that she could look straight into his eyes. "Isabel, I don't know what to say." He paused, at a loss how to put to words what he felt. "You have given me the greatest gift. You have returned my sister. Completely. You have my eternal gratitude and devotion."

He dropped his head, his lips finding hers in a gentle caress. Oblivious to the crowd surrounding them, Rory tightened his hold, pressing his body close to her curves, seeking that perfect fit he knew would mold them together. It was so much better naked, skin to skin, but this would have to do—for now.

His chest swelled to bursting even as he touched the softness of her lips beneath his. How he loved to taste her. His mouth moved over hers in a seductive dance. Her lips parted, and he slid his tongue deep in her mouth, savoring her sweetness. His fingers stroked the ivory smoothness of her cheek. *She is so soft and desirable,* he thought. He felt the instinctive press of her hips against his heavy loins and knew he had to stop.

Regretfully, he lifted his head and said hoarsely, "We will finish this later." He fought to control his immediate response to her, yet still he stiffened like a lad with the merest touch. As much as he'd like to toss her over his shoulder and take her upstairs like one of his pillaging ancestors, it would have to wait. There was a wedding feast to be had.

And later, they would share their own private celebration.

Chapter 18

❖

A short two weeks later, Isabel stood beside Rory at the top of the sea-gate stairs, welcoming the clans gathering at Dunvegan for the noontide feast to launch the Highland gathering. Gowned in a simple but elegant yellow silk day dress, Isabel felt every inch the proud lady of the castle. Only the anxious twisting of her hands betrayed her nervousness at confronting her family for the first time in over nine months.

The castle itself was bustling with energy and excitement. The lilting notes of the pipes beckoned the ear while the tantalizing aroma of roasted meat beguiled the nose. The Highlanders swarming the castle reacted with the expected exuberance: When not feuding, feasting and gaming were undoubtedly what a Highland warrior loved best. Most of the clans had arrived earlier and were already enthusiastically partaking of the renowned MacLeod hospitality in the great hall. If she listened closely, Isabel would undoubtedly hear the clanking sound of flagons slamming on the tables, demanding replenishment.

Amid the celebrating, her heart beat nervously as she watched her family slowly make their way up the sea-gate stairs.

They had arrived.

She fought to control the steady stream of high notes in her voice betraying her nervousness. "Welcome to Dunvegan, Father, Uncle. I trust your journey was uneventful."

"Quite uneventful, Isabel. It is an uncommonly pleasant spring. You look well. Your time at Dunvegan has agreed with you?" Her father kissed her cheek politely, his gaze flickering pointedly over Rory's hand resting possessively at her waist.

"Very well, Father," she murmured, stifling the joy that rose unbidden to her face by looking down at the tips of her yellow slipper-clad feet, lest her emotions be displayed for all to see. She hoped she was imagining her uncle's glare fixed on her pink cheeks.

No such luck.

"You look *very* well, niece—such a becoming rosiness to your cheeks. I feared, from the one short note that I received from you, to find you exhausted from the many tasks that keep you so well occupied. Glengarry and I have been quite concerned about you, yet here you are obviously thriving in your new home. And from the satisfied look of MacLeod here, it appears that your handfast agrees with you both. Such an inspired custom is handfasting, having a year and a day to decide whether a permanent arrangement is desirable. Never know what can happen in a year." He paused dramatically.

Isabel fought to control her temper at the slight to Margaret. Rory dropped his hand from her waist. With a surreptitious peep from beneath her lashes, she detected the inflexibility in his square jaw and the slight muscle twitch on his lower cheek, nearly imperceptible signs of anger that she would not have noticed nine months ago. Isabel knew him well enough now to realize that he itched to attack Sleat for his crass reminder, but Rory would never snap at bait dangled by her uncle.

Instead of the anger Sleat sought, Rory smiled. "I believe my sister made a similar observation just the other day. Though she did remark how long a year could drag on."

Sleat's face turned red as he took Rory's meaning. Isabel fought the urge to giggle. Sleat turned to her with a sharp look. "I trust you have *found* everything you were searching for here at Dunvegan, Isabel?"

His emphasis was not lost on her. So much for biding his time and waiting until they were alone. Obviously, Sleat was not fooled by the short note she sent him with the invitation, pretending not to understand his request for a detailed report. "I find *everything* much to my liking, Uncle." She glanced meaningfully to Rory. "I'm sorry to have worried you, but I have been quite busy the last few months with my duties at the castle and organizing the gathering. I'm sure over the next few days I will have plenty of time to allay your concerns."

"I'm most anxious to hear all that you have to say. Let us not delay our little reunion for too long."

Thankfully, further conversation between Rory and Sleat was prevented by the boisterous arrival of her brothers.

"Good to see you, Bel, I've missed you." Ian smiled warmly and swallowed her in a firm brotherly hug.

At only three and twenty, Ian already possessed the formidable height—without the awesome bulk—of their uncle. Each of her brothers was exceptionally handsome, but there was something special about Ian. Of the three, Isabel supposed he most resembled her, albeit a large emerald-eyed version of herself. Their hair was a similar shade, though his was streaked with a wee bit more golden blond than red from the extended periods of time he spent in the sun. His features, although masculine, were classic in their perfection. Fortunately, he was saved from true beauty by a square-clefted chin and a thin puckered scar that ran down the side of his slightly crooked nose. A warrior's mark that if anything only added to his rugged appeal.

Isabel was taken aback by the genuine emotion she detected behind the undeniable roguish charm. Had he really missed her? Was Rory correct? Had she misread her family's inattention? Hope soared unfettered in her heart. She'd found the respect and sense of belonging she'd dreamed of her whole life with the MacLeods; perhaps she could find some semblance of closeness with her father and brothers.

"I've missed you as well, Ian, missed all of you. We've much to discuss, but that will have to wait until after the feast. Come, let's join the celebration in the great hall." Noticing the eager faces of her carousing brothers, she chided teasingly, "But have care with the MacLeod *cuirm*—if you wish to compete at your best tomorrow."

Laughing at the mock affront in her brothers' expressions at the slur on their ability to hold their drink, she turned and started toward the great hall, Ian on one side of her and Rory on the other.

"I trust MacLeod hasn't decided to permit lasses to participate in the trials this year, Bel. Or maybe he's discovered that the MacLeods would be unbeatable in the archery competition with you on their side?"

Isabel basked in Ian's playful compliment. "Ah, but you should see Rory's sister Margaret—of late, her skill surpasses mine."

"You jest. I did not think you could be beaten." Glancing at Rory, he quipped, "You never know when having a sister skilled with a bow may come in handy."

Startled, Isabel fixed her eyes firmly on his face, but he would not meet her curious gaze. Was that just an innocuous comment, or was he outright acknowledging the arrow that saved his life? Isabel felt a warm burst of surprise and pride.

Ian paused and considered something for a moment, then asked Isabel hesitantly, "But what of Margaret's injury? Does that not interfere with her ability to use the bow?"

Isabel shook her head. "Margaret has an extraordinary natural ability for archery. It is sometimes a challenge for her to gauge the depth, but for the most part she is able to compensate for the loss of vision in that eye." Unable to resist looking at Sleat with a triumphant smile, she added, "I think you will all find Margaret very changed."

Rory seemed tempted to say something, but they had reached the hall and the opportunity for conversation was lost by the overwhelming din of the celebratory feast inside.

By late afternoon of the next day, Isabel was wishing she had followed her own sage advice. In a mistaken attempt to assuage the tension she was feeling from the disrupting presence of her family in the midst of her fool's paradise, she'd imbibed too freely of the *cuirm* and was now suffering the consequences of a blaring headache. But the games were far too entertaining to retreat to the quiet sanctuary of her chambers to rest off the lingering effects of the drink. Besides, watching Rory compete in the various trials of strength and skill made her heart race like an excited girl.

Not surprisingly, the MacLeods, in large part because of Rory, were leading early in the competition. This morning, Rory had easily defeated the field in the swimming competition held in the loch, not an unexpected result given that he'd grown up swimming in those crystalline waters. He'd come in second, barely, in the steep hill foot race behind Alex, who'd then good-naturedly spent the better part of the day teasing him unmercifully for being an "old man."

Isabel eagerly looked forward to the stone toss and the dance competition that were to be held later that afternoon. Tomorrow, the wrestling, leaping, and throwing of the blacksmith's forge were scheduled. But the final day of competition would see her favorite events: the tossing of the great tree trunk and the archery contest. Of all the events, Isabel thought the "caber toss" the most remarkable. A great tree trunk was tapered and cut to a height of about eighteen feet. The warrior ran with the caber balanced against his body, then tossed the trunk, hoping that it would flip end over end to land in a straight line. This was a trial of great strength, but it also required tremendous precision and accuracy. Likely the caber toss trial developed as a result of the Highlander's penchant for novel methods of breaching enemy defenses.

A quick perusal of the happy faces of the clansmen around her produced a satisfied smile. All in all, the gathering was proceeding quite well, even with the arrival this morning of Clan Mackenzie. Her duty of hospitality aside, she was grateful they had missed the feast last night. She had been able to avoid confronting the

Mackenzie chief, the father of Murdock, who was killed by Rory not too far from the clearing where the clansmen were now gathered for the stone toss.

"Enjoying the competition, niece? Your handfast husband is putting on quite a display."

Ouch, the pain in her head just got much worse. Isabel looked around for a graceful means of escape. No luck. Sleat had cornered her in a perfect spot for private conversation. Undoubtedly, he'd patiently bided his time for just such an opportune moment. Thanks to her pounding headache, Isabel had lingered in the shade on the edge of the forest a short distance away from the contestants and other spectators.

Taking a deep breath to bolster her confidence for the harrowing conversation that was sure to come, she ignored his scornful tone and replied, " 'Tis hardly unexpected. The renowned strength and skill of Rory Mor are legendary throughout the Highlands. And of course, the MacLeods are heavily favored this year, as they've won the last two gatherings in a row. But I think you do not wish to discuss games, Uncle."

He raised a brow, surprised by her directness. Lowering his voice, he issued a reprimand in the clipped timbre of a verbal slap. "No, I do not want to discuss the games. I want to know why you have not seen fit to communicate your progress in locating a secret entrance or the flag." He grabbed her arm, as he was wont to do, his fingers pressing into the soft flesh. "I want to know why you have forsaken your duty to your clan."

Her uncle's words were a bitter reminder of her precariously wrought happiness. Guilt swept over her, descending on her conscience like a dark cloud snuffing out the flaming sun. But she reminded herself that if her plan was successful, she would not fail in her duty to her clan. She refused to contemplate what she would do if it didn't work. She tried to shrug off his hold, but he held firm. She lifted her chin defiantly. "I've not forsaken my clan."

"Have you found the entrance or the Fairy Flag?" he asked skeptically.

"No," she admitted.

He lowered his head, locking his cold, unblinking eyes on hers. "Or perhaps you have found it and have decided not to tell me where it is. Do not take me for a fool, Isabel MacDonald. Anyone can see the way you are traipsing about after the MacLeod like an adoring pup. Stupid chit! You have fallen in love with your husband. He was supposed to fall in love with *you*." His blotched face turned crimson with rage.

She stepped back, instinctively retreating from the danger posed by her belligerent uncle. His contorted features, unappealing at best, were positively ugly. "No, you are wrong. I have not found the flag or an entrance, Uncle." Though he was right about the rest. Forcing herself not to flinch, she drew on all the reserves of her pride to hold her back straight and not cower before him.

"You had better hope you find them soon. The only thing keeping the Mackenzies from Strome Castle is my forbearance. Do not deceive yourself. Without my help, your clan will suffer. Badly. And people will die. Ask the Mackenzie how easy it is to lose a son."

Isabel blanched, and her blood ran cold. She forced back the guilt. Her brothers would not lose their lives and her clan would not need to suffer, not if she could convince Rory. Sleat was only trying to scare her with his threats. Never mind that it was effective. "I know well the dire situation of our clan, you need not remind me."

Sleat studied her with a calculating glare. "Yet I do not sense the urgency in your actions. Is he in love with you?"

"I don't know."

"Has the MacLeod spoken of marriage?"

"No."

His eyes narrowed. "Does he suspect you?"

"Of course not. I've been very careful." She tried to move farther away from him. But his hand was still gripping her arm, and he used his hold to propel her forcefully back toward him.

"I am not finished with you, Isabel. I won't be finished with you until you have found what you came here for. Do you comprehend the importance of this mission—the importance of what you were sent here to do? I refuse to allow the future prominence of the MacDonalds in the Isles to be compromised by the whimsical heartstrings of a mere lass. There is far too much at stake. Look over there—" He motioned to the clearing. "See how your husband converses so intimately with Argyll, our clan's most vile enemy. Since the dissolution of the Lordship, Argyll has usurped *our* power in western Scotland. Soon, Argyll and his Campbell clan will be nearly as powerful as the king. We must act now, reclaim our Gaelic heritage for the MacDonalds, before it is too late. You will do what you were sent to do, or you will live to regret your foolish decision." The corners of his mouth lifted in a sinister, yellow sneer. "Perhaps MacLeod would be interested to learn of your traitorous purpose here?" He laughed cruelly at her expression of horror. "I wonder what your adoring husband will make of your explanation—do you think he will forgive you for deceiving him? For spying on him?"

No! You can't tell Rory. Panic gripped her, choking her ability to think rationally. Would Rory understand that she'd had no choice? Would it be enough that she had changed her mind? Could she take the chance? She intended to confess when the time was right—when she could be sure of his affections and had all the parts of her plan in place—but the truth coming from her uncle would be disastrous. She should have anticipated that her uncle would not let her get away without a fight.

"The MacLeod is a proud man," Sleat taunted. "How will he react to having been duped by a MacDonald lass? At my bidding."

Isabel forced a nonchalance to her expression that belied the fierce pounding of her heart. "But if you tell him now, you lose all chance of my finding the flag and an entrance, if it exists. I do still have two and a half months left in the handfast period." Ten weeks to find a solution, and then she could confess all to Rory—before her uncle.

He scowled at her as if he gleaned her true purpose for delay and wanted to refuse, but then he gave a curt nod. "Very well, dear niece," he said, smiling grimly. "But as you now seem to be a reluctant spy in our family endeavor, we shall have a new codicil to our original arrangement. Bring me what I want within ten weeks and I will not tell the MacLeod the true purpose behind your handfast. Fate will decide the future of your marriage, as it will the future of the MacLeods. But if you fail, your handfast husband will learn your little secret."

Isabel lost all pretense of composure. "You can't even be sure there is a secret entrance. And what if I cannot find the flag by then? It must be well hidden. You can't force me to find something that doesn't exist or is impossible to find."

" 'Tis not my problem. Where you fail, others may succeed."

"What do you mean?"

"It is not your concern. You should be concerned only with what you were handfasted to do. When you are ready, send me a letter; my man will find you. Do not think to trick me. My man is familiar with the flag." He turned on his heel, abandoning her to the agony of her own introspection.

What am I going to do? Panic squeezed her chest. She'd thought she would have time to work it all out. But if her uncle told Rory, it would ruin everything. Now she had to find a way to satisfy her uncle, until she had convinced Rory not to repudiate the handfast and to support her father in the feud with the Mackenzies. But what if it didn't work?

It had to work.

But in her heart she knew she could not betray Rory, whether he loved her or not. It was a staggering realization. Would her family ever forgive her failure?

Tears of frustration built behind her eyes and threatened to burst. She wanted to fall to her knees and bow her head in despair but knew she could not risk Rory finding her in such a state. There would be too many questions. Questions she dared not answer.

A sudden rustling noise behind a tree caught her attention, distracting her from the tumultuous quandary of her horrible predicament. She held her breath and stared at the space. Minutes passed before she dared exhale. She could see nothing out of the ordinary, and so returned to the agony of her own burdens.

But her uncle's words came back to her. Was someone watching her? Had her uncle hid another spy in their midst?

Rory watched Isabel's conversation with her uncle with marked interest and growing unease. Isabel would never betray him. Of that he was certain. She cared for him and his family. No one could be that accomplished an actor. But something else was at work. He didn't like the way Sleat was talking to her; he seemed to be threatening her. When Sleat grabbed her arm, Rory decided he'd waited long enough.

It was well past time he found out what hold her uncle had on her.

He approached the edge of the clearing, where she stood under a canopy of trees. "Are you well, Isabel?"

She startled, her eyes jumping to his face. "I'm fine," she said too quickly. "It's too warm in the sun, that's all." She tried to smile, but it faltered.

He picked up a small yellow flower, broke off the stem, and tucked it behind her ear. His mind immediately flew to another time when he'd tucked flowers behind her ear. The day he'd taken her outside the castle walls and they'd made love on the hillside of heather. If only he could stall time. He caressed her wan cheek with the back of his finger. "I noticed you speaking with your uncle."

If he hadn't been touching her, he might not have noticed her slight flinch. "Yes."

"He appeared to be angry with you."

"Yes."

Rory dropped his hand and unconsciously clenched his fists. "If he is threatening you, I will—"

She stopped him with a small hand on his arm. "It's nothing like that."

But something was clearly bothering her. She was hiding something from him, but what? He couldn't help her if she continued to be evasive. "Will you not tell me, Isabel?" he asked, more gently this time.

She turned away, almost as if she didn't want to look at him. "He merely sought assurance that our handfast would be formalized into marriage." She paused, giving him an opportunity to speak. "Assurance I could not provide."

He felt the sting of her accusation, but he could not argue. "Your uncle seems to take an unusual interest in our handfast."

Her eyes flashed. "Shouldn't he?" she challenged. " 'Tis because of him that I am here. And isn't it our handfast that is forestalling the feud?"

She was right, but Rory wondered if that was Sleat's only interest. "Did you tell him?" The words knotted in his mouth, but Isabel understood.

"No. I did not tell him you intend to repudiate the handfast. He'll find out soon enough."

Rory hated this feeling. He wanted to be able to wipe away her hurt. And his own. But he couldn't, not until he had a reason to. Instead he cupped her chin. "Your uncle is plotting something, and I do not trust him." He hated to ask her, but it had to be said. "I want to trust you, but you are making it difficult. Is there a reason I shouldn't?"

Her eyes brimmed with tears, and her voice quivered. "You can ask me that after all that we have shared? Have I not given you my body, my soul, asking nothing in return? Not even the promise of your name."

Her words burned a hole in his chest. "I know what you have given me, Isabel. I treasure it, but I warned you how it must be. It is my duty as chief to ask," he said gravely. "Just as it would be my duty to punish anyone who betrays me."

"Don't you know that I could never . . ." She stared at him, tears streaming down her cheeks. "Don't you know?"

He didn't. "Know what?"

His question seemed to unleash something inside her. As if all the tension and pent-up emotion that had been simmering beneath the surface between them finally boiled over. "Don't you know how badly I wish that you would change your mind, how I wish that things were different, how I would love nothing more than to stay here with you forever? How I can't bear the thought that you intend to marry someone else—" Her voice strangled in her throat. "To share your bed with another woman."

His chest constricted; her pain was his own. "Isabel—"

He moved toward her, but she stepped away. "No, let me finish. You started this, now you will hear what I've wanted to say for some time but was too scared to for fear you would not want to hear it." Her shoulders were shaking, but he dared not offer her comfort. "I'll not hide my feelings any longer, even if it is easier to pretend they do not exist." She took a deep breath. "I love you, Rory MacLeod, with all my heart, and I'll not be sorry about it."

He stilled, the impact of her words reverberating through him. *She loved him.* And though he knew he shouldn't be, deep inside he was happy for it. More than happy. Her words touched a part of him he hadn't realized existed. Selfishly, he wanted her love. He wanted to hold on to her and claim her for his own.

But her declaration had only further complicated an already difficult situation. Perhaps he'd known this would happen. Had wanted to protect against it. He never should have made love with her. Yet he could not regret it, though he did regret hurting her. She was right, he didn't want to have this conversation.

He wiped a tear from the corner of her eye with his thumb. "Oh, lass."

"Have you nothing else to say?" she asked plaintively.

Something hot lodged in his chest. But what could he say? Words that would only make parting more difficult? "I am honored, though it would be better if you didn't."

Isabel flinched. He wanted to reach out to her, but he knew if he did, he might say something he would regret. He knew how dangerously close he was to giving her what she wanted. When she looked at him, heartbroken, raw emotion swimming in her violet eyes, he could almost forget his obligations. Almost.

She held his gaze for a long time, waiting for what he could not give her. Finally, she smiled wistfully. "Easier, mayhap, but not better. I'll never regret loving you." She took a deep breath, looked him right in the eye, and did not hesitate. "In case you still are uncertain, you can trust me. I would never do anything to betray you."

He believed her. How could he not? "Then we will say nothing more about it."

She nodded. Rory pulled her into his arms and placed a soft kiss on her mouth, more relieved than he wanted to admit when she responded immediately. He told her with his mouth the words he could not say. Her arms slid around his neck as she pressed her body closer to his. The kiss deepened as he asked silently for forgiveness for his question. Forgiveness that she bestowed with the sweet caress of her mouth and tongue.

His breath was ragged when he finally pulled away. "We will not let Sleat cast his dark shadow across our day. Aye?"

"Aye," she agreed.

He smiled. "Then let us return to our guests. The MacLeods have some contests to win."

Though he'd spoken lightly, the yoke of duty weighed on him heavily. Never had he regretted more the burden of being chief. A marriage alliance was the only way to ensure the return of Trotternish to the MacLeods. *A marriage alliance* . . . The kernel of an idea took hold. His mind raced with possibilities. But it would require some thought.

He tucked her under his arm, placed a tender kiss on her head, and led her back toward the gathering, her words of love etched forever on his heart.

Chapter 19

❖

"A kiss for luck."

Strong, tanned hands encircled Isabel's waist, lifting her effortlessly from her saddle before yanking her close to the warm, granite-hard body she recognized so well. Isabel tilted back her head and smiled with amusement at the twinkling eyes of the handsome man cradling her in his protective embrace. "I do not think you need any luck, Rory MacLeod. You have won nearly every event, with only the caber toss remaining. It seems obvious that the MacLeods will win the gathering for yet the third year in a row."

A satisfied grin spread across his bronzed face. "It certainly seems that way. Does it not please you?" He feigned a frown and arranged his impudent features into the mock hurt look of a besotted squire who'd displeased his lady.

"Don't play coy with me, Rory MacLeod. You know very well that it pleases me. Although I think you are enjoying the admiring glances of some of the more bold lasses far too much. Perhaps it is time for you to learn a wee bit of humility? Mayhap I should kiss a Campbell for luck instead."

"You will do no such thing if you want the man to live to see another sunrise," he growled in her ear. "Now who is playing coy?" His laughter tickled her neck as his lips nuzzled the sensitive skin. "Kiss me, then, if not for luck then as a favor, like the gallant knights of old who would ride in a tournament with the colors of their lady tied to their armor."

Who could resist such a sweet entreaty? Isabel stood up on her toes and held his arms for balance, touching her lips to his in a chaste kiss.

Rory raised a sardonic eyebrow. "That is not exactly what I had in mind, but given our audience and the lack of time, I suppose it will have to do—for now. But when I win, I'll be seeking spoils worthy of the victor."

With one last grin, Rory turned and strode toward the other clansmen gathering for the caber toss. Isabel knew her eyes were probably shining with sensual anticipation, but she didn't care. Her heart swelled with warmth and pride. Rory MacLeod was a man built to make women gush.

Thankfully, after their uncomfortable confrontation two days ago, things had returned to normal. Though Rory hadn't been fully satisfied by her explanation for her uncle's anger, he had believed her vow of trust. A vow she meant with all of her heart. Even if her plan did not work, she could never betray Rory or his family.

She hadn't intended to tell him she loved him, it just happened. She'd been disappointed that he had not spoken in return, but Rory was not a man to wear his heart on his sleeve. She also suspected that he did not want to complicate her leavetaking, should it prove necessary. But in her heart, Isabel knew that he shared her feelings. Indeed, since her declaration, she'd caught him watching her, his gaze noticeably softer.

She must have been standing there staring for some

time before Ian's voice drew her attention from the magnificent specimen of her handfast husband.

"Come, Bel, you'll miss all the excitement."

"Oh, I didn't realize it was about to start." She allowed him to lead her toward the field. "You've acquitted yourself well in the games, Ian. Are you not participating in the last event?"

"No, Angus is the best of the MacDonalds at the caber toss. But even he does not stand much chance against the MacLeod. Rory Mor's skill is fit for the bards. It's too bad that we are not truly . . . Oh, well." He paused, considering. "Tell me, Bel, is everything well with you?"

Isabel knew what he was really asking. She looked around nervously, this time making doubly sure that no one was close enough to overhear their conversation. Finding nothing amiss, she relaxed a bit and, meeting his concerned gaze, said truthfully, "As well as can be expected given the circumstances of my being here."

"I only ask because, well, you seem quite happy with the MacLeod, and I just wondered whether you were perhaps having second thoughts." Noticing the panic that spread across her features, he grabbed her hand. "Don't worry, I would not say anything to our uncle. Anything you say now will remain between us."

Isabel detected the genuine concern in his voice. Rory *was* right. Ian was worried about her. She desperately needed someone to confide in. "Am I all that transparent? It seems I have fooled no one. Our uncle suggested much the same thing but did not put his concern quite so nicely. I think he fears I may not go through with our plan."

"Will you?"

Their eyes met and held for a moment. Satisfied with what she found, she shrugged. "I don't know what I should do, Ian, but our uncle has not left me with much choice."

"I cannot tell you what to do, little sister, but there is always a choice. You just need to find the one that will make you happy. And I have never seen you as happy as I have these past few days. You've made yourself a home at Dunvegan. Not only your husband, but his entire family has obviously welcomed you. You've changed." He put his hand to his chin, assessing her. "You're happier, more confident"—he paused—"different."

Different from when at Strome. He left the words unsaid, but Isabel knew what he meant. She had never found a place at Strome.

But Ian acted almost as if that embarrassed him. As if for the first time he realized that she'd always been excluded.

Isabel tiptoed into the room. The easy fall of voices broke off. Drat and double drat, she thought. How did they always hear her? "What are you talking about?" she asked.

"Nothing," Ian said quickly.

Isabel scrunched her lips together, and put her hands on her hips. She hated always being left out of everything fun. "Are too," she challenged as only an eleven-year-old could do.

"Run along now, Isabel," Angus said. "I think Bessie is calling you."

"You had friends," Ian said, as if trying to reassure himself.

"Of course."

His gaze sharpened. He didn't believe her. "Who?"

"It's not important."

"Who?" he demanded.

Isabel felt her cheeks heat. She didn't want him to feel sorry for her. "Bessie, Mary, Sari." All servants.

"What of the girls from the village?"

She shook her head.

Ian swore. "I'm sorry, Bel. No wonder you were always following us. None of us realized . . ." His jaw hardened. "We should have, and I'm sorry for it."

Isabel smiled, pleased by his acknowledgment. "It was a long time ago. But you are right, I have found happiness here. Margaret is a true friend."

His solemn eyes grew merry with mischief. "I thought our uncle was going to trip over his tongue when he first beheld bonny 'one-eyed Margaret' without her patch. It was truly a horrible jest he played on her and the MacLeods with that atrocious procession. But 'twas he who looked foolish when she, as ethereal as a fairy princess, stood next to that great toad of a woman Mackenzie that he married instead."

Isabel raised her hand over her mouth to cover her giggle. "His expression was rather humorous."

Ian snorted at her understatement. "Well, Isabel, I do not envy your decision. Either way, you will anger a powerful man. I must admit that I have found much to admire in your handfast husband over these last few days. He is a strong chief, and he has the love and respect of his clan. But mark this: Whatever you decide, be very cautious with our uncle. I think he has something else planned that he has not told us about. Our father suspects Sleat may actually be in league with the Mackenzies. Although our uncle has promised to take our side in the dispute with the Mackenzies over Strome

Castle if you are successful, Father doubts that Sleat will keep his word."

Isabel was taken aback. "Why? What reason does he have to suspect treachery from Sleat?"

Ian sobered. "Father was furious when he found out about the Mackenzies' attack on you. He blames himself."

"Why should he do that?"

"He told Sleat of your letter, where you mentioned the MacLeod's delay in Edinburgh. He believes that Sleat told the Mackenzie."

Was that why Rory had questioned her? It took Isabel a moment to digest the fact that a seemingly innocuous comment in her letter could have led to the attack. "I don't believe it," she said dumbly.

"The Mackenzie's rage at our family and the MacLeods is so strong after the death of his son, Father believes that even if Sleat were inclined to do so, our uncle could no longer rein in the vengeful Mackenzie."

At the mention of the Mackenzie, Isabel shuddered. The old chief had watched her closely over the last few days, and she did not trust him. No matter what Rory claimed about the sanctuary of the gathering, she suspected that Mackenzie was planning something. But so far, he'd done nothing more than stare at her with the same flat eyes of his son. Except that his eyes were glazed with something more—the promise of vengeance.

Ian continued, "Even now, Father seeks an alternative alliance to wage our defenses against the Mackenzies."

Isabel couldn't believe her ears. Her heart fluttered wildly in her chest. She tried to contain her excitement, asking cautiously, "Do you think Father would accept the MacLeod's help?"

"I'm almost certain of it. Could you convince him to do so?"

Isabel grinned. "I think so."

Ian met her smile with his own. "It would be a solution to our problems."

Almost all her problems. She still needed to find a way to return Trotternish to the MacLeods and forestall her uncle's plan to tell all. "Don't say anything to Father yet. I will write as soon as I know something definitive."

"Good luck, Bel. For your sake as well as ours, I hope this works."

The opportunity for further conversation was lost by the excitement surrounding the start of the caber toss.

But Isabel didn't mind. Her conversation with Ian had lifted a huge burden off her. Everything, it seemed, was falling into place.

It was well past midnight by the time Rory made his way up the long, winding staircase to their bedchamber. The celebration that followed the MacLeod victory was still going strong, but he had other spoils to reap. Entering the room, he closed the door firmly behind him. Feet spread, folding his arms forbiddingly across his chest, he grinned. "I'm ready to collect my reward."

Isabel, who'd retired a short time ago, turned from her seat at the table where she'd been brushing her hair to study him blocking the door. He loved the way the candlelight caught the flecks of gold in the flaming locks, tumbling around her bare shoulders in a glossy cape. His body heated as his eyes traveled over her naked arms, shoulders, and décolletage. She'd removed the gown she wore for the celebration, leaving only a thin sark between him and naked perfection. He felt a surge of masculine pride as her eyes flowed across his body—not bothering to hide her appreciation—and lingered on his crossed arms.

"I believe you've already had your reward," she said primly, but Rory caught the gleam of naughtiness in her gaze.

"One wee kiss is not the reward I had in mind," he said, making a move toward her. Laughing, she slipped past his reach, darting to the other side of the bed. He caught a lust-inducing glimpse of a slim bare leg. "Don't play games with me, Isabel," he warned.

"I thought you were good at games," she taunted, leaning across the bed. "Did you not win nearly every contest you entered?"

His gaze fastened on her lush breasts slung forward, swaying enticingly. Blood surged to his already hard cock when he thought of the way they'd bounce as she moved on top of him, riding him.

He moved one way, and she moved the other. When he tried to slide around the bed, she dove across, again slipping past his grasp. "You'll pay for your insolence, wench," he threatened.

Her eyes twinkled mischievously. "I'm counting on it."

She was quick, he'd give her that. But he was done giving chase. He faked to the right, she went left to slide across the bed, and he pounced, pinning her underneath him.

"Captured," he said with a wicked grin.

She made a halfhearted attempt to push him off. Her cheeks were flushed, her eyes bright, and her breathing quick from her exertions. Would he ever tire of looking at her? "Mercy?" he asked.

She shook her head. "Never."

He tsked. "Oh, lass, you try my patience." He clasped her hands above her head, giving him full access to the length of her body. She wiggled, but he had no intention of letting her go. He lowered his head, covering her mouth with his in a long, hot kiss as his hands began to caress the delectable curves of her body. Slowly, he lifted the hem of her sark, sliding his hand up her velvety thigh. He could feel her heart race as he brushed his finger over her heat. Her response to him never ceased to amaze him; he felt how she quivered, waiting for his touch. He knew how she would explode almost the moment that he stroked her.

"Mercy?" he asked again, his finger tantalizingly close to her most sensitive spot.

She peered at him from beneath her lashes. "You are a horrible man, Rory MacLeod."

His grin widened. "Is that a yes?"

"Yes, you shall have your reward."

"And you shall have yours," he said huskily. He lowered his head again, this time sliding past her mouth, over her breasts, and between her waiting legs, where his tongue brought her to quick surrender. Her soft cries of release echoed in his ears, a sweeter sound he'd never heard.

She lay still, languid in the wake of her release. Rory helped shimmy her shift over her head, before quickly removing his plaid and linen shirt. After stretching out beside her, he rolled to one side to watch the delicate flush fade from her pink cheeks. Their eyes met, and a slow smile curved up her lips. "Hmm . . ." Her fingers traced a delicate line down his stomach. The muscles flexed instinctively. "What reward would you have of me?" she asked, her hand moving achingly close to his arousal. Stroking the lines of his stomach, she teased him, her hand hovering just out of reach.

He couldn't concentrate on anything but the elusive grasp of her hand. "Surprise me," he said with difficulty.

She did.

Rather than take him in her hand, she slithered down his chest, kissing and licking along her dangerously slow path. Rory couldn't think; a red haze clouded his vision, and the blood pounded in his ears. He closed his eyes and clenched his jaw, giving her time to find her way.

Oh God, she was so close. He ached for the press of her warm, hot mouth around him, sucking, taking him deeper. Suddenly, she stopped. His eyes flew open. Her mouth was inches from him. While he was watching, her tongue flicked out to lick him. His ass clenched as he fought the overwhelming rush of heat. Their eyes met and held. It was the most erotic, intimate moment of his life.

"Mercy?" she asked.

Rory couldn't speak, he was too damn close to bursting. Her tongue swirled around his thick head. Every muscle in his body tightened. "Mercy," he choked.

She chuckled and finally slid him into her warm mouth. Her soft pink lips surrounded him, pulling him deeper as her tongue slid against him. He showed her how to take him deep and how to use her hand because there was too much of him. Finally, when he couldn't take any more, he pulled her on top of him, entering her in one hard thrust.

He held her hips as she moved up and down, clenching him like a silken glove with her muscles. Rory was out of his mind with need. She arched her back, and he knew she was close. He lifted her harder, faster, until she tensed, shuddered, and broke apart. Rory felt the pressure of his own release build from the deepest part of him. The intensity shook him. Every muscle, every fiber of his being, compressed in one hot moment, tightened, and then shattered into a thousand pieces. She rocked against him, wringing every last drop from his climax.

Rory felt as if the life's blood had been drained out of him. He couldn't have moved if the tower were on fire. Slowly, the feeling returned to his limbs, and the haze faded. It took him a moment to realize what he had done. He'd spilled his seed inside her, a mistake he'd not made since the first time. A mistake that had nothing to do with lust and everything to do with what he knew in his heart. He'd told her with his body, the words he could not say. *He loved her.* But the realization did not change the fact that he might be forced to marry another. And now he might have gotten her with child. Their child.

What had he done?

He reached over and slid a finger under her chin. "I'm sorry, lass."

She pressed her fingers over his mouth. "Shush. Don't." *Ruin it,* he heard her unspoken plea.

He didn't need to say anything. They both knew it would make no difference. If need be, Rory would do what he had to do. But the thought of Isabel bearing his child . . .

It would tear out his heart.

He couldn't allow it to happen. The stakes had grown

too high. He pulled her tight against him, tucking her under his arm and pressing his lips to her head. The idea that had taken hold two days ago could be the answer to all their problems.

The alternative had become unthinkable.

Chapter 20

❖

By late the following afternoon, Isabel had to smother a yawn behind her hand. It had been a long day following a short—very short—night. Peeking out from beneath her lashes at the man riding beside her, she hoped he hadn't noticed. Thankfully, Rory seemed involved in his conversation with Alex and Douglas.

She shifted her bottom in the saddle uncomfortably. It galled her to admit it, but she was beginning to feel sore after not having sat a horse at any length for some time. They had traveled much farther than they'd originally intended—a distance of nearly six leagues—past the coastal village of Bracadale and nearly halfway to Sligachan before turning back toward Dunvegan. The splendor of the spring infusing the countryside had urged them on with its vibrant color and fresh beauty. Shades of lavender from the heather and lime from the grassy moors undulated with the breeze. Isabel welcomed the opportunity to leave Dunvegan and explore Skye, but it was getting late and exhaustion from the excitement of the last few days was catching up with her.

Rory had warned her that it would be too tiring, especially after their vigorous victory celebration, but Isabel had insisted on accompanying him and his men as they escorted her family, Argyll, and the MacCrimmons partway on their long journey south toward Armadale. Now she wished she had heeded his warning. Her mouth twisted. Though she'd never admit as much to Rory. He'd just look at her with that inscrutable expression, but she'd know exactly what he was thinking: *I told you so.*

He knew her so well. At times, it seemed, better than she knew herself.

Isabel's thoughts kept drifting to the night before. Even with the extensive lovemaking of the past few months thoroughly expunging her innocence, she could not prevent the deep blush that crept up her cheeks at the memory of her all too willing surrender to the marauding warrior bent on wreaking new havoc on her senses.

And last night he'd held nothing back, spending himself deep inside her.

She tried not to put too much significance on what had happened, but it was impossible not to hope. Rory was not a man to make the same mistake twice—especially when he'd been so careful after that first night. Was he starting to see her as a part of his future? A future that after her conversation with Ian now seemed possible? All she needed to do was mollify her uncle and find a way to give Rory the land that was the source of the feud—that didn't involve marriage to someone else. Isabel was not without friends in the royal household. Perhaps she could help Rory. But how?

A strong, unusually warm coastal breeze tore an errant lock of hair from its feckless restraint. The red gold silken threads flew haphazardly across her face, tickling her nose and momentarily obscuring her view. Annoyed, Isabel captured the defiant tresses with her fingers and tucked them securely behind her ear.

They'd departed Dunvegan not long after breaking their fast, but the day was nearly gone. The rose-hued sun lingered on the late afternoon horizon as they skirted the woodland and steered their mounts toward Dunvegan village only a few furlongs ahead. Almost home. She could soon relax. The incident in the forest was still too fresh in her mind, and she was glad Rory had insisted they take the longer route around rather than risk another attack in the forest. She wondered if it was more for her benefit. Did he realize how the shadowy darkness of the trees terrified her?

Caught up in her own thoughts, she didn't realize Rory had been watching her. "Tired?" he asked innocently.

Isabel straightened her back and thrust back her shoulders, ignoring the shot of pain in her aching back. "Not at all."

"Stubborn lass." He laughed. "Don't worry, 'tis not much farther."

"Will we be back before dark?"

Rory nodded. "We can pick up our pace when Colin returns."

They'd traveled slowly, enabling Colin and a small party of warriors to scout ahead of them as they rode. Rory was not taking any chances. With the Highland gathering and temporary truce behind them, Isabel knew that Rory anticipated an attack from the Mackenzies. In fact, Douglas had led a small party of MacLeod warriors to follow the Mackenzies early that morning to ensure that they departed Kyle Akin, where they would cross to Kyle of Lochalsh. Rory had also kept a close eye on Sleat, who had traveled in the party with her family as far as Dunscaith Castle. Dunscaith was very close to

Armadale, where Argyll and her father would then cross to Mallaig.

She inhaled the salt-filled air. The sea was close. The *birlinns* moored along the shore in the village would carry them back to Dunvegan.

The deep laughter of men echoed in her ears. The MacLeods were still basking in the glow of their resounding victory. For most of the journey, she'd been subjected to the loud, boastful banter of Rory's warriors replaying every second of the various trials of skill and strength that had taken place over the past few days.

As the stories were mostly about him, Rory kept unusually silent, but he did seem amused by the more exaggerated retellings. Yet even though he seemed relaxed, Isabel knew he was constantly alert to their surroundings. She was watching him so closely, she noticed him tense.

"What's wrong?" Isabel teased. "Are the stories of your legendary skills not to your liking?"

Ignoring her gentle ribbing, he frowned. "Colin should have returned by now."

Isabel felt a shiver of fear creep down her spine, but Rory's presence prevented her from panicking. "Do you think . . . ?" She didn't want to voice her fears.

"I don't know, but I'm not taking any chances." He halted his men and began issuing his commands; the sudden pounding of hooves stopped him. It was Colin, and from the blood running down his arm, Isabel knew what had happened.

"Mackenzies," Colin gasped, his breathing labored from his hard ride. He pointed. "About a score of them, ahead." He looked directly at Rory. "They were waiting by the boats, but now they're heading in this direction."

"Mackenzies?" Isabel echoed. Her blood ran cold. "But Douglas watched them cross the kyle this morning."

"It was a trick," Rory said. "The Mackenzie did not send all his men to the gathering. He must have sent others separately, in secret, trying to catch us unaware." But Rory was never unaware. As he began to shout his commands, Isabel realized that he'd anticipated something like this. If it weren't for her presence, Isabel suspected he'd be looking forward to the fight. He seemed to thrive on the pressure, on the danger. Except when he looked to her; then he looked worried. "Isabel, stay close to Alex. He will lead you from harm." She didn't want to leave him, but he must have read her thoughts. "You will obey me. We don't have much time, they'll try to surround us." Even as he spoke, Isabel could hear the sounds of horses coming from behind. To Alex he said in a low voice, "Take her through the trees. We will meet you at the boats. And Alex, you know with what I entrust you?"

Alex met his brother's gaze and nodded, then spun his horse around.

"You'll be careful," she pleaded.

His gaze met hers, and something passed between them. An intensity of emotion that bore deep into her bones. "Aye, lass," he said gently, "now hurry."

With one long look at Rory, she turned after Alex. The Mackenzies were heading straight for them, having just crested the small rise ahead of them. Arrows started to fly. Her heart pounded with fear. What if something happened to Rory? What if she never saw him again? She should have kissed him, told him that she loved him, but it was already too late.

Rory and his men attacked right in the direction of the flying arrows.

"Hurry, Isabel," Alex shouted.

Only the knowledge that her presence would endanger Rory even more gave Isabel the strength to leave him. She would not make the same mistake she'd made before. Rory was the greatest warrior she'd ever beheld; his skills would not fail him. Still, she could not quiet the voice in her head that reminded her even Achilles had his heel.

The fierce battle cry of the MacLeods echoed in her ears as she followed Alex into the forest at breakneck speed. The light was fading fast. She couldn't repress the shudder of trepidation that moved over her as the memories assailed her. The forest. Dusk. It was too eerily similar. Fear rose in the back of her throat, but she tamped it down.

They rode for a few minutes, but her thoughts never strayed far from the battle taking place behind them or the man who was waging it. *Please, don't let anything happen to him.* Suddenly, she heard a shout behind them.

"Alex! Behind you."

Relief swept over her. It was Rory. He'd followed them through the trees. Her relief, however, was short-lived as an arrow flew by her, missing Alex by inches. Isabel looked behind her to see a handful of Mackenzies hard on their trail. Alex stopped and quickly brought his horse around, positioning himself between her and danger. He raised his claymore just as the Mackenzies descended on them. Isabel heard the clatter of steel as the fighting began.

Alex held them off until Rory could catch up to him.

With the two of them, the small band of Mackenzies didn't stand a chance. Isabel stared in horrified fascination as Alex and Rory methodically, ruthlessly, dispatched their enemy.

They were so close to escaping unharmed. But just as Rory lifted his claymore on the final man, a lone arrow shot from the trees found its mark straight into Rory's gut. He slumped forward over the thick neck of his powerful warhorse. His golden hair draped over the shiny black coat of his destrier. Blood spread across his saffron-colored *leine croich,* staining it a horribly deep, dark, saturated red.

For one terrifying moment, Isabel's heart stopped. Time stood still. *He is dead.* When a piercing, animalistic scream tore shrilly through the clear day, she didn't realize that the sound had come from her.

"No!" Her guttural cry sounded no more than a whisper.

Rory lifted his head, and their eyes met. Wordlessly, he sought to comfort her. He was alive.

Slowly she exhaled.

When Rory spoke, he addressed Alex, his voice weak and raspy. "Another group must have followed. Use the old passage. Hurry." Isabel noticed his knuckles were stark white as he clenched the reins, fighting to hold himself upright on his horse.

Isabel felt panic grip her chest, catching her breath in its tight hold. She felt smothered by an invisible cloak of horror. *This couldn't be happening.*

Alex recognized her panic and brought her back to reality with the cold, calm voice of authority. "Isabel, collect yourself. Do not fall apart on me. Move quickly now, we have to get Rory back to Dunvegan." His words acted like a physical shake. "Do you understand? If we do not get him back, he will die. It is our only chance. We must move now before they have time to surround us."

She nodded. Her voice seemed stuck in her throat.

Alex grabbed the reins of Rory's horse and raced through the cover of the woods. Tears flew from the corners of Isabel's eyes, aided by the force of the wind as her horse pounded through the underbrush. Heedless of the branches scraping her cheeks, she followed Alex at a terrifying speed as he led them north toward Dunvegan through the woodlands, skirting the open coastline and shaggy moors where the Mackenzies had waited. Even now she could hear the wild cries of their pursuers just behind them, excitedly closing in for the kill.

Rory's head bounced awkwardly over the neck of his horse. The thought of the pressure of the arrow on him with each rough stride of his horse acted like a knife twisting in her own stomach. *I can't lose him.* The pain must be excruciating. He would never survive. She'd seen injuries like this before and knew it would be a miracle if he survived even the day.

"Not much farther, Isabel, don't slow down. We're almost there!" Alex yelled, his words almost lost, muffled by the crashing thunder of hooves.

Isabel forced her mount faster. Never very good with directions, she knew if she lost sight of Alex and Rory, she would never find her way out. If the Mackenzies didn't find her first.

"They're up ahead, we've almost got 'em." The Mackenzies sounded close, too close. As if they were right behind her.

"Faster, Alex, they're gaining on us. We'll never be able to hold them off."

"We're almost there."

He headed left toward the coast and led them along the edge of the woods, through more dense underbrush and down a well-covered path that led to the rocky shoreline. They had reached the tiny inlet of the loch just south of the castle. There was nowhere left to go. Above them, perched high on its rock of inaccessibility, Isabel could see the castle not one hundred feet in front of her. So close to safety. But they might as well have been in Edinburgh. To reach the castle, they would have to fly or swim. The loch surrounded Dunvegan on one side, and on the other, the landward side, a cavernous rocky trench fronted it.

"Where are we going?" she shouted ahead to Alex.

"Just follow me."

She could no longer see Rory. Alex had urged Rory's horse ahead, and there was barely enough width on the rocky coastline for the horses to travel single file. *Please let him live.*

Alex led them around the inlet and headed straight for the rocky cliff where the edge of the steep crag met the edge of the trees. Isabel cautiously raised her eyes to the ominous thirty-foot sheer wall of rock and the curtain wall of the castle that rose high above it. There was no way in. Unless Alex planned to scale the wall with Rory on his back, they were cut off by water on one side and inaccessible terrain on the other.

Alex slowed his pace and headed straight for a large, jagged rock covered with dense foliage.

She could hear the battle cries of the Mackenzies behind her. They were hidden from view by the trees on their right, but she knew that any second her party would be visible. And vulnerable.

Her horse followed Rory and Alex as they dove right into the middle of a thicket, turned sharply left behind the jagged rock, and disappeared into nothingness.

A damp, dark chill enveloped her body. She could hear the snorting of Alex's horse in front of her but could see nothing in the darkness. Slowly, her horse followed Alex's destrier as if by instinct. Or scent. She blinked repeatedly, accustoming her eyes to the loss of light. Finally, she could make out stone walls and a damp floor. They'd apparently entered a wide tunnel in the cliff. Alex stopped in front of her and turned, motioning with a finger to his lips for quiet, then continued into the bowels of the rocky cliff.

After a few minutes, they stopped completely and Alex slid from his horse.

"It's safe now, Isabel. We must leave the horses here and walk the rest of the way. I'll return for them later. But now I need your help with Rory."

Rory. Isabel leapt off her horse before Alex could offer her assistance and flew to Rory, who was still slumped over his horse. She thought from his position he must have fainted, but at her touch, he opened his eyes and smiled weakly.

"Rory, oh God, Rory. Hold on, we're almost there." Craving further reassurance that he truly lived, she grabbed him, clasping his arm desperately. Conscious of his injury, she carefully leaned forward around the arrow protruding from his belly and placed her lips on his damp brow. His skin felt so cold. She could smell the metallic scent of blood. Fear unlike anything she had ever experienced strangled her soul. Surely the capricious fates would not be so cruel when they'd only just found each other?

"Isabel, we must get him to the castle."

Wordlessly, she helped Alex slide him from the saddle, trying not to cause him more pain than was necessary. Alex slung an arm over his shoulder, and Isabel supported him as best she could on the other side. Rory moved his feet, but Isabel could tell by the spasms of stiffness that racked his body that each step caused him new agony. Huddled together, they struggled along the treacherously wet path of stone and sand.

"Where are we?"

"In an old passageway built long ago by our Norse ancestors. It is rarely used, and few even know of its existence. Only Rory and I know how to find it. And now you."

She gulped, honored to have been entrusted with such a secret but all the same wishing she didn't know. She still felt loyalty to her family and would rather not be forced to lie.

Exhaustion threatened to crumple her legs; the large physique that she so admired was definitely a detriment at a time like this. Isabel knew by the way he tried to hold himself away from her that he was attempting not to crush her with his weight. With the amount of blood soaking her gown, she feared he would soon lose consciousness—or worse.

Don't fall apart, Isabel. He needs you.

Just when she thought she would not be able to take one more step, Alex stopped.

"We're here."

She nearly wept with relief. Even in the damp tunnel,

sweat beaded on her brow. Wiping it away with her sleeve, she looked around blankly at solid rock.

"I don't understand."

"Look up."

In the roof, perhaps a foot above Alex's head, she noticed a door.

Alex answered her unspoken question. "I'll go up first. You'll need to hold him steady while I try to lift him through the trapdoor. We'll be at the bottom of a hidden staircase that leads to the kitchens in the old keep."

How could that be? She'd been over every inch of that tower. Isabel held her tongue, not wanting Alex to question why she'd felt the need to inspect the castle so closely.

"What is that smell?" She sniffed. "Almost like roasted meat."

"It is roasted meat. A particularly cruel ancestor of mine decided to vent the kitchens into the dungeon to torment the prisoners."

"Are we near the dungeon pit?" she asked. The only entry to Dunvegan's dungeon was located in a small room in the great hall above the kitchens. She repressed a shudder. The dungeon was nothing more than a horrific thirteen-foot-deep hole in the rock where prisoners were tossed and left to die. When she'd first arrived at Dunvegan, she'd had many nightmares about that pit.

"We are very close to the dungeon in an adjacent tunnel. The kitchens are part of the barrel vault that runs the length of the old keep."

"What if we can't lift him up through the door by ourselves?" she wondered aloud.

"Rory would not want me to bring anyone else down here, but if there is no other choice, I'll find help."

But somehow they managed. Rory stirred from semiconsciousness only once, when Alex pulled him up through the hidden door, but it provided them much needed timely assistance up the small staircase. At the top, Alex peered through a small hole in the hidden door to make sure no one was about. Carefully, he pushed open the door and pulled them to safety.

What happened next was lost in the murky haze of confusion that descended when the MacLeods learned that their chief lay dangerously injured. Once Alex checked to make sure no evidence remained of their entry, the cry for help went up and chaos reigned.

Through it all, Isabel refused to leave Rory's side. Vaguely, she recalled holding his hand as someone—perhaps Deidre?—dug the arrow from his stomach and stitched the gaping wound closed. She must have blocked the rest from her memory, because after that she could remember nothing.

Smoky, mist-filtered moonbeams bathed the solar in ghostly semidarkness. Relishing the quiet, Isabel sat patiently at his bedside. Needing to be alone with him, she'd sent everyone else away. Nothing more could be done for him right now; they would have to wait to see whether he survived the fever that was sure to follow such a horrible injury. That he survived an arrow in his gut this long was a miracle in itself, but it had hit in the perfect spot. An inch or two in any direction, and he would already be dead.

She fidgeted restlessly, trying to find anything to occupy her hands. At a time like this, patience seemed unattainable. He looked so helpless, she thought as she bathed his head with cool water.

Long dark lashes fluttered, then opened to graze his brow.

"Where am I?" he groaned weakly, his blue eyes burning with an unnatural brightness.

The fever had arrived.

"Our chamber." She shushed him. "Don't try to talk. You are safe but need your energy."

He tossed his head back and forth against his pillow as if he fought unconsciousness. "Isabel, you must get Alex. I must speak with him, he needs to know—"

"Shh. Sleep, Rory. You need your rest, you can tell Alex in the morning."

"No, you don't understand. I must speak with him now, he will be the next chief." His voice took on a fevered urgency.

The truth hit her hard. *He thinks he is going to die.*

"Please, Rory, you must keep calm. If that is what you want, I'll get him."

"Hurry, Isabel. After I talk to Alex, I want to speak with you. I need you to know something."

She found Alex asleep before the fire in the hall downstairs. He looked awful. She hated to wake him. From the dark shadows of weariness around his eyes, it looked as though he had only just fallen asleep.

She placed her hand on his shoulder and shook him lightly. "Alex, wake up. Rory wishes to speak with you. Hurry, he's quite anxious." Bleary-eyed, a startled Alex followed her up the spiral stairs to Rory's chamber.

She motioned him into the room. "I'll wait outside, he wants to speak with you privately."

Alex nodded and closed the door behind him.

Anxiously, she stood in the hallway, staring at the door. Watching, waiting for any sound that he might need her. She took a few steps closer and frowned. Did Rory know there was a crack between the door and casing that allowed a sliver of light to shine from the room into the hallway?

The sound of raised voices riled her anger. Didn't Alex realize how weak his brother was? What could they be arguing about at a time like this? Rory made a loud gasping sound, followed by a gurgled cough. Isabel leapt to the door, peering through the crack to make sure he was all right. Her eyes flew to his face, and she sighed with relief. His breathing was uneven, but there was a fierce, determined glow in his eyes.

It took her a moment to realize what was happening. Too late, she realized her mistake. She wasn't supposed to see this.

"Reach behind the headboard of the bed and twist the wooden knob that you will find there. It looks like part of a carving. . . . Yes, that's it. Now reach under the bed and you will find a hidden drawer has opened. The box is in there. Bring it out and place it on the bed. Careful." Rory's voice sounded strained but steady.

Isabel's heart was beating at a frenzied pace. She knew she should look away, but she'd already seen enough. She'd learned his secret: where he kept the flag. The solemnity of the moment was not lost on her. He sounded like a king bequeathing his kingdom. *He can't die.*

"Now push the carving of the MacLeod badge and the box will open. Take out the flag."

"Rory, I don't need to do this, you are going to be—"

"I should have told you where it was before. The flag must be kept safe. Now take it out!"

Alex lifted it up and held it right before her eyes. The prize that had brought her to Dunvegan hung not ten feet in front of her.

Somehow she'd thought a magical talisman would look more impressive. The famous Fairy Flag of the MacLeods was a thin, raggedy length of red-and-yellow silk fabric. Her nose wrinkled. It looked oddly familiar. She could have sworn she'd seen it before.

She watched as Alex reverently replaced the flag in its box and returned it to its hiding place. Well, she thought, he did keep it close, as she had suspected. She just didn't realize she'd literally been sleeping on it for the last few months.

Isabel stepped back from the door, troubled by what she'd just witnessed. But she knew she would take the secret of the Fairy Flag to her grave. Her uncle would never hear of its location from her.

Moments later, Alex opened the door. "Rory wants to speak with you, Isabel."

Their eyes met in mutual fear and pain. She knew Alex was thinking the same thing she was. *Please don't let him die.*

Rory's eyes were closed as she approached the bed. His skin glowed pale with a gray tinge in the candlelight, much different from its normal burnished gold. Sensing her presence, he blinked and then opened his eyes. Remarkably, his gaze was lucid.

He must have recognized her fear because he managed a weak smile of reassurance. "I'm sorry."

"Whatever could you be sorry for?" She rushed to his side, taking his hand as she knelt beside him. "You have done nothing to apologize for." Confusion turned to anger when she realized what he was saying. "Don't you dare apologize for dying. You are not going to be rid of me so easily."

"My stubborn little Isabel." He tried to smile, but she could see how his conversation with Alex had weakened him.

"Rory, you don't have to explain anything."

"Yes, I do. It's not good," he said, referring to his injury. He drew a deep breath. "I'm sorry that it could not have been different. Sending you back would have torn out my heart." He winced with pain. "But I need you to know—"

The words stalled in his throat as pain racked his body.

Isabel felt her blood run cold. "Stop. Don't say anything more. You need your strength."

"No," he rasped through clenched teeth, every sound an impossible strain. "It's important. You need to know that you were not alone in your feelings. I need you to know that I love you."

That brought her head up immediately. Her entire body seized with disbelief as her eyes fastened on his. "You l-love me?" she stuttered.

"More than I ever thought it possible to love another."

A wave of happiness crashed over her. For a moment she forgot her fears, allowing the soothing warmth of his words to enfold her. Words she'd ached to hear. But not now. Not at a time like this. Tears blurred her vision. "Why did you not tell me before?"

"I thought it would make our parting more difficult. But I want nothing more between us."

Guilt tore like acid through her veins. Now was the time to say something. If she was ever going to tell him why she had been sent to Dunvegan, this was the time. "Rory, I—"

The words stuck in her throat. Fear wrapped around her chest. Would he understand? A heavy pause hung between them while her conscience warred with practicality. Rory was dying. Anger would only weaken him. What purpose would it serve to tell him now, when he had just declared his love? She dared not risk that his last memory of her be one of betrayal rather than love.

He stroked her cheek, wiping away the tears streaming down her cheeks.

"I love you, too," she said instead. "I will always love you." She pressed her face into his hand and said a silent prayer for forgiveness.

This was the happiest, most terrible moment of her life. He loved her, but he lay dying. It was so illogical, like a flower blooming in the ashes of hell.

She listened to his pained, shallow breathing growing steadier. Until at last he slept.

Chapter 21

❖

The haunting sounds of the pipers playing their eerie lament for their dying chief echoed through the dark halls. The words of Patrick MacCrimmon gave voice to the anguish of a clan.

My pipe hand me and home I'll go,
This sad event fills me with woe;
My pipe hand me, my heart is sore,
My Rory Mor, my Rory Mor.

It seemed as though the entire castle dwelt in a state of limbo for months, although in reality it was only a few days.

Endless days of waiting for the fever and infection to run its deadly course.

Endless days of praying for God to take him, to relieve him of his unbearable pain.

Endless days of praying for God to take her, so she would not have to watch him suffer.

In the end, He took neither.

By some miracle Rory survived, finding the strength to defeat the fever.

Never would Isabel forget those harrowing days when she thought she might lose him. Or the infinite joy she'd felt when at last he opened his eyes and his lucid blue gaze, strong and unwavering, met hers.

He took one long look at her and boomed in a surprisingly strong voice, "Get some rest. Now."

Isabel never thought she'd be so glad to hear that uncompromising voice ordering her about. Ignoring his instructions, she rested her head on the bed and wept with relief. Relenting for a moment, Rory gently stroked her tangled hair. But when her tears had dried, Isabel found herself forced from his bedside, not allowed to return until she'd eaten and slept.

Over the long weeks that followed, Isabel nursed Rory during his recovery, her happiness tempered only by the fact that she knew she might lose him still. He loved her, but he still had not promised to marry her. Each day that passed was like the tolling of a bell reminding her that the time of reckoning drew near. Would Rory go through with the repudiation? His silence on the subject of their future seemed only to confirm her fears.

Her uncle's threat to tell Rory of her perfidy weighed heavily on her mind. Sleat acted with the single-minded purpose of destroying the MacLeods, heedless of her happiness or security. She had no doubt her uncle would hold to his promise if she did not bring him the flag by the end of the handfast period. If he waited that long. Isabel knew she had to do something about her uncle soon. She would do whatever was necessary to protect her secret until she was sure that Rory would not send her back; only then would she dare risk his anger.

Rory had given her his love and trust, and she had not been completely honest with him. She should have told him that night as he lay dying, but she'd been too scared.

Their love was too fragile. There were too many forces
trying to keep them apart. Isabel didn't have much experience with love, nor was she confident that she could
hold the love of a man like Rory. The scars of her past
were too deep to erase with words spoken in the face of
death . . . and not repeated. How could she be confident
in the strength of his love when the threat of repudiation
hung like a reaper over her head?

She needed to buy time. Time to ask the queen for her
help in the disposition of Trotternish and time to dissuade her uncle from blasting a hole right through the
delicate bond of their love. But how could she satisfy
Sleat without betraying Rory?

The answer had come to her unexpectedly, while
praying for Rory's recovery. Bessie walked into her room
wearing an old silk shawl, and Isabel had her divine response.

That was where I've seen it. The flag that she'd
glimpsed through the door looked just like Bessie's
shawl. A plan formed quickly in her mind. She would
write to her uncle and tell him that she'd found the flag.
But instead of the flag, she would give him Bessie's
shawl, or if her uncle insisted the spy retrieve the flag for
himself, she would switch it temporarily. Once her
uncle's spy removed the "Fairy Flag," Isabel would re-
place the true flag and tell Rory the truth as soon as possible.

There were many risks, but she could think of no
other way to satisfy her uncle that would enable her to
stay at Dunvegan. No doubt the ruse would eventually
be discovered, but by then she would have garnered precious time. And hopefully by then the issue of the repudiation would be solved by marriage vows. Vows that,

unlike a handfast, could not be easily set aside. She quashed the wave of guilt at her deception, telling herself it would all work out in the end.

So nearly a month after the attack, when Rory had recovered enough to attend meetings with his men, Isabel sat down at the desk to compose a carefully worded letter to her uncle and another to the queen. Moving some papers out of the way, she glanced down at a letter Rory had left unfinished only that morning. The name leapt off the page: The Earl of Argyll. She read the words that confirmed her worst fears: "I'm recovered . . . must see you to discuss the alliance."

He still intended to go through with the marriage to Elizabeth Campbell. The knowledge stung. But it also made her sure that she was doing the right thing. Repressing the urge to crumple the offending letter into a ball, Isabel carefully put it to the side and began the letters that would garner her precious time.

Though frustratingly weak, after weeks confined to his bed, Rory was anxious to resume at least some of his duties. It was not simply the endless cosseting of women that made him restless, though there was that, but while his wound healed, Rory had begun to implement his plan. It could be a solution to all his problems, one that might enable him to marry Isabel and do his duty to his clan. But even if it failed, Rory knew that he would never be able to let her go. It was time to inform his men of his decision.

Careful not to reopen his wound, Rory slowly made his way down to the library, as Isabel had threatened to do him bodily injury if he attempted to take one step out of the Fairy Tower. But he would not have a council

with his men in his bedchamber. Alex, Douglas, and
Colin were already waiting for him. Rory was glad to
see that Colin had recovered from the injuries he'd suffered at the hands of the Mackenzies. Two of Rory's
other men had not been so lucky, though Rory knew it
could have been worse. It was Colin who'd noticed the
band of Mackenzies following his chief through the forest. He'd pursued, slowing Rory's attackers and enabling their escape. Once Rory, Alex, and Isabel had
disappeared into the rocks, the Mackenzies had fled,
preventing any further injuries.

But it was not the Mackenzies who concerned Rory
right now. It was the reaction of his men, as he'd just
laid out his plan.

"It is a good plan," Alex said. "But do you think the
king will agree?"

"James has been reluctant to interfere in land disputes
between the clans," Rory said. "But my proposal ceding
Trotternish to the MacLeods as part of Isabel's tocher
gives James the opportunity to resolve the matter without actually having to decide the merits of the dispute."

Alex nodded. "Something the king would rather not
do, reluctant as he is to choose between you and Sleat.
James will jump at the easy way out. A dowry is perfect."

"But Sleat will never agree," Colin pointed out.

Rory shrugged. "It doesn't matter. By then the idea
will already be in James's head. Also, it was Sleat who
proposed Isabel as my bride in the first place. Her tocher
was not discussed when we agreed upon a handfast. But
a dowry would be expected with marriage."

"Argyll will be furious if you break the alliance. Can
you afford to anger him? You might not find him as

ready to intercede on our behalf in the future," Colin said.

"I will find a way to mollify him. And any loss of Argyll's support at court will be made up with the support we are gaining," Rory replied. "Isabel's friendship with the king and queen is surely as beneficial as Argyll's influence." Watching her act as hostess at the Highland gathering had made him realize that having Isabel as a wife would be an asset at court. Rory was only sorry he hadn't realized it earlier.

Douglas nodded his agreement. "You forget, Colin, I've seen her at court. I can assure you that Isabel is well connected in the royal household. She was the favorite of the queen amongst her ladies and a favorite of the king as well."

"It's done," Rory said. "I've already written the king." He paused. "And Argyll."

He looked around the table, but if his men questioned his actions, they did not say so. His gaze fell on his brother. "If you have something to say, Alex, do so."

Alex shook his head, but Rory knew what he was thinking. An alliance with Argyll would have all but guaranteed a return of their land. If Rory's plan didn't work, the MacLeods would lose Trotternish. In deciding to break the agreement with Argyll before he was sure of the outcome with the king, Rory had put his love for Isabel above the good of the clan.

He would just have to make sure his plan didn't fail. But right now, if he did not want to collapse before his men, he would return to bed. This short sojourn had sapped his strength. Isabel had been right, though he would never admit it. She already hovered over him as if he could disappear at any time. But Rory understood her fear. And that was what had prompted this council.

He knew Isabel was deeply troubled by his failure to assure her of their future, but as soon as he resolved the situation with Argyll and heard from the king, he would be able to ease the lines of worry marring the smooth skin on her forehead. Soon.

It was a beautiful June morning, the clear, cloudless type of day you dream about in the dark, depressing days of winter. Rory stood near the window in his solar, finishing his morning preparations. Though he'd been out of bed for a few weeks, today he would return to sword training for the first time since his injury, and Isabel was nervous. A roar from the courtyard below drew her attention. Isabel smiled, welcoming the clamorous sounds of life that had been conspicuously absent while Rory recovered.

"Are you sure you are ready to resume training, Rory? It has not even been two months since you were injured," Isabel asked, unable to conceal the worry in her voice.

Rory laughed and replied teasingly, "You know, I have a healthy new respect for Alex, enduring as he did the constant attentions of *three* of you. I consider myself extremely fortunate that Bessie has been kept busy with Robert's bairns or I am sure she would have joined you and Margaret in your endless cosseting. If I stay chained to this keep much longer, I may find myself unable to belt my own plaid."

"Ungrateful wretch!" Her hands landed at her waist. "Margaret and I have allowed you far more latitude than we thought appropriate because we knew you would resist what was good for you at every step. You are a decidedly horrible patient, Rory MacLeod. Need I remind you of the second fever you suffered after getting out of bed too soon last month? And Margaret and I should be the ones complaining for having to look at that black scowl all day long."

Rory grinned broadly at the mock affront in her posture.

Her heart caught as it always did at the sight of the dimpled grin that now lifted so easily. It was hard to believe that not too long ago he used to be as dour as Margaret's Viking. Isabel frowned. Something had been bothering Margaret of late. She'd assumed it was the near death of her brother, but now she wasn't so sure.

Rory almost looked himself, but was he really ready to resume his duties? She admitted that he did look better than he had in weeks, but the signs of his lengthy illness still lingered. He'd lost a considerable amount of weight. Height alone would always make him an imposing man, but the loss of weight created a feral, hungry leanness in him that she could not say was unpleasant or unimpressive. Still powerfully muscled, he seemed more tightly wound. He'd allowed them to trim his hair and shave his beard, and though he'd lost most of the perpetual tan he seemed to have, he would get that back soon enough with the resumption of his normal activities.

The wound in his stomach had healed nicely, thanks to the salves applied by Deidre, but he would bear a large scar where the arrow had torn a gaping hole through his skin. What worried her was that with the resumption of fighting, the wound might reopen.

Cognizant of her concern, Rory turned serious. "I'll

be fine. Don't worry, I know just how close to death I came. I'll not chance another fever. But if you'll recall, you did not question my full recovery last night."

She blushed at the memory of their passionate love-making the night before—the first time they had shared a bed since the night before the accident. "Wretch. How like a man to measure the state of his health by his prowess between the bedsheets. Very well, then, return to your sword practice, but if you do not return in a few hours, I will send Bessie after you."

"With a threat like that, how can I refuse?" Still smiling, he pulled her into his arms and crushed his mouth to hers in a demanding kiss. Instantly intoxicated by the heady taste of him, she felt her body flood with desire. How she loved to feel his lips move over hers. One night of lovemaking could not douse the powerful fire that flared between them, forged by weeks of abstinence. She felt her blood rush; the warmth spread across her body as his tongue swept her mouth.

There was nothing seductive about this kiss, nothing teasing. His mouth moved urgently over hers, searing her with its heat. He knew what he wanted, and so did she. Their shared intent was obvious as their bodies moved together with wonderful familiarity. Her body pressed taut against his hardness, her soft curves molding to him instantly. She felt the press of his hip to hers. His tongue delved deeper, and his hand moved purposefully toward her bodice.

"Rory, are you coming or not?" Alex shouted from below.

Rory lifted his mouth from hers, sanity slowly returning from beneath the haze of passion. Their breathing slowed. When they had time to consider Alex's choice of words, they burst out laughing in tandem. Rory lifted his brow in question.

Isabel shook her head no.

She had something very important to do—the quicker it was behind her, the better.

"Later. Tonight we will finish what we started, Rory. The lions below are hungry. Off with you before they come hunting," she chided.

Reluctantly, he released her from his hold. "I think I'll have a word with Alex about interruptions." He gently kissed her brow in farewell, now anxious to join the other warriors.

Isabel watched him leave, admiring the strength and pride in his carriage. He looked every inch the impressive Highland warrior, astounding for a man so perilously close to death not even two months ago. A sense of inexplicable bliss settled over her. Holding the love of a man like Rory was awe-inspiring. She must do what was necessary to keep it.

She sat on the edge of the bed, putting her hand over her stomach, fighting a sudden wave of nausea. For the past week or two, she'd experienced strange bouts of queasiness, brought on, no doubt, by stress.

This was the opportunity she'd been waiting for to take a closer look at the flag. Sleat had warned her not to try to trick him, and she knew he would be sending instructions soon. She needed to be ready. She had to be sure that Bessie's shawl could pass muster with someone familiar with the flag.

An excited roar boomed from the courtyard below, the sound of Rory as he joined his men. She took a deep breath. It was time. Isabel shook with nervousness. *Just get it over with*. Cautiously she walked to the door, paused, and listened to make sure no one was coming. Hearing no sound, she opened the door and peeked down the corridor. All clear.

Slowly, she moved to the bed, reaching around to feel for the wooden knob in the carving that Rory had described to Alex. She found it easily, turned it, and slid her hand under the bed to locate the opened drawer. The etched metal box was heavier than she'd anticipated, and it took some time to remove it from the drawer. Using both hands, she raised it to the bed and pushed on the MacLeod badge. The lock released with a small pop, and she opened the lid.

Dust and a musty smell gathered at her nose. She rubbed her nose, trying to prevent a sneeze. The famous Fairy Flag of the MacLeods lay folded neatly in the box. Reverently, she lifted it out, letting the soft folds unfurl on the bed. Well, at least lightning didn't strike. That was something. She had touched the flag and was still alive.

Now for the shawl. Fortunately, Bessie had given over her old shawl with no more than a raised eyebrow or two. Lifting the shawl from her trunk, she held it up in front of the window close to the flag for comparison. A sudden breeze through the open window caught the thin silk fabric and puffed it out like a sail. Amazing. It was just as she remembered. Bessie's shawl could have been cut from the same cloth as the flag, except that it looked a wee bit less worn. Slightly darker in hue, the crimson-and-yellow pattern of the shawl was otherwise identical to that of the flag. The shawl would fool even someone who had seen the flag up close. Only a side-by-side inspection would differentiate the two.

This might just work!

Carefully she replaced the flag, returning it to its hiding place. Lifting Bessie's shawl from the bed she turned and placed it in her trunk. She'd just closed the lid when she heard a voice behind her.

"What are you doing?"

Her heart dropped like a stone at the achingly familiar voice. How long had he been standing there? She glanced over her shoulder.

Long enough.

Chapter 22

❖

Rory stood stone still in the doorway, watching Isabel place the MacLeod's precious talisman in her trunk. For a moment, he felt oddly disembodied as he tried to make sense of the sight before him.

"R-rory," she faltered. "You're back so soon. I thought you were training." She ran to him, pressing her soft body against his chest and circling her arms around his neck. But he barely noticed. "Did something happen? Are you feeling well?" she asked, the concern in her voice a bitter mockery.

Shock propelled his inane response. "I thought I saw something in the window." He spoke tonelessly. *I didn't want to believe it.*

The flag. Isabel had the Fairy Flag. But how . . . ?

The truth hit him hard, striking him cold. He looked down at her, not wanting to believe it. Eyes wide, her perfect oval face lifted to his in silent entreaty. That soft mouth he'd kissed so tenderly only moments ago was now trembling. The longing was almost unbearable. He hated his weakness. How could something so innocent and beautiful mask such treachery?

Betrayal.

Rory forced himself not to turn away, though it hurt just to look at her. The pain in his chest was like nothing that had come before. It ripped through him, tearing a fiery path along its trail. He'd take a thousand arrows in the gut before he faced the raw, excruciating agony that was Isabel's treachery.

"You bitch," he growled. Forcefully, he pushed her aside. "How could you?"

She staggered but did not fall. "Rory, you don't understand. I can explain. It's not how it looks."

"I'm sure it's exactly how it looks," he snapped. There was only one explanation. "You spied on me when I told Alex where the flag was hidden." His penetrating gaze fell on her guilt-stricken face, daring her to deny him. But she could not.

His earlier suspicions rushed to the forefront of his consciousness, no longer blinded by emotion. The pieces fell into place, and it all made horrible sense. Sleat's ready agreement to a handfast, Isabel's searching of the kitchens, the tempting, sometimes indecent clothing, and her eagerness to share his bed even when she knew there was no future. All led to one unmistakable conclusion. Isabel was in league with her uncle. She'd come to Dunvegan under false pretenses.

A fresh stab of pain shot through his chest.

She'd never loved him.

She'd lulled him into a besotted trance, bewitching him with her beauty, and led him down a treacherous path he had sworn never to travel. He'd fallen in love with the enemy and allowed his judgment to be clouded by beauty, lust, and love. Worst of all, because of her, he'd broken the alliance with Argyll. He'd chosen a woman over his duty to his clan. And for that failure, he could never forgive her. She'd made a fool out of him.

Blood pounded through his body. The initial tumult

of emotions gave way to an all-encompassing rage. His fists clenched at his side as he felt the pressure building from inside, threatening to erupt in a violent maelstrom. The intensity shook him to his core. He held himself rigid, not trusting himself to move. For a moment, he could have killed her for doing this to him. To them.

"God damn you, I trusted you." His hands gripped her arms as the force of his fury unleashed like a whip.

Her eyes widened. "Rory, please—"

The vein in his neck pulsed as every muscle in his body strained with restraint. "You are in league with your uncle. You came to Dunvegan under false pretenses and planned to steal the flag. The handfast would be your way out."

"Yes, but—"

Confirmation squeezed him like a vise. Something inside him died. She might as well have slipped a dirk into his back while he was sleeping; the effect was the same. He felt as if someone had splayed open his chest, pried out his heart, and twisted it until there was nothing left. Nothing but the cold, aching void where there used to be something beautiful.

He did not let her finish. "You've spied on me and my family, intending to betray us. You've whored yourself and manipulated your way into my life. I assure you, further explanation is not necessary."

She recoiled at his crudely spoken words. But he didn't care. "No, Rory, you have it all wrong. I may have come here under false pretenses, but once I grew to love you and your family, I knew I would not be able to go through with what my uncle had planned—"

"Enough!" he roared. The mention of Sleat had

snapped whatever tenuous control he had over his anger. He thought of how completely he'd fallen for her lies. But he was fooled no longer. "I refuse to listen to any more lies from you. Consider yourself lucky that I do not dress you as the harlot you have acted so convincingly and send you back accordingly. Your uncle might appreciate the irony." He looked at her with all the contempt that filled his blackened heart. "Pack your things and leave before I decide to put you where you deserve—do you know what we do with spies at Dunvegan, Isabel?"

This couldn't be happening. Dear God, what had she done?

The panic that rose in her throat seemed so palpable, she could almost taste it. It thickened her tongue and smothered her breath. But it was not the threat of imprisonment in that dank dungeon that caused her fear. No, it was Rory who terrified her. The thought that he might not listen to her frightened her more than she had ever dreamed possible.

He couldn't send her away. She had to make him understand.

Tears streaming down her face, she clutched at his sleeve, trying to force him to listen. "Rory, please, I would never give my uncle the means to destroy you and your family. I intended to trick him. See, look." She turned around, raced back to her trunk, and pulled out Bessie's shawl. "See, it's not the flag. I intended to send him this instead."

Rory studied the shawl, seeming to recognize that it was not in fact the flag. "It doesn't matter. You spied on me. How do I know that you did not intend to switch that for the real Fairy Flag?"

"It was an accident. I did not mean to spy on you. I heard noises. . . ." She lifted her chin and met his gaze, ready to weather his scorn. "And as to the other, you'll have to trust me. I love you, I would never betray you."

"Trust," he spat. "Never. You will leave here immediately. I wish to never lay eyes on you again."

His voice was like a shard of ice cutting through her heart, stopping her cold. This was the man she'd feared if he'd ever discovered the truth, the emotionless stranger who looked at her with wintry eyes. He stood so close, she could see the golden tips of his lashes, the dark shadow of stubble already appearing on his jaw, and the subtle, angry flare of his nostrils as he spoke. An hour ago, she'd had the right to touch him. To place her hand on his face and lift her lips to his. No longer. He was so close, but immanently unreachable.

She gazed up into his cold, unyielding face. His eyes glinted with steel, his mouth a tight line before the hard square of his determined jaw. "You must believe me that I planned to tell you as soon as I was sure you would not repudiate the handfast. I wanted to tell you the night you were injured, but I was scared. I feared that you would not forgive me."

"You were right," he said stonily. His eyes never flickered.

"You claim to love me, Rory, won't you even hear my explanation?"

He laughed ruthlessly. "Surely you realize that I lied when I said I loved you, Isabel. I felt sorry for you. Sorry that your family had so obviously neglected you. I was grateful for all that you had done for Margaret, and you seemed so pathetically needy. Remember, when I spoke those words I thought I was dying."

Her head jerked back as if he'd slapped her. It couldn't be true. He had to love her. It couldn't be just pity. Could it? She felt the stab of truth. He wielded his weapon well; he knew just how to hurt her. Still, she knew they had shared *something*.

"Deny you love me if you will, but after the happiness we have shared these past few months, I know you must care something for me."

"What we shared was lust, Isabel. Do not confuse it with sentiment or depth of feeling." He boldly looked her up and down as if he were evaluating a horse at market. "You are an extremely beautiful woman with an undeniably alluring body. I assume that it's not a coincidence that Sleat chose you to be my bride." His eyes flared at her blush of confirmation. "He chose well. From the first, I have wanted to bed you, as I would desire to bed any beautiful woman. But beauty wears thin. Even before today I was growing weary of our *temporary* arrangement. Your treachery has only hastened the inevitable."

A beautiful shell. That is what he thought of her. That was all he saw.

Maybe that was all there was.

Stunned by the vehemence of his denial, she could feel his words snuffing out the dreamlike happiness, shrinking her heart until she felt nothing but a profound emptiness. But something in her refused to die—refused to give up.

"Please, won't you give me a chance to explain? I only agreed to help my uncle because he would not help my father fight the Mackenzies if I didn't." Her voice took on a desperate urgency reacting to the finality of his tone. She grasped his arm pleadingly.

He shrugged off her hold. "I believe there was a time for explanation. That time has passed. I warned you never to betray me. There is nothing more to discuss. You spied on me. You've deceived me and deceived my family." He paused to catch her gaze so there would be no misunderstanding. "You are dead to me."

And deep in her shattered heart, she believed him at last. The look in his eyes left no doubt. He was a Highlander. Highlanders did not forgive or forget betrayal.

Past caring, pride all but forgotten, she wanted to get on her knees and beg him to listen, to understand. Paralyzed, she watched their future slipping through her fingers. Her pleas as effective as trying to melt rock. Never had she wanted anything as badly as she did at this moment. *Please don't ask me to leave, please say something, just one word,* her heart cried.

"This handfast is over."

No, not that! And as simple as that, it was gone. As completely as if it had never been. All that remained was a painful burning in her chest where her heart had only hours ago soared with joy.

She watched, transfixed with horror, as he turned on his heel and left the room. The door closed forcefully behind him, an effective exclamation to his words. She collapsed in a heap on the floor next to Bessie's shawl, crushed by the force of the hatred that seemed to radiate from him.

She sank her head in her hands, weaving her fingers through her hair to clasp her head in disbelief. How could this have happened? Isabel felt her soul violently ripped from her body as perfectly and decisively as he had cut her from his life. Her hope and dreams for the future extinguished, she slipped into darkness.

"My poor poppet," Bessie mused sadly when Isabel managed haltingly to explain through the choking tears what had happened.

But there were no magical words of wisdom that Bessie could utter to repair the horrible debacle Isabel had made of everything.

Bessie cupped Isabel's chin and lifted her face, brushing aside the tears that sped down her cheeks. "I know 'tis difficult to hear, Isabel, but I think it is best if you leave now as Rory has ordered. He is angry right now; there is no telling what he might do. The pride of a Highlander is a powerful thing, and by betraying his trust, you have damaged not only his heart, but his honor before his men. Time will be your greatest ally. You need time to think of a way to make him understand, and he needs time to forget some of his hurt."

Isabel knew she was right, but how could she bear to leave? Everything that she loved was here. Even Bessie.

As if she knew what Isabel was thinking, Bessie offered, "I could come with you. Robert would understand."

Isabel clasped her hands and kissed her cheeks, moved by the selflessness of her beloved companion. "Dearest Bessie. Your life is at Dunvegan now; I would never ask you to leave. The decision was mine; I knew what I risked when I agreed to my uncle's plan. I just never dreamed that I would have so much to lose."

Enfolded in the gentle, loving arms of her nursemaid, Isabel allowed her grief to spill over. She wept with the intensity known only to those who have loved greatly— and lost. She wept until the tears refused to fall. Unable to keep the nausea at bay any longer, Isabel retched under Bessie's worried gaze.

Time passed too quickly. She stood at the window, watching as dark clouds gathered across the sky. Watched as the orange sun began its slow descent off the edge of the western horizon. It was almost dark. She knew she should pack her things, but instead Isabel remained fixed at the window. Waiting.

She was vaguely aware when Bessie began to gather her belongings. Picking up the strewn clothing, separating those things she would take with her, and placing those things she would send for later in the trunk before the bed. But Isabel continued staring out the window, waiting as the slow movement of the sun extinguished her last moments of happiness.

Floundering in the dark chasm of heartbreak, she did not immediately process the sound at the door. *No, not yet.* The sobs that racked her body did nothing to dispel the despair she suffered as Bessie rose to answer the knock.

It was not all a horrible nightmare from which she would wake. A silent, grim-faced Colin stood before her, waiting to escort her from their—now his—bower. She managed one last glance around the room, then walked toward the door. She passed the bed, still mussed from their passion-filled night. A stab of searing pain twisted in her gut. Everywhere she looked there were painful reminders—she closed her eyes, blocking out the memories. Quietly, she gathered the meager belongings that Bessie had managed to assemble for her hasty departure and left the room, not daring to look back.

The Viking refused to meet her eyes as he led her down the twisting stairs, through the *barmkin*, and down the slick sea-gate stairs to the waiting boat. She looked around anxiously, praying for a reprieve. Praying for a chance at least to say farewell. But Rory was not there. And either he had not told them or they had chosen not to come, but Alex and Margaret were not there to say good-bye. She bowed her head, willing herself not to cry.

She felt Bessie's reassuring hand on her arm. "I am sure they would be here if they knew you were leaving."

It was uncanny how Bessie always seemed to guess what she was thinking. Isabel managed a wobbly smile. "I am not so sure. Please tell them—"

"You shall tell them when you return," Bessie said firmly.

Isabel knew Bessie was trying to ease her suffering, pretending that she would return someday. But both knew that day would likely not come. After what she'd done, she knew Rory would never forgive her. He'd given her something sacred—his trust—and she'd deceived him.

She fought to control the tears once again as she felt Bessie's strong arms gathering her in a tight embrace. Too tight. Indicating that Bessie, despite her words to the contrary, also worried that they might not see each other for some time—if ever.

Colin cleared his voice, signaling that the time for good-byes was at an end.

"Dearest Bessie, be happy. Robert and his daughters need you. Don't worry about me, I'm strong." With one last kiss on the soft cheek of her childhood, she turned and climbed into the waiting *birlinn*.

Smoky fingers of haze threaded the perfect circle of the iridescent moon above her as the *birlinn* pulled away from the castle. She lifted her hand in silent farewell to the shrinking figure of Bessie poised forlornly at the base of the sea-gate stairs.

The droning sound of the oars dipping and pulling the water filled the silent boat. No one spoke a word. Men who had laughed easily with her only yesterday now acted as if she were a leper. On a *birlinn* full of MacLeod clansmen, she felt completely alone. Isabel sat huddled on the boat, her puffy, tearstained face hidden from the curious stares by the deep hood of her cloak.

She had traveled full circle. Fate had won. Star-crossed enemies they had begun, and star-crossed enemies they would end.

For the last time, she lifted her red-rimmed eyes to the gray walls receding into the mist, hopelessly memorizing with watery vision the grim castle that she had come to love. A fresh spasm of despair filled her heart as her gaze was drawn to the top floor of the Fairy Tower, to that familiar window where she had looked out in happiness only yesterday.

As if sensing the shift of her eyes, a shadow moved away from the window. Her breath caught for an instant. Her heart pumped frantically with hope. *Please give me a sign, any sign.* She refused to blink lest she miss it. She kept her eyes glued to the window in the Fairy Tower, hoping and praying with every fiber of her being for a sign of forgiveness. She stared until the tower slipped into ghostly gray, swallowed by the ephemeral mist.

The dream was over.

Her heart had been cleaved in two—part of her was gone forever, left behind to rot in a much beloved old castle.

Chapter 23

❖

The sound of a door opening shattered the peace of deadening solitude. Rory knew he'd been fortunate to avoid them for this long. Isabel had been gone now for almost a day. Margaret and Alex had shown remarkable forbearance considering the circumstances, but their patience had finally run out and they'd tracked him to the library. He didn't want to talk about it, but he understood their questions. If only he had answers.

Rory directed his gaze back to the fireplace, where he had spent the last few hours staring placidly into nothingness. The sting of betrayal had dulled. Sinking deep into his chair, he took a long swig of *cuirm*, allowing the drink to ephemerally kindle the emptiness smoldering inside him.

They stood beside the chair, waiting.

Finally, Margaret dropped to her knees beside him and took his hand in hers. "What happened, Rory? Won't you tell us why you sent Isabel away?" She lifted the empty jug next to him. "I've never seen you like this, it scares me. Never have I known you to try to dull your senses with drink."

If only it were that easy, Rory thought. He looked down at the confused, heartbroken face of his sister and cursed Isabel MacDonald again. This time for her betrayal of his family; he was not the only one who would be devastated by her treachery. Rory took a deep breath and dispassionately recounted the events yesterday leading to his discovery of Isabel with the Fairy Flag—or what he'd thought to be the Fairy Flag.

Their bewildered expressions mirrored what his had been, so thoroughly had Isabel charmed them.

"I don't believe it," Alex said dumbly.

"Oh, Rory," Margaret said at the same time. "Did she offer no explanation?"

Rory couldn't bite back the burst of sarcasm. "What for? For coming to Dunvegan under false pretenses as a pawn for her loathsome uncle, for spying on us, or for—" He stopped himself. *Making me love her.* He glared back into the fire so they would not see the pain twisting through him. He still couldn't believe he'd been so wrong.

Margaret bowed her head on his hand, and her shoulders began to shake. "Oh, Rory, it is all my fault."

Rory stroked her pale cheek. "Don't be ridiculous. What part could you have played in this treachery?"

Margaret raised her tearstained face to his. "I overheard Isabel speaking with Sleat at the gathering, I heard him threaten her and say something about the flag. I should have come to you." Her hands twisted. "I never thought . . . I knew she was hiding something, I just assumed she would eventually confide in you."

Rory stared hard at his sister, unable to prevent the momentary flash of anger that went through him for another betrayal, from yet another unexpected source. He took another long drink and allowed the moment to fade. It would do no good to lash out at Margaret, not for doing what he'd done himself. Trusting Isabel.

"You should have come to me," he said. "But don't blame yourself, Margaret. You were only showing loyalty to your friend. She was an accomplished liar. You were not the only one she fooled." He couldn't hide the bitterness in his tone.

Alex shook his head, still stunned. "So she admitted coming to Dunvegan for the flag?"

Rory nodded tersely.

Margaret's brows gathered across her nose. "But it wasn't actually the flag she'd placed in her trunk?"

"No, it was an old shawl of Bessie's. Though the resemblance was uncanny. For a moment it even fooled me."

"But if she meant to steal the flag, why did she not do so when she had the opportunity?" Alex asked.

"She claimed that she'd decided she couldn't betray us and was planning to use the shawl to trick her uncle."

Margaret bit her lip, thinking. "Do you believe her?"

That was the question he'd spent the last day trying to avoid. "I don't know. Does it matter?"

"I think it does," Margaret said softly. "She loved you, brother. Of that I am sure. I know that she admitted coming to Dunvegan under false pretenses, but from what you said, she only agreed to help Sleat so he would help her clan against the Mackenzies. It sounds like she had no choice, her clan needed her. I know how important it was for Isabel to earn the respect of her family. She spent her childhood recklessly trying to attract their notice. I suspect coming here was her opportunity to finally prove her worth." Margaret's face filled with compassion. "It must have put her in a horrible position:

being forced to choose between her family and us. But if what she said is true, Isabel chose us."

"Can you forgive her so easily, Margaret, when she chose to ally herself with Sleat. Have you forgotten what he did to you?" Rory demanded.

"Of course I have not forgotten what *Sleat* did to me. Sleat is worthy of your wrath. I, too, burn for revenge. But I shall bide my time and wait for the right opportunity to present itself. I do not excuse what she has done, but I do understand the circumstances. From my own experience, I know how cruel and unyielding Sleat can be. He will twist anything to his purpose. If he wanted something from her, he would not be gainsaid." Margaret paused. "Have you forgotten what she did *for* me?"

"I have not forgotten," Rory replied stonily.

"It doesn't make any sense. I agree with Margaret, Isabel loves you. Why did she not confide in you?" Alex asked.

"Apparently, she started to after I was injured but was scared that I would not forgive her. She claimed that she intended to tell me when she was sure I would not repudiate the handfast."

Alex lifted his brow in surprise. "You hadn't told her?"

Rory shook his head. "Not until I heard from the king."

"It sounds like she had reason, then, not to confide in you?" Margaret asked quietly.

Rory clenched his jaw. "She lied to me."

"Yes, but she also loves you," Margaret said. Taking a deep breath, she added, "And I think you love her."

Rory stiffened, refusing to look at his sister, not wanting to give credence to her statement. Love didn't matter, not without trust. "It's done."

He turned to his unusually quiet brother. "And what of you, Alex? Do you agree with our sister—should I forgive my traitorous bride?"

Alex shook his head, his eyes shining with anger. "Isabel betrayed us all. In your place, I might have done worse."

Rory nodded.

Alex turned to leave the room but looked first to his sister. "Leave him be, Margaret. He has a right to his solitude."

Margaret smiled sadly, leaned over, and placed a kiss on his cheek. "I'm sorry, Rory, I know how this must have hurt you. What she did has hurt me, too. You must do what you think is best. But are you sure there is no other way?"

Rory sat mutely, steeling himself from considering Margaret's question.

"And remember this," she said in warning. "If you do not want her, someone else will."

Rory's fingers tightened around the stem of his goblet until the silver began to bend. His reaction was instantaneous. Violently, he tossed the now ruined goblet to the floor, where it clattered conspicuously in the otherwise deathly quiet room.

Margaret turned and followed Alex out the door. "I think you have your answer, Rory. If what she said about her clan needing Sleat is true, you might not have much time to figure out what you want. Her family may be forced to seek another alliance soon. One that could take her from you forever."

Rory did not give any evidence that he had heard her.

Once again, he sat motionless before the flickering flames of the soul-cleansing fire.

But he had.

Three days later, the MacDonald of Sleat watched from the battlements of Dunscaith Castle as the group of MacLeod clansmen approached over the tangled, grassy moors. He recognized the hooded woman astride the palfrey immediately—after all, he had provided her cloak.

Sleat swore, wiping the back of his hand across his mouth to clear the residue of wine. So, his disloyal niece returned under guard—she must have been discovered. 'Twas as he had expected, then. The chit had failed. Silly wench, to succumb so easily to the wiles of a handsome face. He shrugged with disgust. Well, what could you expect from a woman? Women were good for only two things: providing a substantial tocher and providing an heir. Good thing he was smart enough not to wager his quest for the Lordship solely on the capabilities of a lass. An alternative plan was already in position.

He drew his fingers across his chin, considering her return. Isabel knew where the secret entrance was to Dunvegan—of that he had no doubt. Mackenzie had followed the three retreating MacLeods after the latest attack until they had simply disappeared right into the face of the rocky cliff beneath Dunvegan. The Mackenzie chief had searched the area exhaustively for the entrance, to no avail. But Isabel would be able to find it. He would watch his dear niece closely. And wait. She might be of some use yet.

Another bungled attempt on MacLeod, he thought, disgusted. The man was proving exceedingly difficult to kill. He'd had high hopes that this last attempt might succeed, until his informant had apprised him of the MacLeod's miraculous recovery. Sleat did not believe it was actually magic that had enabled MacLeod to evade death so many times, but he would take no chances. That bloody flag had defeated the MacDonalds before; it would not do so again. Magic or luck, it did not matter, it would run out soon enough. All was ready—soon he would reclaim the Lordship and rule the Western Isles. It wouldn't be long now before his dream was fully realized.

The great Rory MacLeod would not stand in his way.

Chapter 24

❦

Isabel waited for a reprieve that never came. Though her head knew differently, her heart refused to accept that he might not forgive her. Bessie had urged her to give him time, time for his anger to dissipate and understanding to take hold. But Isabel had waited long enough. If she waited any longer, she might find Rory wed to another.

A sharp pain pierced her chest, as it always did whenever she thought of him—which was constantly. She yearned for perspective, the bittersweet dulling edge of time, but it had been only a little over one week since he had sent her away.

That meant enduring five days alone with her uncle, forced to wait for her family to arrive at Dunscaith and escort her back to Strome Castle. Not that she looked forward to the impending confrontation with her father. No, she had failed doubly, letting her family down and losing Rory. But at least the arrival of her family would bring a stay from Sleat's daily interrogations. She sensed that her uncle was merely biding his time, waiting for her to make a mistake. Clearly, he did not believe her story that she was so deep in shock after the attack by the Mackenzies that she could not remember how to access the secret entrance to Dunvegan. Sleat was planning something. If only she could find out what.

She stood, as she had for days, at the window in her bower, overlooking the beautiful loch, staring north past the great Cuillin in the direction of her forsaken heart. Scanning always for a rider, someone to bring her the news she longed to hear.

Instead, a loud rumbling knocked her out of her dreary reverie. Instinctively, she clasped her hands over her stomach as it beckoned noisily for sustenance. Her nose wrinkled at the thought of food. Admittedly, she had not eaten much over the last week. The pungent smells of food turned her stomach, but she knew by the looseness of her clothing that she had lost too much weight. She would need to be strong if she was going to fight for Rory.

Was she going to fight for Rory? Her eyes widened. She felt a bud of awakening in the wintry slumber of her anguish—and a trace of something else that could only be termed excitement.

She had to do something; she could not go on like this. Isabel needed to let him know how sorry she was for what she'd done and find some way to make him understand. If only she could make it up to him and prove that she was worthy of his trust . . . and his love. She headed downstairs toward the kitchens. First, she needed to eat. Then she would be able to think. And plan.

"Good morning, Willie. Are you going somewhere?"

A very distracted Willie had just exited her uncle's solar when Isabel greeted him on her way back from the kitchens. She felt much better after the small meal she had managed to force down and was ready to begin planning.

Startled by the sound of her voice, Willie stumbled, and the stack of missives in his hands flew up in a parchment rainstorm over his head, scattering haphazardly around him on the floor. After a stunned moment, he managed to collect his thoughts enough to speak. "Good morning, my lady."

She did not have the heart to correct his improper address. He looked flustered enough as it was. "It appears you are off to deliver some messages."

"Yes, my lady." He managed to right himself, still staring at her. Recognizing the look, Isabel reluctantly gave up on conversation. She bent down to help him collect the jumbled letters strewn across the rushes. Suddenly, her eyes caught sight of the familiar script and distinctive seal: *Per Mare per Terras*.

Were the capricious fates smiling on her at last?

Her heart beat furiously with anticipation, and her eyes widened when she noticed whom it was addressed to. *Please let this be what I'm praying for!* Carefully, she craned her neck to make sure Willie could not see what she was doing as she slipped the letter between the folds of her gown. Handing the remaining letters to Willie, she smiled with genuine delight—for the first time in over a week. Distractedly, she wished him a good journey and tried not to race up the stairs.

Isabel had been gone for only a little more than a week, and Rory had done nothing more than sit before the fireplace and drink rather copious amounts of *cuirm*. He ran his fingers through unkempt hair, snagging on a few knots along the way, and swept it back from his face.

A wee lass had toppled the powerful Rory Mor. He would laugh if the irony weren't so painful. For a man who prided himself on control and decisiveness, discovering that he was not immune to emotions was a severe blow. Every man had his weakness. Apparently, Isabel MacDonald was his.

The question was, what was he going to do about it?

What he wanted to do was immerse himself in his duties, find a way to repair the alliance with Argyll, and begin plans to resume the fighting with Sleat. Instead, he found himself dissecting every moment of the last few months and analyzing every word of their conversation, unable to focus on anything else.

In repudiating the handfast and sending her away, Rory had acted as he always did: coolly, dispassionately, and decisively. His judgment had been sound. Never had he questioned a decision. But he realized that in this, in determining the fate of someone he loved, he was without experience. He could not simply cut Isabel out of his heart because he wanted to.

She'd wronged him, yes. But when his anger had cooled, Rory realized that Isabel's treachery was not as clear-cut as he'd first thought. She'd handfasted with him under false purpose, but he could not fault her loyalty to her clan. She should have come to him, though he could understand her hesitancy. She had spied on him, but she hadn't taken the flag.

But one realization above all blocked his ability to put Isabel behind him forever. Had she truly chosen him over her uncle and her family?

A knock on the door disturbed his reverie.

He glanced up to see Douglas. "A letter, Chief. From the king."

Rory looked at Douglas blankly, his eyes burning from lack of sleep. It took him a moment to realize what he held in his hand.

Douglas knew as well, for he stood woodenly, awaiting instructions, and would not meet Rory's glance. Slowly, Rory cracked the seal, unfolded the parchment, and began to read. When he'd finished, he let out a pained laugh.

"Well, it appears I have an answer to my proposal."

"Yes," Douglas said evenly, with no evidence of the curiosity Rory was sure he felt.

"The king has agreed to cede Trotternish to the MacLeods as part of Isabel's tocher upon our marriage."

"What will you do?"

Rory shrugged. "I don't know." It was the answer to his prayers, come too late.

"Should I instruct the royal emissary to wait for your response?"

"No, I need some time to think."

Dismissing Douglas, Rory reread the passage that had struck him.

Since our dearest Isabel assures us of her happiness, and has also urged the disposition of Trotternish to the MacLeods in her recent missive to the Queen, we are pleased to do so under the conditions outlined in your letter.

Isabel had written to the queen on his behalf? The small crack in his resolve broke open. She *had* chosen him. And in part thanks to Isabel, he now held the means to reclaim Trotternish for the MacLeods and, at least partially, to avenge Sleat's dishonor to the clan. If he married her.

But could he find the strength to forgive her?

Rory felt a flicker of something inside him. He recognized what it was immediately: possibility.

Chapter 25

❖

The MacDonald of Sleat was furious to find Isabel missing. He did not like being duped, especially by a lass. He'd been waiting for something like this, but she'd outmaneuvered him. Though, surprisingly, he had to admit that his little niece had impressed him. Janet's daughter was stronger than she appeared. Sleat was not completely devoid of familial sentiment. He almost regretted that his niece must be sacrificed. Almost.

But it was necessary. His gaze moved calculatedly to his newly arrived guest. The Mackenzie chief would not be satisfied with anything less than Isabel's death. Isabel's near rape at the hands of the Mackenzie's son, the stupid boy, had been another unfortunate cost of war. Sleat stroked his chin, both thoughtful and philosophical. No, Isabel's death could not be avoided. If she'd done her part, he might have been moved to help her. But, like most women, she'd disappointed him.

It was pure chance that had brought the Mackenzie to Dunscaith only hours after Isabel's disappearance had been detected. A few hours later and there wouldn't be a chance of passing her. Fortunately, Sleat had discovered Isabel's absence almost right away. Another piece of luck. A kindhearted maidservant had thought to entice the girl to eat with special honey-sweetened oatcakes, only to find the chit had disappeared. He'd guessed immediately where she was headed.

"Go after her," Sleat said to the other chief. "But you will have to travel fast to overtake her. And you must not be seen. A few men, no more. If you are patient, she will lead you to the entrance."

The Mackenzie's eyes narrowed. "How can you be sure she returns to Dunvegan?"

Sleat shrugged. "Instinct. She fancies herself in love with him. Besides, where else would she go?" He sneered. "She'll be careful to make sure that no one is following her, but of course you won't be following her."

"I'll ride straight for the place we lost them after the attack. I know just where to wait. I'll follow her inside, and my men will wait for you," the Mackenzie said.

Sleat nodded. "Do nothing rash. We won't be far behind."

With the MacLeod dead and a surprise attack on the castle, victory would finally be his.

Perhaps his little niece had been useful after all.

She was almost there. Back to Dunvegan, to Rory, and to what she hoped was forgiveness. For Isabel held in her possession the means to prove her loyalty to Rory.

Excitement and anticipation alone urged her on, as her body had long ago stopped cooperating. Her shoulders slumped, heavy with a deep, bone-aching fatigue such as she had never before experienced. Usually an excellent rider, she struggled to keep herself upright astride the palfrey. When was the last time she'd been able to feel her backside? It must have been miles ago, hours ago. The insides of her thighs would be sore for weeks.

But she had to keep a steady pace that would get her there as quickly as possible.

Dirt and dust streaked her face. With the back of her arm, she wiped away the sheet of dampness on her forehead. There was little she could do about the beads of perspiration collecting under the large ball of hair bound at the back of her neck. It was too hot. She wore a broad-brimmed hat, but after the long, sunny days in the saddle, even that had been unable to prevent the crimson burn now staining her nose and cheeks.

At least her cramped hands were protected from the sun by the thin gloves she usually wore with her habit. Unfortunately, the fashionable thin leather gloves might protect her from the sun and the midges, but after long hours of constant hard use, they weren't protecting her from much else. The voluminous skirts were hiked up to her thighs to accommodate her riding astride but were otherwise too cumbersome for such a long, difficult journey. She dearly wished she'd been able to find a pair of breeches and sturdy leather gloves, but there hadn't been time.

She had traveled north for two days and nights, over fifty miles along the road—at times path—from Dunscaith located on the western peninsula of Sleat. Two days traveling for a journey that normally took three full days or more. She recalled the nervous excitement she'd felt when she'd cautiously snuck out of a sleeping Dunscaith armed with proof of her uncle's perfidy. The letter she had stolen from Willie was more than she could have dreamed. She doubted even her father was aware of Sleat's plans. With this letter, Rory would have the means to destroy her uncle. It would give him the weapon he needed to extract Sleat from the king's favor.

And in doing so, Isabel would hand him what he wanted most of all—a way to avenge the dishonor done his clan at the hands of Sleat.

And Isabel hoped it would indisputably prove her loyalty to him.

Anxious to leave, she'd nonetheless been forced to wait, making sure that Willie had left to deliver the rest of his messages before she set out—she wanted to make sure no one was aware of a missing letter. But Willie left right after their collision in the hall, enabling her to sneak out that very night.

Now it was late morning on the third day of the journey, and she was only a few furlongs from her destination.

She patted her mount fondly along the side of its warm neck. Her uncle's stables were among the best in the Highlands and Isles. This purloined palfrey was undeniably a magnificent animal. She knew she'd used it badly, but she had no other choice. She had to keep moving, to keep well ahead of any pursuers. She had allowed herself and the horse a few hours of sleep at night but otherwise kept stops to a minimum. She couldn't allow her uncle's men time to catch up to her if they were following. She dared not risk stopping during the day for longer than the time it took to water and feed the exhausted animal.

The meager food supply she had managed to save from her last dinner at Dunscaith had run out yesterday. The persistent headache she'd had since then from lack of food had subsided a bit, but she knew that once she dismounted she would fight dizziness.

At least she was familiar with this part of the road. At times, she worried that her poor navigation skills would lead her down the wrong road. On her first day of travel, she had narrowly avoided taking the wrong fork in the path—heading toward Port Righ instead of Dunvegan—at the base of the great Cuillin Mountains. She was much more careful after that. During the day, she used the path of the sun to keep her heading due north, but navigation was more difficult at night. She dared not stop and ask for directions for fear that her uncle's men would use this to track her.

That they had not caught up with her was surprising. For the first few hours after sunrise on the day she'd left, when she'd known they must have discovered her missing, she'd jumped at every sound, looked warily at every village, and caught herself looking behind her so much that her neck had begun to hurt. She had brought her bow for protection but so far had not needed it. Either her uncle was not aware of where she was headed or, more likely, he must have decided to wait for her father to arrive before following her.

Utter weariness prevented her from noticing the lavish bounty of the countryside spread out like a banquet before her. The hills were scattered with a kaleidoscope of summer wildflowers. Lavender bunches of heather formed a natural border to the road. The sea sparkled on her left, and the green, grassy moors undulated with the gentle breeze on her right. The lush density of the forests beckoned ahead of her.

A sudden inexplicable chill, perhaps the cold wind of remembrance, crept down the back of her neck. This was just about the place where the Mackenzies had attacked Rory.

Dunvegan was just ahead.

She steered her palfrey off the trail and headed into the copse.

She would take no chances. She would have to use the secret entrance. She dared not risk that Rory might refuse her entry to the castle. This time she would not give him a choice: Rory would listen to her whether he wanted to or not.

Isabel focused on the task before her, concentrating on remembering the way to the entrance. The closer she drew to the hidden entrance, the more she checked her surroundings. Nothing. There was nobody following her; of that she was sure. She retraced their steps along the inlet of the loch and paused before the dramatic rocky cliff.

Dunvegan, in all its forbidding splendor, sat perched high on the rock above her. The walls were situated so close to the edge of the cliff, it looked as if it might slide off with only the slightest nudge. The sheer, thick, gray stone edifice hardly offered a warm welcome. But rather than dissuade Isabel from her purpose, the sight of that grimly beautiful pile of rocks filled her heart with bursting joy and brought a broad smile of accomplishment to her weary countenance. Her back straightened as she drew up her shoulders.

Dunvegan. Rory. She'd made it.

Almost.

Isabel held her head completely still, chin lifted, ears alert, eyes scanning back and forth, listening for the smallest sound or flash of movement. Hearing nothing other than the steady movement of the loch on her left and the sound of the breeze flitting through the leaves and underbrush of the forest on her right, she looked carefully once more behind her, then headed for the jagged, rocky entrance that lay hidden before her.

She urged the frightened horse forward, straight into the face of the cliff where it joined with the edge of the forest. Taking a deep breath, praying for strength, she pulled the reins for a sharp turn to the left and slid into the cool, dark dampness of the tunnel.

Chapter 26

❖

Hold fast that which is good.

—I Thessalonians 5:21

Isabel was cold, exhausted, and hungry. She'd waited in the tunnel until the sounds above in the kitchens had quieted before pulling herself carefully through the secret door, winding her away through the darkened corridors, and stealthily making her way to the Fairy Tower.

Unsure of her reception, Isabel approached the tower with burgeoning unease. What would Rory do when he found her in his room? Would he toss her out without listening to her? Or worse? She wished she could be sure she was doing the right thing. But she thought of her misery the past week and a half and knew that she had no other choice. She had to try to make things right.

She paused in the doorway of the Fairy Tower, casting a quick glance around before darting across the entry. She'd just started to climb the stairs when someone grabbed her from behind, yanking her momentarily against a chest as hard as stone. A scream caught in her throat.

Her captor spun her around to face him, and she exhaled. Rory. She was so relieved to find him after all that she'd gone through to get here, after the days of agony that had marked their separation, after thinking she might not ever see him again, that she could have collapsed and burst into tears. Her knees weakened; if not for his support, she would have slid to the floor in a grateful heap.

Then he spoke, and her relief stalled. "By all that is holy, Isabel," he swore, "what are you doing here?"

She shrank from the fury in his voice. Cautiously, she raised her eyes to his. So long had she been anticipating this moment, the rush of emotion in just seeing him again was far more overwhelming than she could have imagined. She took in every beloved detail of his face. The strong, hard lines of his ruggedly handsome features, the brilliant blue eyes, the square jaw, the thick golden strands of his . . . She stopped and frowned. Actually, Rory looked horrible. He looked as though he hadn't slept in days. In truth, he looked as awful as she surely did. Something kindled inside her. Was it possible? Had he missed her? She dared not allow herself to hope.

So desperately did she want to touch him, she placed her hand against his chest, savoring the heavy beat of his heart under her palm. She wanted nothing more than to throw herself into his arms and beg his forgiveness, but she couldn't bear the pain of his rejection. Not again. Not until he'd heard what she had to say. If he would listen.

His eyes were hot as he scanned her face, almost hungrily. For a moment, she thought he wanted her, and her body responded, softening with awareness. He tightened his grip on her arms, pulling her imperceptibly closer, and she felt the heat radiating from his body, smelled the beloved scent of heather and spice. He was so achingly close, it hurt not to press her body against his.

He seemed tight with restraint. His teeth clenched, and she noticed the telltale tic in his jaw. "Well? Explain why I find you here and not at Dunscaith or on your way home to your father?"

"I needed to see you. I know you said you never wanted to see me again, but I have to explain." Before he could argue, she burst out, "When I agreed to help my uncle, I did not know you or your family. I was only trying to help my clan. I should have told you the truth as soon as I realized how I felt about you, but I couldn't. Not while I was unsure of your intentions. Spying on you when you told Alex where you kept the flag was wrong, and unintentional. I'm sorry for it, but even by then I knew I would never betray you or your family." Her eyes raked his face, looking for any indication that her words might have penetrated his steely barrier, but all she could see was a man barely keeping a check on his anger. "I know you have no reason to believe me, so I've brought you proof of my loyalty."

"And this proof of your loyalty is the reason I see you like this? So weary you can barely stand?" His eyes turned black. "Where is your escort?"

She looked down sheepishly, shifting uncomfortably beneath his piercing gaze.

"You traveled almost the length of Skye by yourself?" Incredulous, his voice shook with anger. "Forsooth, don't you realize what could have happened to you? Dear God, Isabel, how could you be so reckless?"

He was livid, but Isabel also detected a thread of alarm in his voice. His hands still gripped her shoulders, and she didn't know whether he wanted to shake her or crush her against his chest. She wanted so badly to believe that he was happy to see her, was she only imagining his concern? Unshed tears burned behind her eyes. "I was desperate. I had to see you. I'd hoped you . . ." *wanted to see me.* She couldn't get the words out.

Something flickered across his face. For a moment, she thought he was going to pull her into his arms and kiss her. Instead, he dropped his hands and turned away, raking his fingers through his hair. After a few minutes, his eyes found hers again. "You used the secret entrance."

Isabel bit her lip. She knew he'd be angry about that. "I was very careful. I feared you would refuse my entry if I came by the sea-gate." She looked up. "I couldn't take the chance."

"I forgot how many of our secrets you share." He reached down to stroke her cheek, wiping the dirt and grime from her face. The gentleness of the movement stunned her. Emotion gathered in her throat, hot and raw. The longing for the closeness they'd once shared was nearly unbearable, the times when she didn't have to stop herself from touching him. "What am I to do with you, Isabel?" He took an ominous step closer. "First you will explain what has brought you here in such haste and with disregard for your own safety."

Isabel felt light-headed with relief. She had a chance.

But sudden fear gripped her, so much was riding on this. She took a deep breath and began. "While at Dunscaith a few days ago, I was helping Willie recover some missives that he dropped on the floor when I noticed Sleat's badge on a letter addressed to Robert Cecil, the first Earl of Salisbury." She paused, waiting for Rory to glean the significance.

She caught the sudden spark in his eye and continued, this time excitedly. "I immediately questioned why Sleat would be writing the queen of England's secretary of state. I suspected that my uncle was trying to find another way to obtain the Lordship for himself. He hinted as much to me in a conversation we had at the gathering. When I found the letter, I realized that Sleat and probably Mackenzie were in treasonous contact with Queen Elizabeth."

"You deduced this from the name on a missive?" Rory asked, clearly impressed.

"I was desperate to find *anything* that would make you understand that I would never betray you. And the letter, well, it just seemed odd. Of course, when I read it I could not believe what I'd stumbled upon. Sleat proposed a new rebellion in the Isles. He offered his service to Elizabeth, actually precipitously referring to himself as the 'Lord of the Isles.' He proposed to unite the Highland chiefs to the queen and keep the Lordship for himself. And destroy the MacLeods in the process. With the MacLeods in shambles, there would be no one powerful enough in the Isles to contest his claim."

Rory shook his head. " 'Tis even worse than I expected. I knew he wanted to reestablish the Lordship, but I didn't think he would commit treason to assure it. I may be at the horn, and do not agree with James's plans for the 'barbarians' of the Isles, but to invite the bloody English into Scotland is an extremely dangerous— and foolish—proposition." He looked back at her, his expression inscrutable. "Do you know what you risked in coming here? If your uncle realizes what you know, your life will be in danger."

"He doesn't know."

"You're sure?"

She nodded, and her head spun with dizziness. Something was wrong, she didn't feel very well.

"Do you know what this means, Isabel? If the king discovers what Sleat has done, he will be destroyed."

"I know."

"And you rode for days to tell me this?"

Isabel nodded again, too teeming with expectation to speak. Would it be enough to prove her devotion? Would he ever be able to forgive her? She forced herself to look at his face. What she saw there made the tears that she'd been holding start to fall. He gazed at her with such emotion, such longing, that her fear abated and the hope she'd been holding inside burst free, overwhelming her with the sheer intensity of emotion.

"I don't know what to say," he said roughly.

"Say that you believe me."

He wiped the tears from her cheeks, his thumb running over her trembling lips. "Aye, lass, I believe you. But unfortunately, without the letter we have no proof."

She reached into her waistband and pulled out the folded parchment. "You mean this letter?" She smiled through the haze of happy tears.

And promptly fainted.

Rory thought his heart had stopped when Isabel crumpled to the floor. He lurched forward, catching her just before she hit the ground. The same fear gripped him that he'd felt that day in the forest. Only when he'd assured himself that she'd fainted did it dissipate—a little. But what the hell had she done to herself?

Carefully, he lifted her in his arms and carried her up the stairs to his solar. Looking at the wan, dust-smeared cheek resting peacefully against his chest, he felt his heart flip. All that he could have lost hit him full force.

When he'd first caught sight of her, he'd been shocked, not only to have her seemingly materialize out of his dreams, but to see her so obviously exhausted. Her glorious hair flew in wild disarray around her pinched face, and dark shadows circled her luminous violet eyes. She must not have eaten in days; her wrinkled gown hung loose about her thin frame. His first impulse had been to take her in his arms and prove in the most basic way possible that she was real, but anger at seeing her like that had checked him.

When he thought of what she must have gone through to reach him, and the risk she'd taken in bringing him Sleat's treasonous letter . . . He shuddered as the possibilities chilled him. If anything had happened to her, he would never have forgiven himself.

The timing of her arrival could not have been more ironic. After the arrival of the king's missive, Rory had made the decision to retrieve his bride. Even if he had to take an army to Strome Castle, he would get her back. But he had another plan and hoped that laying siege would not prove necessary. Putting that plan into motion had delayed his pursuit of Isabel.

He'd still had many questions, but Isabel's letter to the queen on his behalf was proof of her loyalty. Now, after what she'd brought him, there could be no doubt. Thanks to Isabel, he had the means to destroy Sleat and avenge the dishonor done his clan.

He laid her on the bed. Her eyes fluttered open almost immediately, and Rory felt relief pour out of him.

"What happened?" she asked, disoriented.

"You fainted."

"I don't faint." She tried to sit up but quickly lay back down.

He frowned. "When is the last time you ate?"

A delicate flush rose to her pale cheeks. "I don't know."

"I will send for something." He started to get up, but she caught his arm.

"Please, don't," she beseeched. "I don't want anything, not yet. Not until I know that you can forgive me. I'm so sorry, Rory—" Her voice broke. "There were many things I did wrong, and I know I have no right to ask for your forgiveness, but I need you to know that I would never betray you."

He gathered her against him, her damp cheek pressed against his chest as he savored the sensation of holding her in his arms again. "I know."

She looked up at him with watery eyes. "You do?"

"Aye," he whispered, a husky caress deepening his voice. He could forgive her. Deep in his bones he knew that Isabel had not been merely acting over the past few months. She loved him; he knew she would not betray him. He must have accepted that when he sent her away, for she knew far too many of their secrets. If he'd truly believed her a traitor, he would not have allowed her to leave. Was not the badge of the MacLeods "Hold Fast"? *God's blood*, he would hold fast to Isabel. She belonged to him, and he would have her. He could do his duty and have the woman he loved.

Rory bent over her, cupping her chin in his hand and forcing her to meet his gaze. "I will forgive you for not telling me about your uncle's plan, but you will promise me that you will not listen in on any other private conversations—unintentional or not."

Isabel blushed to her roots. "I promise. No more peeking through cracks in doors."

"Good." He swept a lock of hair from her face, looking at her tenderly. "And more important, you will also swear that you will never endanger yourself like this again."

She nodded, tears sliding down her cheeks again. "I didn't know what else to do—"

"Shush." He stopped her with a press of his fingers against her softly parted lips. He'd waited long enough, he had to taste her. No longer able to hold back, he lowered his head, covering her mouth with his in a gentle, seductive kiss. His heart jumped at the achingly familiar taste. She was pure ambrosia; the honey of her mouth mingled with the bittersweet salt from her tears.

But Isabel did not want a gentle wooing. At the first touch of his mouth, she moaned, encircling her arms around his neck, bringing him down hard on top of her. She strained and pressed against him, kissing him harder, with an almost desperate plea.

Rory felt his own restraint snap, responding to the savage cry of her desire. The subtle seduction of moments before was replaced by a violent surge of demanding passion. His mouth moved over hers hungrily, possessively, branding her with his lips and tongue. She belonged to him; he would leave her no doubt. Her mouth opened, and he slid in his tongue, locking with hers in an intimate duel of thrust and parry. He delved deeper and deeper, tasting, exploring, as if devouring the very recesses of her soul.

It wasn't enough. Not until he was thrust deep inside her and she was shaking around him with the spasms of her release. Not until they had burned away the memories of their parting with the fire of their passion.

Even then, Rory knew it would never be enough.

From the first touch of his mouth, Isabel's entire body shivered with relief and desire. She was nearly undone by the familiar taste and distinctively masculine smell of him. That wonderful mixture of salt and heather. She moaned, pressing her body deeper into his familiar hold. Gentle curves against warm, hard muscle.

Her hands roamed his back and shoulders, exploring the familiar ridges of steel. He'd regained some of the weight he had lost from the fever, she realized. But there was still a hungry leanness to him that had not been there before the attack. His muscles bulged under her fingertips, and a spark of awareness surged through her. The heat between them flamed instantly, as if it had never been extinguished. As if it had merely lain dormant, smoldering, these last two weeks. There was an urgency to their movements that recalled the long separation.

Isabel felt the familiar anxious tingling low in her belly; she instinctively shifted her hip toward his. Rory clutched her sore bottom, holding her firmly against the solid proof of his claim. The pain of the saddle was forgotten in the hazy warmth flooding her senses.

Suddenly, his hands were everywhere, cupping her breasts, molding her hips, sliding down her thighs. His mouth pressed against her neck and shoulders, scraping the delicate skin with his rough beard. Her skin prickled with gooseflesh, she wanted him so badly.

She felt his fingers expertly work the laces of her gown. He pushed the filthy gown off her shoulders and pulled it over her hips to drop to the floor. Next went her stays and bolster. His fingers slid under the thin linen fabric of her sark, tauntingly tracing the curve of her breast. Isabel felt singed wherever he touched. When his mouth deliciously followed the path of his hands, she wriggled uncontrollably. She felt her hose slide off, felt her sark lifted over her head, until she lay completely naked. Awareness tinged her skin pink.

But she was beyond embarrassment.

And Rory had completely exhausted his reserves. Isabel was mesmerized by the power of the desire that flooded his eyes as they roamed her naked body.

His voice was rough with emotion. "You are so beautiful, my love."

He unfastened the brooch that held his plaid and pulled his wrinkled *leine croich* over his head.

It was her turn to admire him. Boldly, her eyes raked the flat stomach lined with muscle, the broad chest, the muscular arms and legs. The sheer size of his stiffened arousal. He was spectacular.

"So are you," she said huskily.

"It's been too long."

Her mouth felt too dry to speak. She nodded.

He slid down on top of her. At the touch of his skin to hers, Isabel melted. She felt sweetly damp and hot where their bodies joined. When his length pressed into her belly, she circled her hips against him encouragingly, sliding her damp opening against the head of his arousal.

"Isabel, if you do that again, I may unman myself." His voice was gruff with desire.

Isabel ignored him, reaching for him, grasping the velvety skin firmly in her hand. She moved her hand to the rhythm he had taught her. She watched his face stiffen, his jaw clench as if in pain. Wantonly, she increased the speed. Mesmerized by the feeling of control over this powerful man, she watched his flat stomach muscles clench. She could feel the pressure building beneath her hand and rubbed her thumb over the hot drop that escaped from his hold.

"Damn you, love. We'll see how much you enjoy such torture."

Rory yanked her hand from him and roughly pinned both her hands above her head with one hand. She knew his strength; she would never be able to break free. Even if she wanted to. His golden hair spilled forward across his eyes, but she caught the wicked grin he gave her, and it sent another shiver up her spine.

His tongue traced a path down her chest, flicking to nudge her nipples erect. Blowing, raking his teeth lightly across the tips. She writhed beneath him with pleasure, her hips rising to search for his length. He moved back, refusing her request. His mouth enveloped the tip of her breast, and he sucked gently. Isabel felt the sharp sensation of pleasure at the squeeze of his mouth, but she wanted more. Much more.

Rory increased her agony as his mouth slowly, exquisitely, trailed down her belly. Licking and flicking her blazing, sensitive skin with his tongue.

His hand reached down between her legs. Her anticipation caused her breath to catch. She couldn't think about anything other than his hand, his mouth. Anything but how much she wanted him to touch her.

He teased and taunted. Brushing, but not stroking the pulse that was clenching with desire. His mouth left feather kisses along the teasing path of his fingers. She lifted her hips to his mouth in silent entreaty.

"How does that feel, love?"

"Please, Rory."

He chuckled. "Tell me how much you want me."

"Please, I want to feel you touch me. I want you inside me."

He groaned. "I think you have learned your lesson in torture, my love."

His finger slid inside her as he began to bring her to heaven. She closed her thighs against his hand, increasing the pressure, the sweet friction that would make her shatter. She knew she was close, and her mind went black as the rush of heat and sharp spasms signaled her release. Quickly he moved over her, releasing her hands and driving into her in one all-consuming thrust. Isabel gasped to feel the strength of him inside her. The heavy, thick way he filled her. The sensation intensified the power of her climax as the spasms came harder and faster.

He grasped her hips, lifting her to meet his long thrusts. Isabel arched her back, urging him to take her harder, deeper. She needed to feel the force of his passion, to feel how much he needed her.

Rory sensed her urgency, and his hips pounded against her, wild with unbridled desire. He'd never been so rough with her before. She tightened against him again as wave after wave of sensation exploded inside her.

He threw back his head and sank deep into her, pulsing as the force of his release gripped him in its shuddering hold. He held her deep, allowing the waves of her own passion to ebb gently around him, until, strength depleted, he collapsed on top of her.

Naked flesh to naked flesh. Chest to chest, two hearts

beating frantically together. He rolled to the side and gently moved a strand of damp hair from her eyes.

The tenderness in his gaze took her breath away. When she thought of what she'd nearly lost, Isabel could not prevent the tears that spilled down her cheeks. She might not know what their future held, but he'd forgiven her. It was enough.

He looked confused. "What's wrong? Was I too rough with you?"

She shook her head and smiled. "I'm just so happy."

He took her chin in his hand and dropped a light kiss on her nose. "You're exhausted." He tucked her under his arm and started issuing orders. "First food and a bath, then we sleep."

For once, Isabel was only too happy to follow his command.

Chapter 27

❖

A chill at the back of Rory's neck stirred him from the viselike arms of slumber, but the warning had come too late. Falling asleep with Isabel after nearly two weeks of sleepless nights had dulled his senses, severely limiting his instincts. He woke to the cold press of steel against his neck and the malevolent, glassy-eyed Mackenzie hovering over them.

Rory stilled. The invigorating blood rush of battle swept all vestiges of sleep from his body. Every nerve ending flared, primed to attack.

Seeing that Rory was awake, the Mackenzie chief jostled Isabel. "Get up, whore."

He wanted to reach out to protect her, but he dared not move. Not yet. Not with the blade so close. It took a moment for the haze of slumber to clear enough for Isabel to realize what was happening. Rory watched her eyes widen with fear.

"Move slowly, love," Rory soothed. "Stay calm."

The Mackenzie sneered, his expression teeming with the promise of vengeance. "I said get up, whore."

Rory swore. "Do as he says, love."

Isabel clutched a sheet to her nakedness and rose from the bed. The moon lit the sensuous curves of her figure to perfection.

The Mackenzie did not move the sword from Rory's neck, but his eyes devoured her near nakedness. His grayish tongue darted out to wet his lips. Lust transformed his features into a mask of depraved cruelty. Rory felt every muscle in his body clench. Rage surged through him. Killing the man who dared threaten his woman would be a pleasure. But first he needed to create a diversion.

Unfortunately, Isabel seemed to have the same idea. Rory could see how terrified she was, but heedless of the risk, she drew the Mackenzie's gaze to her, innocently allowing the sheet to fall low on her breasts. *Damn.* A hot burst of anger erupted inside him. She'd sworn not to endanger herself. He was going to throttle her when this was done. The only thing that kept him from doing it right now was that he knew she was trying to sacrifice herself for him, and her distraction was working. Too well.

"How did you get here?" Rory asked, though he'd already figured it out.

The Mackenzie's eyes still gorged on Isabel's body, but at least he did not move to touch her. "Why, I followed the gel, of course."

"That's impossible!" Isabel exclaimed. "I made sure I was not followed."

"You were careful to make sure no one was *behind* you. But I had an advantage. I knew where you were headed—where you had disappeared last time. So I waited for you to come to me."

Isabel cursed softly and turned to Rory. "I'm so sorry, it's all my fault."

Instinctively, Rory moved to reassure her, only to stop at the pressure of the blade against his neck. He sat

back. "You couldn't have known, love." He turned back
to the Mackenzie.

The castle was silent. It was a good sign. "Where are
the others? Did you come alone?"

The Mackenzie shrugged. "Patience, MacLeod. All
things in good time." He threw a lascivious glance at
Isabel. "Some things can't wait."

The Mackenzie was too eager to kill them. Rory's
mind worked quickly. It might work to their advantage
if the Mackenzie had followed Isabel inside by himself
or with only a few men. But Rory knew they must work
fast. Sleat would not be far behind. He drew the Mackenzie's attention back to him. "What do you want?"

"Why, the Fairy Flag, of course. To start with." The
Mackenzie leered again at Isabel. Rory fought the urge
to rip the lewd smile from his face.

"Never," Rory said evenly. Cool authority rang clear
in his voice, despite the presence of the claymore pressed
to his neck.

"We shall see." The Mackenzie turned to Isabel.
"You, whore, bring me the flag. And no tricks, I know
what it looks like."

"Never." Isabel met Rory's eyes, her voice imitating
the calm authority she had heard in his.

"You dare defy me? You, the strumpet that lured my
son to his death? I will enjoy watching you beg. How
much do you care for your former handfast husband?"

The Mackenzie flicked his claymore, and the razor-
sharp sword sliced a deep gash across the top of Rory's
bare shoulder. Rory didn't flinch, but Isabel cried out
with horror as blood gushed from the wound.

"We'll see how determined you are to defy me as I cut

him apart limb by limb. How long do you think you'll be able to stomach his pain? By the time I'm done, you'll be begging me to cut his throat."

Pleasure transformed the Mackenzie's face as he spoke. The quest for revenge had deadened the man; there was nothing left in his soul but evil. Rory knew that the Mackenzie would kill them, with or without the flag. He did not doubt his ability to take the man one-on-one, but if the Mackenzie turned on Isabel . . . He needed a distraction—and not the one Isabel proposed—so that he could get his weapon.

His gaze moved around the room from the fireplace to the chair to Isabel's trunk that she'd never sent for—

His gaze jerked back. The fireplace. Isabel's trunks. A slow smile slid over his face. He would give the Mackenzie what he wanted.

Rory turned to Isabel. "Isabel, love, we have no choice. Give him the flag." He pointed to her trunk. "It's in my trunk over there."

Rory saw relief and understanding flash in her eyes. She moved toward the chest, pulling the sheeting along with her to cover her nakedness. Slowly, she opened the lid and retrieved Bessie's shawl from the stack of linens. Reverently, she held up the shawl for the Mackenzie to see. When her eyes looked to Rory's, he flicked his glance over to the fire.

She nodded, and he knew she understood.

Isabel took a seemingly innocent step toward the fireplace. "Here it is." She held it up for Mackenzie to see, then quickly crumpled the thin silk into a ball.

"Give me the flag, gel, or I will sever his head from his body. Now!"

Rory waited, making sure the Mackenzie's greedy

eyes stayed on the "flag." A few seconds were all he needed.

"Here, if you want it—catch." And before the Mackenzie realized what she was about to do, Isabel tossed the shawl into the crackling flames of the fire.

"No!" the Mackenzie yelled.

He lunged for the piece of cloth, using his claymore to lift it from the flames, and Rory rolled off the bed naked and pulled a dirk from beneath the pile of his discarded clothing.

"Get back, Isabel," he ordered softly.

She ran to the far corner of the room, as far from the Mackenzie's reach as possible.

But there was no need; the distraction had worked.

With the Mackenzie's gaze focused on the "flag," Rory was afforded the precious seconds he needed to attack. The familiar hot rush of blood and clarity of mind descended on him, as it always did in battle. Dirk raised, Rory lunged toward the Mackenzie. He moved with lethal precision, his eyes narrowed in on the kill.

Too late, the Mackenzie realized his error. He turned at the last minute to ward off the blow, but his efforts were futile. Rory would not be denied—he easily blocked the swing of the Mackenzie's sword. With the steely determination of a man intent on protecting the woman he loved, Rory plunged his dirk deep into the heart of his prey.

The Mackenzie's eyes rounded, and his mouth opened in surprise. The horrible sounds of a gurgling death echoed in the room as he remained pinned by the dirk against the fireplace. Rory released his hold on the dirk, and the Mackenzie chief slipped to the floor, his face a death mask of shock, his cold, flat eyes fixed on eternal nothingness. Like those of his son months before.

It was over.

Isabel ran into his arms. "I thought he was going to kill us."

Rory smoothed her hair. "I would never let anyone harm you." But the fierce pounding of his heart told him danger was much closer than he would have liked. There were still no sounds of an attack, but he would have to be ready. The Mackenzie had not come alone.

She looked up at him with tears in her eyes. "Oh, Rory, I'm so sorry. I swear I didn't know he was watching me."

His fingers pressed against her lips. "Shush, love. I trust you." He held her out to look at her, a black scowl suddenly descending across his handsome face. "But I thought we agreed that you would not do anything reckless ever again. Allowing that sheet to slip was no accident."

He could see the color spread across her cheeks, knowing very well to what he referred. She tried to look contrite. "I had to get that blade away from your neck. I could think of no other way to distract him."

"I know what you were trying to do, but next time save your seductions for me. And only me."

She frowned. "If you'll recall, I tried, but you were immune. Frustratingly so."

Rory shook his head. "Nay, lass, never immune." He pulled her close again and kissed her, telling her with his mouth and the hardness of his body how much she affected him. Reluctantly, he broke the kiss. "Later. I have to raise the men and see to the safety of the keep." His mind was racing. He realized that the Mackenzie must have traveled fast to arrive before Isabel, but he could not be sure how far the rest would be behind.

"The entrance?"

Rory nodded. "Aye, it's where they will try to enter." He turned away to gather his clothes when he heard Isabel gasp.

The sheet she held was covered with blood. "Your shoulder, it's bleeding."

" 'Tis nothing, just a scratch." One that hurt like hell.

Their eyes met. He knew she wanted to argue, but there was no time. "Just see that you don't get any more."

He dropped a quick kiss on her mouth. "I'll do my best."

It was easier than Rory expected. The thirst for revenge had driven the Mackenzie to act precipitously in anticipation of Sleat's arrival. The guardsmen who had accompanied the Mackenzie were waiting for the return of their chief by the secret entrance, only to be surprised by Rory and his men. When Sleat did arrive, there would be no one left to meet him. No one left to pass on the location of the secret entrance. Within a few hours, Rory had secured the keep and returned to his room. Isabel was waiting with a needle to stitch up his wound.

Later that morning, they sat across a small table that had been set up for Isabel to eat in his chamber. Rory stretched out his long, muscular legs, sat back in his chair with a goblet of *cuirm,* and watched her, reluctant to take his eyes off her lest she disappear. He still couldn't believe she was here.

"I don't think I have ever seen you enjoy a meal more," he said, amused.

Isabel looked somewhat shamefaced, aware that she had attacked her platter with a rather unladylike gusto. "I'm afraid I'm quite ravenous. I've been fighting bouts of nausea for the past couple of weeks." She wrinkled her nose. "I can't abide the smells of certain foods, especially herring," she said with a shudder.

Just like my mother when she was . . .

Rory froze, forcing himself to stay calm, but his pulse quickened with possibility.

She couldn't be. But he, more than anyone, knew that she could. The memory of their night of celebration almost two months ago when he'd lost control and spilled his seed deep inside her. His heart dropped. *Their child.* Could Isabel be carrying their child? Emotion gripped his chest with an intensity that stunned him. He wanted it with every fiber of his being.

He took a long sip of *cuirm*, his fingers squeezing the goblet so hard that his knuckles turned white. As casually as he could muster, he asked, "Isabel, do you remember the night after the gathering?"

She looked at him questioningly, her brows a perfect V above her tiny nose. "Of course."

He held her gaze intently. "Have you had your flux since then?"

She tilted her head, considering. "No, I don't think so. Why—" She broke off with a sharp intake of breath, and her hand flew over her mouth as understanding dawned. She looked at him, eyes wide with disbelief. "A babe?"

" 'Tis possible," he said, his voice thick with emotion.

Her hand dropped to cover her stomach. "Dear God, how could I not have guessed? I've been so worried about everything else, I never even considered . . ."

Rory could have put his face in his hands and wept. From joy, that something so precious could have been created from their love. And from regret. *I sent her away. I could have lost them both. Never again.* He stood up and pulled her into his arms, cradling her gently against him, overwhelmed by what he could have lost, but had now been returned to him.

"Oh, Rory, I'm sorry," she sobbed.

He tilted her chin to his, peering deep into tumultuous seas of violet. "What foolishness is this? Why would you be sorry?"

"I know you did not want a child to complicate matters."

Rory smiled. "A bairn will not complicate anything." In truth, he could think of nothing more perfect.

"But what of the alliance?"

"There is no longer an alliance with Argyll. I'd decided some time ago that I could not let you go."

She looked as though he'd handed her the moon. She realized what it could have cost him. "But what of Trotternish?"

Quickly, he explained about the letter he'd received from King James. Rory knew that James would be angry about the Mackenzie's death, but the king would not fault him for killing a man who'd attacked him in his own bedchamber.

A huge smile spread across her face. "So my letter to Queen Anne helped?"

"Coming on the heels of my letter to the king, I'm sure it did not hurt. Although with what you've brought from your uncle, I think James would have been persuaded to our way of thinking in any event." He looked deep into her eyes. "So you see, I knew before you'd arrived that you would not betray me." He smiled. "Not that I'm not pleased with what you brought me. But I'd already made plans to come after you."

"You did?"

"I wrote to your father. In fact, I think we can expect him soon."

"My father, here?"

"I hoped to persuade him that a marriage, a real marriage this time, would be to his benefit. I believe I made him an offer he couldn't refuse."

Her eyebrows drew tight together. "What kind of offer?"

"I offered him my support against the Mackenzies in his defense of Castle Strome."

She threw her arms around his neck. "You agreed to do that for me?"

Rory grinned. "In truth, 'twas not a very difficult decision. The Mackenzies are no friends of ours, especially today. And with your letter, I may have some influence with the king soon."

"So by marrying me, you will be able to reclaim the land you've sought."

He knew what she was thinking. "Aye, but that is not why I want to marry you." He had to tell her how important she was to him. "You are a MacLeod, you are part of my family." *I was lost without you.*

Her brows knit together across her nose. "I don't understand. You repudiated the handfast."

"Aye, love, I'm sorry for that." More sorry than she would ever know. Those were dark days indeed. He pressed a soft kiss on her mouth. "But don't you remember the bard's tale? Only a MacLeod can touch the Fairy Flag."

Isabel tossed back her head and laughed. "I wish you had thought of that before you sent me back to my uncle, it would have saved me quite a lot of heartache," she said sternly, but the amused twinkling in her eyes ruined the effect.

"I must admit, I didn't think of it until later. But I think I always knew that you belonged to me. From the first moment I saw you." He smiled at her look of disbelief. "Maybe it didn't always seem like it, Isabel, but it was there."

Thank God he'd recognized it before it was too late. Isabel had opened up a part of him that he hadn't known existed. The life of a leader was a lonely one indeed. Consumed by duty and responsibility, Rory had lost sight of what was truly important. His sister's happiness, his brother's, and his own. He'd been wrong. Isabel wasn't his weakness, but his greatest strength.

The intensity of emotion that he felt for this tiny lass humbled him.

Rory drew her into his arms and looked straight into her eyes, so there would be no mistaking his next words—words that would bind them together forever. "I love you, Isabel, with all of my heart."

Much later that evening, after tearful reunions with Bessie, Margaret, and Alex, Isabel sighed deeply and snuggled back against the warm, solid strength behind her. Awash in the sensation of happiness so complete, it took her breath away. She felt his arms tighten instinctively in response—drawing her even closer. Her bottom slid perfectly into the natural bend of his hips and legs. One arm slid snugly under her breasts, the other wrapped almost protectively around her still flat stomach.

A babe. Isabel still could not believe it. The discovery of the tiny life growing inside her had moved her beyond words. Never could she have imagined the intensity of emotion that had come with the knowledge that she was carrying Rory's child. She was bound to this man in a way that she could not have comprehended a year ago. That such a blessing could spring out of such difficulty was a profound testament to the strength of their love and the power of forgiveness.

Her head still spun with all that had happened. He'd forgiven her, saved her from death at the hands of a madman, declared his love, and given her the gift of a child. All in the space of one day. An impressive feat, even for a man like Rory MacLeod. But it was what he'd almost given up that had struck her to the core. She'd been astonished when he'd confided that he'd intended to marry her even if the king had refused his request to include Trotternish in her tocher. He'd risked his duty for her. Knowing what that choice could have cost him humbled her.

Rory had given her so much, more than she'd ever dreamed possible. A place in his family, a new understanding of her own, a child, and, most of all, his love. Without him she would be incomplete—the impressionable, vulnerable child she had been before she came to Dunvegan.

She could feel his even breathing on the back of her neck. Having assumed he was sleeping, Isabel started at the sound of his voice.

"What are you thinking about, my love?"

Isabel smiled. "That I have never felt so gloriously happy. I think I could stay in this position for the rest of my life."

Rory moved over her, rolling her on her back so that he could look in her eyes. Gently, he kissed the tip of her nose. "Hmmm," he murmured, tracing feathery kisses down the side of her cheek. "Perhaps I have been derelict in my duty, then." His tongue darted between her parted lips, sweeping the inside of her mouth.

Instantly, she felt the tingling waves of sensation spread through her limbs like a warm caress. Just the arousing taste of his mouth and he could leave her begging for more. "How do you mean?" she managed to ask through the haze of desire already spiraling through her body.

His mouth grew more demanding as he rolled on top of her and began vigorously seducing her with his lips and tongue, leaving her breathless. After a moment, he lifted his head and grinned. "We are not yet married and already you grow content with one position."

"Rogue. You know that's not what I meant. And you definitely haven't been derelict in your duty." She pushed him away with a laugh. "As to the other, now that I think of it, I don't recall being asked to marry you." She cocked a brow. "Are you so sure of my response?"

An endearingly befuddled expression crossed his face, before it was replaced by an arrogant grin. He sat up against the headboard and folded his arms across his chest. Isabel sucked in her breath. He was beautiful. All that strength. The smooth, tanned skin stretched taut against the rock hard muscles of his arms and shoulders. She would never tire of looking at him, delighting in the fact that he was hers.

"You have to marry me," he pointed out, "for the child." His gaze slid down her nakedness, resting on the rounded curve of her backside. He frowned. "Your hips are too narrow. I worry that our braw laddie will be too big for you."

She savored a thought of their child for a moment, before she processed what he'd said. Her brows shot up. "And how can you possibly be sure that the babe will be a boy?"

Rory chuckled. "Of course *he* will be a boy," he said, as if any other alternative were impossible. He drew himself up even more proudly. "We will call him John."

Isabel shook her head. One day he would have to learn that there were just some things even he couldn't command.

"Are there any other reasons I should marry you?" She was almost afraid to ask.

He'd finished his teasing. The playful arrogance was gone, replaced by a soft expression that warmed her to her toes. He lifted her chin to hold her gaze. "I've saved my best argument for last."

She waited, her breath caught firmly in her chest.

"Because my life would be meaningless without you. You are my light. I made the biggest mistake of my life when I sent you away, and a curtain of darkness descended over my soul. I love you more than I ever thought possible." He moved his hand over her stomach protectively. "I vow my eternal devotion to you and our child."

Isabel was held spellbound by the deep, unerring love she beheld in his tender gaze. The stars at last aligned, shining bright in the twinkle of his eye.

He kissed her mouth softly. "Isabel, you have taught me what it is to love. Will you do me the great honor of becoming my wife?"

Unbridled joy spread through her. Her eyes blurred with tears of happiness. In his sparkling eyes, unveiled and brimming with emotion, she beheld the wondrous promise of a new beginning. A promise of forever.

Their love was not fragile as she'd thought—it was strong enough to weather the slings and arrows of the capricious fates that had brought them together. She would never doubt it again.

She nodded and said simply, "I thought you would never ask."

Epilogue

Ye have heard that it hath been said,
An eye for an eye, and a tooth for a tooth.

—Matthew 5:38

Holyrood Palace, Summer 1603

Rory shifted impatiently in the audience chamber of Holyrood Palace, waiting for the presentations to begin. Sensing his disquiet, Isabel glanced up from the sleeping infant in her arms to give him an encouraging smile.

"Rory, Margaret will be fine. Don't worry. She's in good hands." Isabel indicated the dour Viking positioned protectively at Margaret's side.

"I know," Rory said, returning her smile. His heart swelled, studying the beloved countenances of his wife and child. A more perfect picture he could not imagine. If possible, motherhood had made Isabel even more beautiful, bringing a serenity to her expression and a maturity to her bearing that had not been there before. She bloomed with the confidence of love and of being loved in return. And the tiny cherub in her arms . . . He felt emotion squeeze his throat. Gently, with the back of his finger, he swept the velvety soft cheek.

Rory's love for his wife and devotion to their child grew more powerful with each new day that dawned. He'd found a peace and contentment that he hadn't realized existed. He thanked God for his good fortune and for the strange twist of fate that had brought Isabel to Dunvegan.

His gaze turned to his sister, resplendent in her court finery as she waited at the end of the room to take her turn down the aisle. Margaret's golden blond ringlets caught up high on her head dangled becomingly down her back—glistening silvery white in the flickering flames of the ceiling candelabrum. His mind turned to a day not so long ago when he'd witnessed a very different kind of procession. "Margaret has gone through much worse," Rory said, more to himself. "She's stronger now."

Or perhaps she'd always been strong, and it had just taken Isabel to remind them of that fact. Isabel, who with her unwavering faith had made this day possible. Holyrood was the final stop on Margaret and Colin's extended wedding journey across the Highlands. As promised, Isabel and Rory had joined them for support. Rory knew it couldn't hurt Margaret's chances for acceptance at court to have the new royal favorites by her side—warning the king of a treasonous plot tended to have that effect. Still, though he knew how important this day was to Margaret, he'd fought it, unable to ignore the shadow of uncertainty.

"Rory, if you don't stop frowning like that, you are going to terrify all the ladies," Isabel teased.

He folded his arms across his chest and set his jaw in a hard line. "Good. Perhaps it will remind them to curb the lash of their harpy tongues."

Her eyes narrowed. "You promised . . ."

He scowled. "Aye, I did." Was there anything he would not do for his wife? The fact that he was at court right now probably answered that question. "Though 'twas not a fair fight."

Isabel gasped with mock affront. "Do you impugn

my honor, Sir Knight?" she asked, a teasing reference to the rumors that the king intended to bestow a knighthood upon him.

"No, just your methods of persuasion."

Isabel shrugged, eyes twinkling. "It worked, didn't it?"

"You are an impudent wench, Isabel MacLeod."

"You'll have to remind me of that later." She giggled and turned back to watch the proceedings.

Rory held his breath as Margaret's name was called, bracing himself for the jeers. Isabel slipped her hand into his and gave it a squeeze in silent communication. He watched as Margaret urged her shoulders back and allowed Colin to lead her down the aisle toward King James and Queen Anne, the newly crowned king and queen of England.

"Is *that* the one-eyed woman?" he heard someone say, and tensed. The same voice continued, "But she is so *pretty,* such a fey creature."

More murmured voices followed her down the aisle.

"I thought she was maimed?"

A male voice entered the fray. "Why would Sleat repudiate *her* to marry the Mackenzie lass? Perhaps 'tis he who suffered the loss of an eye." Laughter joined the stranger's words.

Rory exhaled. As his sister floated regally by, Isabel turned to him with an *I told you so* shining in her lovely violet eyes.

His heart squeezed, overcome with love for the woman who had already given him so much.

They had come such a long way together. Ironically, brought together by the events of that horrible summer day four years ago when Sleat had cast Margaret off in that cruel spectacle. Sleat was no longer a thorn in his side, as he was currently enjoying the "hospitality" of the king's guards. Although Rory knew Sleat would not stay imprisoned by the king forever, the MacDonald chief no longer concerned him.

Rory had everything he wanted.

Looking at the proud face of his sister, the beaming face of his wife, and the angelic face of his precious daughter, Mairi—whom Isabel insisted on calling John—Rory felt the last embers of vengeance dying in his heart.

He had won. Happiness was undoubtedly the best revenge of all.

Author's Note

❖

"The War of the One-Eyed Woman" happened much as I described it. The MacDonald of Sleat's cruel repudiation of his handfast to Margaret MacLeod started a bloody two-year-long feud. History did not provide the cause or extent of Margaret MacLeod's eye injury, so I opted for giving her a happy ending. I thought after the horrible way she was treated by Sleat that she deserved one.

Rory MacLeod married Isabel of Glengarry probably earlier than 1602. Unlike Sleat and Margaret, there is no evidence that Rory and Isabel were handfasted prior to marrying. And although there is no mention of love between Rory and his wife, the eleven children they had together suggests at the very minimum a unity of purpose.

Of late, there has been some debate about the way handfasting has been portrayed by novelists. Some argue that there was never any such thing as a probationary marriage and that the popular romance concept of "a year and a day" is pure fiction. They argue that a handfast was basically a betrothal and that once the "betrothal" was consummated, it became a marriage. Perhaps this was the "legal" definition, but I think that in practice a handfast probably was a sort of "probationary" marriage. "The War of the One-Eyed Woman" certainly suggests this. In nearly every book I used to research this story, I came across some reference to handfasting, and it was always assumed to be a sort of probationary marriage (with marital privileges).

The Fairy Flag of the MacLeods is merely a wispy scrap of fabric now, but it is still quite something to behold. It hangs framed in the great hall of Dunvegan Castle, which is still the seat of the present MacLeod of MacLeod.

Until the mid–eighteenth century, Dunvegan was accessible only by sea. Now there is a beautiful entry on the landward side of the castle. Although it seems that there should be one, there is no evidence of a secret entrance to the castle. Dunvegan is a wonderful place to visit, and the dungeon, as I described, is quite horrible. And a rather cruel MacLeod chief did have the kitchens vent into the dungeon.

Although there was no record that James VI brokered Isabel's marriage, there is evidence that she was part of Queen Anne's retinue. And as Rory was indeed "at the horn" around this time, I thought their marriage *could* have been a diplomatic solution by King James to unite the feuding MacDonalds and MacLeods.

The Lordship of the Isles represented the height of Gaelic political power and culture in Scotland. For almost 150 years, under the leadership of Clan Donald, the Lords effectively ruled a large part of west Scotland and the Isles independently of the rest of the country. The Lordship forfeited to the crown in 1493. There were a couple of attempts to revive it, including the purported attempt I described in a letter to Queen Elizabeth by Donald Gorm Mor, the MacDonald of Sleat. The fall of the Lordship ushered in the period of Highland history known as "the Age of Feuds and Forays" and a shift in power from Clan Donald to Clan Gordon and Clan Campbell.

Finally, King James was already in England by the time Margaret made her appearance at court in the summer of 1603. King James left Edinburgh for England on April 5, 1603. He returned to Scotland only once—in 1617.

Looking for more sexy Scottish adventure?

Turn the page to catch a sneak peek at the
second pulse-pounding book in the
Highlander series

❖

*Highlander
Unmasked*

❖

by

Monica McCarty

Lochalsh, Inverness-shire, June 1605

It was going to rain. Perfect. Meg Mackinnon pulled the wool *arisaidh,* the full-length plaid she'd wrapped around her for protection from the elements, more firmly around her head and once again cursed the necessity for this journey. They'd only just begun, and already she was dreading long days on horseback, navigating the treacherous tracks of the drovers. Even had her father been able to arrange one, a carriage would have been useless along these paths. The "road" from the Isle of Skye to Edinburgh was barely wide enough to ride two abreast. The cart that carried their belongings had proved to be enough of a burden on this rugged terrain.

Meg had at least a week of discomfort left before her. It would take them that long to reach Edinburgh, where she must begin her search in earnest for a husband.

She felt the familiar flutter of anxiety when she thought of all that was ahead of her. Her father had entrusted her to find the right man for her clan; she would not let him down. But the responsibility inherent in her decision weighed heavily on her. The pressure at times could be stifling. A wry smile touched the edges of her mouth. Perhaps a week of travel wasn't long enough.

Yet part of her couldn't wait until it was all over. It would be a relief to have the decision made and behind her. Of course, then she would be *married*. And that brought a whole new bundle of anxieties.

Meg glanced over at her mother riding beside her and felt a pang of guilt for dragging her so far from home. It was difficult enough for Meg to leave her father and brother; she couldn't imagine how her mother must feel.

"I'm sorry, Mother."

Rosalind Mackinnon met her daughter's gaze with puzzlement. "Whatever for, child?"

"For taking you away from father at a time like this." Meg bit her lip, feeling the need to explain. "I just couldn't bring myself to accept—"

"Nonsense." A rare frown marred her mother's beautiful face. "Your father is much better. A trip to court is exactly what I need. You know how I love all the latest fashions, the latest hairstyles"—she smiled conspiratorially—"and all the latest gossip."

Meg returned the smile. She knew her mother was only trying to make her feel better, though she did love going to court. Meg, on the other hand, hated it. She never fit in the way her mother did. Partially, it was her own fault. She did not share her mother's enjoyment of frippery and gossip and was not very good at pretending otherwise. But this time, she swore she would try. For her mother's sake, if not her own.

"Besides, I'll not have you marry a man you do not love," her mother finished, anticipating the apology Meg had been about to make.

Meg shook her head. Rosalind Mackinnon was a hopeless romantic. But love was not the reason Meg had refused the offer of marriage from her father's chieftain.

The offer which, had she accepted it, would have dispensed with the need for this trip.

But Meg's choice of a husband was dictated by unusual circumstances, and Thomas Mackinnon was not the right man for her. He was an able warrior, yes, but a hotheaded one. A man who reached for his sword first and thought later. Meg sought a strong warrior, but a controlled one. Equally important, she needed a clever negotiator to appease a king with growing authority over his recalcitrant Highland subjects. Tensions between the two ran high. The time of unfettered authority by the chiefs was waning. She must find a husband who could help lead her clan into the future.

But the lack of political acumen was not the only reason she'd refused Thomas. She also sensed too much ambition in him. Ambition that would jeopardize her brother's position as the next chief.

Above all, she needed a fiercely loyal man. A man she could trust.

Love was not part of the bargain. Meg was a realist. She admired the deep affection between her parents, perhaps even envied it, but she recognized that such was not for her. Her duty was clear. Finding the right man for her clan came first. And second.

"I don't expect to be as fortunate in marriage as you, Mother," Meg said. "What you and Father have is rare."

"And wonderful," Rosalind finished. "Which is why I want it for you. Though just because I love your father does not mean I always agree with him. In this, he asks too much of you," she said with a stubborn set to her pointed chin. As Meg had never heard her mother speak against her father, it took a moment to register what she was saying.

Her mother shook her head. "And now he expects you to sacrifice your future happiness," she lamented, as if a daughter marrying for the good of the clan were anything out of the ordinary. When in fact, Meg choosing her own husband—albeit one who met certain specific criteria—was the oddity.

"Truly, Mother, it is no sacrifice. Father asks nothing of me that I don't want myself. When I find the right man to stand beside Ian, he will be the right man for me."

"If only it were that easy. But you cannot force your heart to follow your head."

Maybe not, but she could try.

As if she knew what Meg was thinking, Rosalind said dismissively, "Don't worry. Just leave it to me."

Warning bells clanged. "Mother . . . you promised not to interfere."

Her mother stared straight ahead with a far too innocent look on her face. "I don't know what you are talking about, Margaret Mackinnon."

Meg's eyes narrowed, not fooled one bit. "You know exactly—"

But her words were lost in the violent crash of thunder as a deluge of rain poured from the skies. The ground seemed to shake with the sudden fury of the storm.

Her mother's terrified scream, however, alerted Meg to the fact that the shaking was from more than just a storm.

Still, it took her a moment to comprehend what was happening, so suddenly had it begun. One minute she'd been about to take her mother to task for her match-making ways, the next she was in the midst of a night-mare.

Out of the shadows, like demon riders on the storm, the band of ruffians attacked. Huge, savage-looking men in filthy shirts and tattered plaids, wielding deadly claymores with ruthless intent. They seemed to fly from the trees, surrounding Meg's party in all directions.

Her cry froze in her throat, terror temporarily render-ing her mute. For a minute, she couldn't think. She watched helplessly as the dozen clansmen her father had sent along to protect them were locked in a battle of un-tempered ferocity against at least a score of brigands.

Her blood ran cold.

There were too many of them.

Dear God, her father's men had no chance. The Mackinnon clansmen had immediately moved to pro-tect Meg and her mother, circling them as best they could in the confined area. And one by one, they were cut down in front of her.

Meg gazed in rapt horror as Ruadh, one of her fa-ther's chieftains, a man she'd known her entire life, a man who'd bounced her on his knee and sung her songs of the clan's illustrious past, was unable to block the deadly strike of a claymore that slid across his belly, nearly cutting him in two. Tears sprang to her eyes as she watched the light fade from his gaze.

Her mother's scream sliced through the terror, jolting Meg from her stupor. The moment of panic dissolved in a sudden burst of clarity. She gathered her courage, with only one thought. Protecting her mother.

Heart pounding, Meg leapt down from atop her horse and grabbed the dirk from Ruadh's lifeless hand, his fingers still clenched around the bloody hilt. The weapon felt so heavy and clumsy in her hand. For the first time in her life, she wished she hadn't lingered so long indoors with her books. She had no experience with weaponry of any sort. But she shook off the bout of uncertainty. It didn't matter. What she lacked in skill she would make up for in raw determination. Clasping the dirk more firmly, she moved to stand before her mother, ready to defend her.

They'll have to kill me first, she vowed silently.

But a bit of her bravado faltered when another of her father's men fell at her feet. The way it was going, it might not be long before they did. Only six of her father's men remained.

The *arisaidh* had slid from her head and rain streamed down her face, blurring her vision. The pins holding back her hair were long gone, and the wavy tendrils tangled in her lashes, but Meg hardly noticed, focused as she was on the battle. The battle that was tightening like a noose around them, as their circle of protectors quickly diminished.

She bit back the fear that crept up the back of her throat. Never had she been more terrified, but she had to stay strong. For her mother. If they were to have a chance to survive.

Meg's action seemed to snap her mother from her trance, and she stopped screaming. Following Meg's lead, her mother slipped down from her horse. Meg could see her hands shaking as she pulled Ruadh's eating knife from his belt.

She turned, and Meg's chest squeezed to see the resolve on her mother's face. To see the direness of their circumstance reflected in her gaze. Even drenched, her hair and clothes a sodden mess, Rosalind Mackinnon looked like an angel—albeit an avenging angel. Though forty, her beauty was undiminished by age. *Dear God, what would these vicious brutes do to her?* Meg swallowed. To them both?

Though Meg knew her mother must be thinking the same thing, her voice was strangely calm. "If you see an opening between them, run," she whispered.

"But I can't leave you—"

"You will do as I say, Margaret," her mother said, and Meg was so shocked by the steel in her dulcet tone that she simply nodded. "If you need to use the knife, strike hard and do not hesitate."

Meg felt an unexpected swell of pride. Her sweet, gentle mother looked as fierce as a lion protecting its cub. There was far more to Rosalind Mackinnon than Meg had ever realized.

"I won't," she said, feigning courage. But what chance did two women, and two particularly diminutive ones at that, have against such strength and numbers?

A filthy, hulking ruffian lurched for her mother. Without thinking, Meg stabbed his arm. At least three of the ten inches sank deep in his skin, opening a wide gash in his forearm. He roared in pain and backhanded her across the face. Stunned by the blow, she lost her grip on the dirk and it dropped to the ground, where he promptly kicked it out of her reach.

Meg's hand instinctively covered her wet cheek, soothing the hot sting.

"Bitch," he spat. "You'll die for that." He turned, lifting his claymore in a deadly arc above her head. Her mother moved to defend her, slicing his shoulder with the eating knife. Easily blocking the blow with his forearm, he shoved her mother harshly to the ground. Meg watched in horror as her head landed squarely on a rock, connecting with a dull thud.

Horror rose in her throat. "Mother!" she screamed, rushing to her side. Meg shook her listless body, but her eyes wouldn't open. *Dear God, no!*

She sensed him, or rather smelled his rank stench, approaching behind her. Anger unlike anything she'd ever experienced flooded her with rage. He'd hurt her mother. Grabbing the knife that her mother had dropped, Meg turned on him, surprising him for a moment. She stabbed him again, this time aiming for his neck. But he was too tall, and without leverage, she managed only to nick him.

She'd lost her advantage.

A vile expletive ripped from his mouth. She felt his enormous dirty hands on her as he grabbed her and tossed her to the ground. His hard black eyes fixed on her. A sneer curled his lip, revealing coarse brown teeth. Shivering with revulsion, she huddled in a ball as he started toward her.

"I'm going to enjoy this, you little hellcat."

Meg scooted back in the mud, but he kept coming. Laughing. She could feel the heavy pounding of her heart in her chest. She glanced around, but there was no one to come to her aid. Those who remained of father's men were locked in their own battles. She grabbed fistfuls of mud in her hands and tried tossing it in his eyes, but it only made him more furious.

They couldn't die. What would happen to Ian? She felt the hot prickle of tears in her eyes. Without Meg and her mother, there was no one to protect him. *Think,* she told herself. *Use your head.* But the logic and reasoning she'd always relied on failed her. There was no escape.

In the black glint of his merciless eyes, Meg saw only death.

Please, she breathed.

And in the skip of two long heartbeats, the answer to her prayer exploded through the trees on a fearsome black warhorse.

A knight. Nay, a warrior. Not in shining armor, but in the yellow *cotun* dotted with bits of mail that identified him as a chieftain—though his size alone would have set him apart. Even without his padded war coat, Meg knew he would be one of the largest men she'd ever seen. Tall and muscular, with a chest like a broad shield. As if forged from steel, every inch of him looked hard and forbidding.

And dangerous.

A trickle of fear slid down her spine. For a moment, Meg wondered whether she'd merely exchanged one villain for another.

Their eyes met and held. She gasped, startled by the most crystalline blue eyes she'd ever beheld, set in a face of rugged masculinity partially hidden beneath the heavy stubble of a week-old beard.

The entire exchange lasted only an instant, but she quickly read the absolute command in his gaze. A look that was oddly reassuring despite his ferocity.

For the first time she noticed that he was not alone; perhaps half a dozen men had ridden in behind him. A more fearsome band of warriors she could not imagine. To a one they were strong, well muscled, and utterly ruthless looking. *Broken men,* she knew with an instinctive certainty. Men without land or a clan who roamed the Highlands as outlaws. Yet for some reason, they did not inspire her fear. Her eyes returned to the warrior. Because of their leader? she wondered.

With no more than a tilt of his head and the dart of his eyes, the warrior issued his orders. His men moved as a unit, swiftly taking their positions with the discipline of Roman centurions and an ease that belied their rough appearance.

Despite their lesser numbers, Meg knew without a doubt that the tide of battle had just turned. This man would not be defeated. Only a fool would challenge him.

With his men in position, the warrior headed directly for her. Finally realizing that something was wrong, her attacker glanced over his shoulder. The horrible laughing stopped. Taking advantage of the distraction, Meg ran to her mother's side, gently pulling her back toward the trees, nearly sobbing with relief to see that the color had returned to her cheeks and her eyes had begun to flutter. All the while, she kept her eye on the man who was their savior.

With one hand reaching over his shoulder he drew an enormous claymore from the baldric slung across his back as if it weighed no more than a feather, though the blade alone would have reached to her chin. Still using only one hand, he raised it high above his head, wielding the weapon with remarkable ease, and landed a heavy blow to the ribs of her attacker. Meg heard the crunch of bone as the villain crumpled to the ground.

After leaping off his horse, the warrior pulled a dirk from the scabbard at his waist, and unhesitatingly drew his blade across her tormentor's throat. Relief washed over her. She should regret the loss of life, but she could not. Their eyes met, and she felt a connection so strong, it startled her.

"Thank you," she mouthed, too shaken to sound the words.

He acknowledged her gratitude with a nod. Then, with a fierce war cry—the words in Erse, which she could not make out—he raised his sword and charged headlong into the fury of the battle, wielding the blade with deadly finesse and accuracy, cutting down all who stood in his path.